Calafia's Kingdom

Also by Joan Druett

A PROMISE OF GOLD
Judas Island
Calafia's Kingdom
Dearest Enemy
Finale

THE MONEY SHIP
The Launching of the Huntress
The Privateer Brig
The Dragon Stone
The Midwife's Apprentice

WIKI COFFIN SERIES
A Watery Grave
Shark Island
Run Afoul
Deadly Shoals
The Beckoning Ice

OTHER FICTION
A Love of Adventure (*Abigail*)

NON FICTION
The Notorious Captain Hayes
Eleanor's Odyssey
Lady Castaways
The Elephant Voyage
Tupaia, Captain Cook's Polynesian Navigator
Island of the Lost
In the Wake of Madness
Rough Medicine
She Captains
Hen Frigates
The Sailing Circle (**with Mary Anne Wallace**)
Captain's Daughter, Coasterman's Wife
She Was a Sister Sailor
Petticoat Whalers
Fulbright in New Zealand
Exotic Intruders

A Promise of Gold

Book Two

CALAFIA'S KINGDOM

CALAFIA'S KINGDOM

THE SECOND BOOK IN AN OLD SALT PRESS TRILOGY
published by Old Salt Press, a Limited Liability Company
registered in New Jersey, USA.

For more information about our titles go to
www.oldsaltpress.com

ISBN 978-0-9941246-8-5

First published in this form 2018

ONE

IT was the first of September in the year 1848, and the gate to Eldorado lay ahead.

Captain Jake Dexter's charts were inadequate now, and when a sloop beat out and hailed them he negotiated for a pilot with some relief. He turned out to be a grizzled old customer with a seamy face and not many teeth, but Jake had been told that a deserter from some whaleship named Richardson had acted as the pilot here for the past fifteen years, and while he hadn't introduced himself, this fellow's deep knowledge seemed to mark him as that man. "Haul in port mainbraces," he said, and Jake was content to leave him to his work.

The entrance to the Bay of San Francisco was framed by a grand vista of hills and mountains that marched boldly down to the sea, creating a panorama that Jake Dexter found unexpectedly dramatic. The water was like a glinting jewel, set in a coronet of peaks and valleys, reflecting stands of cypress trees, the golden-browns of rounded hills, and the heavy granite-gray of cliffs. Waves dashed up against the rocks, splashing rainbows, and seabirds flew in patterns close to the sea. Another tack, and the brig *Gosling* sailed into the great curve of the bay … and Jake stared, astounded.

He had heard that about twenty whalers called here each year to load with firewood and fresh water at an island called Yerba Buena, but that otherwise the bay of San Francisco was usually deserted—but today many more than twenty ships were riding in the harbor. And the way they were riding was strange... A chill lifted the hairs on the nape of his neck as he stared from one vessel to another. The unexpected fleet was huddled untidily, as if the whims of the winds and the currents had more to do with the way the craft lay than the decisions of men. And they looked more like derelicts than ships.

The *Gosling* seamen, who had been exclaiming loudly from aloft, were now eerily silent. Every man was shading his eyes at he stared at the abandoned vessels—for abandoned they certainly were. The silent hulls were splodged with bird droppings, and streaked with rust stains beneath davits, catheads, and hawseholes. Their yards were struck or left hanging all awry, and there was not a sign of movement about any of the decks.

Then the brig passed the entrance to an inlet, and Jake saw the United States frigate *Savannah*, looking much as he had seen her last, in the harbor of Valparaiso, in June. This time, though, she was not flying a host of flags. For a horrified moment he thought the great man-of-war was as abandoned as the other craft, but then he saw a signal raised, and a boat begin to lower. Captain Mervine, it seemed, had recognized the *Gosling*, and was as anxious to see Jake as Jake Dexter felt to ask questions of him.

Wondering how long the frigate had been here, Jake turned to the pilot. The old man, it seemed, had been watching his grim expression, because he grinned and said, "The *Savannah* only keeps her sailors, sir, by the threat of flogging and worse. Ain't nothing else what anchors here but loses all his men, on account of they all run off to the diggin's. And the same'll happen to you, sir. Drop your anchor you may, but lose your men you will."

2

Jake said with confidence, "I don't believe that will happen."

"No? Ha, you'll see different, just like all the rest. A man can dig a thousand a month up in them fabled hills. You're sure you want to drop anchor, Captain Dexter?"

"Go ahead," Jake said curtly, and the old man went back to issuing directions, which Charlie Martin, the first mate, relayed to the men. A stream of orders, and the brig heeled to an anchorage seaward of the abandoned ships. The anchor hit the water with a splash.

Silence. Even the brig's disorderly Ecuadorean passengers were quiet, as every man on board studied what lay on the shore. Small squat buildings were scattered about the brown slopes, some of them clapboard, most of them adobe … and yet there was no sign of life. The only movement was the jerky swing of the arms of a distant windmill. It was high summer, but the air was dank with the after-chill of the dawn fog, and Jake shivered, despite his heavy pea-jacket.

Suddenly the passengers moved, in unison, as if they had come out of a communal spell. Shouting all together and jostling one another to get to the gangway rail, the South Americans demanded passage to shore, saying that they had paid to get all the way to San Francisco from the Tombez River, and not just to the harbor.

"Fine," said Jake, delighted to see the last of them, and the two whaleboats and the two dinghies were dropped into the water, piled up with bodies and their dunnage, and rowed to the beach. Three trips, and they were all gone. Never, thought Jake sardonically, had a rich man got rid of his poor relations with more pleasure.

Turning, he found the pilot at his shoulder, waiting for his money, as bargained. It was handed over, and the old man spat on the silver dollars, and tucked them away in the depths of his garments. Then he stepped to the gangway rail to drop down into his sloop, which had followed them into the harbor.

Jake stopped him, saying, "Are there any American whalemen here?"

"Aye, sir, the *Flora*—there she is, over there at Whalemen's Harbor. But it ain't no use going a-calling, for she be as deserted as the rest. See them empty davits? She come in June, the *Flora* did, and the captain saw the danger, tried to get away a-fore he lost his men, but too late. Crew mutinied, refused duty, gagged the watch, escaped off to the mines. Captain and mates saw naught could be done about it, so off they went off theirselves to the hills."

"Dear lord," said Jake, shocked. "They just abandoned their ship?"

"Aye, they did. Mind you," the old man said with an air of world-weary experience, "she was twenty-six months out, and had taken only seven hundred and fifty barrels of oil. Ah, the rainy season is nigh, and they'll be back. I'll warrant them chains and cables be sufficient strong to last till they come."

Jake found that equally hard to credit. The deserted ships all looked as if they would never get to sea again. Then he saw that the boat from the frigate would be alongside within minutes.

Turning back to the old pilot, he hastily asked, "Tell me—you must hear talk—are any New Bedford whalemen expected here?"

"Not here," the old man said. "The *Minerva* was here, but the captain managed to get her away, with good luck, a good crew, and good judgment. He told me he intended to sail to Valparaiso to get rid of his oil and load merchandise, which he will carry here in the expectation of a grand profit—which he will get, believe me. The masters what have managed to bring off that trick have sold their entire invoices for very large money, and that's what that captain expects. But he won't be here for some weeks."

"What about other ports? Monterey, perhaps?"

"The *Isaac Walton* is lying in Monterey, or so Captain

4

Mervine told me, she being there discharging her oil while she still got some men. Then maybe her captain will go in for the provisioning trade, too. Others be plying the coast, carrying passengers in place of oil, and another one be up at Sutter's Fort, all done up for the boarding house business."

"The … *what?*"

"At the Embarcadero of Sutter's Fort—one hundred and fifty miles upriver. No need to be astounded," said the old man, dourly amused at Jake's expression. "The wind blows fair upriver from February to October, and the river be a noble one. She's navigable all the way up to the fork with the American River and after that to Pueblo San Marco on the Feather, when the wind is right. I've seen 300-ton barks sail up to the Embarcadero with ease—anything can sail the Sacramento what draws less than fifteen feet. This brig would make it easy, even now at the end of the dry season. I can pilot you there, if you want, and don't you doubt I can do it, for I were the first mate of that very same whaler that be a boarding house at Sutter's now."

Jake said blankly, "But I thought you were Captain Richardson?"

"What, me?" The old man found this very amusing. "No, no," he said. "Paddack's the name, late first mate of the whaleship *Humpback*, and I do think, yes, that I have seen this brig before. Off Judas Island, was it not?"

Jake shook his head. So here was the first mate of the ship that had brought Miss Harriet Gray to Judas Island, and whose captain had tricked her into going on board the *Gosling* and then had left her stranded—coincidence beyond coincidence, he thought with disbelief. But when he thought about the call of the siren gold, he decided that maybe it was not such a coincidence, after all. Then he was distracted by the arrival of the *Savannah's* boat, with Mervine himself on board, and when he turned back for another word, he found that Paddack had jumped into his sloop, which promptly tacked away.

5

Mervine was scrambling up the side, his face even redder than remembered. "What do you think?" he cried. "Ain't it a scandal?" Straightening as he arrived beside Jake, he swung out an arm and pointed a furious finger. "See that bark?" he demanded.

Jake looked. The bark that Mervine indicated seemed no different from the rest of the derelict fleet. He said, "Yes?"

"*Amity*, her name. She came in late yesterday, and this morning her master found but six men still on board. He's on board the *Savannah* right now, laying a complaint. Oh, we'll punish the scoundrels when we find them, confiscate their gold, make spread-eagles of them all!"

"That's why the *Savannah* is here in San Francisco?" Jake said, astounded. "To catch deserters? But you told me in Valparaiso that you were on a mission to the Indian Ocean!"

"The need here is greater, Captain Dexter! We was summoned by no less than Colonel Mason himself, because deserters must be caught, and deserters must be punished!"

Then the frigate's commander lowered his voice. "I've lost more than a dozen men myself, and I am right ashamed to say it," he confided. "Scarcely half an hour had elapsed after dropping anchor before the officer of the watch noticed that the gig had disappeared, and with her the first half-dozen of our men. No sooner had he raised the alarm than there was a general rush to a lighter that was lying alongside, and off ten more men went, off over the side like so many eels. In vain was the guard turned out, because by the time another boat was lowered, than they had all shown a clean pair of heels. There's a seven-hundred-dollar bounty on each of their hides, and I assure you, sir, that they'll be sorry for themselves when they are handed in."

"Jehovah," said Jake Dexter, and then saw that Harriet had come on deck, freed to come out of the afterquarters by the departure of the last of the Ecuadoreans. She was looking for him, Jake saw, as if she had something to tell him, but then she sighted their visitor, and her anxious expression turned into one of surprise.

"Merciful heavens, it's Captain Mervine," she said.

Jake said to Mervine, "You remember our supercargo, Miss Harriet Gray?"

"Of course I do, of course! The famous actress, the beautiful Titania! Good morning, Miss Gray!"

Harriet inclined her head and shook his hand.

She did look beautiful, Jake thought. Her waif-like face was pale, and her wheat-colored hair tumbled about her shoulders, but Captain Mervine had no trouble dismissing her from his mind. Turning back to Jake, he urged, "Come ashore with me, Captain Dexter."

"To shore? But why?"

"I'd value your opinion, sir. Tell me what you think."

The boat pulled for a narrow gritty beach. Some of the Ecuadoreans were there, wading through shallow water as they made their way along a bluff, but Captain Mervine led Jake directly up the hill. The wind cut to the bone, despite the warmth of the exercise, and Jake climbed with his hands in his peajacket pockets, listening to Mervine's heavy panting.

At the top of the hill it was even colder, and there seemed to be nothing in sight except short brown-gold grass on the slopes and brown-gold dirt exposed in the gullies. Then, as they walked, signs of habitation appeared — rows of houses, mysteriously only half-built, all at the same stage of construction. It was as if some strange pestilence had carried off all the carpenters, bricklayers, and roofers. There were even ladders left propped against half-built walls, and stacks of shingles alongside the eaves of raftered, gaping roofs. Dogs cringed at corners. Two Ecuadoreans who had made it this far were staring about with bewildered looks.

"Fifty!" Mervine barked in Jake's ear.

"I beg your pardon?"

"Fifty houses a-building — according to plan they were,

7

rising according to a timetable when I left this place in May. The price of manual labor in California has always been high—from one to three dollars a day, with master workmen being able to command five dollars. On the discovery of gold on the American River, this changed at once, wages being tripled and quadrupled by the minute. Soon, tradesmen were being paid eight dollars a day, the highest in the land, but where are they now? Up the mines, sir, up at the diggings! A few hung back, but then the news of a buster nugget got out—a nugget weighing four pounds, worth one thousand and sixty dollars! And that news, Captain Dexter, sent the rest on their way."

Jake stared about, his hands curled into fists in his pockets, thinking that the scene reminded him of the landing stage at Tombez, when he had called there in July. The village had been completely emptied of men, a mystery that had been solved when he had learned that they had all rushed to California on a ship that had called by for provisions, carrying the news of gold. And here, in San Francisco, there was the same sense of hurried departure.

He said, "Is anyone at all in town?"

"Only the traders who are making money out of supplying the miners as they stream into the port on the way upriver to the hills, along with their clerks and servants, who are only kept pinned here by high wages. Do you have any idea what salesmen and shopmen demand from their employers?"

"No, I do not, Captain Mervine."

"From two thousand, three hundred dollars per annum, to two thousand, seven hundred dollars—with board and lodging! And mere boys have the sauce to demand pretty much the same, their seniors being all up in the hills—it's a scandal, Captain Dexter, a scandal! The officers at the garrison in Monterey are forced to go without servants, not being able to afford the outrageous rates—they have to cook their own dinners! Even Colonel Mason has to take his turn to cook! Is it any wonder, sir, that the general aspect of this town is so sad and forlorn—that stores are shut, buildings abandoned? Houses empty? Businesses dead? Tell me what you think."

Jake grimaced, thinking that the abandoned ships in the harbor had certainly looked forlorn. "Those seniors—the tradesmen and artisans who were building the houses and printing the newspapers. Did they leave the town all at once, in a body?"

"In a flood, Captain Dexter. Two thousand men left this budding city in June, sir, two-thirds of them American. Then after that, in July, another two thousand followed in their wake. And is that latest two thousand American? No, sir, that they ain't. The men who flood through here on the way to the diggings, Captain Dexter, are men all intent on robbing the territory of rightfully American gold, and they are not Americans, sir. They are Peruvian, Chilean, Ecuadorean, sir, Russian, French, and—for God's sake, and pardon me, sir—the miserable Mexicans and bloody arrogant English! Our natural-born enemies, sir, come to steal our rightfully won treasure, come to loot the territory what was won with American blood! They expect to leave amazing' rich in just a few months, and they have no intention whatsoever of becoming United States citizens. Barefaced robbery of what is rightfully American, Captain Dexter!"

"Dear me," said Jake.

"We fought a war, beat the Mexicans, made California rightfully American—for this?"

"It's certainly ironic."

"Worse than that, Captain Dexter, it's a scandal!"

They were walking again, more slowly, and the streets widened and became uphill and downhill, often with one side of the road a full few feet higher than the other. There was a deserted meat market, fenced with rawhides on wires, stinking most foully, and then substantial buildings, many

9

made of stone ... but still, still no sign of life.

So where were the traders who were making a fortune out of supplying the miners? Behind their counters and inside their warehouses, Jake supposed—unless they were in the mines themselves, having run out of stocks. Or maybe out of customers, he mused, the season being so late. It was beyond belief, this silence and sense of desertion, almost dreamlike in its weirdness.

Jake shook his head, and said, "And yet, in Valparaiso, Captain Mervine, you swore there was no gold."

"Well, there is." Mervine made it sound like a personal insult. "Colonel Mason and Lieutenant Sherman went into the hills to make a survey—and Colonel Mason has just come back with a report of what the gold in them hills is like."

Jake waited. "And?"

"You've no idea," Mervine said sourly. "Sir, you ain't got a notion. Two ounces is a usual day's work. While Colonel Mason was watching, two men dug seventeen thousand dollars' worth, just in the space of an hour."

Jake said softly, "Jehovah." Even now, it didn't seem possible that the wild tales he had heard in Tombez did, after all, have such a solid foundation in truth.

"In one hour?"

"And that was with naught but Indian baskets for sieving the nuggets out of the dirt. Them with machines like gold-washing pans and dirt-washing cradles can work out even more."

"And all this is in Colonel Mason's report?"

"He writ everything down and tomorrow we sail for Monterey, to escort the schooner *Lambayecana* out of Monterey to Paita. There will be a loyal lieutenant on board that schooner, who will carry that report, along with a tea caddy of gold samples, all the way to Washington."

"So Colonel Mason can ask for reinforcements?"

"I beg your pardon?"

10

"You told me in Valparaiso that if the gold did indeed exist, Colonel Mason would claim it all as the property of the United States government."

Captain Mervine coughed, a loud sound that echoed among the deserted stone façades. "If we capture any deserters—and we will board all outgoing ships to search for deserters, I assure you of that!—then we will certainly confiscate their ill-gotten gold, and make spread-eagles of them all, sir, flog them till their bones are chalk! But," he added with vast distaste, "Colonel Mason has been forced to admit that that be the extent of our powers. The placer has proved to be fully five hundred miles in length—and there's the problem of desertion, too. He can't trust his troops, I am ashamed to say. But what allurement is a private's pay of six dollars a month compared to the tales coming out of the mines? Colonel Mason's force is small enough to start with, but his count of loyal officers and men diminishes by the day."

This was exactly what he himself had predicted, Jake remembered. However, he kept his counsel.

For a moment the only sounds were the thud of their boots, and the echoes that came back from the blank buildings. He saw some more Ecuadoreans, these men in a group, consulting together. As he watched, a couple of men he didn't recognize joined them, and waved their arms as they talked in a knowledgeable kind of way. They were locals, he supposed, because they looked so Spanish, being dressed in gaudy jackets and calcineros, with high-crowned sombreros on their heads. He hadn't seen a man who looked like an American yet. They were all, he supposed, in the hills.

Mervine's thoughts were running in the same direction, it seemed, because he growled again, "It's a scandal, Captain Dexter, a scandal. Back in April the place I left was bustling and American. Why there were two newspapers, two! Now both have failed, sir, and from what? Starvation, that's what, for no paper can survive when the writers, editors, printers and readers have all gone off to the mines. Gold fever," he mumbled like a curse. "A disease, that's what it is, a disease."

San Francisco certainly looked as if it had been emptied by a plague. Jake wondered what other towns on the coast had been left deserted like this. Monterey, evidently. Perhaps Paita, Callao and Talcahuano were in the same state as Tombez and San Francisco, emptied by the fever. And what about Valparaiso? When he had left there, in June, the rumors were just taking hold.

"The October rains will fetch all the men back," Mervine prophesied, but the prospect didn't make him look happier. "The town will be bustling again—until February, when the rains stop. Then they'll all head back to the hills, and more foreigners with them. Damn it, sir, and beg your pardon, Captain Dexter, but it sure bites hard that the gold in this territory should be taken away by the very men we fought to keep out!"

"But it seems impossible to stop the South Americans from coming in, Captain Mervine," said Jake. He was thinking of the load of Ecuadoreans he had carried here—at what he had expected to be an immense profit.

"You think so? But that's why Colonel Mason is sending that report to Washington!"

"It is?"

"Of course! Once red-blooded American boys hear about that gold, then they will come in their thousands, and kick the foreigners out."

"You're expecting another war?"

"Wa'al," said Captain Mervine, and coughed. "Mebbe they won't actually kick them out, being too busy digging all that gold, but the American boys will dilute the multitudes, sir, outnumber the foreigners, make California American, the way it should rightfully be."

Jake contemplated the devious notion. After the loyal

12

lieutenant arrived in Washington with his enlivening yarns and his tea caddy of gold, would New York and Boston be emptied out, too? On one hand, it was unimaginable, and yet ... yet, looking around, it seemed eerily possible.

Mervine barked, "And it is your patriotic duty, sir, to do the same!"

"I beg your pardon?" said Jake, astonished.

"Your duty as an American, sir, is to take your brig upriver, and add to the quota of American citizens in the Sacramento valley. Show the flag, sir, wave it high!"

"Jehovah," said Jake, having trouble not to laugh. The crew of his brig numbered just fourteen — not including Harriet's brother, Royal Gray, who by Mervine's logic should not be counted, because he was English. His men were an energetic and virile lot, but the amount of diluting they could do was very limited.

But Mervine was perfectly serious. "The Sacramento is a mighty stream," he said. "Fully navigable for a hundred and fifty miles, sir, all the way to Sutter's Fort, on the fork with the American River. That's where the news of the gold was first bruited about, sir, the first gold being found on Sutter's ground, at his mill, which is about fifty miles up the fork. Most vessels go no further, because most of the business goes on at the Fort, or on the Embarcadero, but it is possible to sail as far as Pueblo San Marco, an old town half a day upriver, on the junction of the Feather River and Cache Creek, famous in the region as the gateway to the mines."

Jake was silent, thinking that if Sutter's Fort was as busy as Mervine said, it could be ideal for the scheme he had in mind. Then he wondered about duties and taxes — items that he was always anxious to avoid.

He said, "What's the state of law and order there?"

"Shocking, Captain Dexter, shocking! The alcalde, Robert Ross, ain't nothing better than an English adventurer what was appointed by the Mexicans, which is an ever-living scandal in itself. But he has his rules, sir, and his

13

regulations, so Colonel Mason was forced to admit that he do the best what he can."

"Regulations? What regulations?"

"Wa'al, there ain't too many of those, Captain. Alcalde Ross has the same trouble with keeping deputies as we have with keeping sailors and soldiers, sir, and without deputies, what could even a proper American do, huh?"

"Interesting," said Jake, very thoughtfully.

"So you'll go, Captain Dexter—take your brig upriver to Sutter's or even further, to Pueblo San Marco? The season when the prevailing winds blow upriver is still with us—but not for long, so you'll have to make up your mind now. And face it, sir, there ain't no point in stopping here in 'Frisco."

Jake Dexter looked around again. A shut door in the imposing façade of the store to his right carried a tattered notice.

It read, CLOSED ON ACCOUNT OF GOING TO THE MINES.

"You're absolutely right," he said.

TWO

JAKE Dexter did not return to the brig until after Harriet had gone to bed, as he had been pressed to take his supper on the frigate. She lay listening alertly until she heard his voice in the mess cabin, but even then it took a long time to get to sleep. She was very tempted get up and tap on the door to his private quarters, but knew it was wrong – the wrong time to try to tell him her squalid secret, and the wrong place, because it would be misinterpreted.

So she lay there, feeling oppressed, beset with foreboding and doubts. The distant thumps as the abandoned ships touched each other when the tide changed seemed unutterably doleful.

None of the men shared her mood. Chilly San Francisco fog drifted past her sidelights in the morning, but she could hear young Valentine Fish in full voice, with the watch singing lustily along.

> *Ohh ... 'Frisco be a damn fine town*
> *A very famous city*
> *Where all the streets are paved with gold*
> *And all the prospects pretty.*

"I see no gold," Harriet said tartly to her brother, Royal, Royal after she arrived on deck. The morning fog still

15

dangled from the sky, so that the town itself was lost to sight, let alone any gold that might be lying around in the streets.

"It's not here, dear sis — it's in the hills."

"So they say," she sighed, and stared at slowly swirling gray mist. The wood of the rail oozed dampness under her palms. She had a woolen shawl about her shoulders, and yet it was only the second day of September. What would winter be like?

She shivered, beset with foreboding and desperate for reassurance. She had eaten breakfast alone, picking at her food while she waited for Jake Dexter to join her, but he hadn't come into the mess cabin. She wondered what he was doing, and when she would have a chance to talk to him in private.

"California is the modern-day Eldorado, Hat," Royal enthused on. "People will talk and sing about this great phenomenon forever. It will go down in history, like the Crusades."

"But I just can't credit that every man who comes here goes away with a fortune," she objected. "Have we heard any firsthand stories from men who've actually found this miraculous gold? No, we have not. All the stories we've been told are of men who have chased after the enlivening yarns, along with the farfetched yarns themselves. Like the stories Honest Mill Mason was told by the sailors from the ship that called at Tombez, the same tales that he passed on to us, firing up the crew to come, they are tales told by other men, men who have been to the fair and seen the elephant. So how do we know that the elephant exists?"

"Such eloquence," Royal scoffed. "But it's the tales, true or not, that will bring adventurers like us to California, adventurers in their thousands — and Colonel Mason knows that well, shrewd fellow."

"Colonel Mason?" she said, startled. She thought the name was vaguely familiar, but couldn't pin it down. Then

16

she remembered the dinner on the steam bark *Nympha*, and Captain Mervine's loud talk about the mythological gold, and how Colonel Mason, who was in charge of the garrison at Monterey, would regulate the rush for gold—that is, if the gold happened to be truly there.

"Colonel Mason has been in the hills, and has written a formal report about the wealth that men are digging. It's nothing less than the truth, all facts and figures, but in fact it is the most fanciful gold tale yet—because it's bait to bring thousands of Americans to California. Once the report gets to the States, or so the good soldier reckons, New York and Washington will empty out, as Yankees flood to 'Frisco to get this gold for themselves. And, by coming, they will dilute the alien populations, and California will be made truly Yankee."

"Dear lord, how devious," she said, and thought *How American*, which was what their father would have said.

"But it will work, Hat, it will work. The good Colonel Mason has written down yarns that might sound farfetched, but his lieutenants and various experts have attested to their truth. He reveals, for instance, that back in May a man reported twenty-three ounces of gold that he washed out in the space of eight days. His officers was dismissed the flakes as common mica, but when assayed they were pronounced by a judge to be the genuine metal. It was then, he said, that he started to take the reports seriously. So he and Lieutenant Sherman took a party reconnoitering in the so-called diggin's, Hat, and came back with all these enticing, truth-attested yarns. Plus, dear sis, a tea caddy full of nuggets—lumps weighing an average of a quarter of an ounce."

"Oh, marvelous," she derided. "But New York and Washington are many thousands of miles away—all the way round Cape Horn!"

"Not too far away, Hat, because the news will reach the States this winter, in plenty of time for American argonauts to arrive here in the spring. At dawn the *Savannah* will sail to

Monterey, to escort the Mason report on the first stage of its journey to Washington, along with that tea caddy. Cheese in a mousetrap, nothing but bait. Americans!" he said, and laughed, just as their father would have laughed. "They think themselves so subtle."

"If they don't like aliens in their goldmines, Royal, *you're* not going to be very welcome."

"But I'm a true-blue member of a true-blue American Company, Hat!" said he, with another chuckle. "Anyway, as I said, the frigate sails in the morning. And," he added casually, "Jake Dexter goes with them."

Her heart missed a beat. "But why?"

Royal shrugged. "Who knows? But I do hear gossip that Jake Dexter has a wife in New England, and is anxious to speak with the skipper of the whaleship *Isaac Walton*, which is at anchor in Monterey, and find out how she fares."

Harriet said nothing; she couldn't. Her fingers felt cold and numb with their tight grip on the rail. It was as if the fog had crept through her skin and into her blood ... it was impossible to feel any emotion, for all she could feel was the sullen thud of her heavy pulse in her ears. It was like the time her father was killed, the terrible numbness that preceded grief. She loved Jake Dexter — but now she could not tell him that ... she could not humiliate herself by revealing that all she wanted was to be his mistress ... Which was all she could offer him, because of her sordid secret.

She didn't even notice Royal move away, not until Chips, who was chairman as well as the brig's boatswain, loudly declared a meeting of the *Gosling* Company. Then she blinked and roused herself, and realized that she was alone.

Jake came on deck looking energized, as if he had come to a long-awaited decision and was feeling all the better for it. Harriet neither thanked young Crotchet when he brought her a stool, or remembered sitting down on it. Long strings of ducks hooted in the slowly clearing sky, and she watched them and listened to their lonely calls, instead of listening to Bodfish's monotone as he read out the minutes of the last meeting ... the meeting where the *Gosling* Company had voted to come to California.

The men evidently paid little attention, too, for the voice that moved that the minutes be accepted was impatient. Then there was silence. When Harriet looked up everyone was watching Captain Dexter, and every face was expectant.

He said, "I guess you've all heard of Colonel Mason's report."

"Aye, sir," said Chips. All the men were nodding.

"It certifies that the gold yarns that Honest Mill Mason told us up the Tombez River are nothing but the truth. Men in the lower mines are digging an average of two hundred dollars a day. You might have heard of a Mormon trader called Brannan, who started off the gold rush by running about the streets of San Francisco waving a little quinine bottle of gold. In Valparaiso, I was told that he was merely trying to drum up sales of the mining goods he had in his store at Sutter's Fort. If that was his motive, then it was very successful—he did trade that week to the tune of thirty-six thousand dollars. But his story of gold was never a lie. The gold was real, and it came from up the American River, which is a fork of the Sacramento."

He stopped, and looked around. Everyone watched him, and no one said a word.

He said, "Sutter's Fort is the staging post for the mines. It is one hundred and fifty miles up the Sacramento River — but I am told that at this time of the year it is possible to sail the brig up the river all the way there, and that is what I propose we do."

Some of the men, being seasoned mariners, objected, and Harriet listened to Jake's patient voice go on and on about seasonal winds, tide, drift, and bottom. There were marshes and sandbars, he said, but all of them were negotiable. She watched the men's faces become eager as they came to understand that sailing the *Gosling* up the Sacramento River would get them one hundred and fifty miles closer to the fabled gold. It was obvious that they couldn't wait to get to the hills ... that they were as anxious to quit the brig as their Ecuadorean passengers had been.

But what would happen to the *Gosling* after the men left their brig moored at Sutter's Fort, and trudged off into the hills? And what would happen to her?

Harriet's hands were clasped tightly in her lap as she struggled with shameful self-pity. She had coped on her own in a foreign land in the past, she told herself fiercely. She looked up at Jake, her shoulders consciously squared, and found his thoughtful gaze on her face.

Had he been reading her mind? For he said, "We must decide what we will do after we get to Sutter's Fort. There's a substantial landing place, called the Embarcadero, about twenty minutes' walk from the Fort, which is two miles inland, on a tributary of the American River. Mooring the brig and getting her snugged down won't be any kind of a problem. And then—well, even though it is late in the year, Sutter's Fort must have the most potential for profit of any place in the world. The job is decide how we can get some of that profit for ourselves."

The men were frowning at him, their expressions blank and bewildered. Obviously, in their minds, the only decision to be made was how fast they could get into the hills.

Jake tapped one foot on the deck, and said, "We have a fortune right here."

Silence. Uncomprehending silence.

"The provisions," he prompted. "The foodstuffs that we charged for passage from the Tombez River to this place — the meat, fruit, flour, and vegetables the Ecuadoreans loaded in exchange for berths in the hold. We could sell them through an agent, or we could sell them ourselves. Either way, we'd make thousands of dollars."

Abijah Roe cried out, insulted, "You want us to set up as *greengrocers*, sir?"

"But we came here for gold, sir!" exclaimed Tib Greene.

"For gold, yes. But do we get it with hard work, or the easy way?"

"Easy, sir?" said Chips, very doubtfully.

"Let me give you an example," Jake said. "The flour we valued at fifteen dollars a barrel at Tombez will fetch fifty dollars at Sutter's, or even more if we bag it up into one or two-pound lots. There's more — oranges, for instance. When they were brought in at Tombez, Bodfish gave a note to the value of sixty dollars for eight thousand of the fruit. At Sutter's Fort, we can charge fifty cents. Each. Fifty cents for each and every fruit. Coconuts would go for two to three dollars apiece, and bananas will sell for fifty cents each. And the payment would not be in coin. Gold is the currency, there. In Sutter's, or so I hear, they are in need of provisions, but have plenty of gold."

Gold. The word dropped into the astounded silence, as warm and heavy as the metal itself.

"Gold, not coin, is what men deal in, at Sutter's Fort," said Jake. He nodded, looking from one man to another. "A teaspoonful of dust buys a pound of flour, a pinch buys a drink, a nugget a meal ... and a palmful of nuggets buys a passage up the Sacramento River."

Harriet found her voice. "Passengers again?" she cried.

Jake smiled ruefully. "Mistakes have been made, I agree. The Ecuadoreans were worse than I could have possibly imagined a load of passengers could be."

"Especially the Murietas," she said bitterly. Without her realizing it, her fingers lifted to touch the scar where Joaquín Murieta's knife had cut her cheek. The Ecuadorean bandit had done it after invading the after cabin, when he grabbed her hair and threatened her with the knife, with the foulest of intentions.

"Especially the Murietas," Jake agreed, his voice very

even. "If we vote to take passengers upriver the fare must cover nothing more than a berth in the hold or a plank on the deck. It's for three or four days only, and the passengers will all have to carry their own food."

His eyes were fixed on her face, his expression wry. It was as if he was trying to send her a reassuring message, but Harriet knew that he wouldn't be there. Instead … if Royal had told the truth … he would be in Monterey. But perhaps Royal was wrong…

Hope flickered, only to be destroyed. "Mr. Martin," said Jake, "will take the *Gosling* up the river, with a local pilot to assist, and I will meet you at Sutter's Fort."

No one seemed surprised. So, thought Harriet wearily, they had all heard the gossip that he was going to Monterey to get news of the wife he had left back in New England.

She said, "How are you going to rejoin us, if we're all that way inland, Captain? And what happens if there … if there is trouble on the brig?"

Jake said, "There won't be any trouble—because of the passenger who will take over the second mate's stateroom, and who will be eating at the cabin table."

"*Who?*" Her voice shook.

"The alcalde of the Feather River district—a kind of lawyer. Alcaldes are in charge of keeping law and order, so he will be there to prevent any trouble. He's an Englishman, Robert Ross by name, so you should have a lot in common. I know I can rely on him to protect you."

Jake was trying very hard to be reassuring, she thought, and looked down at her tightly clasped hands.

When she didn't speak, he said, "It's only four days' ride from Monterey to Sutter's Fort, I'm assured of that. I … have to go to Monterey on a private matter, but then…"

Valentine interrupted, crying, "But what about the diggin's, Captain?"

Jake sighed, and said, "You're really determined to try the mines?"

"Aye, sir!" And there was an echo all about the deck.

Jake paused, frowning as he chose his words.

Then he said, "You've all heard the wonderful stories, but I want to warn you that it won't be easy. The season is very late, and the rains begin in October. The rains, I hear, are not to be taken lightly—they come in cataracts. Once they've commenced in earnest all the trails will be impassable, and the men in the hills will be trapped for the whole of the winter. Many will starve, some will die of disease or accident, and none of them will be able to dig. At the most, there is seven weeks of the digging season left."

Seven weeks! Harriet could feel the sudden urgency running through the company. The passage up the river would take four days, and then they would have to wait for their skipper, and then God alone knew how long it would take to get into the hills and stake a claim.

A babble set up as all the men tried to talk each other down. Jake had to raise his voice to be heard. He shouted, "There are alternatives!"

"But if we wait till February, all the good claims will be gone, sir," Dan Kemp objected.

His crony, Tib Greene, seemed just as anxious. "Why, good lord, sir," he said, "we've all of us put up with wet and cold, it don't make no difference to us."

"You certainly know your own strengths," Jake allowed. "Form a mining party if you wish, but remember this—*I am not having the brig abandoned!*"

His voice rose with this last, and Tib, being Tib, caved in at once. "Abandon the *Gosling*, sir?" said he. "Why, good lord, sir, that be the last thing on anyone's mind."

Jake snapped, "I'm glad to hear it. I presume, too, that no one wants to pass on the opportunity to make a fortune out of our cargo?"

"Absolutely not, sir, and that is the truth," said Tib. "But the fact is, Captain, that I am plumb confounded. There's the mining party, and the greengrocery, and the shipkeeping,

23

too. That's a big program, sir, and we don't have enough time or enough men to do it all at once and altogether."

All the men were nodding in agreement. "But the answer is obvious," Jake argued. "All we need is a little organization of our forces."

And then he began to sketch out what he planned.

He went on and on, about one part of the Company going into the hills to establish a claim and build a cabin, and then digging in till spring, while another party stayed on board to do the trading. Then he discussed the prospect of turning the *Gosling* into a moored boarding house. To him, he said, it seemed too good a chance to turn down, considering that they had the hold fitted out with berths already. He had been reliably informed, he said, that the usual charge for accommodation was fourteen dollars a week, no food included. Just as with the Ecuadorean passengers, the lodgers would have to provide their own mattresses and blankets.

The men contributed lively comments, but it seemed to Harriet as if none of it had anything to do with her. So after a while she stopped listening.

At dawn there was another fog, but still the *Savannah* prepared to make sail. When Harriet came on deck all the *Gosling*s were at the rail watching the frigate weigh anchor, so she joined them, standing aft, a little apart.

The rail under her hands was clammy, and the foggy air was cold on her face. The shouts from the frigate seemed muffled by the damp air. Birds cried out far above, and the distant sails as they dropped were luminous with mist. Harriet could distinguish the rows of men in the yards and hear the bo'sun's whistle. Then, a clangor as the chain rattled up and the ship hove short.

And slowly, slowly, the *Savannah* began to move.

A cannon from the Presidio on shore thudded hollowly and the frigate replied. Harriet could smell the heavy sour

24

smoke. The big flag fluttered, sagged, and then flew out as it took the breeze. The fog, like the flag, lifted with the rising wind, and low sunlight was suddenly glittering on the tips of little waves … struck sparks from brass fittings, shone starkly on the black snouts of cannon. Another salute. Harriet saw the frigate lurch as she fired. Then, she came about, and Harriet could see the elaborate stern. The sails filled, and the frigate hauled around … and sailed out of the harbor.

She was gone, taking Jake Dexter with her.

THREE

OVER the course of the day, the passengers arrived for the upriver voyage, while Harriet watched from a secluded corner of the afterdeck, where she could see without being noticed.

It was a varied invasion, the men who straggled on board being as wide-ranging in their variety as the people in Harriet's audiences in London and the provinces. Four glum Yankee merchants arrived first, and she could hear them grumbling about the scandalous cost of the fare. Soon they were followed by the skipper and officers of the latest abandoned vessel, still all fired up about the crew that had skipped in the night. Then there was a huddle of furtive men in tattered remains of American uniform, evidently come out of hiding with the departure of the *Savannah*, and some kanakas with them, presumably Hawaiian seamen from the island traders that had sailed into port to sell provisions, and had not been able to sail out again. There were a few South Americans, too, better equipped for the Californian winter than the Hawaiians.

There were black men, looking like their seaman, Davy Jones Locker—perhaps, she thought, they were escaped slaves, too. Silent pig-tailed men came from the East, and Harriet was reminded of her husband, Frank Sefton, and how he had abandoned her without a word, to head off for China. She wondered what Frank Sefton had found there, and hoped that he had found plenty to suit his corrupt and devious ends, because he had talked of coming to California, too. Then, the last man arrived, and proved to be the alcalde.

Charlie Martin brought him into the mess cabin, where Harriet was sitting at the table. She looked up to see Charlie come in through the double doors, hauling at his beard because of the grave responsibility of getting the brig upriver. Then her eyes widened, for the figure that trotted in behind him was a sight from one of the many pantomimes of her past.

Robert Ross was a middle-aged fellow, a fat little man with a paunch. His legs, by contrast to his rotund middle, were as skinny as sticks, but despite their comical shape they were crammed into the tight Spanish trousers with buttons down the sides, and open flaps at the ankle, that she knew were called calcineros. He wore a folded serape hanging off one shoulder, but not in the usual brilliant colors. Instead, it was striped in black, gray and ginger — as if, she thought, he had chosen it to match his flowing beard. When he swept off his sombrero, a yellowed pair of small blue eyes was revealed, along with a large port-wine nose.

"Why, Gawd'n bless me," he said in thunderstruck tones. "A lady!"

To Harriet's disbelief, despite the Californian costume, and though Charlie introduced him by a Californian title — Don Roberto — this strange fellow's accent was pure Cockney. "Miss Gray belongs to London, too," bragged Charlie, as Harriet rose to her feet. "Perhaps, Don Roberto, you have viewed Miss Harriet Gray on the stage?"

"Miss Harriet Gray?" Don Roberto enfolded Harriet's hand in a warm grip that was as moist as his little blue eyes. "I've been Mexican since the memorial year of 1839, through a most remarkable set of circumstances, Miss Gray! But do I know the name? Yes, ma'am, I believe I do!"

Harriet said nothing, smiling politely. What had she been doing in 1839—when she was just nine years old? She had played the circuit as a cherub in board-and-feather wings, and she had acted the juvenile in *The Orphan of Geneva*. Her first success had been her warbling of a song called Home Sweet Home, in a performance of *The Maid of Milan*—but she refused to believe that this fellow had ever heard her sing it, or had ever seen her on the stage.

"London, London," he was saying, and to her disbelief he had actual tears in his eyes. Letting go of her hand so he could mop his face with a huge handkerchief, he gushed, "Such recollections that dear word do bring back! I've been in this here California nigh on ten years, come looking for adventure, Miss Gray, for a fortune!—but how I miss that dear city."

"But why California?" she couldn't help but ask.

"By circumstance, my dear Miss Gray! I arrived in that memorial year of 1839 wiv a letter of introduction from the British consul at..."

There was a clang on deck, and a few shouts, hailing the arrival of the pilot who would guide them up the river. Charlie made a muttered excuse and disappeared back up the steps.

"...consul at Lahaina," Don Roberto said. "Found the Mexicans exceedin' 'ospitable, so I bought sixty thousand acres along with a castle at a most excellent price up the Feather River, just across from Cache Creek, and I've been 'ere ever since, Miss Gray, never regretted it, neither, as I have sponsors, you know, old Californians, great patrons..."

Harriet stopped listening. Surely this garrulous fellow would soon run to a stop?

But he didn't.

The brig anchored at sunset when they were thirty-five miles from San Francisco, at a pretty place called Benecia. Harriet went on deck to look at the fine view of grazing lands that Benecia offered, free to go out in the open air despite all the male passengers on deck, because of the official nature of her escort, which was a blessing, even it did mean she had to put up with Don Roberto's monologue. However, as she soon perceived, there was not going to be anything like the trouble she had experienced with the arrogant Murietas and their Ecuadorean companions, as this lot of passengers paid her no attention whatsoever.

Instead of eyeing her with salacious looks, the men were fully engaged in gawping at the llamas — which was extremely unusual. Ever since the five animals had been loaded at Tombez as prospective pack beasts for California, they had seemed perfectly happy in their pen on the foredeck, lying down whatever the weather and eating whatever fodder was given them, humming to each other, and enjoying being fed, watered, and occasionally patted by Bill, the steerage boy, who had been put in charge of them. Otherwise they had been ignored. The South Americans who had voyaged to San Francisco on the brig had not been at all interested in the animals.

But this complement of passengers was behaving quite differently — quite oddly, in fact. They were fascinated by the strange beasts, and were very orderly about it, lining up along the deck to take their turn at contemplating the llamas. It was as if, thought Harriet, they were at some exotic zoological garden.

The llamas were polite and orderly, too, standing up with their long necks inclined, regarding the passengers down their noses with long-lashed curiosity — but then the passengers dared to touch them, and tousle their wool, which they found irritating. And, being llamas, when they became irked they spat.

The passengers who were within range scattered in cursing disarray, and swiped at the smelly green splodges on their shirt fronts. Then the four merchants complained about it to Charlie Martin — at length and in detail. Harriet

29

watched the poor fellow yank at his beard as he listened, making conciliatory noises but obviously at a loss to know what to do. Royal, being the man who had bought the llamas from the Peruvian Indians, was appealed to for some kind of solution, but he merely spread his hands, laughed immoderately, and walked away.

The llamas, the merchants complained, not only spat, but they stank. In fact, the whole brig stank, along with the crew, undoubtedly on account of living with the llamas for so long. It was pointless for poor Charlie to protest that Benecia stank, too, as the slaughter yards were very close to the beach, as the slander continued. The *Gosling*s got the vessel snug for the night in a wounded silence, and no sooner had full dark descended than the brig was attacked by a horde of bloodthirsty mosquitoes.

Within minutes the merchants were back at the after-house door. It was the stench of the brig, the crew and the llamas that attracted the insects, or so they complained. The watch, slapping at mosquitoes, retreated to corners where they lurked, offended, and Charlie was too distraught to eat much in the way of his supper, which meant that Bodfish became sulky too, banging about in the pantry because of what he thought of as an insult to his cooking.

Bodfish was still making a ruckus in the pantry again next morning, when Charlie was topsides, supervising the watch as they weighed the anchor. As Harriet and Don Roberto were eating breakfast the brig stood up with the tide in her favor, sailing into Suisan Bay, and as soon as they had finished they stood at the rail to view the amazing scenery.

Within one bend the brig was surrounded by vivid marshland, a gold-red-green sea of marsh and tall bulrushes. Bulrushes?

"Toulies," said Don Roberto.

Standing on the deck of the brig seemed more at times like standing on the floor of a dray. Ducks and geese rose hooting into the pale air. It didn't last long, however, as within another broad reach they were sailing up the Sacramento proper. Sailing! For Harriet, it was a marvel. As a child she had learned beyond doubt that the current of a river flowed always to the mouth, and so surely the *Gosling* should be going backwards? Instead, however, she was sailing sweetly against the direction of the rippling flow, her topsails set and puffed full.

As Jake had promised, the Sacramento was a noble stream, a full hundred yards wide even at this dry time of the year. The banks were noble, too, lined with long stands of oak trees and sycamore, many with trunks with a girth of more than six feet. Beyond the trees — more trees, and rolling slopes of gold-brown grass. Then elk were glimpsed, bounding about in the undergrowth. The passengers demanded, one and all, that the brig haul aback while they lowered boats and went off a-hunting. Those with pistols fired them off to emphasize their point, and Charlie, again completely at a loss, gave in and let them have their way. So, the brig loitered about while the hunters headed off into the nearest marsh, and the men who stayed on board made wooden pick-handles and sheet-iron washers.

Just as the tide turned against them, the huntsmen returned with their bloodied booty, which they shared out freely, declaring they had cooked and eaten their fill on shore. The truth of this was confirmed by the sight of their camp fires all gone out of control. Harriet wondered with alarm what effect this would have on California, but Don Roberto informed her that the toulies caught alight all the time, and no harm was wrought. Then, just as the fires went out, proving the Cockney correct, the brig grounded on a bar.

Next morning the crew was on deck at dawn, struggling to get the brig back into deep water. They took kedge anchors and dropped them ahead, and returned and heaved at the windlass to haul the brig up to the kedges, but all they accomplished was to lose a chain and anchor. They came

31

back on board downcast enough, and ate supper and went to bed with nothing more than a minor scrap with the most belligerent of the passengers. At three in the morning the westerly wind blew fresh and the tide was on the full, so Charlie called all hands on deck and they managed, at last, to get the brig afloat. Then, once the brig was securely moored to a handy oak, the men lowered boats and fished for their lost anchor. It was afternoon before they returned in triumph, to unloose the brig, and set off upriver again.

And all the time Don Roberto talked. My God, thought Harriet, how the little fat Cockney talked. It was as if he'd been forced into silence since that memorable year of 1839 and now the dammed talk was all pouring out.

"Sixty thousand acres," he told her repeatedly, while she scarcely listened, wondering what lay ahead for her in this crazy land instead—wondering how Jake was faring in Monterey, what news he had heard of his wife. When he had told her his story—how his young bride had fallen into the shipowner's bed the moment Jake's ship had been topgallant down on the horizon—Jake had seemed bitter enough. But now, she thought drearily, he had forgiven his errant sweetheart, unknowing that she, Sefton's discarded wife, had been foolish enough to fall in...

"Other men have done it, yes," said Don Roberto. "But I've been a true pioneer in California, about the first Englishman to buy a tract of land, if not the *very* first. I have a fort, too up the Feather River where it be narrow enough to bridge, not as large as Sutter's Fort, but an efficient citadel. It bars the way to a great estate, belonging to a prominent old California family, the Vidries, who produce fine beef and wine. It would be a scandal and a disaster if the gold diggers strayed onto Vidrie land, Miss Gray—but my fort is there to stop it. My fort also overlooks the trails to the diggings, much of which I adjudicate. A proper fortification was necessary, Miss Gray, for the state of lawlessness in California is beyond belief."

He looked about the empty mess cabin where they were sitting, and then lowered his voice. "A rumbustious lot, the Americans — the trappers and hide and tallow traders, why, you ain't got a notion. Drunken, I call them, but shrewd enough, too, and some of the wide ones have been wide enough to see the opportunities, ma'am, and settle like meself in this new land. Some even become an alcalde like me, wiv jurisdiction over a province and a whole town, Pueblo San Marco! Ain't that strange enough, a native-born Londoner reaching the position of alcalde?"

"Yes indeed," Harriet agreed with great sincerity.

At six in the evening the brig reached a settlement called New York, and Harriet and Don Roberto went on deck to view this unlikely city of the west. New York was at the junction of two fine rivers, the Sacramento and the Joaquín, and it was made up of two huts and two riverboats. The *Goslings* had a good laugh about that, but then the merchants laid another complaint. While everyone on the decks slapped at bloodthirsty mosquitoes, they complained about young Bill.

Bill, they all declared, had been stealing. He was nothing but a nasty common little thief. They demanded to know where he had come from, and when they were told that his father had been a Yankee beachcomber, and he had been born in the tropical Pacific, they guessed, darkly, that he was a runaway from the penal colonies of Australia.

The basis of their slander was that Bill had more money stowed away in his pants than any little rascal had any right to own — he had more dollars, fips and levies than any normal boys should have in his pockets. Where had this wealth come from? But when the merchants had demanded to know, the steerage boy refused to say. Instead, he defiantly informed them that there would be a lot more where this had come from.

So two of the Yankee merchants took over and collared

33

him, pinioned his squirming form and poked fingers into his pants pockets. Bill wriggled and screeched and kicked and bit, and both men let go with a curse, whereupon he shot like a bullet into the rigging, and did not stop until he reached the foretop. Then he turned, steadied, adjusted his breeches, took aim, and pissed with startling accuracy right down on the heads of this tormentors.

Both Harriet and Royal found this excruciatingly funny. Harriet laughed until the tears poured down her cheeks, which was a welcome release for all her pent-up emotions, and the American merchants stared and muttered, and declared her behavior scandalous. Then the *Goslings* found out how Bill had made his contentious fortune — he had been charging the passengers money to line up and look at the llamas! The *Goslings* had their own laugh, then, and the traders muttered foully.

Don Roberto did not laugh. Somewhere, since 1839, as Harriet deduced, he had lost the robust quality of English humor. Or perhaps he didn't even notice it, being so lost in his enjoyable production of an endless flow of information.

"A pueblo, now, you may not be familiar with that word, Miss Gray," he said at supper, "for pueblo is Spanish for village."

His suzerainty, Pueblo San Marco, was situated on the Feather River, a half-day's march downriver from his fort, at the end of a well-marked trail that had been worn out of the terrain by numberless muletrains. Pueblo San Marco, or so Harriet learned, was a half-day's sail upriver from Sutter's Fort, and was where Don Roberto did most of his work as an alcalde. He received a fee for his legal responsibilities, it seemed, and it was easy money, too, for official proceedings in California were a great deal less complex than the workings of the law in London.

"For a start," he said, "there ain't no writ down legislation."

"Merciful heavens, is there not?"

"And the jurisdiction of the alcalde is just about boundless. The old Mexicans devised the system, and it ain't been changed since. They established each pueblo by selecting a site and marking it out, and then selling the land in fifty-vara lots. Then they appointed an alcalde and gave him the money they'd got from selling the land, to start off the town. Whenever an alcalde needs more money all 'e 'as to do is mark out some more land and sell it. Easy as that," he assured her, and nodded profoundly at her expression.

"But what about crime, Don Roberto? You told me yourself that the state of California is lawless beyond belief. What do you do with a thief—and what if a man commits murder?"

"All you need for a jury is eight good men—if you need a jury at all. There ain't no jails, I grant you that, but who needs a jail where there is a tree, and that tree has a good strong branch, and you 'ave a good strong rope to hang from it?"

"But what if the man is innocent?"

"Ah, but that's simple, too. If there be any doubt at all, any suspicion voiced that the charges be unfounded, then the man is given twenty-four hours to quit clear of the alcalde's province—a full day and night. If he is still present at the end of the deadline, then it is taken as a confession of guilt, and we string him up without argument. I told you, it's easy!"

"Good heavens," said Harriet, thinking that there was no logic in this at all.

However, she didn't comment, not wanting to trigger another monologue. As usual, though, Don Roberto needed no encouragement. He opened his mouth, and she braced herself for another flood of talk.

35

FOUR

At supper, much to her relief, Charlie announced that he was pretty sure they would make Sutter's Fort next day. The old pilot, he said, had assured him of that.

The old pilot? It was the first time Harriet was aware that they were being navigated up the river, as the pilot had made no appearance in the afterquarters at all. Where did he sleep? And where did he eat? With the tradesmen of the brig, in the steerage, Charlie said. The old man preferred it that way.

Then, that night, it rained, so that when Harriet arrived on deck in the morning the trees and grass were washed and shining in the early sun. Beyond the hills and clumps of trees the mountains were a distant gray and mauve. The passengers lined the rails, staring at those distant promising hills, and the *Gosling*s paused often in their work to gaze at the enticing vista, too. Harriet looked around for the pilot, and thought he must be the old, hunched man who was standing at the main shrouds with his back turned towards her. She shrugged, and looked away — but then looked back, trying to pin down a sense of familiarity.

And yet it was impossible that she had ever seen him before. This old man knew the river, and knew this California, so obviously he had lived here a very long time —

and she'd never met anyone from California before. All seamen looked the same in their weathered old age, she told herself, even if that seafaring happened on a river instead of on the sea—they all got seamed in their water-beaten faces. She had never heard his voice, as he only spoke to Charlie, and then only to convey curt instructions.

Then she forgot the little mystery, as Don Roberto trotted up to her side. He grinned as broadly as if he had done something magnificent, threw out an arm, and cried, "New Helvetia!"

Harriet said blankly, "I beg your pardon?"

Infuriatingly, the garrulous little man merely smiled. Then she could hear the men aloft calling out. The passengers all rushed at once to the starboard rail, though there seemed nothing unusual in the scene. The river was the same, the mud was the same, and the gold-colored grass was the same. There was the usual smell of mud, and the autumn warmth was as humid. The scattered clumps of tall, thickly foliaged trees looked just like the stands of oaks they had been passing for many miles. For a few moments there was nothing but shouting and commotion, while Harriet could see no reason for it all.

But then…

In the middle distance, set on a rise overlooking the plain—walls, the thick solid adobe walls of a fort. Harriet could glimpse the blunt witches' hat shapes of two corner bastions, a huge high gate that seemed designed as an iron portcullis, the terracotta roof-tiles of a square building inside those walls, and a bright proud flag.

She looked up to the rigging, envying the *Gosling*s their vantage places, and saw Royal up the main topmast, his arm flung out, his beard jutting. He looked medieval, like a herald from old Outremer, and the outline of the fort was almost Arabic, too. Don Roberto had told her that Captain Sutter had built it in 1838, the same memorial year that Don Roberto had arrived here, but it looked much, much older

37

than that, like some ancient defensive structure from the time of the Crusades.

The trees thickened as the brig sailed on slowly, slowly, towards the Embarcadero, and then Captain Sutter's Fort was lost to sight behind the trees. There was a path running alongside the riverbank, but it could only be glimpsed in snatches, whenever there was a gap in the thicket. Harriet saw ox-drawn carts, horses, men hunched over with the weight of burdens on their backs, a half-beached riverboat with a notice up that said TRADING POST, and then the larger hull of some ship, wedged tightly into a clump of bushes so that she couldn't see the sternboard.

The pilot was talking in Mr. Martin's ear, issuing instructions, and Charlie shouted out orders. The brig slowed and slowed as the topsails left the wind, and then surged towards the squared timbers of the Embarcadero. A pause—and then the gangway dropped.

Just as at San Francisco, the passengers rushed about, jostling each other to get on shore first. Harriet scarcely noticed their departure, or see the old pilot go off down the plank. She was staring at the Embarcadero, at this fabled gateway to … what? And a shiver of foreboding lifted the hairs on the nape of her neck and trickled down her spine.

Because this did not look at all like Eldorado. It was impossible to believe that this was the gateway to a promise of gold. This, surely, was still the frontier, she thought, even though men gave it names. Sutter's Fort. New Helvetia. Eldorado.

Boatmen were shouting and swearing, wagoners were whistling and halloaing and cracking their whips while their horses strained to haul heavily laden carts, and groups of horsemen were dashing to and fro. People on foot moved about in masses, heading this way and that, on errands that were impossible to guess. There was no feeling of mission here, or of American enterprise and energy. Whips cracked but for no apparent reason, and all the shouting, or nearly all, was in Spanish. Would Colonel Mason's report make the difference to this that Royal reckoned it would? Again, Harriet shivered.

Then she was distracted by movement in the field on the other side of the Embarcadero, just across the broad promenade from where the *Gosling* was moored. There were soldiers working there ... with strings and stakes. She was reminded of the day she had found the *Gosling*s digging for pirate treasure on Judas Island, because they had marked out the ground, too, according to a treasure map Jake Dexter had found in an old journal. But surely these soldiers weren't digging for gold? They looked more like surveyors. They even had the little handcart to carry all their gear that surveyors were accustomed to use—but they were definitely soldiers, and hard-used soldiers, too. Their regimentals were scruffy, muddy, and ragged, and they had a dogged look about the way they carried out their work.

What the devil, she thought, were they doing?

"They're laying out the town," said Don Roberto.

"What town?" said she, bewildered.

"The Embarcadero, ma'am! They're laying it out American style, streets numbered one way and lettered the other, all neat and tidy-oh, United States fashion." He waved a short arm and cried, "Don't you see the future, Miss Gray? Can't you see the promise? This will be the most capital town of California, one day!"

Harriet shook her head.

"Come, Miss Gray," he said, and clicked his tongue. "Come and see what marvels we have now, and put your mind to picturing what the future will bring—within two years, Miss Gray, if not sooner!"

They walked down the gangplank, and were instantly absorbed by the throng that packed the promenade, buffeted and crowded from every side, becoming two motes in a maelstrom of men. The going was treacherous, and Harriet had to hold her skirts high to avoid the mud and heaps of steaming horse manure, most of which she glimpsed only just in time. Then they turned off the Embarcadero, heading inland, and the going became a little smoother and dryer.

For a long time, even though they were walking straight towards it, the fort didn't seem to get any closer, and she remembered someone—Jake?—saying that Sutter's Fort was two miles from the Embarcadero. The walls seemed to float on the near horizon, with the outlines of great mountains making an ethereal backdrop in the distance. Again she was reminded of a medieval citadel, an impression that was accentuated by the creek that curled about the north wall like a moat, and which was crossed by a chunky little bridge.

Their footsteps rattled on the bridge, and then all at once, so suddenly that Harriet was overtaken with surprise, the walls were looming over them, more than two feet thick at the level of her waist, and three times her height. Though they were adobe, they seemed as massive as stone, tan-colored where the whitewash had flaked.

"Sutter's is bigger than Fort Laramie!" Don Roberto declared. "And the fort at Monterey? Wivout a word of a lie, Miss Gray, the fort at Monterey is just a little heap of log huts compared to Sutter's!"

And there was a military presence here, too. The broad, well-worn path ran on past the fort, leading to a double-storied adobe building that sat about a hundred yards away, which Don Roberto told her that was the army barracks. Harriet could see a fenced corral in front of it where the troop's horses were held, presumably, though it seemed to be empty of horses at the moment. So where were all the soldiers? In the mines, obviously—but were they still loyal to their officers, or had they been lured into desertion by the call of the siren gold?

Instead of asking, she followed Don Roberto, as he turned through the gate of Sutter's Fort. The portcullis overhead was made of huge timbers, studded with spikes, and the gate had a guardhouse on each side, with small, barred windows. When they emerged from the dark shadow, Harriet found herself in an enormous courtyard, made of bare beaten earth, sheltered by large trees in several places, and dominated by a massive two-level dwelling place that stood in the middle.

The courtyard was as full of noise and color as the Embarcadero. It was like an ancient Eastern market, Harriet thought, for every trade was carried on in full sight of the crowd, and men talked at the tops of their voices. Gamblers had set up shop under red-striped calico awnings, with red curtains looped back at either side, and they rang little bells to get the attention of prospective speculators. Traders who had set out trestle tables laden with picks, pans, tools and provisions were bawling out their allurements, too. More noise came from the lines of men who were waiting at the beehive ovens were set here and about, steaming red-hot with the loaves that sweating bakers made to sell. Whole carcasses revolved on spits, while other fires smoldered under metal grills cooking gobbets of meat, buccaneer-style. When the meat was cooked, the roasters and grillers rang their own bells, and men lined up at their fires, too.

Adobe cottages had been built against the inner sides of the surrounding walls, and many of these seemed to be manufactories, for Harriet saw blacksmiths sweating over forges, and coopers shaving staves. There was a candle-making house, a room where Indian women patiently worked at blanket looms, another where Indian men made whiskey, brandy, pisco, kitchens that turned out smoked hams, and stone-walled pantries where butter was churned. There was even a room where tanned hides hung, stinking most distinctively.

Most of the tanning had been done in a hut over by the American River, Don Roberto told her—near the field where the soldiers were laying out streets. Curing hides and tallow-making had once been the prime industries here, but the discovery of gold had put paid to that. Now the surveyor-soldiers lived in the tanning hut, and the tanning room here was hired out by night as accommodation, despite the all-pervading stink.

Harriet said, puzzled, "Why don't the soldiers live in the barracks?"

"All the buildings are hired out for the hotel trade," Don Roberto informed her, the army building being no exception.

Several of the cottages inside these walls had been accommodation for Sutter's vaqueros, but in May the herdsmen had been turned out to make room for the bales of goods, and barrels of flour, grain and meat that had been brought upriver to meet the huge demand that had so abruptly arisen. And now that the goods had all been sold, they were rented out, too. There was an old ship moored at the Embarcadero that was turning huge profits as a boarding house. Even Sutter's house was not exempt, Captain Sutter being up at the mines.

"They pack 'em in so tight in the attic," said Don Roberto, "that when one man wants to turn over in the night, he has to call out for them all to turn, and the way they call out is to holler the word *spoon!*"

"Good lord," said Harriet. And how much did men pay for this uncomfortable accommodation? One dollar a night, or two dollars if two meals a day were included, or so Don Roberto told her. But that price, he reckoned, would be much higher in the season to come.

"You just wait till Colonel Mason's report gets out in the States! The mines will close down soon, when the rainy season starts, but in February it will be different. You may think is bustling and crowded now, but you just wait, Miss Gray, for the memorial season of 'forty-nine, and then you'll truly see doings, you just wait and see."

FIVE

THE path back to the Embarcadero was as crowded as before. As she walked closer, Harriet could see *Gosling*s in the rigging—getting ready to set up the brig as a store and maybe even a boarding house, she supposed, and wondered tensely yet again what would happen to her in this gold-mad region while the Company was busily making their fortune.

Then they were abreast of the trampled fields again. When Don Roberto headed in the direction of the three surveyor-soldiers, Harriet hesitated, but then she caught up with him, driven by curiosity, holding her skirts high to keep clear of the mud.

"Who ordered them to survey this field?" she asked.

"Captain Sutter, of course! He might be Swiss or whatever, but he has a great head for business, which be the kind of head that's needful in this place."

If he was Swiss, a great head for commerce was only to be expected, thought Harriet wryly, but didn't have the chance to comment, as they had come up with the soldiers.

The trio looked no less morose at close quarters, and stank even worse than llama spit, undoubtedly because of their living quarters. Their horses were grazing in a rough corral nearby, and looked as muddy and miserable and insect-bitten as their owners. It was a miracle, she thought, that any of them were there at all, either horses or men, the enticements of the mines being such a contrast to their present state.

The three soldiers were all officers. "Lieutenant William Warner," the first introduced himself. "William Tecumseh Sherman," said the second. The third was Lieutenant Ord. Breathing shallowly through her mouth, Harriet shook three exceedingly muddy hands.

The soldiers were delighted to meet her—not that they recognized her name. They had very little company, they said, and never the company of a lady. Perhaps because of that, they competed to talk. Not only did have have to do this confounded muddy surveying job, they informed her, but they had to fend for themselves, as well. Lieutenant Warner was the ostler, and looked after the horses, Lieutenant Sherman did the cooking, and Lieutenant Ord was supposed to clean the dishes. This last was a bone of contention, the other two lieutenants having just found it that he simply wiped them down with grass from the horse paddock.

"Lieutenant Sherman," said Don Roberto, in the first gap in the flow of chatter, "was assistant to Colonel Mason during the investigation what led to the famous report on the mines."

"Actually, ma'am," said Lieutenant Sherman, more dour than ever, "I was cook on that survey, too." He sniffed at his drooping moustache, which matched his straggling black hair.

"But the gold was truly there in the hills?"

"Ma'am," said he heavily, "the Colonel estimated that since May more than ten million dollars' worth of gold has been taken out of the hills."

"Ten million? Merciful heavens, surely not!"

"Ma'am, I assure you that I do not tell lies."

All the officers' smiles had been replaced by offended

44

scowls, and Don Roberto's frown was equally disapproving. Harriet said very hastily, "I do assure you, sir, that I was merely marveling, and that I most sincerely do not doubt your word, not for a single instant—"

"Men in them hills, ma'am," said Ord with emphasis, "are running around like hogs in an oak thicket, picking up nuggets the way hogs grub up acorns."

"Good lord," said Harriet. "Is that really so?" Then, very quickly, as she realized that this, too, could be taken the wrong way, "It is so very hard to believe that—"

"Men are picking up ten ounces a *day*," said Warner. "They calculate on making a dollar a *minute*."

"Seven men staked a claim within my jurisdiction," said Don Roberto. "Back in July, high in the mountains that overlook the Feather River. And do you know how much they have dug from there since?"

"No, I do not," confessed Harriet.

"Well, Miss Gray, they've dug three hundred pounds of gold, all but twenty, and that in seven weeks."

"And it's facts like that which make up the colonel's report," said Lieutenant Ord.

"Those tales and other tales like them," said Lieutenant Warner. "And when those tales all get about back east, well, you know what will happen."

"They will come in their thousands, and render this a bustling city," said Lieutenant Sherman.

Harriet looked about at the trees, the fields of neglected corn, the tanning shed, and the muddy corral. The fort in the distance seemed like a mirage-like delusion.

She said, "Why you are laying out the streets right here, at the Embarcadero, and not at the walls of the fort?"

"The situation, ma'am!" Lieutenant Warner cried. "The confluence! American River one way, Feather River the other, and fabulous mines on both of 'em. This place will be a second New Orleans!"

The officers were as animated by the grand prospects for

45

the Embarcadero as they had been about the tales of gold. These three men, morose as they were, displayed a most remarkable loyalty to their country and their flag, Harriet mused. Their fellow officers and the soldiers they had led had deserted in their dozens, but these three men had proved stalwart despite the mud and slovenly conditions.

Then she had another thought. Because they were going through such an ordeal, they *had* to believe in their cause. It was like the story of the man who boasted about his new carriage despite its many faults, because he didn't want to look a fool for having bought it. These men *had* to believe in the future of the Embarcadero, to make their present parlous state worthwhile. This, she meditated, made their claims somewhat less believable.

Don Roberto had been watching her face. "Look past the mud, Miss Gray, and try to imagine this place at this time next year," he urged. "The memorial year of 'forty-nine will go down in 'istory. There will be stores and shops and manufactories where you see nothing but mud and grass — taverns and taps and groggeries, too, saloons and restaurants and theaters! This city might turn out to be low-class and fast-paced, the miners bein' all men wiv no women's sensitivities to hold them back, and men bein' men, they want to do more when they find their gold than shout EUREKA! The Embarcadero will provide everything they need to celebrate in style, and because of all that it will become the boomingest town in the land."

Harriet had stopped listening. Her mind had seized on the word *theaters*. My God, she thought in a rush of wild inspiration, the three lieutenants and Don Roberto could well be right, and if they were right...

Theaters. If the gold seekers came from the big cities, from New York, Philadelphia, Charleston, Cincinnati, they would be men accustomed to the stage; they would know their actors, and their plays, and have their favorites. And they wouldn't just be members of a prospective audience, they could include managers and owners, too … and in the theatrical business, as in any enterprise, it was the investors who raked in the profits, while the actors, even the stars, had to be satisfied with ten shillings a night with board and lodging and stabling for horses and the occasional benefit…

She said with urgency, "How does one claim land in California?"

The four men stared at her as if she had taken leave of her senses. Then Don Roberto said, "Why, Miss Gray, surely I have explained the system before?"

She shook her head, because if he had told her, she hadn't been listening, and he launched himself into his usual self-important monologue. "No claim be more than one hundred feet square, no man can own more than one current claim, no man shall have a claim and not work it, unless his tools are left there as a sign, all claims must be soundly staked with a notice, no man can jump a well-staked claim or one with men or tools upon it, all disputes taken to the local alcalde who decides the rights on payment of a fee."

"Yes, yes, Don Roberto," she said impatiently. "But I didn't mean that—what I want to know is how I can buy a piece of this land that these gentlemen are surveying."

All four could not have looked more astounded if Lady Godiva and her horse had come strolling by. "You, Miss Gray?" Don Roberto hooted. "*You?* Buy land?"

Harriet bit back exasperation and said, "I would have to ask the *Gosling* Company first, but I am sure they will agree, once they hear what I have to say."

"*Gosling* Company?" he said swiftly, his little eyes going shrewd.

"Yes," she said, hoping she wasn't breaking a confidence. "We—all the people who live and work on the *Gosling*—we all belong to a joint company, like … like the mining companies you talk about, Don Roberto. We have meetings with minutes and motions, and take votes, and everyone agrees to go along with the majority decision."

He was staring at her, his expression speculative. Then he said, "But why would you want a bit of this land?"

"You've just been extolling the future of the Embarcadero," she said acidly. "Have you changed your mind?"

"Of course not, but…"

"All the Company wants to do is make a fortune, like everyone else."

The men all looked at each other. This, it seemed, made more sense than anything else she had said.

Lieutenant Warner said with an air of benevolence, "And which plot do you fancy, ma'am?"

She looked about and pointed at random. "That one."

They all looked at the patch of mud, and the strings and stakes that marked it out. Then Lieutenant Sherman looked at a chart. "On Front Street, facing the waterfront," he said. "On the block between I Street and J."

Giving the lot a description seemed, somehow, the make it more real, and the men, accordingly, more cooperative. Don Roberto said helpfully, "You will have to buy it through the alcalde of this place—Sutter's son 'imself."

"Do you know him?"

"Of course I do, Miss Gray, of course."

"Can you arrange it?"

"Most certainly, ma'am."

At a fee, she was cynically certain, but was too inspired to let it spoil the moment of excitement. She said, "How much should we offer?"

"A thousand."

"What? But that's terribly expensive!"

"It's a bargain," said Lieutenant Warner, and the others all echoed, "A bargain."

"Then I shall call a meeting and talk to the Company the moment I am back on the brig."

She prepared to take her leave, but Lieutenant Ord forestalled her with a clearing of his throat. "What, if I may

48

ask, ma'am, would you intend to do with your purchase?"

"We'll build a theater on it, of course," she said. "What else?"

The transaction took a full four days, and still Jake Dexter had not arrived. He was still not back on the fifth afternoon, when Harriet stood poised in the middle of her plot of ground. The *Gosling* Company watched from the rail of the brig, some indulgently, some wisecracking to fit the occasion. Harriet waited, hammer in hand, and Don Roberto trotted up to her and handed over the precious notice.

She nailed it to the stake with her own hands while the *Gosling*s threw their hats in the air and cheered with simple high spirits. Then Harriet stepped back to admire it. The words were in English.

NOTICE
THIS PIECE OF GROUND, FORMERLY PART OF THE
RANCHO OF SUTTER'S FORT AND CONTAINING ONE
THOUSAND SQUARE FEET OF LAND, IS HEREBY
CLAIMED FOR THE PURPOSES OF A THEATER.

At the bottom it was signed by Mr. Sutter Jr. and Don Roberto Ross.

"Congratulations," said the latter, and shook Harriet's hand.

Harriet laughed for joy—and all at once she felt a tingling at the nape of her neck. Without doubt, she knew there was someone behind her, studying her. She heard a well remembered chuckle, and turned quickly—and there was the tall, familiar figure of Captain Jake Dexter.

He was standing by a hard-ridden horse, holding the reins. He was sun-scorched, and wind-scorched, and insect-bitten, and he had his hat pushed back, and he looked wonderful. He was grinning down at her with his crooked eyebrows slanted, and for the life of her she could not hold back the welcoming radiance.

She exclaimed, entirely without thinking, "Oh, Jake, oh Jahaziel, it's so, so good to see you!"

And she was poised to throw her arms about his neck when a hoarse voice from further up the Embarcadero path said, "Ah, there thee are, Captain Dexter. You owe me thirty dollars for piloting your brig upriver."

And all at once she knew the old pilot's voice, and in that dreadful instant she remembered where she had known the old man before. Not in California, but on the whaleship *Humpback*. The same whaleship whose captain had tricked her — a paying passenger! — into going on board the *Gosling*, by pretending that he would be following soon after. Instead, the *Humpback* had fled to the open ocean, abandoning her to Jake Dexter's mercies and an unknown fate.

The old man had been dirty and taciturn and unsociable on the whaleship, too, and had seldom come down in the cabin. Harriet stood rigidly, feeling like wood, and with dreadful inevitability, she heard him say spitefully, "Afternoon, Mrs. Sefton."

Mrs. Sefton. She had travelled on the whaleship under her married name — the name Jake Dexter had never heard before, because she had never told him she had a husband.

Oh God, she thought, and turned to face the horrible old man.

"Mr. Paddack," she said numbly.

"Ah," he said, and nodded. "So you know me now, at last, Mrs. Sefton, for Paddack indeed be the name. I've been up the Feather River, Mrs. Sefton, being as I thought it timely to go and see your husband — or perhaps you disremembered, too, that Colonel Sefton be a settler up the Feather River? I thought to meself that he might be uncommon pleased to hear that his wife was in California, and interested in the happenstance, too, that you don't sail on the brig under your married name. And I was right, for he paid me well for the information, Mrs. Sefton, and he ain't far behind me, as he said he'll be coming to fetch you to live at his ranch."

Then he spat, to one side but barely missing her skirts. Harriet, feeling sick, turned away.

The first face she saw was Don Roberto's. His expression was strange, almost aghast, but she didn't have the strength to think about it. Instead, she thought numbly that all her fears about what would happen to her after she was left to her own devices in California had been pointless, because her husband would come and fetch her, and she would go and live with him on his ranch. It was an end to her worries, but a prospect that filled her with terror.

At least, she thought drearily, Jake Dexter didn't have the problem of what to do with his uninvited passenger any more. He would be able to forget her, and go ahead with making a fortune here, and then forge on with his reconciliation with his wife.

So, when she looked up at him, she expected to see ill-hidden relief.

Instead, she saw shock, and contempt.

SIX

JAKE wondered bleakly if the dreadful day would never come to an end. As he returned to the brig *Gosling* from Sutter's Fort, he looked forward to being alone, to try and come to grips with bitter disillusionment. Instead, Don Roberto stepped out from under a tree, and insisted on trotting alongside.

He strode in an angry silence, trying to make it obvious that he wished to be alone, but the tubby little Cockney alcalde hurried to keep pace. "Colonel Sefton is most prosperous settler," he rattled on in anxious tones. "Like Captain Sutter's son, he came late to the Sacramento Valley, didn't arrive until last autumn, but he's done well, very well."

"From New Zealand, I suppose," Jake muttered.

"No, Captain Dexter, not New Zealand, though he did mention... He came to California all the way from Canton, China, with a Chinese servant, and a Chinese ward too — quite a novelty, for these regions. He bought hisself an estate — a hacienda — across the Feather River from Pueblo San Marco, in my area of jurisdiction, and I can vouch that he's both rich and respectable."

"Respectable?" Which he himself was not, Jake brooded. When he thought about the monies he had stowed in Hong

Kong and Singapore and Manila, he was definitely rich. But that did not signify. Richness did not bring respectability.

"He has fitted in, sir, fitted in — is thought of very highly by the Californian dons, his particular friends bein' a most influential family named Vidrie, who have a great vineyard up Cache Creek, and much grazing lands, too. Colonel Sefton has prospered 'ere, Captain Dexter, he even 'as a bank, Sefton's Bank for Miners, in Pueblo San Marco…"

Jake stopped listening. He didn't want to know any more about the man who had turned out to be the husband of the girl who had boarded his brig under the name of Miss Harriet Gray. Instead, for the hundredth time, he silently cursed the day he'd forgotten his vow to never carry passengers.

When he turned onto the gangway that led to the deck of the *Gosling*, he expected the alcalde to take the hint. But Don Roberto scurried after him.

"I had no idea that Miss Gray was married," he said in worried tones.

Neither had Jake — not until that awful moment on the Embarcadero earlier that day, when that horrible old man had stepped forward and identified Harriet as Mrs. Sefton. He stopped in the shadow at the break of the poop deck, not far from the door that led to the afterquarters, determined not to invite this intrusive little official into his cabins, and snapped at the alcalde, "What difference does it make to you whether she is married or not?"

Don Roberto flinched at the deliberate rudeness. "Miss Gray, yes, I knew she were from New Zealand last, though she be a Londoner, like what I am, and Colonel Sefton told me that he'd once had great property in that colony — "

The tubby little Londoner broke off, looked around the empty decks, looked again at Jake, and said, "I had not a notion that Miss Gray were married, otherwise I would never 'ave allowed her…"

Jake waited, but the infuriating little fellow had drifted

off again. He sighed, and said, "Allowed Miss Gray to do what?"

"There was a small matter of business, a signature…"

Again, the meaningful fade into silence.

Jake said impatiently, "When she signed for that plot of land on the Embarcadero, you mean?"

"Yes, Captain Dexter."

They both looked across the Embarcadero to the trampled fields where three army lieutenants had marked out the land into rectangles with stakes and strings.

Then Don Roberto went on, "Miss Gray told me that she bought it on be'alf of a Company, or I would never 'ave allowed her…" Again, he broke off, and then said, "Is that true, Captain, what she said about your ship being run by a Company?"

Jake said with open fury, "The *Gosling* is mine!"

The alcalde flinched again, but said gamely, "So she wasn't telling the truth about the Company, Captain Dexter?"

Jake bit back irritation. "We do have a *Gosling* Company, yes." As everyone on the *Gosling* knew, it was run in the old swashbuckling style, according to the method set up by the buccaneers, but he said, "It's no different from the mining companies you deal with, sir. When a man joins this ship, he becomes a shareholder in a joint endeavor, where everyone works for the benefit of all."

"And Miss Gray, I mean Mrs. Sefton?"

"She was a passenger on the brig, sir," Jake snapped. "A *passenger*, sir, and nothing more than that."

"Ah, aha, I am pleased to 'ear that," said the alcalde, seeming very relieved. "From what Miss Gray, I mean Mrs. Sefton said, I got the impression that she was a member of your Company."

Jake grimaced, and admitted, "Yes, she does have a share."

"Oh. Oh dear." The Londoner paused, looking around

the darkening decks again, and lowered his voice. "When you speak to Colonel Sefton, Captain, when he comes to fetch Miss Gray, I mean Mrs. Sefton, it might be a very good idea not to mention that."

"*What?*" Jake couldn't imagine for a moment why he would want to tell Harriet's husband anything at all.

However, when the alcalde said nothing, he couldn't help asking, "Why?"

"It could get uncommon … complicated … have unpleasant consequences…"

Don Roberto broke off abruptly, and Jake realized that the brig's steward had joined them.

He turned and barked, "What is it, Bodfish?"

The steward's expression was embarrassed, and his hands were twisting together. "Ah … sir, there's company in the transom, waiting."

In his private quarters? Jake sighed, wondering what else this awful day held in store, and said curtly, "Who is it?"

"When I said company, sir, I didn't exactly mean guests." The steward's eyes avoided Jake's puzzled glare as he said unhappily, "To tell the truth, sir, it be Miss Gray."

Oh God, he thought. He had gone to a great deal of trouble and expense to arrange hotel lodgings for Harriet in Captain Sutter's house in the fort, and had trusted Bodfish to get her there. He said savagely, "What the devil does she want?"

Bodfish looked miserable, and Jake didn't wait for an answer, knowing it would be just an unhappy mumble. Turning to the alcalde, he said brusquely, "I'm sorry, Mr. Ross, but I must ask you to leave."

The alcalde coughed. "Don Roberto."

"I beg your pardon?"

"It's the Mexican custom, Captain. I have lived in this 'ere territory since the memorial year of 1839, and I became a Mexican citizen, sir, on account of which I am an alcalde.

55

And being by law a Mexican citizen, I prefer to be known by my Mexican title — "

Jake said nothing; he merely stared. Don Roberto started as if he had come all at once to his wits, and with a lot of offended flaunting of his serape he trotted off down the gangplank.

When Jake turned again, Bodfish wasn't there. Knowing his captain's mood, he had made himself scarce. Jake sighed, braced his shoulders, and opened the door to the after-quarters, then stepped down the short flight of stairs that led down to the cabins that had been built under the poop. Because the deck above was so high, he scarcely had to duck his head, despite his six-foot height.

At the bottom of the steps was a passage, with two doors off the right-hand side that led to the staterooms that were usually assigned to his officers — his first mate, Charlie Martin, and Abner, Charlie's second-in command. Until today, however, Charlie's room had been Harriet's room, Charlie had had the second stateroom, and Abner had lived in the steerage. That, thought Jake grimly, was about to change.

There was another door at the sternward end of this corridor, which opened to the lobby to his private cabins, and he went through this into a transom cabin, across the stern, which was his sitting room. And Harriet was sitting on the long sofa that was built under the lovely gallery of stern windows, her head bent in the position he knew so well, the light from the lamp that hung from the skylight shining kindly on her downcast lashes and her hair.

She must have heard him, he knew, but for a long moment she did not move, and he stood and watched her. At that moment all he wanted was to sit down beside her, and take her in his arms, and bury his face in the curve of her neck. Hot angry craving racked him — and then she looked up.

The spell was broken. He folded his arms as he stood over her, and said curtly, "Why aren't you at the hotel?"

She said, "Jahaziel…"

He snapped, "You mutiny, Harriet?"

Her lips twitched, making him angrier than ever, and she said softly, "Yes, Jake, I am."

"Well, you can take yourself out of here and get over there right now. Bodfish will escort you — the way he was supposed to, earlier."

"I won't go until we've talked."

"Talked." The word was bitter. "You mean you've concluded at last to tell me the truth?" Then, unable to keep back the violence, he shouted, "Didn't I have a right to know you were married?"

He saw her lips press together. Then she met his eyes, and said quietly, "Of course you did, and though I have never told you lies, I should have told you more of the truth, and I'm so sorry I didn't tell you, more sorry that you will ever believe."

She paused, and looked down, her lashes fluttering as if she was fighting to hold back tears, and then she looked up again, and said, sadly, "Of course I should have told you. When I first came on board the *Gosling* at Judas Island, I should have told you everything. But it didn't seem right, back then, and after that … once I had joined the *Gosling* Company, it didn't seem important any more. And there was always so much else to talk about. I enjoyed teasing you so, and I was … so happy on the *Gosling*. For the first time in over a year I was happy. Can't you see that I was scared to spoil the happiness by telling you my problems? When you're at sea the outside world seems to far away and unimportant … and then when I realized that it was unfair for you not to know my true situation, and was trying to get you alone so I could talk … Royal told me that you were off to Monterey to learn about the welfare of your wife, so how could I bother you with my story then?"

He shouted, "I asked about my wife when we were in Valparaiso, too, if that holds any interest!"

He was shaking, almost out of control, shaking with rage and humiliation that he should have been cheated twice. Back when he was just twenty-two years old, he had married his childhood sweetheart, and built her a house, and then a rich shipowner had sent him off on a long China voyage, in charge of his largest ship ... and as soon as he was away, that owner had taken over not just his wife, but his cottage as well. Jake had had his revenge. He had turned pirate. He had stolen the ship and bought the *Gosling* with the proceeds from selling his prize. It meant that he could never go back to New England—but he didn't care about that. The wide Pacific was his realm, and was all the ocean he needed.

But then, an enticing waif had boarded the *Gosling* and demanded passage to Valparaiso. He had resisted, but she had tricked him—tricked them all, by joining the *Gosling* Company, and demurely proposing that they sail to Chile. And over the passage, he ... he had fallen in love with her. He had fallen in love so deeply that he wanted to claim her for his own—which meant dealing with the problem of the treacherous little wife in New England. And what he had heard in Valparaiso had encouraged him.

"And at Monterey I was told that the rumor I'd heard in Valparaiso was true," he said bitterly. "I was given a newspaper that told me everything I needed to know—that my wife had divorced me, that I am now an unmarried man. That *she divorced me* for stealing her lover's ship, *she divorced me* for causing a public scandal, *she divorced me* because I'm officially labeled a pirate, and now she is remarried, to that same lover who stole my house!"

Harriet said, "Oh God, dear God." Her voice was shocked, her face so white he could see the pink line of the healed cut on her cheek. Then, incredibly, he saw her try to smile.

She said softly, "It must be a wonderful house."

He nodded curtly, unable at that moment to speak. He'd built that house with his own hands, honor-built, sailor-built, paid for with money from his last voyage as mate and the legacy left by his parents. He had invested in the best bricks and cedar shingles; he had run to the extravagance of sixteen-paned windows and to the devil with the resulting taxes; he had pictured it filled with exuberant children, with a shell and coral wreath fastened to the front door to tell passers-by that this fine house belonged to a seaman.

Then he heard Harriet say, "I am so sorry, so very sorry, Jahaziel."

Sorry? He'd been delighted when he had heard for certain that he was no longer a married man, when the captain of the New Bedford whaleship *Isaac Newton* had shown him the newspaper with the notice of the divorce.

The last time Harriet had said she was sorry she had kissed him—and it had turned into a passionate embrace, the most ardent he had ever known. He shouted, "How often do I have to tell you not to call me that!"

Harriet flinched; at that awful moment he felt as if he had struck her. She cried, "Can't you find it in your heart to forgive me? Won't you listen, and *please* try to understand that I *can't* stay here, alone in California, at the mercy of … of… Please, *please* don't send me away from the brig!"

He said curtly, "You have to go."

"Jake, I can't—I can't, because…"

"I don't have any choice. Sefton's your legal husband. He owns you."

She cried, "Never!" She was up on her feet, trembling, close to him, and his world narrowed to her wide, stricken eyes. "You have no right to punish me by sending me back to that man. I have done nothing to deserve being shamed so utterly. Can't you understand that I was *ashamed* to tell you I was married!"

"Ashamed?" Jake's echo was blank. Then he was

reminded of past nightmares, the endless awful self-questioning. Had his wife been ashamed of him — was that why she'd fallen so readily into the bed of another man?

He shouted, "No decent woman is ashamed of being married!"

"No?" she demanded. Her breasts were rising and falling. Then she said passionately, "Jake, I didn't expect to be ashamed. I, too, thought that marriage implied honesty, responsibility and loyalty. I married Frank Sefton gladly because I thought I loved him, and I thought he loved me. For God's sake, Jake, I was only sixteen, and he was a man of the world, more than forty, the same age as my father — he was wealthy, a landowner. He'd come to New Zealand from Philadelphia, and invested heavily in New Zealand land, so everyone respected him as a laird, a lord ... and my father approved of him highly, he was greatly in favor of the match. I knew there was some kind of business deal involved, something that was perhaps devious, a plan that had been hatched by Frank Sefton and my father, but I thought little about it, and my father assured me that everything was fine, that it was just a legal ploy, and he ... he arranged everything. Arranged marriages are perhaps more common in England than they are in America?"

This last was wistful. Jake stared at her in angry perplexity. Arranged marriages in New England were unheard of, in his experience. He had thought they only occurred in exotic Eastern countries.

He said tersely, "What kind of business deal?"

She paused, choosing her words. "I know you will find this hard to believe, but Frank Sefton married me for my English nationality. As I said, he had invested heavily in land in New Zealand. In 1840, when the British took over, they started setting discriminatory taxes to force American investors out. Most went, but some, like Frank, hung on. They were hoping for a change in policy. Instead, the British administration set up even sterner measures. Americans were forced to sell—to English nationals, at the same price they had bought the land originally. So," she said, and sighed, "my father and Sefton devised a way round it. The day before our wedding, Sefton signed over all his holdings to me, putting them into my name—as a kind of dowry, he said. For that twenty-four hours, I was very rich. If I hadn't married him, he would have lost all his investments … but I did go ahead with the marriage. I trusted him and I trusted my father … and a lawyer had witnessed the transaction, so I thought everything was fine."

Jake frowned, trying to puzzle this out. Then he said slowly, "Sefton gave you everything?"

"All his New Zealand property. But it was only to get around the system that punished Americans by making sure they couldn't profit from speculating in New Zealand land. As an English national, I could sell the land at whatever price I liked."

"And that is why you are ashamed, because you were party to such a devious plot?"

His tone was scornful, and he saw her flush. "No! I was only sixteen, and I didn't understand what was going on. Sefton shamed me the day he left me. He left me just two days after we were married, Jake. My father died the second day—and … I was there when it happened. After they had carried the body away I went back to Sefton's house to wait for him to come home, but instead I was told that he'd sailed away. He'd gone—he'd left me, without a word."

"To California."

"No. He—he talked at times of California, yes, but the ship that he ran away on was going to Canton in China."

Canton. That, Jake remembered, was what Don Roberto had said. He said in a low, bitter tone, "You can't pretend that you're not married just because your husband sailed off to make his fortune. Men all over the world do that—and their wives don't considered themselves deserted."

"But do they leave their wives homeless and destitute?"

61

Her eyes were wide and shining with fury, and she looked so frustrated that for an instant he thought she was going to fly at him, and try to shake him into understanding.

She cried, "I don't know how he did it, but somehow Sefton sold everything that he had given me, all the lands and investments that were in my name. He sold them all at a gratifying profit, and then he took all that money away with him when he sailed to China. He even sold my horses – and took the money my father had given me! Frank Sefton cheated me and shamed me, and left me destitute and despised as an abandoned wife, without family, without friends, in a foreign land, and with a father just buried!"

Jake was silent, listening to the heavy thud of the blood in his throat. Then he said, "Why didn't you tell me all this before?"

"Because I didn't want you to despise me too! Because..." She stopped. Her eyes left his and she looked down, her demeanor suddenly shy. She said very softly and wistfully, "Can't you see that I wanted you to think well of me, Jahaziel – and not as an abandoned wife, the reject of another man?"

Then, slowly, she gazed up at him. Her lashes were long and shadowy, her eyelids heavy, almost blue, her lips just a little parted, the lower lip gleaming just a little, enticing. The bodice of her gown was cut in the English style, so much more revealing than any dress a New England woman would have worn, and he could see the sweet upper curves of her pert breasts, and guess at the inviting thrust of nipples. For the long space of a heartbeat he moved towards her. Their breaths mingled, her eyes shut even further; he almost pulled her into his arms.

Sense returned in a rush. She was an actress, she was trying most deliberately to seduce him into forgiveness and give her his protection – from her legal husband. A man who had every right to her, while Jake had none.

He jerked back a step and snapped, "I don't believe you.

If Sefton had given you all his New Zealand property, how could he sell what he no longer owned?"

She cried, "I don't know! I've never worked out how he managed it—and don't think for a moment that I haven't lived it over and over in my mind. I don't know how he did it, but Frank Sefton somehow left me penniless. Even the house over my head had been sold! I had to borrow money to pay for Father's burial!"

He was silent, and she looked up at him with huge appeal in her eyes, and said, "Please don't make me go back to a man who treated me like that."

He sighed, a sigh that came from deep, deep inside him. "I have no choice. He's your legal husband. He owns you."

"How can you call a man who treated me like that a *husband*?"

"It makes no difference what I call him. The fact remains that you are married—and I do not rob other men of their wives."

Harriet whispered, "Oh God, you think I am making it all up—exaggerating." Her eyes shut for a long moment while he stared at her, and grappled with his own bitter pain.

Then she opened her eyes and said tonelessly, "I'm a member of the *Gosling* Company. You can't send me away without consulting the men."

"You want to call a meeting so you can tell them what you've just told me?" he demanded incredulously.

"No. We have to call the meeting to discuss the future of the land I bought for the purpose of building a theater."

A theater. The word infuriated him. At a time like this, he thought savagely, she was intent on her career. *At a time like this*, when he was racked so cruelly with disillusionment, she could think of a theater.

Bodfish and Charlie had told him about it, how Harriet had called a meeting of the *Gosling* Company the same night the *Gosling* had moored here, how she had told them that

63

she'd found a chance for a wonderful investment. Just as she had promised when she had persuaded them to sail to Valparaiso, she had said, *I can put a piece of most profitable business your way.*

She had charmed and persuaded them all, and Don Roberto's recommendations about the golden future of Sutter's Fort and the Embarcadero had done the rest. The men had collected one thousand dollars out of their own pockets, in the innocent belief that when their skipper returned and they had a proper meeting, the Company would repay what they'd shelled out.

"Once it was your brother's alpacas that were going to make the Company a fortune," Jake jibed. "Do you really think a theater will do better?"

"It wasn't my fault that the alpacas weren't on the plantation where Royal had left them. And," Harriet added, though a little reluctantly, "it was not Royal's fault, either. And we were telling the truth! If the Indians hadn't stolen the alpacas, and we had managed to carry them to New South Wales, the merchants who own the woolen mills in Bradford, England, really would have paid us a reward of five hundred thousand dollars. Royal lost a lot more than the Company did—he spent a year of his life in Peru collecting those alpacas, and he paid for them out of his own pocket."

"But why in the devil's name did you think that I would want to build a theater?"

She sat down again, staring up at him earnestly. "You're clever and shrewd, Jake, and I really expected you to see the possibilities. The Company listened to me, so why don't you? A theater here in the Sacramento Valley can't help but do well! Don Roberto assured us that Sutter's Fort and the Embarcadero have a great future, and I've already told you that men turn to theater in foreign places."

That, he thought unwillingly, was true. In Monterey, Colonel Mason had shown him a playhouse the soldiers had made. It was perhaps the first theater in California—or that was what Captain Mason had boasted. It was set up in a wing of an old adobe hall, with pit, scenery, a stage, and a wooden drop curtain.

Harriet was watching him, her eyes intent on his expression. As if she had read his mind, she said swiftly, "Now that we have the land, the rest is easy. You've concluded already to moor the brig here for the winter and leave a few shipkeepers on board, while the rest of you dig into the hills and watch over a claim until spring. The shipkeepers can easily fill in the time by building the theater. We'll have the timber, once the berths in the hold are dismantled, and we'll have custom enough, once February comes. Why, the passengers on the river passage were happy to pay coins to Bill—a young boy, for goodness' sake!—to line up and view the llamas in the pen on the foredeck! Can't you see that they would line up to be entertained by actors, too?"

"And who would be the actors on this stage you think we should build? Royal, perhaps?"

She flushed, and said, "No, not Royal."

"What? Your brother does not share your great vision?"

She bridled at his sarcasm, and snapped, "Royal wants to try his luck at the mines."

"What? Well, then, what players would you employ? Surely not Crotchet or Valentine?" He took angry pleasure in sardonically naming the two most scatterbrained young men in the Company.

"Crotchet and Valentine are talented shantymen, but— as you know perfectly well—they wish to try the diggings too. But," she said with spirit, "there are always players to be hired."

"You expect me to believe you—that there are actors willing to be hired for a few dollars a night, when there are so many enticing tales of the gold that's lying the hills ready to be taken?"

65

She said resentfully, "You told the men at a Company meeting that there are fortunes to be made in California without going to the mines, that you can make a lot of money in other ways than digging."

That was true, and because it was true, it made him even angrier. He said, "And you? Would you go on the stage, for the entertainment of men?"

At that she went bright red with fury, and shouted, "Don't act the righteous prig with me, Jake Dexter. I have been entertaining men, as you put it so nicely, since before I was born! My mother acted Rosalind in the morning, and I arrived in this world in the afternoon! You forget I come from a stage family—I learned my first words from listening to my mother, father, aunt, brother, on stage! I learned to read from the scripts of comedies and melodramas! And how you can act the righteous Yankee? And condemn me out of hand because of what I do? You're a self-admitted pirate, an adventurer, a fortune-hunter! And the men who come here won't be so very different—they may be lawyers, physicians, ship captains, and army officers, farmers, and merchants, journalists, and whalemen, but they are all adventurers, too. And they will all pay good gold, the lot of them, for one night's fun watching a drama on stage!"

"Ah yes," said Jake bitterly. "We're all adventurers, and we all need our grub-stake, and no one more than you. You learned your eloquence from your family too, no doubt, and no doubt these were your impassioned arguments when you duped my men out of a total of one thousand dollars, just to set yourself up in the theatrical trade."

She went white again. "You bastard," she whispered. "You utter, utter bastard. I would never, ever, deliberately dupe your men, and you know it."

"Oh yes? What I do know," he said with savage pain, "is that you came here to talk to me because of the theater, and for no other real reason. You didn't really stay to explain your silence, or even to beg my forgiveness or my

66

protection. What you wanted was to make sure of your theater, to get the thousand dollars that you need to back your scheme."

She stared up at him, her eyes wide and unseeing, her arms folded so tightly over her breasts that he could see her knuckles stand out like stones. Then she said in a shocked toneless voice, "You don't really think that, you can't."

He said nothing. He was unable to move, or do anything but watch her with that awful rage and pain seething inside him.

She shivered, and looked down at her clenched hands, and whispered, "Oh dear God, what will the men think of me?"

And still he was silent. For a long moment the only sounds were the bumps of the brig against the wooden wharf, and the low silky rush of the Sacramento River flowing against the brig's hull. Again he was tempted to forgive her, to take her as his mistress, to give her his protection and a theater … or to sail away with her, for ever. His arms even unfolded, but before he could sit down and draw her against his shoulder, she stood up with an abrupt movement, and walked out of the transom cabin with short, quick steps.

At the door, she glanced at him over her shoulder. "Tell the Company that they will get their money back," she said crisply. "I will repay this debt, the way I repaid all the others. In New Zealand."

Then, before he could stop her, she was gone. He heard her steps on the gangplank. He heard Bodfish hailing her, and the steward's hurried footsteps as he pursued her. Then Bodfish's worried voice faded with distance as they went off together.

And nothing after that, nothing but silence.

After a long moment Jake moved.

He looked about stiffly, not sure what he sought. He caught sight of the brandy bottle. Then he sat down.

SEVEN

BODFISH held her arm with one hand—undoubtedly because Captain Dexter had ordered him to make sure she didn't run away, Harriet thought drearily—and kept on mumbling platitudes in an embarrassed kind of fashion.

Harriet was silent, too distracted to listen. She thought that Bodfish must have overheard a lot, which he would pass on to the men. That was mortifying enough, but much worse was the panic. She couldn't stay in California, not where Frank Sefton would find her and take her to his house or desert her again according to his whims, she just couldn't—but how could she get away?

Before they left the Embarcadero, it was dark, and the two miles to get to Sutter's seemed a much longer trudge than it had been by day. As the sun had gone down, a thin fog had drifted up from the river, and clung, and what had been a clearly marked road became a bewildering trail of half-light and deep darkness. Harriet stumbled, holding up her skirts to save them from being filthied by unmentionable things in the dark. Then her footsteps echoed as they walked over the bridge, and the fort loomed up suddenly, out of nowhere, just as it always did.

There were Indians crouched close to the gate, some with blankets pulled over their heads. They all smelled of spirits, and one reached out to pluck at her skirts as she passed. Harriet stepped away quickly. Then she and Bodfish walked under the massive portcullis that hung over the entrance, and stepped into the huge compound that was framed by the tall, massive walls.

Smoky red fires flickered all about beneath the mysterious dark shapes of tall trees. A sharp voice called out in Spanish, in words that sounded like a challenge. Neither Harriet nor Bodfish answered, and Harriet quickened her steps. She could smell manure and scorched meat turning bad, urine and sweat, of both horses and men. The gamblers still plied their trade in their tents with red curtains, under the shifting light of small cressets, but only a few men responded to the ringing of their little bells.

Very few men, in fact, seemed to be awake. They were either asleep, or looking for a bed. Coming to Calafia's kingdom, Harriet reflected, was a tiring business — but then her mind turned and nagged at her awful problem again. How in the name of dear Providence was she to get away from California before Sefton found her?

They were at the outside flight of steps that led to the upper storey of Captain Sutter's house. Harriet silently followed the bobbing shape of the basket Bodfish was carrying to the second-floor entrance.

When she arrived in the yawning room just inside, she was at once aware of the presence of many men. She could see them lolling about on benches as they tried to sleep upright, or sitting crouched over small books or packs of cards. Some were writing, perhaps letters home or journals.

There was a massed creaking from the ceiling where men slept cramped together in the attic, caused by a lot of shifting and turning, accompanied by lamentable groans from the wakeful ones, and the sawpit sound of concerted snoring from those who slept. Though it was cold, the air was so stuffy it was almost unbreathable.

Bodfish stopped at the far side of the room, and Harriet

watched him as he tapped at a door. The door, she knew, led to the room where there was a bed that Jake had booked for her. Before this summer it had been Captain Sutter's pantry, and the room she was standing in was his dining room, where he had entertained Californian guests. As Bodfish tapped the door creaked open, but no one appeared. Instead of a questioning voice all Harriet heard was more snoring.

Bodfish pushed her basket towards her, muttering that he would bring the second basket in the morning. Harriet roused herself and took it from him. Muttering a goodnight, the steward made to leave, but Harriet softly called him back.

"Tomorrow, when you come with the other basket," she said. "I will have the money, I promise." He merely nodded, mumbling awkwardly again, and Harriet found herself alone.

She moved hesitantly into the room and shut the door. It was immediately pitch dark. She stood with her back to the door, her basket at her feet, and waited while her sight adjusted. It felt like the night of the day of her father's burial, the night she had abruptly found herself without a roof over her head. Then she had removed to the hotel where her father had lived—she had taken over his room, and found in the morning that she not only had to pay for her night's lodging, but the unpaid bill for her father's past lodging, as well.

But she refused, refused, *refused* to wallow in self-pity. She had managed then, and she would cope with this, too. Instead of weeping she concentrated on getting her bearings, listening to the female snoring from the bed in the other corner, discerning which bed was hers. A man in the loft above cried out hoarsely in his sleep, and other men cursed him for waking them up. It sounded as if an awkward brawl broke out, because there was some shouting and commotion, but then, abruptly, all was quiet again. Harriet moved stiffly.

Her bed had a thin straw mattress and no blanket. She undressed to her shift and lay down on her spread cloak, with her two woolen shawls over her, and a third one folded as a pillow. She did not close her eyes, but stared into the noisy darkness, instead.

California … she had to get away from California. She thought of San Francisco, and the abandoned ships she had seen in the harbor. It seemed evident that few ships, if any, managed to get away from these shores. A captain only needed to drop anchor to lose all his men, all of them run off to the mines.

California was a golden trap, and she … she had no money. Paying over her last ten sovereigns to buy her share in Jake Dexter's *Gosling* Company had been a desperate gamble. Oh, dear God, she thought, but refused to cry.

When Harriet woke up she found she had wept in her sleep, for the shawl where her head had lain was damp. Outside the gray sky was weeping too, sending drizzle down the single window. The humped shape in the other bed was silent.

Harriet got up and dressed stealthily, reluctant to face any kind of conversation from her roommate. There was a washstand in one corner, with one pitcher, one bowl, and a looking glass, a comb and a toothbrush. All these last three were chained to the stand—to prevent theft, she assumed. The jug and bowl were empty. Harriet took up the pitcher, and hesitantly opened the door.

Men sat hunched in chairs under blankets, while others were curled in tight spaces on the floor. Above, in the attic, there was a commotion as the men there awoke. Some were even singing, apparently glad enough to be here even if the hills were veiled in streaming rain. Cautiously, she opened the outer door, and made her way down the outside steps.

There were more men out in the compound, rain blackening their hats, waiting in yawning queues at the well and the smoking beehive-shaped bread ovens. Before she joined the line for water Harriet walked out to the entrance. She could see the Embarcadero in the two-mile-long distance. The brig was still moored snug, and a schooner had joined her, tied up just astern.

Harriet turned for the well. When men spoke jocularly to her as she waited, she scarcely heard them, and did not reply. Then, slowly, her head bent, she carried the water to the house and back up the stairs to her room.

The other occupant of the room, she immediately saw, was awake. This female was sitting on the edge of the other bed, contemplating a tumbler of clear liquid that she held raised in one hand. She wore only shift and petticoat, which did little to veil an exuberant figure. She was middle-aged — or at an age that she no doubt considered *interesting*, and her abundant coarse hair was dyed black.

Harriet said rather cautiously, "Good morning."

The woman turned to look at her, peering up through all that hair, before giving her attention to the tumbler again. As well as liquid it held teeth. As Harriet watched, unwillingly fascinated, the teeth were extracted, popped into the waiting mouth, and then the liquid was drained.

The lady smiled radiantly when she came up for air, evidently having waited until her mouth was properly equipped before returning Harriet's salutation.

"Good morning!" she cried. "Though that statement be not true — I see that I do verity an injustice. It's not good at all, for I hear and see rain, and — hist! — we miserable folks be all drenched again."

Harriet's mouth fell open. She couldn't help it. Not even on the provincial circuits had she encountered such an eccentric figure. Her silence did not seem to worry her audience in the slightest, however. Instead, the woman looked about, grabbed up a gown, and commenced to haul it over her head. Like Harriet herself, she did not bother with corset stays.

"Does my manner of speech intrigue you?" she demanded from within the folds. "I have a gift for rhyme, and cannot leash the facility — it demands to be ever unleashed!" Then she wriggled manfully, emerged red-faced and panting, and said, "Mrs. Abiah Marchant!"

"Miss Harriet Gray," said Harriet. The woman had a pronounced Yankee twang, so she did not expect her name to be recognized. And neither it was. They shook hands, American style, and Harriet became all at once aware that the liquid in the glass had been gin.

This didn't worry her. Throughout her childhood she had been used to sporting men and drinking women. Instead, her mind was abruptly touched with hope, for here was not only a fellow female in a world that was so greatly dominated by men, but a female, moreover, who spoke English — American English notwithstanding. Here, perhaps, was the key to her escape from California.

She said, "Have you been in Sutter's Fort long?"

"Naught but four weeks, Miss Gray."

"But how did you get here?"

"By ship," Mrs. Marchant said airily, and waved an eloquent but meaningless hand. Then she allowed Harriet to read the journal she had kept on passage. To Harriet's further bemusement it turned out to be a tiny handmade book, stitched together and measuring no more than two inches either way. Its contents — of course, thought Harriet — were in verse.

> *May the eight, eighteen forty-eight*
> *On the good ship Sylvia I my berth did take*
> *To california for to go*
> *To seek my fortune, weal or no...*

"Merciful heavens," said Harriet, and turned another midget page.

"Ain't it a wonder?" quoth the complacent diaress.

Harriet nodded, beyond words, and continued reading.

The diary ended in 'Frisco.

The hills of california are very high and green
But the adobe buildings are thought to be mean
The journey is over, this journal is done
The captain's wife yesterday bore him a son.

"I am in the throes of composing another versifying journey," said Mrs. Marchant. "Based on my own travels, but none the less most fanciful. 'Twill be the story, Miss Gray, of a young miner misguided enough to bring his wife to this extempore place. On their very wedding day he catched the gold fever, and couldn't make up his mind 'twixt love and lust for the yellow dust, and carried her along, the dithering fool. How romantic the tale will be! Like the captain's wife, this young miner's lady will bear him a son, and expire soon thereafter."

"Is that what happened to the captain's wife?" asked Harriet.

"Who knows, Miss Gray, who knows?"

"But I can't imagine why the heroine of your tale consented to come along—or what you are doing in California, either."

"But the poem tells you," hooted Mrs. Marchant. "I came to make my fortune, of course!"

And at that, she produced a visiting card, which Harriet took rather warily. It announced that Mrs. Marchant taught the gentle art of painting on velvet.

"*Here?*" said Harriet.

"But the gentle pursuits are of the most essential in this rough land, Miss Gray! Without the presence of the gentle arts the men of California will be lost beyond redemption in the pursuit of unlawful pleasures and indulgence in enervating vice."

"But here, in Sutter's Fort, *velvet painting?*"

"No, not here," said Mrs. Marchant, for the first time sounding impatient. "The rains will come, they come today, for just look to see the rain hold sway—and for certain I'll do better business in San Francisco, as the inhabitants return to await the drought of Spring. And then ... and then, aha, we will see."

Harriet ignored this last, seizing on the possibility of a return to San Francisco. The port might be only the first part of a journey away from this land, but it was certainly a step in the right direction. She said swiftly, "How will you get to San Francisco?"

The lady ignored her, however. "Breakfast," she said compellingly. "I hear the merry bell, that tells us preparations go well."

Harriet hadn't heard any bell, but went with her, assuming that the lodging fee Jake had paid on her behalf included the stipulated two meals a day.

The dining room turned out to be a long outhouse tucked against the northern wall of the fort, hard up against a kitchen. It was deafeningly noisy, crowded with men. Greasy deal tables took up the length of it, and the benches on either side were full of bellowing customers who voiced their impatience by hammering with their jack knives on the table top. Some men lay on the floor rolled up in blankets, while others sat and scratched their heads, evidently still in the places where they had slept all night. Other men walked around kicking bottles and bags.

Harriet stood in the entrance, feeling dazed. A stout, important looking man emerged from the doorway that led to the kitchen, looked about him, spied Mrs. Marchant, and hailed her in a roar. This, Harriet gathered in the flurry of introductions, was Mr. King, the man in charge of the restaurant. He had bought the right to this business from Captain Sutter's son, and undoubtedly had made a pile out of it, for he looked so smug and prosperous.

He ushered them grandly to a smaller table that was set at the end, crosswise to the fore-and-aft tables, and three chairs were drawn out. Harriet sat in one, and Mrs. Marchant sat in another, with Mr. King on her other side. Then, in procession, the food arrived, borne on huge tin platters by sweating pig-tailed Chinese cooks.

Meat—roast meats, fried meats, and huge elk steaks, chops sliding about in quivering gravies, sliced meats and hashes. The smells of grease and sweat were overpowering, and a greasy steam rose into the rough-hewn rafters. Hard bread and biscuits and *frijoles* were served up too, and molasses in little dishes, but there was not a fruit or a vegetable to be seen.

As Harriet watched the dishes go by, Mr. King and Mrs. Marchant were indulging in vivacious banter, with not a single pause for her to insert a question about getting to San Francisco. The air was redolent with flirtatiousness as well as steaming meat, and Harriet deduced that Mr. King and the versifying Mrs. Marchant were somewhat more than acquaintances. Perhaps Mrs. Marchant saw the fortune she desired in the person of this stout fellow, she thought, for Mr. King certainly believed that he would reap a great fortune out of California.

He would make it out of the accommodation trade, or so he informed Harriet, speaking in a bellow that was quite unnecessary, because the rest of the room was unnervingly silent. All the men at the table were eating like wolves, sparing no time for talk. As Harriet watched in disbelief men poured molasses onto platters of meat and then demolished the mixture with their knives, with no resort to spoons or forks. The only sounds were the rattle of the dishes and clatter of knives, the champing of jaws, and Mr. King's bellowed monologue.

In just this short past season, he boasted, feeding the men who rented the rooms in Sutter's house had reaped a profit of no less than one hundred and fifty thousand dollars American. And he expected to make a great deal more in the rush of 1849, as he declaimed at the top of his voice, because

77

he planned to build a hotel of his own, somewhere on the Embarcadero where the soldiers were surveying the streets.

Harriet said very quickly, "Have you bought land for it, yet?"

"In the Spring," he boomed. "In the Spring."

"But why not before that?" she countered. If she sold him the ground she had bought for the theater, some of her problems would be solved, she thought. She had the deed to the land, and the ground was properly staked and claimed. She could ask a little more than one thousand dollars, and get funding for her escape as well as the repayment for the *Gosling* men.

"Spring, Miss Gray, will be time enough."

"But won't you build your hotel this winter?"

He laughed, and pounded the table with his fist. "It rains here in cataracts, ma'am, that rain out there ain't nothing yet. No, no, off to 'Frisco I do go, and with me my dear new friend, Mrs. Marchant."

He slapped a large thigh in an affectionate fashion and received a playful push in return. "And I'll draw up my plans while I am there," he cried. "It'll be a true Yankee hotel, in true-blue United States style. Carpets!" he boomed. "Bar rooms stocked with the most expensive liquors money can buy!" Then, while Harriet stared at him in suspense, waiting her chance to insert another question, a bell rang.

The men at the table stopped eating, all at once and together. It was only fifteen minutes since the bell to start eating had rung, but the men all stood and walked out of the room with many regretful over-the-shoulder glances. Some picked their teeth as they went, while others hauled out tobacco cuds from secret places in their clothing, and shoved them back into their mouths.

"Fifteen minutes is time enough," said Mr. King, reading Harriet's stunned expression. This, it seemed, was one of the secrets of making a tremendous profit. The Chinese cooks came in and hastily wiped down the table and went back for more huge platters of meat, hard bread and biscuits and *frijoles*, and little dishes of molasses. There was, it seemed, a second sitting, and a queue of eager men awaiting the bell to take their places.

The bell rang. Even Mr. King had to stop his talking as men shoved and fought to get to the benches, for the noise was so deafening. Harriet, however, had a voice that was trained to overcome the ruckus of the noisiest of pit audiences.

She shouted, "If you are going to San Francisco, how do you get there?"

"By ship, of course," he bellowed.

"But what ship, pray?"

"The old ship, the boarding house ship, the one set up on the Embarcadero!" His voice rang out all at once as the men silenced and set to their chewing, and his laughter was even louder as he surveyed Harriet's expression. "Didn't you see her?" he demanded. "They come here at the start of July, and snugged her down at the mooring and turned her into a boarding house—and they've done well, mighty well. Now that the rains have come they've been setting up her rigging, on account of the folks what run her have made what they reckon is enough of a fortune, yes, and they sail downriver for San Francisco tomorrow, taking a mighty load of fare-paying passengers with them, and after that to the seas beyond. Home to the States, they are going!"

They were? Oh dear Providence, Harriet thought, here was her chance of escape. She had no desire to go to the States, but once in New York or Boston it should be easy to get back to London. She opened her mouth to ask price, time, date, to offer her piece of land—for what? One thousand dollars plus how much? One hundred and fifty? But Mr. King wasn't listening, being distracted by the arrival of a bowl of steaming stew, which was placed on the table in front of him.

This was evidently a treat, judging by Mrs. Marchant's

exclamations and Mr. King's complacency, and Harriet nodded when Mr. King lifted an eyebrow, offering to fill her plate.

She said rather breathlessly, "Mr. King…" and he said, loudly, laughing, "They might've made their fortunes, yes, but they be going one year too soon, they are, for this time next year even greater fortunes will be made in the lodging trade. Bath tubs!" he cried.

"I beg your pardon?'

"In my new hotel. It'll have bathrooms."

"With tubs?"

"Bath rubs—long tubs. Tubs what a man can stretch his bones in."

Harriet blinked, utterly confounded. She opened her mouth with little idea of what she was going to say, and Mr. King forestalled her, saying, "Like the stew?"

She hadn't tasted it. "It's delicious," she said.

"It's coon," he said, beaming.

And Colonel Frank Sefton walked into the room.

EIGHT

FRANK Sefton. For a numb moment Harriet's mind went completely blank. Then her husband took off his hat and his fair hair gleamed in the light from the doorway, and she knew him.

Mr. King sighted the newcomer with a shout. He rose to his feet, exclaiming a welcome, and Mrs. Marchant had her hands clasped together in delight. Harriet swallowed on a dry throat, feeling sick. It was New Zealand all over again. It was like the day when her father had brought this admirer to her attention as the most popular figure in Auckland, and Colonel Francis Sefton looked just as he had, back then.

He was urbanely handsome. Harriet felt a weird relief. She had lain awake so many nights wondering why she had been such a fool to be attracted to such a man, and now she knew the reason. As always, Frank was elegantly dressed. His suit was more than damp, but of excellent quality, and his face was sleekly shaven, as smooth as the day he'd first declared himself enchanted.

His manner, too, was just as courteous. He bent over Mrs. Marchant's tremulously extended hand with elaborate gallantry, then turned to Harriet. He said, "I came the very moment I heard of your arrival, dear Harriet, I crossed the river at once, and boarded my schooner and ordered sail set

81

at dawn."

She stared at him. His words seemed meaningless, because she knew, beyond doubt, that he would have been stunned and appalled to find that she, his deserted wife, had somehow arrived in California. But he, being Frank Sefton, would somehow turn the embarrassing situation to his own advantage.

Belatedly, she became aware of the smooth, oily fingers still holding hers. She pulled away, and wanted to wipe her hand on her skirt, but he was staring at her. For the first time, she realized that his eyes were protuberant. Had they always bulged a little, like this?

"Yes, I have a schooner, Harriet, a ship of my own," he said, as if she had asked. "She is moored this very moment at the Embarcadero. You will soon see what a beautiful craft she is! She is but newly built, my lovely schooner, made for the river trade, and is nameless yet, but now that you have come at last to join me, dear Harriet, the name for my beautiful schooner is obvious. A perfect name for the crowning jewel of my success in this land! Harriet, my dear, you have not a notion, you will not believe that a man could do so well in such a brief time. I have a bank, a ranch, but I am not just a *ranchèro*, you know, for I have all kinds of profitable speculations in Pueblo San Marco, up the Feather River—what I have accomplished is astounding, even for me. I have beaten my own record!"

Had he always been so smug ... so pleased with himself? Harriet blinked, and then thought that the complacency was indeed part of her memories. Now, she found it offensive, but back then it hadn't detracted in any way from his glamour. Mrs. Marchant, beside Harriet, was palpitating at the thrill of being in the presence of so elegant a man; she was just like women of Auckland, when Colonel Sefton had been the most eligible bachelor in the colony.

"My dear Harriet's arrival could not have been better timed," he told Mrs. Marchant. "I have such invitations, extended by the first family of the upper Feather, Californian dons named Vidrie. We will have fandangos, bear baiting, bull fighting, and all the variations of that Californian sport, and we will extend many invitations of our own. Do say, my dear Mrs. Marchant, and you, Mr. King, sir, that you will be free to attend one or two of these occasions?"

Mrs. Marchant fluttered. Obviously, she would have adored to sigh an affirmative. Mr. King, however, cleared his throat, and said with ill-hidden pleasure that no, it wasn't possible, as they were leaving Sutter's, bound for 'Frisco the very next day.

"Perhaps next spring," he said gruffly. Mrs. Marchant's palpitating had made him a trifle possessive and jealous, Harriet meditated … but her mind was too preoccupied to pay very much attention, because she was thinking about the ship that was bound to San Francisco the very next day. All she needed was the money for her fare and a chance to get away unseen.

She said to Sefton, forcing herself to smile coaxingly, "Do you have to sail upriver so soon? Surely not, when I have made such friends with Mrs. Marchant. Delay a day, please do, so I can enjoy her society for another few hours."

If he noticed that these were the first words she had spoken to him, he did not allow it to mar his complacency. He smiled the dangerous, pouting, rosebud smile she had almost forgotten, and scolded, "Harriet, Harriet, after all this time, surely you will consent to come quickly to the home I've prepared for you in this land?"

"But I must see Royal, too…"

"Ah, yes, Royal," he said. His face was the smooth face of a gambler who had the winning cards tucked up his sleeve. "What wonders we have to show your brother, truly. But he has signed up, it seems, with a mining company — or so I have learned. Such dreams of gold as he harbors — a fortune-hunter, always! He will come to the hacienda to stop

83

a while, my dear, once he has made the strike he expects so confidently, and you will see him at your leisure then. But my fortune, dear Harriet, is even more golden, golden with promise! Cattle, horses, grazing lands, I can't even begin to enumerate them all."

None the less, he did enumerate them. So he had not seen Royal yet, thought Harriet, after having worked this out—and remembered that Sefton was supposed to have provided at least half the funding for the alpaca venture, money that had never materialized. Instead, it was Gray money that had been lost, which was why Royal was penniless now. Was that why Sefton was anxious not to see him?

"How the Californian señoritas will envy my wife's blonde beauty!" he was rhapsodizing to Mr. King. "But I shall not allow the men to look, for I am wild with jealousy already, dear Harriet, as wild as I was when no letters came in reply to mine."

"*Letters?*" she cried. "*What* letters?"

"Letters go a-missing, you know that," he scolded. His mouth was pouted and cruel again. "I assure you I speak no less than the truth when I say that I made every effort to get word of your welfare. How could you believe any less of me, when I am your lawful wedded spouse?"

Harriet felt sick, thinking *liar*, but unable to voice it, because no one would believe her in the presence of this plausible man. She didn't have another chance to argue about leaving Sutter's Fort so soon, either, because the bell rang at that moment, and with a clattering and commotion the second sitting was forced to leave the hall.

"Come, my dear, you must pack your belongings," Sefton said, standing up, and she found her arm gripped in an implacable hand, pushing her into the current of men flooding through the door. He steered her to the foot of the stairway to the first-floor entrance of Sutter's house, and then, thank God, he let her go.

Harriet ran up the stairs. Her last glimpse of Sefton was of him standing in the rain, watching her alertly. Surely he wouldn't stay out there in that weather? Her basket stood beside the washstand with the chained toothbrush and comb where she had left it the night before. There was no packing to do, because she had never unpacked it. She shut the door and collapsed onto the edge of her bed, her arms tightly folded, hugging her breasts as she tried to stop the shuddering, tried to make plans.

The door clicked open. Harriet's heart tried to jump into her throat. But it was just Mrs. Marchant. The woman shut the door again, came over and sat beside her, and whispered piercingly in her ear, "You could've knocked me down with the veritable feather, I vow! Everyone knows of Colonel Sefton, he is second only to Captain Sutter in prominence in this territory. But no one knew, and I must confess it, that Colonel Sefton's vast property included a wife! Tell me," she said, putting her arm around Harriet's shoulder in the most confiding manner possible, "do you have a reason for calling yourself *Miss Gray?*"

Reason? Harriet could think of several without thinking at all—that is, if she felt like trusting this garrulous eccentric.

Instead of confiding, however, she said carefully, "Miss Harriet Gray is my stage name."

"You're an *actress?*" It was a shriek, right in her ear. Harriet flinched.

"Yes, I am," she said, rather weakly.

"Oh, Miss Gray." Mrs. Marchant let her go, to clasp her hands before her bosom. "Such poesy sublime, Miss Gray! And, ah yes, I must confess my little secret, that I myself, yes, me, have oft-times longed to tread the Thespian planks. I have faltered often on the threshold of drama's shadowy land, drama's hands have beckoned me, thrilling from the strand."

"They have?" said Harriet. She felt enmeshed in an illogical hallucination.

"And furthermore, Miss Gray, I must confess it—though it is naughty of me to convey a trade secret—but at times I too have played a role, with grass as a stage and the moon and stars as lighting. It was in the very best of causes, the salvation of souls. Certain camp preachers vied to procure my services as an actress, in their mission to find sinners and persuade them to repent. You have not a notion how often I have stood and listened to the sermon and the homilies, and when the preacher cried out, Repent! I were the first to cry, I do repent, I do! Oh, the times I have been reformed, Miss Gray, the times I have fallen to my knees and cried, Amen! And Glory, Glory! And the preacher has cried out to the congregation to follow my example, Miss Gray, and my example never failed to find others."

"My God," said Harriet, staring at her. Not for the first time, it occurred to her that Mrs. Marchant was no better than she ought to be, and was probably an adventuress, and perhaps a sporting woman, too.

With that thought she made up her mind, and said in a swift low voice, "I'd be in your debt for ever, Mrs. Marchant, if you would lend me some money."

"Money?" Mrs. Marchant's eyes went wide. "What for?"

"To escape. To get away from here."

"To get away from Colonel Sefton?"

"Yes! I'd go as far as Judas Island, if needs be," Harriet said bitterly. Uninhabited Judas Island, where she had first met Jake Dexter, held terrible connotations ... of cracked flagstones, a destroyed church, skeletons, and ancient terror, but it was far enough away to be out of Frank's reach.

"Judas Island?" Mrs. Marchant blinked, astounded.

"It's in the southeastern Pacific, but I meant it as a figure of speech," Harriet said, feeling desperate. "What I mean is, I'd go anywhere—anywhere! But I need money to do it."

"But your husband is a rich man. Don't you have any money at all?"

"Not a penny. Not a cent."

"Ah." Again the sound was long-drawn. Then Mrs. Marchant said, "How much do you need?"

"Enough to pay for passage to wherever that ship that leaves in the morning might be going." Harriet paused, her eyes intent on Mrs. Marchant's speculative expression, and added, "I can give you security in the form of a deed to some land—land that I think Mr. King might be willing to buy for his hotel."

"Here?"

"Yes, on the waterfront of the Embarcadero. On the street that they are going to call Front Street."

Silence. Then, as Harriet watched, Mrs. Marchant's face became roguish again. She said in another piercing whisper, "You have an ... arrangement, perhaps, with another man? Your heart lies with another?"

Oh Jake, Harriet mourned, because an arrangement was the most unobtainable of her dreams. Nevertheless, she lowered her lashes, put on her ingénue look, and said demurely, "You have guessed my secret, Mrs. Marchant."

"Ah..." And Mrs. Marchant's manner became conspiratorial.

Within minutes, it was all worked out. Money in hand, Harriet stole to the door, wearing her cloak and three shawls, and with her basket over her other arm. The room beyond was empty, and there was no sign of Sefton at the bottom of the outside stairs. The whole compound, mercifully, was almost empty. The rain had driven everyone indoors.

Within a hundred yards Harriet was drenched and cold, shivering despite her rapid pace. It was still the first week of September, but it felt as if winter had come early. The path was mired with mud and slimed manure already, and she remembered how Don Roberto had described to her how the trails into the diggings became impassable by the end of October.

Down by the waterfront the scene was even more

miserable. The three lieutenants who had been laying out the streets had gone, perhaps packed up until spring. Harriet slipped and stumbled in places, but finally she got to the foot of the gangplank that led up to the deck of the boarding house ship.

She hesitated, looking up at it. After the dashing little *Gosling*, the hull seemed huge. There was mud dripping from the planking, no doubt the result of the months of being moored here. She had scarcely noted the ship before, because it was so well hidden in the riverside thicket, but now, unpleasantly, she was beset by a feeling of having been here before. She paused, looking around, trying to find the reason for the horrid sensation. A hundred yards up the path the brig *Gosling* was moored, and beyond the brig, Sefton's schooner. Harriet moved quickly, darting up the gangplank and onto the ship.

When she arrived on deck she was immediately assailed with still more insistent misgivings. The deck planking was in two layers, the top one being chipped and stained with grease and blood; there was a brick furnace built behind the foremast, the whole deck stank, of old...

Of old oil, and whale blood. *She was on a whaleship.* She was instantly transported to the miserable passage across the southern Pacific, to ... Judas Island, where the captain of the whaleship *Humpback* had tricked her into going on board the brig *Gosling*. He and his wife had sent her onto the brig by pretending that the captain of the *Gosling* would be happy to carry her to Valparaiso. And then, the instant he had seen her step on board, the captain had put on all sail and fled, taking the passage money she had given him to take her to Chile.

Oh God, she thought, she felt sick. The ghastly Mr. Paddack—the same man who had recognized her, and had gone to Colonel Sefton to be paid for the information that his wife was here, the same horrible old man who had betrayed her—he had been the first mate of the *Humpback*, and yet she had never wondered how he had got here... But even that thought dissolved in her overriding horror at the realization that she was on the *Humpback*, and that all her plans for escape were doomed.

Then she saw the short, bow-legged figure of Captain Smith heading her way. Close behind him came Mrs. Smith, her huge breasts swinging the way they always had. Harriet swallowed on a dry, clenched throat, remembering how Mrs. Smith's chin had always been thrust out belligerently, like this, like a boot.

Both captain and wife stopped short in front of her. Mrs. Smith nodded curtly and said, "I cannot say I am glad to see you, Mrs. Sefton, for we're a deal too busy for callers. You have to go away, as it ain't convenient."

"It was never convenient!" Harriet cried. It was like a terrible delirium; she wanted to pinch herself, because then she might wake from this nightmare. Oh, dear God, how these people had tricked and cheated her, and now, some-how, incomprehensibly, these dishonorable swindlers were here to frustrate her again.

"Why did it have to be you?" she shouted, shaking. "Why did it have to be you, you godless and dishonest cheats? Why did my luck have to be so foul? Your excuse for sending me on board the *Gosling* was that you were bound home about Cape Horn, and didn't feel like honoring the bargain you had made with me. You had my money, but you didn't want me, and so you foisted me onto Captain Dexter, you tricked me, and made fools of us both! So, where is my money now? And why, why, *why* are you here?"

"What money?" said Mrs. Smith, unmoved. "We got you to the eastern Pacific, and we don't owe you a cent. We spoke a ship and a-heared about the gold, steered this way, profited by that, but it ain't your business whatsoever."

"Isn't it?" said Harriet drearily. "Even though you *crooks* have cheated me and ruined my life?"

Without waiting for an answer, she turned and walked away. It was not until she stumbled that she realized she was weeping with frustration and rage. She was still holding the money that Mrs. Marchant had given her. She turned when she arrived on the path, and walked blindly to the *Gosling*.

There was a man on the path, coming towards her. She stopped short. It was Jake. He stopped. They faced each other in silence. He looked haggard, dreadful, unshaven, wonderful.

She said tentatively, "Jake?"

He said nothing. Instead, his eyes moved to look at something behind her. She heard the steps then, and knew who it was before Sefton's hand gripped her upper arm. When she turned her head Frank Sefton's face was bland, but the tight clutch of his fingers was vicious.

He said in his smoothest, most urbane voice, "Captain Dexter, I owe you a debt of gratitude. You could not have done me a greater favor than to bring my dear wife to my side. Name your price, sir, name your price! All you need to do is send an invoice to my bank — Sefton's Bank for Miners, in Pueblo San Marco, and the bill will be honored at once."

Harriet said nothing; she couldn't. Her mouth was parched with the desperate words that she could not voice, and her mind was leaden with despair. Jake looked so … so unforgiving. He stood quite still, his expression grim and wary. The rain dripped off the brim of his hat, but he did not seem aware of it.

"I don't need payment," he said. The words were bitten out.

"Of course you do," said Frank Sefton, smiling savagely. "Or are you implying that my wife was something more than a passenger on your ship?"

Jake's mouth set. He glanced at Harriet and then back at Sefton, and bit out, "Mrs. Sefton was just a passenger, sir."

"Then I must pay her fare."

Jake said nothing, but he nodded.

"And I have this for you."

Harriet felt Sefton move, as he reached with his free hand into an inside pocket. He brought out a folded paper, which he handed to Jake.

Jake didn't take it. "What is it?" he said curtly.

"A note for one thousand dollars, sir."

"For your wife's passage?" Jake frowned, puzzled.

"But this is not for that, sir. I am determined that my wife's crazy theatrical notion should not leave your men in unnecessary debt. She should never have purchased that lot of land, and she certainly should not have borrowed the money from your crew."

It took a long moment for the suave words to sink into Harriet's mind. Then, with a lurch, she cried, "How do you know all that?"

Sefton ignored her. Instead of answering, he said to Jake, "My Harriet was such a bewitching little girl when I met her. Such a pretty young charmer—and I see that charming *naïveté* yet. She thinks to build a theater in this place, how ridiculous can she be? Look at the rain, silly goose," he said to Harriet while she stared at him. "Picture the way this place will be in one month's time, naught but a tract of swamp, just the way it was last winter, just as it will be next year. Build a theater in this place? What nonsense!"

Harriet said in a hiss, "How did you find out that the idea of a theater was mine, Frank? *Who told you?*"

Sefton stared at her with his mouth in a little pout, but Jake moved abruptly, forestalling whatever he was going to say. He snapped, "Was it your wife's idea to give the money to me?"

"Of course, Captain. Who else?"

Harriet shut her eyes, because Jake was staring at her with bitter hurt, as if he hated her, and she couldn't bear it. Then fury saved her, for the moment. She opened them

91

again and shouted, "Frank, answer me! How did you know I paid one thousand? And how did you know that I borrowed it from Captain Dexter's men—and how in God's name do you know that *I* was the person who bought that lot of land, that it was *I* who signed the bill of sale?"

Sefton's eyes went red, the whites flushing the way she remembered. When she tried to pull her arm out of his grip he held still more tightly, and she knew she would have bruises in the morning.

However, his voice was just as bland when he said, "Take it, Captain Dexter, take it. As Harriet's husband I hold myself responsible for all her debts and obligations."

Jake snapped, "Keep the draft."

"You're a fool if you don't accept the money. According to law, I don't have to pay you at all—because my wife signed for it. But I honor my wife's debts."

Harriet stared, remembering other documents she had signed so thoughtlessly, then cried, "What exactly, is my signature worth?"

"Harriet, my dear," said Sefton, and gave her a little shake, which looked innocent enough, no doubt, but hurt. "Your signature is worth precisely nothing. *Nothing.* That is what I am trying to explain."

Nothing. Her signature was worth nothing? Surely that wasn't true? Her signature had seemed important enough when she had signed all Frank's documents, the day before their wedding. Harriet's mind seemed trapped in a circle, endlessly seeking some kind of sense.

"But how did you know that it was my signature?" she said, but was too weary with despair to wait for the reply. She looked at Jake yearningly, desperately, and said, "Take it. It wasn't my idea, truly, I swear—but please take it."

Jake shifted. He looked the way she felt—caged, frustrated, racked with useless longing. He looked a full ten years older than the man she had known on the brig.

He said, "But—"

92

She said, "Please." And watched him slowly, very reluctantly, take the draft from her husband's hand. Then she allowed Sefton to lead her away.

NINE

Harriet's grip on the rail of her husband's schooner was convulsive as she stared numbly at the Embarcadero, thinking that the scene did nothing to distract her from misery.

Instead of high autumn, it looked like mid winter. It was almost impossible to believe that a place would become a mire of ankle-deep mud so quickly—almost impossible to believe that just twenty-four hours ago she had watched three army lieutenants mark out streets, and listened to their great prophesies that the Embarcadero would become a booming town, because now the great tract of land was swimming with mud. Only the top halves of the stakes they had used to mark out the lots were visible, and it was impossible to pick out the single post she had hammered into the ground herself, claiming a piece of land for the purposes of a theater.

Just forward of the schooner was the *Gosling*, but she felt too embarrassed to look properly at the brig where she had been so happy. There were very few men on the decks, and none of them looked her way. But even if they had smiled, and called out, it would have made no difference, she drearily thought. Bodfish had called on board, carrying the basket she had left behind on the brig, the one with the rest of her clothes, which he had promised to bring to the fort in the morning. Obviously, he knew that the situation had changed. But he'd had nothing to say, hadn't met her eyes, and had seemed very glad to leave after dropping the basket at her feet.

Sefton had been gone an hour, taking the money she had borrowed from Mrs. Marchant, but it was only a respite, and not a chance for escape, because there was nowhere for her to go. She had watched him go to Sutter's Fort, and now she watched him walk back along the Embarcadero. His steps, as he came up the gangplank, seemed unnaturally loud. He was smiling his little pouted smile. Then, deliberately, without a word, watching her all the time, he put his hand in an inside jacket pocket, and when it came out she saw he had the deed she had given to Mrs. Marchant for security. After flipping it at her, he stowed it in his inside pocket again. Harriet said nothing, turning away, and when he headed to the deck cabin on the afterdeck, she stayed at the rail, even though the rain started to drizzle down once more.

There was something very odd about the schooner, she thought. That it should be luxurious was only to be expected, considering the money that Sefton boasted he had lavished on the vessel. Compared to the *Gosling*'s crew of captain and fifteen hands, however, it seemed to be woefully undermanned. Harriet had counted just five seamen, commanded by a sailing master called Driver. Harriet had called him *Captain* Driver when she had been introduced to him, and had been sharply corrected by Sefton, who informed her that though Mr. Driver might be in charge of the set of the sails and the pilotage, but he was not in charge of the ship, because Sefton himself was the captain. Surely this was both illogical and probably dangerous, because Frank Sefton had been a soldier — a colonel in some American militia — and never a mariner. But Harriet also thought that it was typical of him to insist on being the cock of the roost.

What did Mr. Driver think of being relegated to a subordinate position while he did all the actual work? Harriet found it impossible to tell.

Like the five seamen, he had a furtive look, as if he had no right to be up the Sacramento Valley. And, as for the seamen, she was convinced they were deserters, because they were wearing remnants of navy uniform. So why were they working for Sefton, instead of mining in the hills? They had been driven out by the oncoming rains, she supposed, but were too frightened to retreat to San Francisco, where the officers of the garrison and the U.S. frigate *Savannah* were hunting down runaways—and if they were deserters from the *Savannah* herself, then the punishment after being caught was a savage flogging.

Then, to Harriet's surprise, she saw passengers start to trail up the gangplank. Considering what she had heard about the exodus from the hills at this time of the year, she would not have expected that so many would have wanted to take passage upriver to Pueblo San Marco. After all, as she remembered from Don Roberto's stream of information, it was popularly known as the gateway to the mines—which were about to be closed for the rainy season, surely. Then as Sefton arrived beside her again, she drew her shawl more tightly around her shoulders, trying to shrink away, without it being obvious.

Thankfully, he was not there to taunt her, this time, but to greet the influx as they came up the gangplank. The men who were willing to pay to get up the river so late in the season turned out to be a motley lot of merchants, Spanish Californians, Mexicans, and captains of abandoned ships who were searching for their runaways. Not only were they the same kind of men who had taken passage on the *Gosling* from San Francisco to the Embarcadero, but some of them were the same characters.

Harriet nodded politely as they passed her on their way to one or the other of the two lavishly furnished deck cabins, and wondered what gossip they had heard.

Instead of following them, Sefton lingered, and she tensed again—but he was there only to boast, as she soon found to her relief, his topic being the vast riches he expected to make out of the schooner.

"I expect to average one hundred and thirty passengers per journey," he bragged. "And calculate that after subtracting Sundays, I should carry twenty-five thousand people between here and Pueblo San Marco over the 1849 season. And at twenty dollars per head that means five hundred thousand dollars from fares alone, without counting the money made by carrying freight." With a smile that seemed almost genuine, so pleased with himself was he, he announced, "I confidently expect to make a million-dollar profit—in just one year, Harriet, just one fleeting year."

Which was just another sign of this crazy California, thought Harriet, but managed somehow to produce a faint, dutiful smile in return—something that was made easier by him taking his departure, after informing her that he must take over command of the ship for the departure from the Embarcadero.

And no sooner had he gone than a familiar figure trotted up the gangplank—just in time, as it was about to be raised.

"Don Roberto!" she exclaimed.

"I owe you an apology, Miss Gray, I mean Mrs. Sefton," he said with a little bow. "I was ignorant of your standing, that you are married to one of the first men of the territory. I 'ave to admit that…" he broke off, and then said in a rush, "I didn't know you was a single woman, ma'am, but how could I, when you didn't call yourself Mrs. Sefton?"

"Miss Harriet Gray is my stage name, Don Roberto."

"You know that Colonel Sefton is a neighbor of mine?" said he. "He bought hisself a rancho across the river from Pueblo San Marco, in my area of administration, ma'am. He has a bank, the Sefton Bank for Miners, in Pueblo San Marco, and influential friends, the old dons, people by the name of

Vidrie. If I had only known, Miss Gray..."

"But you didn't, Don Roberto."

"No, I did not," he agreed, and sighed heavily. Then he tottered a little as the schooner unmoored and got underway.

There were some more moments of clumsiness as the schooner cleared the brig *Gosling*, and she gazed longingly at the decks as they passed. "They're setting up as a boarding house," said Don Roberto. "Or so I am told."

"Yes, I know," said Harriet sadly. Then she wondered who had told Don Roberto what the Company planned.

It was no use asking, because she knew she wouldn't get an answer. "Tell me more about Pueblo San Marco," she urged instead. She had probably heard more than enough on the passage to Sutter's Fort, but she hadn't been paying much attention at the time. Now, she thought cynically, she had an excellent reason to be interested, because Pueblo San Marco was the closest village to the hacienda where she was going to be incarcerated with her husband.

And Don Roberto, just as on the upriver journey, needed no encouragement to talk. She heard again about how he had bought sixty thousand acres since arriving in this territory in 1839, being a true-blue pioneer in the frontier-breaking business; she heard about his fort at the place on the Feather River where it was narrow enough to bridge, a half-day's march west of Pueblo San Marco—and how the little castle was necessary, because of the shocking state of law and order in this land.

And she heard again about his miraculous elevation to the post of local alcalde, which, as he explained yet again, was a kind of sheriff, only more powerful, there being only alcaldes here. And for everything he did, including the verdicts he handed out, he received a fee, and as well as that he got all the money from the land he had surveyed and then sold to speculators. As he delicately indicated, Colonel Sefton did not have all the wealth of Pueblo San Marco to himself.

"I'm sure I already knew that, Don Roberto," she said.

"And then there is all my investments…"

The wind was with them, if not the current, and the rain had tautened the sails so that the schooner scudded swiftly. The upper river was a streaming landscape of brown-green water with a ripple on its surface, clumps of trees in thickets along the banks, rolling golden hills of grass that were rapidly mildewing with wet, and then, in the distant fastnesses, the blue and purple-gray foothills of the sierras. In the middle of the afternoon they passed an Indian encampment, a miserable place in the rushes by the river. Women and children lifted their heads to stare as the schooner slid by. Because they were so close, Harriet could see their expressions of dumb endurance. The children seemed bluish with cold, and their coverings were scarce and pitiful.

Harriet stared, horrified, and didn't hear Sefton arrive until he spoke.

He said, "Waste not your sympathy, dear Harriet."

"I beg your pardon?"

"They're better off now than they was before," contributed Don Roberto slavishly. He might reckon that he was nearly as rich as Colonel Sefton, but that didn't stop him from being Sefton's toady, or so Harriet had noticed.

The Indian houses were made of plaited willow thatch and piled-up mud, apparently built over holes in the ground. There were no men at all, just women and children, and she wondered where the men had gone. Then she remembered Tombez, the port in Ecuador where she and the *Gosling* crew had first heard about the gold. There had been no men on the Tombez River, either, because they had all run off to the diggings of California.

But surely the Indian men would come back, now that the rains had begun? Uneasily, she thought of the Indians who had crouched in corners at Sutter's Fort, wrapped in scarlet blankets, armed with old, rusty, worthless muskets that they had exchanged for their bits of gold. Many of them had been drunk.

Then she heard Sefton say, "They have benefited greatly from the discovery of gold."

She said, "I find that hard to believe."

"You contradict me, before you have heard the facts? When you have no idea of the way they lived before? Many of the rancheros employ them to work in their claims, which is a great improvement to the way the Mexicans treated them."

Don Roberto said, with an inappropriate smile, "The Mexicans put a bounty on their heads."

Harriet exclaimed, *"What?"*

"The Indians stole valuable horses," said Sefton, sounding as if he approved of the barbaric law. "For food, Harriet, imagine that—for food! They learned too fast about guns and grog, learned bad ways from rogues and scoundrels. So the administrators of Sonora and Chihuahua felt obliged to take extreme measures. As Don Roberto told you, they paid a bounty for Indian scalps. As far as I know," he said, smiling, "they still do."

Harriet looked at the Indian encampment and said softly, "Oh, dear God."

"Two hundred dollars for the scalp of a warrior," said Don Roberto. "One hundred for that of a woman."

"But how can those who pay the bounty tell the difference between a man's scalp and a woman's?" she cried.

Sefton was looking thoughtful, and Don Roberto pulled his beard a little, for once lost for an answer. Then Frank Sefton shrugged, and said, "You would have to ask the Indians. The chiefs of rival tribes profit from the bounty, you know, as well as Mexican bounty hunters."

Oh dear God, she thought, *what kind of country is this?*

The schooner tacked about yet another bend, and the

encampment was lost to sight. The countryside was empty again, quiet and tranquil — so deceptive, she thought. It was a landscape of high banks and russet-colored thickets, of great evergreen oak and sycamore trees with long branches that spread out low to touch the face of the water. Dark purple pine groves marched down the broken sides of the hills, and beyond the hills great rock faces, gray and black in the lowering light, and a hint of lofty, snow-capped mountains.

They arrived at Pueblo San Marco near sunset. It was pretty in the fading light, but smaller than Harriet had expected after Don Roberto's boasting. There were ten or twelve heavy old adobe houses built on terraces along the side of the nearest hill, surrounded by vines. Thirty or forty Yankee-style clapboard cottages that had been much more recently built were scattered along another terrace, halfway up a little tributary stream, which was headed by an ancient looking stone watermill.

The end of the landing place connected with a wide road that ran along the waterfront, and continued on its way out of town. This road, Don Roberto informed her, was the gateway to the mines, and ended at his fort, which was where the Feather River was bridged, and the trails to the mines began. Men had to walk out of town, or ride, as Pueblo San Marco marked the spot where it became impossible to sail or row any further, the river being too narrow, and the current too strong.

In town, this thoroughfare was lined with about twenty substantial buildings, one with a bold notice on its roof proclaiming that it was Sefton's Bank for Miners. Other establishments, which grandly called themselves café-restaurants, advertised gaming and drinking, as well as the provision of meals. There were three boarding houses, and several stores, one run by a boot-maker who, Don Roberto said, had made more money out of selling double-cleated knee-high boots than many a miner had made from gold. As a sideline, he said, this rich cobbler employed a man to sell serapes, paying him the huge amount of a hundred dollars a month—partly because the cobbler had stipulated that his employee should speak English as well as Spanish, the American prospectors being good customers for the Californian blankets, too.

"And you're the alcalde of all this bustle and enterprise?"

"And of the Feather River, right up to Cache Creek."

The schooner steered for a long wooden embarcadero, which was vacant save for a number of casually tied small boats. In the height of the season, said Don Roberto, it had been packed with vessels, this being as far as the river was navigable. The craft had brought goods to stow in the large warehouses that had been erected nearby, as well as hundreds of fortune-seeking miners.

The passengers hadn't stayed long, just long enough to stock up with provisions and tools and boots before heading along the road to his fort, and then dispersing into the hills. Soon they would be all flooding back again, some to overwinter in town, but most to head back to Sutter's Fort and San Francisco. This was the trade Sefton had sized up when he built the schooner, Harriet thought.

Down went the gangplank, and the passengers streamed away from the schooner. Don Roberto was the last to leave. In contrast to all his smug boasting on the passage, his expression was unhappy as he took Harriet's hand to bid her goodbye.

"I do wish I had known more," he said, after looking around to make sure that Sefton was not within earshot.

"I beg your pardon?"

"Before I encouraged you to buy that land on the Embarcadero at Sutter's Fort."

"But you got your commission, didn't you?"

"Of course, Miss Gray—I mean, Mrs. Sefton."

She said, exasperated, "I do wish you wouldn't call me

that."

"And I do wish you had told me that Miss Harriet Gray was just a stage name, ma'am."

"What difference does it make?"

"If I had known you was married, it would've been very different, I do assure you of that!"

"Why?" she cried.

But Frank Sefton was coming along the deck, having left it to the sailing master to have the sails stowed and the schooner made snug, ready for the next profitable sailing. And without saying another word, Don Roberto was off down the gangway, fleeing into Pueblo San Marco.

TEN

AT that precise moment the sun went down, and it became night, with more rain. As Sefton led her down the gangplank of the schooner with his fingers curled about her upper arm, Harriet heard orders echoing about the decks. Then they were on the wooden planks of the landing. She heard the hollow sounds of their steps.

Sefton urged her along the wharf to where a boat was waiting. It was a ferryboat, and she remembered that his ranch was across the river from the village. A small man was waiting for them, a lantern in his hand. When she got closer, Harriet saw that he was Chinese. His name, Frank said, was Ah Wong.

Ah Wong said nothing, but he bowed a lot and smiled all the time, seeming most intensely nervous. Then Harriet was in the boat, her baskets on either side, and her heavy wet shawl clasped tightly around her shoulders.

She watched Ah Wong as he hauled the boat to the other side of the river. He stood in the middle of the boat to do it, grunting as he hauled at a rope. It was a double rope that apparently stretched all the way across the river, and it appeared to work with a number of pulleys. Despite the pulleys it looked difficult, and the Chinese man was small and thin. Frank, however, made no attempt to help. Instead, he sat in the bow, looking forwards. Ah Wong had to reach up for the rope, and the wide sleeves of his loose blouse fell back past his elbows. Those elbows were thin and sharp, but the arms were corded with knotty muscle. He was a lot stronger than he looked.

Then, with a bump, they arrived on the other side, and Frank gripped Harriet's arm again, to help her out. On the bank horses awaited them, one with a side-saddle, meaning she was expected. Harriet mounted without help, and followed Frank and Ah Wong into the darkness. Tired though she was, she had no trouble keeping her seat, despite the unknown landscape. And though the wet night was very black, the horse seemed to know the way.

She knew they were near the house when the hooves of her horse suddenly rattled on gravel. She could smell wet dirt, a garden, and then the stone smell of wet adobe. The hacienda loomed up, massive in the darkness. There was a lamp set on either side of the entrance, and the door between them was huge.

Her horse stopped, and Harriet slid down slowly, feeling stiff and very, very apprehensive.

Sefton got to the door before she did. She saw him watching her over his shoulder as he pushed it slowly open. His expression was strange, gloating, enigmatically sly, and she felt more guarded than ever, the hackles on the back of her neck prickling. The door swung wide. There was no one behind it.

When she reluctantly stepped inside, the entrance hall smelled strange, of some heavy, erotic perfume, like burning sandalwood, flowers and musk. The room took up the whole front of the house, so that its front and its sides were whitewashed adobe. Along the two ends and in both front corners there were large, elaborately carved chairs and sofas, with small tables bearing figurines and lamps. Otherwise, this foyer was unfurnished—except for the screen that divided it off from the room beyond it, a screen that came

105

from a continent that was not America.

The screen was about twenty feet wide, and rose all the way to the high, raftered roof. It was made of some dark, glossy wood, and its panels were so intricately carved that Harriet could glimpse fragments of light from the room beyond, betraying where the carver's chisel had gone all the way through. For a moment it reminded her of a map Captain Dexter had shown her, a map drawn by the old pirate-navigator Schouten, of coastlines embellished with bears, dragons, llamas, and serpents, because at first glance, the carved images in the screen writhed the same way. Then she saw that these were images of Oriental men and women … in strange, contorted postures, twined together, their faces lifted in ecstasy. The carvings were obscene.

With a sick lurch, Harriet tore her eyes away, then realized that she was alone in the strange, wide hall, with only chinks of light and darting shadows for company. Sefton had disappeared around the left-hand end of the screen, and gone into the room behind it. Harriet looked about apprehensively, holding her wet shawl tight … and heard the ghost of a taunting giggle.

It sounded like a child, and it came through the chinks of the beautifully carved, prurient screen. The laugh was high-pitched and feminine, and something rustled as the unseen female giggled. Harriet heard Frank's soft gloating voice, but could not distinguish the words. Her skin crawled with a sense of being watched; she knew she was being inspected from the other side, as someone peered at her through the chinks cut into the screen. Sefton called out in a louder voice, and she spun round with fright … and the phantom laughter sounded again, from that end of the other side of the screen, from this, followed by rustling back and forth like autumn leaves, and Harriet's hair tried to stand on end.

A door at the right-hand end of the screen opened, and she bit back a scream. Ah Wong stood there, his manner apologetic. He had one of her baskets in each hand.

He said, "M-M-Miss?"

Did he have a stutter? Harriet gasped, "You gave me a fright."

"...a fright." It was so unexpected, this echo, that she flinched again. She wondered if she had imagined it, or if it came from behind the carved partition. But the room behind the screen was silent.

Ah Wong said more clearly, "So sorry, very sorry, miss." Then he ducked his head, and said, "Please follow."

She followed him through the door at the right-hand end of the screen, glad to get out of the hall, but dreading what might happen next. They were in a long, wide, dimly lit passageway, that apparently ran the length of the house. Her heels rattled on a wooden floor, setting up echoes. Then Ah Wong opened a door and stood to one side.

The doorway led to an enormous bedroom. An icy cold bedroom. One lamp was lit, but there was no fire in the drafty grate. The floor was made of short pieces of wood set in a crisscross pattern, and was waxed. Parquetry, she thought. The furniture was huge, black and ornately carved, somehow Chinese in style, and the bed was huge, too, a gigantic bed with tapestried curtains, as if to hide what went on inside.

Ah Wong said, "M-M-Miss?"

Harriet jerked round to look at him. "Yes, Ah Wong?"

He had put down her two baskets. "Excuse please," he said, and smiled very humbly, showing teeth that were big in his thin face. "Colonel come soon, please, very soon, please," he said, and backed out of the room.

As the door closed the lamp flared up and almost went out, but then burned steadily again. Harriet listened as the soft footsteps shuffled away. The door was solidly shut, but had no lock or latch. She turned her gaze, shivering, to the bed.

It was a four-poster bed. Of course, she thought,

clenched tight inside. She knew what those four posts could involve. The bed was heaped with quilts and she could see the sag of its canvas bottom. It was, she thought, very old … was it made of a wood called ebony? There was a table, too, with spread-out legs carved like dragon feet, twirled carving on the supports of a wash-stand, a commode with a velvet seat … all ebony? Great-aunt Diana had had furniture like this, made in some Oriental land. But this—this was old California.

Then Harriet realized why this room reminded her so of her childhood. It was because she felt so vulnerable, so intimidated and dwarfed by the size of the room and the fittings. She felt the child that she had been on her wedding night. It was terribly cold, and she was shivering in long, almost convulsive, shudders. The quilts on the bed looked inviting … deceptive, she knew. Frank would come soon, her lawful wedded husband. He would come as he had the night of their wedding, smelling of tobacco and brandy, gloating over her body with merciless self-indulgence.

The following morning he had gone into town, leaving her shocked, her innocence destroyed. Now, she knew that he had gone back to the lawyer, and spent the day selling everything that he had put in her name, including the house over her head, and the two racehorses that her father had given her as a dowry. She, herself, had spent the day in a numb daze, coming to terms with the fact that her husband did not adore her at all, that he simply regarded her as his property, to use as cruelly as he willed.

When he had come into the bedroom again, late the second night, for a long time he hadn't touched her, pacing about the bed instead, ranting about the hated British and the loathed administration, terrifying her with his venom, letting her know beyond a shred of doubt that he hated her, too. Then, when he had forced himself on her, she had tried to fend him off. Humiliatingly, he had enjoyed her panicked resistance, taunting and pinching her to make her fight harder. But then he had got bored, and...

Harriet's mind veered away from the terrible memory. She undressed slowly, her fingers numb and clumsy, remembering the long, cruel, contorted hours before Frank Sefton was sated. Once she was down to her shift she put on two nightgowns and a bed gown, making sure she was a clumsy bundle of clothing—as if, she thought wryly, fabric was any kind of protection. Then she crept under the quilts, and waited, cold and tense inside, watching the door.

She heard his step ... and then she heard a giggle.

The half-hysterical little sound came from the passageway on the other side of the door, coming closer, closer. She heard the same light steps she had heard from behind the screen, oddly uneven, stumbling footsteps, off this way, off that, off along the passage, punctuated by the giggles. Then the sounds faded—and Frank Sefton laughed, right outside the bedroom door.

The door opened. Harriet bit her lower lip to stop the scream that rose inside her. Sitting bolt upright, the covers clutched about her, she met Frank Sefton's hot stare.

His silhouette was outlined by a lantern in the corridor. He had taken off his jacket and his stock was all awry. She saw the unblinking shine of his eyes and the dark excitement in his cheeks, and his obvious arousal. The lantern flared, and she saw the tip of his tongue poke out and circle his lips. Harriet's heart thumped with panic against her ribs. A door along the passage slammed.

And the lamp by the bed flickered and went out.

Again, she nearly screamed. The room was in darkness, and Sefton's silhouette in the doorway was all that she could see.

Then, slowly, the door shut, and she couldn't see a thing.

ELEVEN

WHEN Harriet woke the creeping sense of being watched was with her again. She dared not move, or even open her eyes. Instead she lay quite still, every muscle taut as she listened. She heard the soft sound of someone breathing, and held her own breath as she waited.

She was lying on her right side, facing the window, tangled in all the clothes she had worn to bed, still protected by layers of cloth, because Sefton had not come into the room. Bright light shone on the other side of her eyelids. Then, fractionally, she drew her lashes apart. A dusty yellow quadrant of light sprang from the window, ruled off with shadows of iron bars.

She turned her head, and someone was there. She gasped with fright, and then recognized Ah Wong. He was standing by the bed, watching her, his expression sad, strangely disappointed.

She sat up in a quick defensive motion, gripping the bed gown about her, and said, "I didn't hear you come in, Ah Wong." Then, just as uncannily as the night before, she heard his faint echo, "...come in, come in..." and she cried, "What do you want?"

He flinched visibly, and she immediately felt sorry. He looked so small, so easily hurt, as he stuttered, "I sorry, I bring..."

He seemed to have lost the word, and looked around wildly for it. Harriet looked too, and saw the tray that had been placed on the table. "Breakfast?" she said.

"...breakfast, breakfast..." Ah Wong seemed to be tasting the word. Why did he do this?

Then he said hesitantly, "Colonel, sir, he told me ... when eaten, yes, he will take you inspection of the ranch."

Harriet said nothing. So Frank couldn't wait to show off his wealth, his possessions, his great success in this land, she thought.

She nodded, and Ah Wong went. She watched the door swing shut and then she dressed and ate. She was very hungry, as she hadn't eaten since the previous morning, but she kept on stopping to listen, listening to the house. Outside her barred window trees rustled and unseen cattle lowed, but the house was perfectly silent. The sun shone as quiet as dust.

When she had finished and washed, Harriet hesitantly opened the door. The passageway was empty. She walked slowly to the entrance hall. It seemed even more cavernous in the daylight, and was empty. The big front door was open, and two horses waited outside on the drive, one of them with a side-saddle. She was about to step outside when a door at the left-hand end of the partition opened, and Ah Wong materialized.

He looked about anxiously and said, "Colonel not ready yet, tell me to ... to tour you the hacienda."

"Oh," she said, confounded, but followed him back through the door. It led along a stone alleyway to a courtyard, and she saw then that the house was built in the old Mexican style, in a hollow rectangle. There were mosaic tiles about the small fountain in the center of the courtyard, and Harriet wondered if it became so cold in winter that the fountain froze up.

When she asked, though, Ah Wong didn't answer,

instead whispering to himself, "...fountain, fountain..."

At the back of the courtyard there was a kitchen and a stone scullery, but no maid or cook. Ah Wong sometimes answered her, and sometimes not, but she gathered from his fragmentary sentences that the wives of some of the vaqueros came in to cook and clean. Then they were walking down the passageway that led to the bedrooms. All the doors were shut save the one to her room, and there was not a sound from behind any of them.

When they were back in the hall, Harriet pointed at the screen, and said, "What room is that on the other side?"

But instead of answering, he whispered, "...other side, other side..."

Oh God, she thought. Suddenly she was at the end of her tether, harried and desperate, and his taunting echo seemed to epitomize her loneliness and fear. She shouted, "Why do you imitate me, Ah Wong? Why do you repeat everything I say?"

The little man looked utterly aghast, and she was immediately conscience-stricken. He clasped his hands so they disappeared in the folds of his blouse, and blurted, "Oh, sorry, please, sorry." He seemed terrified, and darted glances everywhere, staring fearfully at the screen as if he expected, too, that someone might be spying on them through the crannies.

Then his eyes jerked back to her face, and he whispered, "I came to this land for self-improvement, Mrs. Sefton, please forgive that I try so hard." He was shivering with anxiety, she saw with wondering pity, and drops of sweat stood out on his face. "I seek true euphonious English speaking," he hissed then. "For how may I learn the good English from—from an American?"

Harriet said blankly, "Merciful heavens." The notion that Ah Wong found Sefton's cultivated Philadelphia accent not worthy of imitation was remarkably diverting, and she trembled, incredibly, on the verge of laughter.

112

Then she heard a rustle from behind the screen, and a footstep. Harriet whirled around, and Ah Wong scurried out of the anteroom.

A young woman came out from behind the screen, a petite Chinese girl. She had very dark almond eyes, and was exceedingly beautiful, her perfect face like a flower. Then she spoiled the image by lifting her hands to her mouth and giggling—looking at Harriet, openly finding her amusing.

As Harriet turned away, embarrassed, Sefton came in. He was as dapper as always, though he smelled of sweat and horses. "Mei-Mei, my Mei-Mei," he said lovingly, and held out his hands to the Chinese girl.

"Mei-Mei," he said, looking from the girl to Harriet and back, "meet Mrs. Sefton."

Harriet bowed her head and smiled. The Chinese girl ducked her head in return, but not before Harriet saw the flash of hatred. Then the girl bent low, sliding her palms down her silken thighs, and when she straightened her porcelain, perfect face with its tiny bow of a red-painted mouth was unreadable.

Sefton said, "I bought Mei-Mei in Canton, and paid for her passage to California. In China girls are sold or put to death—imagine! In China, the people despise such pretty blossoms, but here her beauty is paid due homage. And see, because of me, she wears nothing but the finest silks."

Mei-Mei's silken draperies were in pastel shades, in several layers. As Harriet watched in utter disbelief, Sefton turned the girl round and round, like a doll, removing the layers. One by one the silk draperies were removed, until the floor at her feet was swathed in fine fabric. At the end, Mei-Mei was wearing nothing but loose trousers.

The trousers were also made of silk. They were pale straw-yellow in color. "See her lovely breasts?" said Frank Sefton, turning the girl around so Harriet could see, holding Mei-Mei's bare back against his chest. "In China, such breasts are likened to pigeons."

113

Pigeons? Mei-Mei's breasts were round, polished pale gold in color, with dark brown pouting nipples. Sefton caressed them with his palms, watching Harriet with a small smile, his hands revolving slowly, hypnotically. Mei-Mei leaned against him and did not seem to mind. Harriet felt sick, but could not look away.

Then Frank said abruptly, "Do you wonder about Mei-Mei's feet?"

There was a feverish note of excitement in his tone. Sefton stooped and picked up Mei-Mei and put her on a chair. Because the Chinese girl was so small her feet did not touch the floor. Then, still more incredulously, Harriet watched as Colonel Frank Sefton, the urbane, suave man-about-town, the arbiter of fashion and correct behavior, kneeled on the floor in front of the chair in the humblest of postures, and with his own hands removed one of Mei-Mei's little black velvet slippers.

Underneath, the foot was tightly wrapped in bandages, but its shape spoke clearly of past ill-usage. The toes had been broken and bent up underneath to sit tightly in the curve of the instep. The result was a crudely club-shaped object that reminded Harriet of a stallion's phallus, but Mei-Mei's face revealed nothing but pride.

"It's a most strange custom," Sefton said pensively. He shuffled on his knees to one side, so that Harriet could have an unimpeded view of the obscenity that had been done to the girl's foot. "When Mei-Mei was the perfect age, when she could walk but her little bones were still very soft, her feet were broken and fastened like this. The pain must have been unendurable. Even now, if the bandages are removed, she suffers the most excruciating agony…"

His tone was reminiscent. Harriet's skin crept. His fingers hovered over the travesty of a foot, tugging at the bandage as if he was making up his mind whether to reveal the deliberate deformity or not, rubbing and cupping the phallic shape of it—and Harriet abruptly couldn't stand any more. Before she knew it, she had run out of the house, and had sprung up into the saddle of one of the horses.

It was the one with an ordinary saddle. She yanked up her skirts, and threw one leg over to sit astride, and kicked hard. The horse flinched, and then took off. Gravel spurted, and then she was pounding across the path and up over the nearest hillock, urging her steed into a wild gallop.

The horse's hooves pounded up slopes that were lush with clover and wild vetches, over hills that waved high with wild oats, and cleared thorn hedges in wild leaps. A wild exhilaration seized her. The rhythmic jolt and thump was soothing, and the rush of cool air felt almost like normality. Harriet ducked her head to avoid overhanging branches, but did not really care if she was knocked off the horse.

Sefton's place was prosperous, she saw in a blur; the land was certainly fertile, and it was obvious that he had invested well. She galloped over lush oat-grass pastures, past hay barns, grazing cattle, and staring vaqueros. Then, as she gained a sense of territory, and found her sense of direction, she guided the horse to the path by the river, heading for the place where the ferryboat had landed the night before. She wanted to see in the daylight what she had passed in the dark.

The river was the same powerful serpent that she remembered, rushing green, with brown in the curl of the current. The wild oat grass grew lavishly, as yet not halted by the chill of autumn, and groves of thick oak towered over the landscape. Then Harriet reined in. She had arrived at the beached boat. The scattered buildings of the town of Pueblo San Marco lay on the other side, fifty yards away, across the river. The double rope of the ferry was like two strands of a spider's web, and at the other end, Harriet could see the schooner, moored up to the wooden embarcadero.

At the far end of the town the road marched into the hills, alongside the river for a little while, and then leaving

115

the river to climb past clumps of red oak, and head for the distant dun slopes. That, she thought, was the way to the diggings, but the road, as far as she could see, was empty. Then a movement caught the corner of her eye, and she looked at the river again—and the brig, the brig *Gosling*, was coming round the nearest downriver bend.

She saw the dashing vessel with preternatural clarity, while her breath rushed in her ears. Jake Dexter had changed his mind, he had decided to abandon the muddy Embarcadero at Sutter's Fort, and come instead to this place—to Pueblo San Marco. Harriet was scared to blink, in case the brig vanished, for fear it would turn out to be a vision, but then she saw the *Gosling* take in sail, and edge to the wooden landing, just downriver of Sefton's schooner.

Her eyes blurred with tears. It was as if a knight had arrived—a guardian. The brig might be on the far side of the river, but while the *Gosling* was in sight it was possible not to feel so bereft and alone. Jake Dexter had come to watch over her, even though he now knew she was married. To Sefton.

Sefton. Belatedly, Harriet heard the pounding of his horse. She heard it thump to a stop, and turned her head and watched her husband vault down from the saddle. He looked perfectly unruffled, and was scarcely panting at all. Then, as she watched, he went very still.

For a long moment he stared at the *Gosling*, as the brig worked to a snug berth against the piles of the embarcadero, and she could sense the cold, devious mind at work. Then he roused himself. With a decisive movement, he turned, came over, and reached up. Hard fingers nipped her arm. "Come, my dear," he said. His rosebud mouth was pouted in the little smile she hated so much. "You must pack your clothes—you have been summoned," he went on. "I have just received a message from Don Manuel. The Vidries insist that you go to stay with them this very day, so you must ready yourself for the five-hour ride to their house."

116

TWELVE

ONCE the job of unbending sails, swaying down the yards, and striking the topmasts was well underway, Jake Dexter left Charlie Martin to oversee the work. Taking Chips, Abner and Bodfish with him, he went in search of the alcalde.

Though small in appearance from the river, Pueblo San Marco was uncommonly crowded with men and mules. Past the squared timbers of the mooring place, the grass of the riverfront was steaming, as summer had returned for the day, and the sun had come out—and the bank was crowded with miners.

Men were hunkered down in circles under the trees, smoking and sharing reminiscences, while others leaned against the struts of little wagons piled with well-worn tools, standing with their arms folded while they listened. Others were doing their laundry in the river, or sitting cross-legged as they mended their clothes.

They had all come out of the hills, which was a bad sign, Jake thought. The *Gosling* Company had voted overwhelmingly to stake a claim and then wait out the winter until it was fit to dig, and it looked now as if it was a poor decision. There was nothing he could do about it, though, as his rule was to abide by the majority vote. Otherwise, the whole idea of a cooperative ship's company wouldn't work. It was because of that majority decision that he had the three other *Goslings* with him — Abner, because he would head the mining party, Chips because he was the chairman of the company, and Bodfish, who was carrying the minutes book with him, because he was the secretary.

The substantial buildings across the other side of the broad dirt road might not have had glass in their windows, but they did have wrought iron bars, Spanish style. The wooden sidewalk, complete with hitching rail, was a more modern kind of convenience, though the street was so crowded that most men had to walk along the dirt road, battling for space with an incoming mule train. Getting across the walkway into the stores or saloons meant another jostle, and so the crowd constantly eddied, like a river beset with contrary currents.

It was a motley multitude that had to be battled to cross the street and get into the stores. There was the occasional hatchet-faced Yankee, and there were also Indians in ragtag collections of European garments, with red and yellow handkerchiefs about their swarthy necks, and trappers in buffalo hide coats, too, but most of the men pushing by were as olive-skinned and black-haired as the Ecuadoreans Jake had carried as passengers from Tombez. Until Colonel Mason's report of the huge riches that could be found here reached New York and Washington, he mused, California was dominated by the descendants of the Spanish.

Jake certainly found a Yankee presence, though, once he had gone into a few stores, and accosted the men who manned the counters, to inquire about the whereabouts of the alcalde's office. Dressed in straw hats and loose frock shirts, they drove hard bargains with miners who were eager to replenish the stocks of food and gear that had been used up in the hills. The stuffy air inside was raucous with shouting — for coffee and tobacco, bread and brandy and bowie knives.

And, though nuggets were handed over as casually as buttons, it seemed that gold was not all the currency here. Abner, who had gone into the bank, rejoined Jake to report that there was a man in a railed off corner inside, busy with weights and scales as he exchanged gold for Chilean silver dollars. The bank's profit was a high one, he said with his brows high — the teller was offering just twelve dollars for an ounce of gold, when the rate was supposed to be sixteen. Men who objected were told that coins were as scarce as cockerels' eggs, and if they didn't want to pay that rate, would they please move over so that other customers could get to the desk.

The bank had double-thick bars on its windows, the bars placed so closely together that it was as dark as a stormy evening inside, said Abner. Theft, obviously, was an ever-present problem — so where was the alcalde who set the rules and enforced civil order? Jake had expected it would be a lot easier to find a flamboyant and self-important figure like Don Roberto. Finally, however, he spied a notice in the front of a store that sold boots and serapes, that directed him up a narrow set of outside steps that led him to the second floor of the next-door building, above a tavern which he already knew had a particularly nasty reputation as the resort of thugs, called the Shades.

Bodfish, Chips and Abner trampled up the steps behind him, crowding the little lobby at the top as he knocked on the door. A peevish voice called out in the well-remembered and extremely irritating Cockney accent, and Jake opened the door.

It was tough for them to all get in, because the room was not much bigger than the hall outside. The single window, which overlooked the busy thoroughfare, was barred, just like the windows of the bank and the stores, but because it lacked glass the sounds of the traffic and the carousing in the tavern below were as loud as they were in the street. Not only was Don Roberto hard to find, Jake meditated, but his quarters didn't match his bragging.

The alcalde was standing behind a desk that was piled with papers, bent over as he sorted through documents. Without looking up, he said irritably, "I'm busy, I'm busy, I 'ave to be off." Then he straightened, and as he recognized Jake Dexter his expression became guarded.

Jake introduced Chips, Bodfish, and Abner, but it was obvious that Don Roberto wasn't bothering to listen, because the instant he had finished the alcalde said, "Have you seen Colonel Sefton?"

Jake frowned. "What if I have?"

"You didn't tell him about your Company ... the shares...?"

"Why should I? It's none of his business."

The alcalde shrugged, yet seemed relieved. Then he said, "I'm busy, as I said. I've been called away on urgent business. What do you want?"

"Abner would like a copy of the regulations for staking a claim."

"It's a funny time of year to go into the diggin's."

"That was our decision."

Don Roberto shrugged again. "Your funeral," he said, then fossicked around, produced a roughly printed bulletin, and shoved it in Jake's direction.

Jake read it, aware of the others crowding to read it over his shoulder. It was a list, itemizing eighteen Articles of Law, number one being the system for appointing an alcalde, "who shall have the power to appoint a deputy or deputies." From there, it moved on to the alcalde's responsibilities if a crime should be reported, the first of which was to ascertain how the accused man wished to be judged. Once arrested, it seemed, he had the choice of being tried by the alcalde, or by a jury of eight picked men, duly sworn in by said alcalde. Jake wondered which would be worse, trial by eight random rogues, or the judgment of Don Roberto.

Article VI was the first item on the list that dealt with

mining affairs.

"Each individual locating a lot for the purpose of mining," it read, "shall be entitled to twelve feet of ground in width, running back to the hill or mountain, and running forward to the center of the river or creek, or across a gulch or ravine, lots in all cases commencing at low-water mark, and running at right angles with the stream where they are located."

Once a claim was staked, according to Article VII, it was not necessary to be seen working it, just as long as the parties who claimed the lot were "represented by a pick, shovel, or bar," and if said pick, shovel, or bar "be stolen or removed, it shall not dispossess those who located it, provided he or they can prove that they were left as required."

If the claim wasn't worked for a whole week, however, then it was considered abandoned, even if the tools were still there.

"So we'll have to keep a-moving from claim to claim," commented Abner. "To make sure that each is worked at least once a week."

"No, no!" cried Don Roberto, demanding rudely, "Don't you know how to read?"

He pushed past Abner and thrust his thumb at Article VIII. "See?" he said, and read it aloud, assuming that Abner was illiterate. "No man or party of men shall be permitted to hold two locations at the same time."

"But that ain't fair," Abner exclaimed. "Eight of us only allowed one claim among us?"

"It's the law," Don Roberto sniffed. "See it for yourself— it's written-down law."

"And I don't want the party splitting up," Jake Dexter warned. In winter conditions, survival could depend on them working together. He stared at Abner compellingly, and his scar-faced second mate reluctantly nodded.

Article IX dealt with the irritating habit of throwing dirt

121

onto the next-door mine, simply forbidding it with no mention of punishment, while Article X allowed the damming of a stream, as long as any other men who might be affected could keep on mining their lots.

"Good lord," Jake said then, involuntarily. He had just read Article XI, which baldly pronounced that, "No person coming direct from a foreign country shall be permitted to locate or work any lot within the jurisdiction of the Feather River." He thought of the Ecuadoreans he had carried to California — the bandit Murietas, in particular — and laughed.

He said, "How the hell are you going to stop foreigners who are determined to get into the hills?"

Don Roberto looked sulky. "Plenty of Americans will come after Colonel Mason's report gets to Washington."

"Yes, we all know that, but people in other countries read newspapers, you know. How the devil do you think you can keep the hills exclusively for the use of true blue Americans?"

"Me and my deputies'll 'ave our methods and ways, sir!" the alcalde snapped. "The frigate *Savannah* will be stationed in San Francisco Bay throughout the season, and Captain Mervine..."

"But," Jake pointed out, "you, yourself, are English."

"Mexican, sir! I'm a Mexican citizen, I would 'ave you know, and I would be obliged if you'd hurry up and get out of here. I have urgent business in the hills!"

"So you said, Don Roberto," Jake agreed, and returned to his leisurely reading of the bulletin, while the alcalde angrily shuffled papers on his desk.

From Article XII onward, the regulations went back to issues of law and order, but Jake carefully scanned through them to make sure there was nothing else relating to the staking and retaining of a claim.

Anyone who stole items worth a hundred dollars or more was considered just as vile as a man who took the life of another, he found, because the thief was hanged just as speedily as the murderer, once the alcalde or the jury had pronounced him guilty — though there was an interesting codicil stating that if the jury couldn't make up its collective mind, then the accused, whether killer or burglar, was given twenty-four hours to quit the territory. If he was still around at the end of the deadline, then it was considered an admission of guilt, and he was led by a rope round his neck to the nearest stout branch.

As if anyone would still be in the territory, given that kind of choice, Jake thought with derision. It was as mad as the idea that aliens could be barred from the mines.

"Well," he finally said, and straightened with the paper in his hand. "That seems clear enough, so I'll bid you good day, sir."

"Hang on a minute," Don Roberto snapped.

"I beg your pardon?"

"You don't take that list, you don't, not unless you pay five dollars."

"Five dollars? For this?" Jake looked at the document again. It was one sheet of flimsy paper, and the printing was so bad that the letters leaked ink.

"It says so, right there," the alcalde snapped, and took the bulletin away from Jake to jab his finger at Article XV, which stated, sure enough, that the regular fee for anything Don Roberto might do in the execution of his office was liable for a fee of five dollars in coin, or one ounce of gold dust.

"And a list of regulations is considered the same as a legal writ?" said Jake incredulously. He turned to Bodfish, and said, "Copy it out, and then return it to the alcalde."

Don Roberto went red in the face, and shouted, "But I ain't got time to 'ang around while he writes down every word!"

"Then lend it to him," Jake said. "I will personally guarantee, sir, that he will get it back to this office — and despite my reputation, Don Roberto, I assure you that I'm an honest man."

And with that he left, abandoning Bodfish to his task, and Abner and Chips with him, to make sure that Don Roberto didn't prevent the copying. Through the barred window, he had seen Tib and Dan out in the street, each of them shouldering a bag of the grain he had ordered them to bring into the village.

When he arrived beside them, they were standing in the middle of the road, staring dumbfounded at the humanity that streamed back and forth. Tib said, "What d'you reckon, sir? Ain't it an amazement, for a little place like this?"

"It's the gateway to the mines, remember," Jake pointed out.

With no more ado he led the way up the winding track that bordered the village stream, up past the clapboard houses to the heights where the old stone mill was set picturesquely in a grove of big trees. It was a steeper climb than it looked, and he could hear the two seamen panting as they labored after him with their burdens.

He stopped at the top, and looked down to where the brig was moored. The air was crystalline, like clear white wine, and the leaves of the trees on the hill were turning to wine colors, too, dark red and yellow gold. Many of them were fine oaks, and he could see the thick carpeting of acorns under their widespread branches.

The weather was brilliant, but the Feather River wound as silver as ice, and he thought it wouldn't be long before the first snow. Then he heard a hail from the mill, and prepared to do business.

The miller was from Maine, a regular Yankee. He had come overland, he said, and during the last part of his trek he had been with the Mormons. His dungarees were dusty in the sun, and his hands were whitened, too. The millstones ground with a harsh regular sound and the stream rippled, its water shooting off sparks of light.

He was polite enough, but pulled a long face when he

saw the sacks of grain, and was told there'd be ten more a-coming. "Ye'll have to wait to have them ground," he said.

Jake didn't mind, because there was enough flour on the brig to last the first few weeks. However, he said, "Why?"

"Colonel Sefton has priority."

"What do you mean?"

"He's just sent over six hundredweight from his rancho, and I have to drop everything else to attend to it."

Jake frowned. "It's that important?"

The miller laughed. "*He's* that important—important to me, Captain, on account of he's the owner of this here mill."

"But the mill looks so old—really old. Obviously, it was here when he arrived. He's bought it since he's come to Pueblo San Marco?"

"From a Californian Don, or so I heard." Then, when Jake made no answer to this, the miller went on, "He pays me in a percentage, and I'm doing right well, I am. But I'm sure you understand my position, Captain, that I have to be careful to make sure he keeps treating me good."

Jake shook his head. "What the hell *doesn't* Sefton own?"

"What doesn't he own?" The miller's laugh was genuinely amused. "Whatever of this here town what Don Roberto does not."

Jake turned, and stared down at the town. So which of the taps and saloons of Pueblo San Marco did Sefton possess, and which of them belonged to the fat little alcalde? It didn't matter, he decided grimly. If Sefton was raking in the money, then Harriet was safe…

Yet, there was a deep uneasiness inside him. He turned back, and checked, "Colonel Sefton is a prosperous man?"

"Prosperous?" the miller repeated, and turned his head and spat in the stream. "Oh aye, folk would say that Sefton were remarkable prosperous," he said. However, his voice had become heavy, and his face was as expressionless as his stones.

"Others might wonder," he went on in a lower voice,

"why the crookedest street in Pueblo San Marco is named after Colonel Frank Sefton."

As Jake was threading through the crowd at the bottom of the path, intent on getting back to the brig, he saw the man in question himself. Frank Sefton was coming out of his bank, his head turned as he talked to the man who was with him. Stopping beside the thicket of trees that sprouted where the stream ran off toward the river, Jake watched from under the low shadow of his hat.

Sefton's middle-aged companion was an image out of old Spain, a Spanish Don of the old Californian school. He was magnificently attired in a waist-length velvet jacket, azure in color, with silver buttons and scarlet lapels, that fitted closely over a snowy white frilled shirt. His calcineros were velvet, too, the same scarlet as the trimming of his coat, while the silver buttons on the seams were left undone from just below the knees, to show off the azure satin lining, as well his embroidered deerskin boots.

Like all the Spanish-looking types in the crowd, he wore a sombrero, jauntily placed to one side, but his hat gleamed like new varnish in the sun. He also wore the usual black handkerchief about his throat, with the corners placed carefully over the back of his neck, but this, like the striped sash about his waist, was made of the finest silk.

Sefton was talking volubly to this impressive figure, and the Don had his head bent as he listened with courtly attention. Slowly, deep in conversation, they moved off along the sidewalk, followed by the Don's servant, a man with watchful eyes and a long moustache, who carried a musket over his shoulder.

As Jake watched, the trio progressed across the street to the end of the embarcadero. The crowd made way for them, he noticed, but thought that the respect was for the Don and not for Colonel Sefton. Then they boarded a ferryboat, and bobbed off across the river.

He turned to the nearest bystander, tipped back his hat when the other nodded, and said, "Who was that?"

"Don't you know Colonel Sefton? Everyone knows him."

"I was wondering about the Californian with him."

"Ah, Captain, that's an old identity in this area, head of a family what owns a big spread up Cache Creek—which stream is a tributary that runs off the Feather up where it ain't navigable any more. A great vineyard, he has, and a pueblo of his own, and many miles of grazing land, all of it owned by the family for centuries, as far as I can tell."

"And his name?"

"Don Manuel Vidrie."

THIRTEEN

FIVE days later, Jake set out with the mining party on the well-worn mule trail to Don Roberto's fort.

He had decided to take charge of the party himself, which meant that at the age of twenty-six he was the oldest. The rest were the younger, hardier ones, the adventurous young fellows—all the young ones of the brig except Bill, the steerage boy, who had begged to come but had met a staunch refusal from his skipper. God knows what the little beggar would get up to while he was away, Jake brooded, but after all the hassle the boy had given him over the two years since he had shipped him at Capricorn Island, he certainly wasn't going to watch him die in the California hills. Charlie Martin could watch him in Pueblo San Marco, instead.

Charlie had been equally mutinous about being left behind. But, since Jake had changed his mind, and decided to go into the hills, he was the only one who would run the brig as a trading post and boarding house. Was Charlie, a seafarer and no man of the land, likely to be a good boarding house keeper? Jake sighed, and shook his head, not at all sure he had made the right decision.

However, he'd settled affairs as best he could before he left. Bodfish, as steward, purser, and secretary of the *Gosling*

Company, would handle the accounts, and Chips, as carpenter, boatswain, and chairman of the Company, would maintain the brig, carrying out running repairs as needed … while … while what? While Jake, with the rest of the Company, was digging in for the winter in the hills, staking a claim and then making sure that it wasn't jumped in the spring.

Had he made the decision for entirely the wrong reason? Jake had his head bent as he set one boot in front of the other. The casual comment Abner had made in Don Roberto's office about splitting up the party and staking a number of claims had been worrying him. Once the party was in the hills and away from the alcalde and Jake's supervision, they were all too likely to separate into smaller groups, which could be fatal. Throughout the harsh winter, each man would need the support of all, and so a strong leader was needed, to keep them together. So it was logical that their skipper should head the group, with Abner just the second in command.

But Jake also had a nagging feeling that he had had a different, personal, reason for coming with the mining party and leaving Charlie to cope with the boarding house and the brig, one that wasn't nearly as right or as logical. He grimaced, wishing he had foresight, and was able to see what was going to happen to them all. If everything went wrong, and he regretted what he'd done…

The boys trooping ahead of him felt none of his doubts. Instead, they were chatting, whistling, and singing as they strode along the wide, rutted track, the mining implements they carried rattling cheerfully. When mule trains passed them, the miners and mule-skinners called out jokes and jibes, openly amused that anyone should be going into the diggings so late in the season, but the boys still looked and sounded brightly hopeful.

They would have dug their pile before the 'forty-niners even got into the hills next year, they sung out boastfully, and only cheered when the miners laughed.

The boys even knew exactly where they were going. The Company had chosen which *arroyo* the party would try first, after a lot of discussion and the taking of a vote. It had the nursery rhyme name of Bedstead Gully, which might be a nonsensical title, but was not a silly choice. More than seventeen thousand dollars' worth had come out of there last month, according to reliable information. They had also been told that everyone who had mined there had left the gully. Come spring, the best claim would be theirs, and the prospect of the hard, wet winter they had to endure before that didn't daunt them at all.

Jake, by contrast, had only premonitions of disaster — and yet he had done all he could to guarantee their survival, if not their success. The gear that they weren't carrying themselves was packed on the five llamas. The beasts trotted serenely ahead of Jake, making soft plodding sounds with their fat-insulated hooves, as graceful as woolly swans with their long necks bobbing in rhythm to their pace. Their pack saddles were thick, soft cloths, with the local leather bags called parfleches slung over them. These held tents, and salt and dry provisions, and tools for cutting down trees and making a shelter. One of the animals carried a stove. Others carried three gold-washing cradles, carpentered by Chips, who had made all three for less than twenty dollars. A well-used common cradle cost three ounces of gold or forty dollars in coin to buy in the stores. Such were the fortunes, Jake mused dourly, that could be made from California.

The miners who had already come into Pueblo San Marco had been helpful. They had shown the *Goslings* how to pan for gold, and how to wash for it in a cradle, too. They had told them the camping tricks — how to dig a ditch about a tent to take off the rain, and how to throw the dirt against the tent walls to make them more windproof. There had been a note of pity about it all, though. Those men reckoned they'd done the wise thing by coming out of the hills, even though they lost their claims by abandoning them. By contrast, the boys who were whistling along the track ahead of Jake reckoned they were the canny ones. But spring was six months away, brooded Jake. They would be dug in and out of contact with the outside world for six cold, wet months, while Harriet ...

He doggedly set one boot before the other, battling worry and foreboding and angry jealousy, listening to Valentine's cheerful song. Then, abruptly, he found he was alongside Royal Gray.

He contemplated Harriet's brother with little liking — Royal, too, had kept him in the dark about Harriet's married state. And he had gone across the river to Sefton's ranch to see how she was a-doing only because Jake had insisted.

Jake said curtly, "Sefton does well?"

"You know he does well." Royal's expression became resentful. "You saw his bank. He has an interest in just about everything in Pueblo San Marco. I saw his hacienda and his cattle. My brother-in-law is rich and getting richer every moment of every day."

"But," Jake pointed out, "you did not see your sister."

"How could I? She wasn't there. I told you, she's with a family called Vidrie. Don Manuel Vidrie happened to be in Pueblo San Marco on business, and when he heard about Harriet, he insisted on sending her back to his mansion for the winter. Sefton had much to say about them, all praiseful, and in town people told me that they are the first family of the area."

"But Sefton isn't with her."

"I told you that, too. He will join Harriet the moment his business allows it. He's a devoted husband, I assure you."

"And did he recompense you for the alpaca venture — the one where you lost all your money?"

"I didn't ask," said Royal. His eyes didn't meet Jake's probing stare. Then he moved away, before Jake could ask him why a devoted husband would send his wife away when they had just been reunited.

Perhaps Royal wondered about that, too, Jake thought—but it was unlikely that Harriet's brother would trouble his mind about it, because the way things had turned out suited his personal plans. If Harriet had still been on the brig, then Royal would not have felt free to join the *Gosling* party that was headed for the mines.

Time trudged by, while Jake went back to his brooding about his dubious motive for joining the party himself. He had always intended to stay on the brig, but at the last moment he had changed his mind, for there was no point in staying on the *Gosling* when he could not even keep a distant eye on Harriet, yet was tortured by constant reminders of her ... not the least being her hairpins. He had found those straying pins everywhere, in deck planks and sofa cushions.

Now his hand wanted to slide into his peajacket pocket and touch his little hoard of pins again, but instead he increased his pace. He had been told it was just a half-day trek, but darkness was nearly upon them.

Twenty minutes later, to Jake's relief, Tib called out that he could see the river. A few more strides, and he saw the rushing water himself, the bridge that spanned it, and the square, squat shape of Don Roberto's fort on the other side. Two of the corners of the walls about this little castle had medieval-looking bastions, tall, with conical witch's hat roofs, and arrow slits high up. Like Sutter's Fort, the house that guarded the river was a relic of the past.

The road to the bridge was wide, and very rutted, and Jake could see a track off the road that led to a grassy embankment, well cropped. The mule skinners camped there, he thought, rather than pay Don Roberto whatever extortionate fee he charged for stabling. Then the boys were crossing the bridge, stepping carefully, because the cold waters were very high, lapping at the planks. Soon the bridge would be impassable, and Don Roberto's link to Pueblo San Marco lost.

There was a notice at the far end of the bridge, with a graphic representation of a death's head and crossbones, and a warning in both Spanish and English of the penalty for the crime of trespassing onto the grassy hills that undulated away from the other side of the river.

"What the hell?" said Tib.

They all stood and looked at it. "Warning off cattle thieves?" hazarded Dan.

"Warning off prospectors," Jake decided. The trail into the mines branched off the mule road on the other side of the bridge, but with the coming season men would be keen to try new ground.

Giving up the pointless speculation, they all turned for the entrance to the fort compound. The huge wooden door in the outer wall was firmly shut, but after the *Gosling*s had hammered and shouted a while, a shuffle of steps sounded from the other side.

The gate creaked open slowly, to reveal an ancient vaquero with a lamp in his hand. When he stood aside, they all pushed past him, into a cobbled courtyard. Don Roberto was not at home, the old fellow objected. The alcalde, it seemed, was still in the arroyos, on the urgent business he had rattled on about.

Jake informed the vaquero that that was a shame, as Don Roberto had been expecting them, and the old retainer shut up after he was given twelve dollars as payment for the night's lodging. However, he made no effort to get them acquainted with the accommodations. Instead, after stowing the coins away, he shuffled off into the darkness, headed for some fireplace in one of the half-dozen cottages that were built hard up against the north wall of the courtyard.

Jake found a lamp in one of the llama packs, and lit it. Don Roberto's house was square, like the outer fort, and obviously deserted. No lights showed in the narrow glassless window-slits. He told Dan and Tib to go inside and light a good fire, and then turned his attention to the llamas.

Stables were built against the southern wall, just to the left as they came in the entrance, and with Royal, Abner and Davy, he drove the animals inside. The stalls were all empty, and the air reeked of old urine and mildewed hay. When the llamas skittered unhappily, Jake didn't blame them.

Taking the first couple of parfleches into the house was equally depressing, as the interior was as dark and unwelcoming as the courtyard. The house had two levels, but only three rooms, two below and one up above. The smallest room, which was the one at the front, measured no less than forty feet one way, but just twelve feet the other. It was completely unfurnished. The next room held a battered billiard table, an equally battered sideboard, and nothing else. The room above, on investigation, proved to be Don Roberto's living apartment, which was crammed with heavy old furniture, all of it in a damaged state.

Each room had its own enormous fireplace. When Jake went back down the stairs, he found Tib and Dan in the front room, rummaging purposefully in the pile of wood that was stacked beside the grate. Jake stopped short and pushed back his hat in puzzlement, but then it became evident that the two young salts were looking for snakes, because they found one. The machete that Tib wielded cut off its writhing head at the same instant that Dan fired a pistol at it. Miraculously, neither of the two friends was hurt.

When Jake left they were back to feeding the small fire they had lit, and when he arrived with the next load they looked very much more comfortable. The fire was now a roaring large one, and they were cooking beans and bacon.

Tib and Dan had found a bottle of liquor in the sideboard in the other room, and by the time the llamas were unloaded and the rations cooked, the atmosphere was merry. The grub went down well with hard bread, and then most of the men went to slee. They lay spread out like spokes of a half-wheel, their feet to the flames, their heads on parfleches.

Not Royal, however. He took the bottle into the billiard room, and by the time Jake followed him, he was sitting cross-legged like a djinn on the table. There was a fire in that grate, too, and he held up the bottle to the light. It was a fine brew, whatever it was, perfectly palatable and with a decent knock — or so he said. Wind whistled in the chimneys, setting the flames to leaping and twisting, but Royal was tipsy and cheerful.

"Come, thou monarch of the corn," he declaimed to the upheld bottle. "Agile Bacchus in Kentucky born! Cup on!" he cried. "Cup on!" Then he tossed it.

Jake, who was standing in front of the fire, caught it and drank, and Royal looked pleased. "An odd old customer, Don Roberto, don't you think, Captain?" he said. "One of London's odder gentlemen."

Jake said nothing. Though he had listened to a great deal of what the Cockney said, he thought he scarcely knew him.

Undeterred by silence, Royal rose to his feet and took a pose, albeit rather unsteadily. "What a house!" he cried, with a wide, theatrical gesture:

It's mostly a muddle of tumbledown walls
And the carpetings flap in the stormy squalls
The tiles on the roof all knock like hell
And you pay good coin when you ring that bell
The dogs all yap and the llamas make a din
But it's a damn fine house, for the shape that it's in!

Then he spied someone coming into the room, jumped down to the floor, and cried, "Sing, sir, sing—join me in a song!"

When Jake turned, he expected to see Valentine or Crotchet, but instead to his surprise it was Davy, the ex-slave who had come on board the brig at Tombez, a year or more ago ... who had grabbed the martingale chains as the brig bobbed outside the bar, and had been hauled on board

135

by the foredeck lookout.

There was no way of telling how he had arrived there, as he had been battered beyond comprehensible speech by the men and dogs who had chased him, but somehow he had made it all the way to Tombez from a slave plantation in Guyana, on the other side of the isthmus. And every man on board had recognized it as a miracle. Not only had the newcomer been respectfully dubbed "Davy Jones Locker," but he was been adopted into the *Gosling* Company.

The silent black man was grinning widely, the happiest Jake had ever seen him. "Sing?" he said. "I tell you sing, I show you the way we do it in Guyana."

Then, to Jake's amazement, the tall, thin man vaulted up onto the table, while Royal jumped down to give him room.

Then he began to dance. It was a dance like nothing Jake had ever seen, an agile jangle of long arms and legs, accompanied by a meaningless scrapbook of phrases, "…slap, clap, slap, clap, wind do this, rain do that…" It was intoxicating, and Jake couldn't help it—like Royal, he began clapping in time, while Davy danced, bent over almost double at times, then throwing himself backward, arms weaving, long feet kicking, hands clapping, and beating out the strange broken rhythm on his thighs.

all at once, it was over. Davy jumped off the table and stood there, laughing.

Jake was laughing, too, surprised into good humor— and Royal said impulsively, "My God, Jake, we might have misjudged my sister. I didn't believe her when she insisted that building a theater at Sutter's Embarcadero was the way to a fortune, but with a dancer like Davy we would have had a natural for the stage. Maybe," he said, and laughed, "we should've gone for the idea. The *Gosling* theatrical company, what do you think of that?"

Jake stared at him. The *Gosling* Company a theatrical company? It was a preposterous idea—as crazy as the actual fact that he, once a respectable Yankee mariner, was now a disreputable pirate. Yet he had already travelled such a long, strange path as a fortune-hunting adventurer that metamorphosing into the manager of a theatrical company was just another step, he cynically thought.

Then he heard Davy laugh. "The stage, sir Royal, you think the stage for me, you really figger white folks would pay to see a black man dance? Why, even black folks wouldn't do that!"

Then, shaking his head and laughing some more, he left the room.

When Jake looked back at Royal, the Englishman's expression was stunned. He said, "Is that so, Jake? Would a black man really not be allowed on the stage?"

Jake shrugged. He didn't know, but Royal's incautious remark had made him wonder if he really had been too hasty. He remembered Harriet's furious words. *You're a shrewd businessman, Jake … I thought you'd see the potential.* He also remembered the sea of mud at Sutter's, but still he felt uneasy.

Royal muttered, "You Americans make me feel so damn foreign. One time, we acted in a play written by an American, a fellow called Washington Irving, a humorous dramatist of the finest water. He told my father he had to write his plays twice, once bawdy enough for English audiences, and a second time to sober it down enough to suit his home-country folk. Can you credit that?" he exclaimed, just as if Jake were not American. "And I heard, too, that in Cincinnati women and men do not picnic together, for they'd commit the indecency of sitting on the same grass — so perhaps, yes, I have to credit another story, that American women make little pantaloons for their pianos, so the piano legs won't offend their friends. Tell me, Jake, how could Americans have developed so differently, when their country ain't even a century old yet?"

Jake snapped, "You had no scruples about marrying your sister to an American."

"What?" Royal's eyes became evasive. He looked at the door as if he wished they were not alone, as if he wished someone else would wake up and come in. He found the bottle and tipped it to his mouth, and then muttered, "I don't know what you mean."

"Harriet told me that her marriage was arranged by your father. That it was a piece of business between your father, yourself, and Colonel Sefton."

"My father and I made no money out of it, I assure you," Royal said with dignity. "Sefton was a fine match. I told you, he's rich. His cattle and horses are the finest I've seen. And Harriet, remember, is an actress — an actress! Back in England, the most she could hope for from a man as rich and well-thought-of as Sefton is an offer to set her up in a house. Rich men and nobility don't *marry* actresses, you know."

Harriet wasn't good enough to marry — because she was an actress? For a moment Jake trembled on the verge of hitting Royal, but instead he shouted, "You think he's so well heeled — but what about the alpaca expedition? Wasn't it Sefton's idea that you should go to Peru and collect a herd of the animals?"

"I do admit that, yes, it was indeed his idea, and he was the one who worked up the arrangement with the merchants of Bradford, that they would pay us one hundred thousand pounds if we succeeded in getting a flock to Australia."

"But did he provide the funding?"

Royal looked more uneasy than ever. Then he muttered, "But he would've paid me back, I'm sure, if I had managed to produce the bloody animals. It wasn't his fault that I lost them all — that the Indians stole them back."

"Did you ask him for the money, when you went to the ranch?"

Royal winced, and muttered, "No, but..." Then, in a stronger voice, he said, "But it has nothing to do with Hat's marriage!"

"No? I thought money had everything to do with it! She

138

told me," Jake said deliberately, "that Sefton married her so that his investments in New Zealand would be in English hands."

"My sister didn't marry against her will, I assure you of that! Sefton was besotted with her, or my father would never have taken part in the arrangement."

"She said that he married her so that he could profit from his investments — take the profit that was forbidden to Americans."

"She told you that? But did she also mention that Sefton gave her all his New Zealand property *before* they were married? For God's sake, Jake, you might think that we were all as devious as hell, but the fact remains that Sefton signed it all over to her *before* the ceremony, and that if she'd changed her mind and decided not to marry him after all, he would have lost all his investments! Tell me, does that sound like an untrustworthy man?"

"And yet, somehow, Sefton managed to sell it all and leave her destitute — and that despite the fact that it was legally her property. Or so your sister told me."

"Look," said Royal, and put the bottle down on the table to spread his hands helplessly. "I don't know what happened after I left New Zealand. I sailed to Peru the same day as the wedding, straight after the ceremony. She was happy and smiling when she bid me goodbye, Jake. Sefton looked as prosperous there as he does in California now — there were lands, a fine house, the horses my father gave him as her dowry. And I *know* that he gave his properties to her, as I witnessed her signature, along with my father, and there was a lawyer there, the same lawyer who had drawn up the documents. It just ain't possible that he sold it all without her say-so, without her signature, so I just don't know how it happened."

Jake said nothing for a long moment. His mind was tugging at the word *signature*. Abruptly, the scene at the Embarcadero when Harriet had sailed away on the schooner was as vivid as when it had happened. He could even feel the rain and smell the mud, hear Harriet's voice as she cried out to her husband, *Is my signature worth so very much?*

And Sefton had answered, *nothing*. Her signature, he said, was worth precisely *nothing*. At the time, Jake had scarcely registered the contempt in Sefton's voice, but now he remembered it very clearly.

He said slowly, "There is something very underhand about this."

"But didn't he pay you back the money Hat borrowed from the men to pay for that patch of land on the waterfront at Sutter's? The land she intended for a theater?"

Jake was silent, thinking. He had the note for one thousand dollars still. Over the past five days he had gone past Sefton's Bank for Miners often, had even stepped inside it once or twice ... but somehow he had not been able to bring himself to exchange it for money, though he had paid back the men who had loaned it to Harriet out of his own pocket. Why? Because, as he realized grimly now, he had recognized that note as a boastful taunt, a gesture of contempt.

He said, "I don't believe he would have given me the note, if you hadn't told him that it was Harriet who signed the bill of sale."

"What?" In the flickering firelight, Royal's expression was startled. He said, "I didn't tell him that. I assumed that you did."

Jake shook his head. When Sefton had called on the brig that foul morning, he had merely informed the arrogant bastard that his wife was in a room at Sutter's Fort, and not on the *Gosling*. Then, when Sefton seemed disposed to stay and ask probing questions about how exactly his wife had happened to be on the brig in the first place, he had simply told him to get the hell off his ship.

Puzzled, he said, "Then how the devil did Sefton find out about it? When he gave me the note he knew it all—that

Harriet had signed the bill of sale, that she had paid one thousand dollars, which some of my men had advanced to her out of their own pockets. He even knew that she intended to build a theater there."

But Sefton could have learned the last from the notice on the stake that claimed that piece of ground, he remembered — a notice that said, *This piece of ground, formerly part of the rancho of Sutter's Fort and containing one thousand square feet of land, is hereby claimed for the purposes of a theater.*

Nevertheless, he demanded, "How did Sefton learn all that?"

"God knows," said Royal frankly. "For I don't."

"Who else knew all the details, then?"

Royal was quiet a long moment, staring into the fire. He was back in his sage-like attitude, cross-legged on the table top with the bottle held in both hands. Then he said, "The men knew, of course, because Harriet had called a meeting of the *Gosling* company to discuss it. And the three surveyors who laid it out knew, too. And Don Roberto."

"Don Roberto?"

"Yes. He organized the sale."

Don Roberto, thought Jake.

"Of course," he said grimly.

FOURTEEN

THE day dawned pink and murky, and by the time the llamas were loaded a cold rain had set in, a gusty drenching rain that made every surface unpleasant to touch.

When they crossed the bridge to get back to the trail, the llamas jumped about, looking restive, and the men had to drag them across. The river had risen a foot in the night, and the foaming current that covered the planks was ankle deep. Obviously, it had rained cataracts up in the hills. Another day, and the bridge would be impassable.

Where the mule track from Pueblo San Marco ended, a narrow trail led immediately uphill, heading into the mountains. It was very hard going, but still the boys who were trooping ahead of Jake were chatting, whistling, and singing, the mining gear they carried rattling cheerfully as they mounted this first of many upward slopes. As the party tramped down the slippery shingle of the other side of the hill the wind whistling down the ravine was freezing, but the boys seemed to care about it as little as the llamas did. The llamas had their lashes lowered to keep the cold from their eyeballs, and their wool was fluffed up, and for the first time they looked at home.

Davy Jones Locker was at the head of the procession. Jake watched him stalk up the next slope with the leading llama, a long-limbed mythological figure with a brilliantly striped serape billowing about his triangular back. Another crest was reached, and the party scrambled down the shingle slope on the other side. The going became slippery and treacherous. Loose stones rattled down to the stream at the bottom, a stream that had to be forded. The water was even icier than the wind. Tib Greene slipped and stubbed his boot and with a fizzing curse he fell, wetting himself almost all over. Dan Kemp hooked him out with a grip on his collar, and Tib shook himself like a dog, and trudged on. At the top of that hill the wind gusted nastily, turning Jake's bones to ice, but Tib, like the llamas, did not complain.

"It's like Peru," said Royal's meditative voice, and Jake glanced around to see Harriet's brother beside him. "Once one of my vaqueros was kept out all night, an Indian in the Andes, and when he came in he was frozen solid in his saddle. We carried him in, horse and all, to warm by the fire. It was a strange and wonderful sight to see that horse thaw out. It dripped, it steamed, it moved, and the Indian fell to the ground, restored to life."

Those in hearing laughed, but not Jake, and Royal picked up pace so that he moved on ahead. Then the path narrowed, becoming no more than eighteen inches wide, hard up against a sheer cliff that was streaming with water. Overnight, that water could turn to ice. The men sidled cautiously, strung out along the cliff, but the llamas moved with confidence.

Abner slipped once and cried out with fear, and Tib Greene grabbed him just in time. There was a strange sense of ambush, perhaps because the land was so empty, or because the weather was so grim. All the men were tense, Jake saw, not nearly as happy as they had been at the start of today's trek. He himself kept breaking step to look about.

The rocks dripped, and soaked foliage hung low. Every precipice was half hidden in cloud. Once the clouds drew apart with a stray gust of breeze, revealing the full extent of the cliff face they were traversing, and Dan Kemp swore in a yell of fright. Stones rattled ahead, and the roar of a hungry hunting bear rumbled about the hills. Everyone froze, and then the bear roared again, further away.

They moved on, into the mountains. Again the path became so narrow that the men were forced to sidle with their fronts to the rock face, holding onto clumps and crevices for balance. The llamas, despite their burdens, were the surest footed of them all. This particular cliff face was pocketed with the nesting burrows of a multitude of swallows; in summer, Jake thought, the going would be more dangerous than ever. Perhaps even the llamas would take fright at the diving and swooping of the birds. Far below, huge conifers spread ancient branches, veiling whatever was beneath them. Pebbles rolled away from the boys' boots as they descended the terraces that zigzagged down the sheer side of the mountain, and then, at last, the party was in the valley at the bottom.

The basin was surprisingly lush, thick with grass and ferns. It was possible to see where the miners had pushed a way, because of the cleared patches where their mules and horses had foraged. Where the growth was still thick the going was slippery, slicked by many layers of conifer needles. A creek ran along the bottom, as water did in all the arroyos, and occasional holes showed where men had tested the ground for traces of gold.

After a mile or so, the valley opened out, and Davy was faced with a choice of paths. He stopped, and everyone gathered around, while Jake hauled out the map one of the incoming miners had given him. When he looked about to check his bearings, he realized that he hadn't needed it, not really, because every little track was marked with a notice, clearly if badly scrawled, and often bearing a frivolous name. One board pointed the way to Olé Olé Hole, another to Pancho's Fortune; there were Old Dead Bar and Black Man's Luck, and Dry Bones Gulch, and Bedstead Gully.

When Jake pointed this last one out, Davy led the way, and the others followed. The trail was very narrow, so that they had to push through thickets and scrub. Boughs flicked heavy moisture at their faces and fern soaked their feet and legs. Then, from ahead, Jake heard an unearthly wailing.

He stopped short. He could see Joseph Fayal showing the whites of his eyes in fright, and Dan Kemp swore. Royal, just behind Jake, whispered, "Oh, my God, what is it?"

It was a weird concert that shrieked with pain and rage and loss. Then the wind gusted … and brought with it an appalling charnel smell of burning flesh and hair. The terrible screaming rose in volume, and Jake began to run.

He ran up the gully towards the terrible noises. He heard some of the men call out for him to come back, and then Davy and Valentine and Crotchet were running alongside him. A thicket rose about them. Jake shoved through the tangle of bushes — and stopped short.

There was a wide open space before him, where an Indian encampment was built. The Indians were dancing, dancing about a fire, dancing in the rain. They threw their torsos back and forth while they shouted out their terrible screams. Bedraggled black hair streamed about their contorted faces, and they danced in wide circles about a fire. And the thing that was burning on the fire was a body.

Jake understood then that it was a funeral pyre. He stood irresolute. Though the trail to Bedstead Gully led through this encampment, he felt as if he was intruding on something immensely private. A gust of rain fell, and the flames drew back with a hiss, revealing that the body was dressed in a blanket. Grease spat and black smoke billowed, and huge smuts whirled with the gust. The dancing Indians threw more fuel into the flames as they circled — bowls, baskets, food.

Then Davy ran into the encampment before Jake could stop him. He started to move after Davy, but Crotchet's hand held him back. "Better not, Captain," he said in his

French accent, and Jake remembered that Crotchet—whose real name was Crozet, and who hailed from Lower Louisiana—knew Indians better than he did.

So Jake stood and watched as Davy walked up to a young woman. The girl was crouched by the head of the pyre, and Davy crouched down too, to talk to her. The girl had something on her back, like a hump. Then Jake realized it was a cradle board with a baby in it. As Jake watched the ex-slave took his bag off his shoulder and opened it, and gave the woman some food. Jake thought—hoped—that she would eat it or save it, but instead she threw it into the fire.

It was like a signal. The whole heap of burning branches collapsed, and the corpse shriveled and collapsed, too. Everything disappeared entirely, and Jake realized that the fire had been built over a pit in the ground, and that the ashes and embers had fallen into the hole. When he looked at Davy again, the tall black man was coming back.

Valentine said, distressed, "Why did she burn that grub? There's a hard winter ahead, so how could she waste food like that?"

Davy shrugged, and set off back to where the other men were struggling with the terrified llamas. They resumed their trek, and then, thank God, they were out of the broad valley where the Indians lived, and heading into a ravine. Jake followed Davy, listening to the men hauling the llamas along. The Indians were out of sight, but not the smoke, not the smell, and not the loud mourning.

Tib came up with Jake and demanded, "What was they doing, Captain?"

"It was a funeral pyre, Tib."

"They were burning a *body*?"

"Aye."

Davy said, "He was the chief, the girl's husband, the body, he."

"So why burn him? Did he die of some disease?"

The defile was narrowing fast, becoming no more than a

thin corridor between two tall, sheer cliff faces. Slow echoes drummed back from the tramp of their boots. Davy said, "He did not die a natural death, that poor man, he."

"What do you mean?"

"I saw his head. I saw his skull bones. He had no skin or hair …" Davy was lost for the word, and pulled at his own crinkly hair, grimacing.

A flicker of movement caught Jake's eye, and he tipped back his hat to stare ahead. There were mules, horses, men at the far end of the defile, coming towards them in single file. Above the head of the cavalcade a huge boulder stood suspended at the top of the crevice, wedged insecurely between the two cliffs. One day, it would fall down and block the path.

"What do you mean, his skull bones?" said Valentine Fish.

"The—the men who killed the chief, they took away his hair, with the skin." Davy's voice held bewilderment.

"Oh, God," said Royal.

Valentine said, horrified, "He'd been *scalped?*"

Scalped, Jake thought with revulsion. Then he was distracted by a growing sense of incredulity. The men coming along the defile towards them were close enough to recognize. The first was Don Roberto, the Cockney alcalde. He sat astride a mule, riding with the grace of a sack of corn. The six other men in the party rode horses and led more mules. The pack beasts were heavily laden with parflesches that bulged hard, as if they were packed full of gold dust.

"God!" said Royal again. "That's…"

"Yes," said Jake grimly. The six men were the Murietas. The last he had seen of them was when they had left the brig at San Francisco, and glad indeed he had been to see them go, for of all the Ecuadorean passengers they had carried from Tombez, the Murietas were the most vicious.

Bandits, definitely bandits—what the Californians called *desperadoes*. And of the six Murietas the worst, by far, was their leader, Joaquín Murieta.

Royal demanded, "So why the hell are those bandits riding with Don Roberto?"

Jake wanted to know that, too. For a moment he wondered if the alcalde had them under arrest, but that was obviously impossible — there was only one Don Roberto, and there were six of the Ecuadoreans.

Then the cavalcade stopped. The two parties were confronting each other.

Joaquín smirked, his moustache writhing, and said, "Capitán," but Jake ignored him.

"Don Roberto," he said grimly.

The space in the defile was a little broader here, and men and beasts milled restively, the pack mules nuzzling at the llamas with a curiosity that was almost human. There was sweat mingled with the rain on the alcalde's face, and his hands fiddled nervously with the reins. His eyes hunted the landscape, rather than counter Jake's stare.

Jake said, "You've been on alcalde business?"

Don Roberto's mouth opened. His tongue touched his lips and then he said defiantly, "I told you I had urgent business to attend to in the hills, Captain Dexter."

"Aye, I remember that — but now I wonder what that business might be, when you travel with such men." Jake nodded at the laden mules and their fat heavy burdens, and said, "And I think that looks more like the result of digging business than proper alcalde business."

"Whatever kind of business it be, it ain't your business whatsoever! And whatever you say, whatever you think, Captain Dexter, the business — and these men — be all legal. These men are my lawful legal sworn-in deputies, and you just take notice of that!"

"Dear God." It was Royal's voice, awed. "What monstrous fool would give legal authority to such blatant rogues?"

Jake could hear the mutters of agreement from the rest

of his men. However, he didn't look around, but kept his stare on Don Roberto's sweating face.

"I need deputies!" the alcalde shouted furiously. Spittle flew out of his mouth to join the rain. "I 'ave to 'ave deputies, and these be fit men! They have their own headquarters in the Shades tavern, below my offices, and they provide armed escort to anyone who needs them, and is willing to pay. And because of my pressing needs, I have procured their services, and deputized them proper. I need deputies what can dig, and deputies what can guard my mule trains against robbers, and these men are willing to do all that. And I deputized them for the season because I need 'em regular, and not just when they're not protectin' other men, claim jumpin' bein' so popular!"

Jake paused, turning this over in his mind with increasing uneasiness. Not only was it unbelievable that this fat little alcalde should give the Murietas the kind of credibility that allowed them to pretend to protect people from the thuggery that they probably had committed themselves, but he also remembered that he and his men planned to take over abandoned claims.

Would this pompous little fellow consider it claim jumping? He remembered the clause in the regulations that stated that a claim was considered abandoned when it had not been worked for a week, but thought that in these unpoliced hills the alcalde could make up whatever rules he liked.

He said, "What claim jumping do you have in mind?"

"Which one, he asks," said Don Roberto, apparently to his mule, and laughed mirthlessly. "Even at this time of the year there ain't a week what goes by wivout someone or other sending for me to complain that his mine has been jumped, and the lord alone knows what it will be like when the diggin' season starts next year. And this be my jurisdiction, so what else can I do but do something about it? I have to stir myself right away, drop everything else, drop

149

all other activities, that's what, and travel to the disputed claim, that's what, and listen to all the clamor and shouting and then decide the rights of the business. And 'ow am I suppose to make up my mind while all them distractions is going on? I need time, that's what I need, but time ain't what I got, so I make the time instead."

Then he sniffed peevishly at the sweat and rain on the end of his nose. Jake frowned, trying to make sense of what sounded like sheer prevarication, while his men muttered in puzzlement, too.

Then he said slowly, "Is that why these mules are carrying so much gold?"

"Who says it be gold?" Don Roberto sniffed again, and then said defiantly, "Well, you're right, I do admit, yes, that it is indeed gold what them mules are toting. I'm carrying it off for safe-keeping, to stow in the vaults of the bank while I ponder the merits and demerits of the case, and when I decide who rightfully owns that gold, then that person or persons will get it all entire. With the exception of my fee, of course," he added, apparently as an afterthought. "And my deputies get fees, too—for I have to 'ave deputies! I need them deputies to dig all the gold out of the disputed claim, to pan it and bag it, and then load the mules up, and escort the mule train to Pueblo San Marco, and no sooner that be all over and the gold all safe in the vaults of the bank, than another claim gets itself jumped, and the business starts all over again."

Bank? Which bank?

Jake snapped, "And the bank—does it get a fee as well, in the form of a percentage, perhaps?"

"But of course!" Don Roberto bellowed. "You can't expect Colonel Sefton to look after all that disputed gold for nothin'!"

So the unasked question was answered. Jake pictured all the gold piled up, waiting in Sefton's bank vaults, while Don Roberto made up his mind at his leisure. So much could happen while Don Roberto paused and thought and prevaricated — the contestants could die, or move on to other places, or make a pile somewhere else, and forget about the gold in Sefton's vaults.

And was Sefton honest? Jake, remembering his conversation with Royal the night before, didn't think so at all.

He said grimly, "I have a note myself, writ on Sefton's Bank for Miners."

If Don Roberto was surprised or intrigued by this, he certainly didn't betray it. When Jake produced the folded draft the alcalde merely shook it open, glanced at it, and handed it back.

He said indifferently, "It'll be good, good as gold."

"You're sure of that?"

"Of course I am. Colonel Sefton is a substantial man. Any of his notes is worth every cent of its written value."

Jake lifted a brow and said, "I'm more interested in the reason Sefton gave it to me. He said it was repayment for the money Mrs. Sefton borrowed from my men to buy that piece of ground on the Embarcadero at Sutter's Fort."

Don Roberto shifted in his saddle. Every one of his boys, Jake observed, was staring at the alcalde, too, waiting, as he was, for an answer. The silence dragged on and Don Roberto looked everywhere except at Jake. His expression, oddly, was embarrassed.

Then he muttered, "I do admit, Captain, yes indeed, when I realized the true state of affairs I wished myself most heartily in another place. But it was not my fault. It was Mrs. Sefton's deception. How I was to know she was married, when I had not a notion that Miss Harriet Gray was just a stage name? How I was to know what I blunder I had made, when I sold that lady 'er own husband's land?"

"What!"

"Yes — Colonel Sefton owned that very piece of ground at Sutter's, he got it as collateral on a failed loan. Even though he don't believe in the future of the Embarcadero the way I do, he owned that bit of land what Mrs. Sefton chose, because it had been a guarantee on a loan what was never repaid. So I sold your Company 'er own husband's land, and allowed her to sign for it. How's that for an awkward coincidence, Captain?"

Jake said softly, "Oh Jehovah." So that, he thought, was how Sefton had known that Harriet had signed the bill of sale. That was how he had known every detail of the transaction.

Then Don Roberto went on, "So it's most uncommon generous of the Colonel to think to repay the money, for by law he don't 'ave to. The money *and* the land are legally his."

Jake frowned. "That can't be true."

"But it is, I assure you."

"But it doesn't make sense! If I conclude to keep the land, it is mine, because the *Gosling* Company bought it and paid for it, so by right and by law, it's ours."

Don Roberto hooted, "But you can't!"

"And why not? The men told me that you recommended the purchase as a fine investment, that it was your persuasions that helped them make up their minds to lend Mrs. Sefton the cash. Did you lie about that?"

"I did not tell lies!" the alcalde shouted. His mule whickered, and the horses moved restively, their ears flicking at the llamas who snorted and puckered thick threatening lips. Don Roberto ignored all this, staring at at Jake and shouting, "That land will do well, I warrant it! It's a very fine investment, even if you don't build anything on it! It may be swamp now, but within a year a city will rise up on that spot, a town to rival New Orleans!"

"Then," said Jake, "there is no reason at all why I shouldn't tear up that draft and demand the deed back from Colonel Sefton, so that the Company can do what they like with this valuable land."

"But you can't!"

Don Roberto's voice became a wail, and the llamas and

the horses and the mules all whickered again. The animals seemed very nervous, Jake thought, and then he imagined he heard thunder. The rain started up again, harder than before, but he kept his stare on the alcalde's face.

Then Don Roberto said angrily, "What do I 'ave to do to make you understand? Can't you see it, no matter how I explain it? Mrs. Sefton had no right to sign that bill, she had no right to sign anything legal, for a wedded woman's signature ain't lawful. It ain't valid, for everything she owns belongs to her 'usband, by legal right! Sefton still owns that land, for his own wife signed for it with a signature that ain't valid. He don't even have to return the money, for once she signed for it that land became his, land that he owned already!"

Jake froze, abrupt understanding rushing inside him. When Don Roberto nodded curtly and tugged the mule out of his grip, Jake scarcely noticed it, just as he scarcely noticed the mule train trotting off, accompanied by the Murietas on their horses. The rest of the *Gosling* mining party was heading up the defile, but he stood in the shadow of the suspended boulder, lost in increasingly apprehensive thought. Then, with a lurch, he pulled himself together, and looked around for Royal, who was at the rear of the *Gosling* party, talking to Valentine and Crotchet.

Running up in pursuit, he stopped Harriet's brother short with a hand on his arm. Valentine Fish and Crotchet stopped, too, looking inquisitive, but Jake ignored them, saying tensely to Royal, "That's how Sefton managed to sell all his property in New Zealand, even though it was all in Harriet's name, that's how he did it!"

"What?"

"When she told me he married her for her English nationality, she spoke nothing but the truth. He took a gamble when he gave her everything the day before the wedding, but not much of a gamble, because she married him, which gave him all his property back—with the added

153

advantage that he was now able to sell it in the name of an English national. Because he married her, he was able to avoid the restrictions against Americans! My God, once she married him, she was doomed."

Urgency filled him. He looked around wildly, and said, "I must go back."

"But you can't—what would you do?"

"I'll find her. I must. She could be in danger, because she's of no use to him now. At the very least, he could abandon her, just as he did in New Zealand. That's why he sent you off to South America on that alpaca-collecting scheme! To get you out of the way!"

He saw Royal frown, and then slowly turn white. But before Royal could speak, from right above, directly overhead, the hunting bear roared.

Men yelled from both ends of the defile. The Murietas had turned their horses and were shouting and pointing. Then they were wildly firing their guns. Pablo looked up and screamed. Jake looked up too—he was directly under the boulder, still holding Royal's arm. He heard Valentine and Crotchet shout, and then their steps as they ran away from the shadow of the suspended stone, back toward the alcalde and the Murietas, out of the way of a sudden rattle of loose stones.

High above, the bear roared again. Hugely. Right above Jake and Royal. It was on top of the suspended stone. Then it plunged down the cliff face, setting stones rolling, falling with the falling shingle. Jake yelled and shoved, pushing Royal ahead of him, rolling frantically forward as the bear plummeted onto the back of the hindmost llama.

The llama shrieked like a woman, horribly. It collapsed under the dreadful weight, broken-backed, screaming. The bear snorted, its muzzle full of blood, and all the men fired guns at once. Jake threw himself flat, forward, hauling Royal with him, and glimpsed Valentine and Crotchet running away to the rear. The bear growled and shook its great head

154

while the llama still screamed and its fellows bolted. And the rock above thundered like the bear.

The rock moved. The whole world shuddered as the great boulder shifted and shrugged in the niche in which it had been set for so long. Then it fell, taking half the cliff with it. With a mighty crashing that went on and on, mud and stones slipped and fell. When at last the commotion was over, there was only an echoing memory of the terrible double scream as the bear and the stricken llama were crushed.

Valentine, Crotchet, Don Roberto and the Murietas were on the downriver side of the defile. Tib, Dan, Pablo, Joseph, Jonathan, Pablo, Davy and the four surviving llamas were on the Bedstead Gully side of the ravine, trapped by the rock fall. Even if they changed their minds, there was no way out until the rainy season that had just begun was finished.

And Jake, with Royal, was with them. Like the others, he was trapped on the trail to Bedstead Gully, unable to go back until spring.

FIFTEEN

BEDSTEAD Gully turned out to be a surprisingly pleasant place, though hazardous underfoot, because of all the holes the miners had dug, many of which were now grassed over, so that the pitfalls were invisible until a man actually put his boot in one.

The prospectors of the 1848 season had certainly been busy. Jake marveled at how thoroughly it had been dug, with scarcely a spot about the banks of the stream that had not seen the attentions of a pick, crowbar, or shovel. It was obvious that if any gold was ever here, it had been taken away. That was a thought he kept to himself, however, as the gully was a good place to build a log cabin and settle in for the winter. The bubbling stream ran too fast to be iced over, so would supply them with endless fresh water, and the thick groves of oak on the hills promised lumber for the hut.

The first night, they made camp under an overhang that kept off most of the rain. The party stretched out with their bedrolls and blankets, using saddle-cloths for mattresses and pillows, a good fire burning at their feet. Nevertheless, the night passed in a long, uncomfortable doze that could not possibly be called a sleep, and when they roused at dawn, they were so heavily covered with dew that it shook off like a shower when they stood. Many more nights like this, Jake thought, and they would be all dead of fever.

With ferocious efficiency, he set about ensuring survival. Tents were pitched, and moats dug around them, and the dirt slung up against the saturated canvas to keep them in shape. Then he had to hassle the men into cutting logs and building a cabin, because they wanted to dig for treasure, instead. As Abner pointed out, the clay they had dug out of the ditches was the bluish color that held the best promise of gold. The previous prospectors hadn't hunted hard enough, or so he reckoned, having heard stories in Pueblo San Marco about men who picked out seven or eight ounces a day from places others had given up as useless. This, he said, was because the gold was in pockets, which were crevices between blocks of slate, where gold that had been washed down from the heights by the heavy rains of millennia had collected. It was impossible to tell where they were, he said, so finding them was a matter of luck—and he was certain he felt lucky.

Everyone except Davy felt the same way, and muttered about being forced to cut down trees and carpenter the timber, instead of prospecting. Thank God, Jake thought, that he had come, or they would have all been dead within a month. Then he tongue-lashed them into leveling a square of earth on a terrace, halfway up the nearest slope. Soon after that, though, he didn't have to argue any more, because as fast as the holes for corner posts were dug those holes filled up with icy mud, making it obvious that digging for gold was out of the question until spring.

At last the men saw the logic of putting their energy into felling trees, and then cutting the logs to length. Three weeks more, and they were living in a watertight log cabin. It might have had a mud floor, but it did have a hearth, so they could have a fire inside, which was kept burning every hour of the day and night.

Because of the unfailing fire, the levelled earth dried out, and became a decent floor, particularly after flour bags had been spread out as a carpet. And, also because of the fire, they could cook civilized meals—cooked by the man who was on cooking duty, according to a daily roster that Jake devised. Again he had to exert his force of will, just to make sure that the rota was followed—and how he missed Bodfish, who normally did that kind of thing. Other jobs on the daily list were the gathering of firewood, and the collection of water from the stream. The first barrel of meat to be emptied had been cleaned and scrubbed until every trace of salt and grease was gone, so they could have a scuttlebutt of water that was fit to drink, just inside the door. There was even a lean-to stable for the llamas, though Pablo and Joseph had argued that it would be warmer with the llamas inside.

The nine of them argued about a lot of things, and discussed other things, too. The boys talked of sending out a party in the higher hilly fastnesses where there was snow instead of mud, but Jake talked them out of the dangerous idea of packing up and heading out, being determined that they should not split up until it was safe to do so. It was boring, dug in at the placer, waiting out the rain for spring, but at least—as he pointed out—they were dry and warm. And there was plenty of food, because as well as having a good supply of provisions, they were able to fish and shoot game.

All they had to do was wait.

In Pueblo San Marco, waiting out the winter was every bit as boring. Valentine and Crotchet had been lucky to get back to the brig when they did, for once they got to Pueblo San Marco, they were trapped in town. If anyone wanted to try to get to Colonel Sefton's ranch, the river was running too high to be crossed, and Sutter's Fort was naught but swamp, so there was no point in taking a boat downstream.

But at least, unlike the *Goslings* at Bedstead Gully, the

shipkeepers were not alone in their tedium. The streets were crowded with men who'd come upriver or down from the hills to wait until spring. Many of them lived as boarders in the hold of the brig *Gosling*, but they were not encouraged to stay on board in the daytime, so throughout the day and far into the night they lounged about the streets, fighting, drinking, and telling tall tales about the gold. And most of them gambled, a lot. Nine-pin billiards was very popular, particularly with the South Americans. However, the biggest game in town was monte — monte in the Peruvian style.

And the biggest place to play the game was Abrigo's café-restaurant.

Abrigo was a native of the area, a hugely fat man who had been running his establishment for God alone knew how long. He owned the place outright, and worked for himself with his wife as cook and croupier, and must have been reaping an incredible fortune — or so Crotchet and Valentine reckoned. Nonetheless, he looked poor. Abrigo looked poor and dressed poor, too. He wore duck trousers instead of calcineros, perhaps because he couldn't cram his bum into his national dress. His shirt was thin and wet with sweat even in the coldest weather, and was invariably so short of buttons that it revealed a large brown hairy paunch. Valentine reckoned that the paunch had more expression than Abrigo's face.

Abrigo's appearance fascinated Crotchet, too ... but not as much as the monte tables. The last time he had played monte was on the brig during the passage from Tombez to San Francisco, when the Murietas had set up a gambling saloon in the steerage, and he had done rather well, so he regarded the game of monte with affection. For him, it held a golden promise.

Monte was a simple game, relying entirely on guess and good luck. Skill had nothing at all to do with it, though cheating was a definite factor. The table top was marked into four rectangles, and a card was thrown into each rectangle, face up. The players then bet on the suit and color of the next card to be faced, laying down their bets beside the card with the suit or color of their choice. Then, the betting done, that fifth card was turned over. Those who had guessed right got back their bet plus an equal sum, while those who had guessed wrong had the pleasure of seeing their hard-won gold deposited on top of the bank in the center of the table.

The base of the bank was a solid pile of Chilean silver dollars, intermingled with the coins of a dozen different countries, while the thick frosting of this very rich cake was dully shimmering gold dust, sometimes decorated by little bags of nuggets. Valentine had seen miners put these bags onto the table, the result of dreary months of digging and panning, and go away with nothing, just leaving the bank heaped higher.

He had also seen a Californian lose every sou he owned, then sell the fine indigo cloak that had draped his shoulders to another customer, and lose that money as well. A wide-awake looking Yankee who was watching, too, confided that it happened all the time — that whenever he was in need of horse, a saddle, spurs, or a serape, he was always able to find a bargain at Abrigo's café-restaurant. "As soon as I see a Spaniard thoroughly pigeoned and eager to try his luck again," he said, "I go outside and take a squint at his horse and its trappings, and I generally get what I want for less than a third of its value."

On the other hand, Valentine had witnessed some surprising runs of luck. With his very own eyes he had seen a boy who looked no more than ten years old come in with a handful of dollars, and go away with a bulging wallet. During the past season professional gamblers had regularly sent twenty thousand dollars back to England — or so he was reliably told. An even more popular story was of the young man had come upriver, stopped at Abrigo's, and won nearly ten thousand dollars during the course of just one night. A wise fellow, he had sold his un-used tools, and taken himself off down the river again, his winnings securely stashed in a parflesch that he had slung over one shoulder.

And Crotchet thought he could do just as well as that—for the Company.

"Five hundred dollars," he said coaxingly at supper.

Because there were so few of them—just Charlie, Bodfish, Chips, Abijah, Cookie, and the mutinous steerage boy, Bill, plus Valentine and Crotchet—the shipkeepers ate their meals together in the mess cabin of the brig, and so the two boys had a captive audience for their enticement.

"What for?" said Charlie.

"For a stake," said Crotchet.

"You want *Gosling* Company funds—for gambling?" Abijah's voice was scandalized.

"But we'll win," said Valentine, with boundless optimism. "Crotchet's luck is famous."

"I know I can double the money, or even better. Would not it be wonderful, if I came back with three thousand?"

"Luck," quoth Bodfish, his expression wise, "is not altogether reliable."

"And those tales you tell were probably made up by Abrigo himself, to draw in more custom," said Chips, even more wisely.

"Why don't you come to Abrigo's and watch?" asked Valentine. "And then you can judge the truth for yourselves."

"The devil's drawing room and the devil's tickets are not my idea of entertainment," sniffed Abijah Roe, and Valentine and Crotchet rolled their eyes at each other.

Then Crotchet, like some diffident magician, began to play a game of knucklebones, tossing heavy gold bones up in their air, catching them on the back of his hand, tossing them again. The rattle was loud in the silence, and every man seated about the table had his eyes fixed on the tumbling gold shapes.

Then one missed its mark. It fell onto the wooden table

top with a thud, and rattled to a stop. Bodfish picked it up and held it up to his nose as if to sniff it.

"What is this?" he said suspiciously.

"Gold, of course," said Crotchet.

"And where did you find five nuggets like this?"

"Won them at Abrigo's, suh."

And the boys got their stake of five hundred dollars.

They ambled into Abrigo's at a little after ten that same evening. Though they were wet with rain, Crotchet seemed in no hurry to commence his assault on the tables. Instead he gambled with a little of his own gold, and then stood back to study others as they gambled more.

Valentine was content just to watch. As he watched, a greasy French beaver trapper laid down half a hat of gold dust and took that fur hat full of dust away. A Californian lost his dust, then the silver spurs from his heels, the gold buttons from down the seams of his calcineros, the serape from his shoulder, and finally the horse at the hitching post outside. The caballero went off then, as dignified as ever, and Crotchet quietly took the vacated place at the table.

That was when Valentine became nervous.

Crotchet played cautiously and won a little, and then lost what he had gained. Valentine, at his shoulder, watched anxiously every second of the time. Then, without even waiting for his luck to change, Crotchet began to play with *Gosling* money. Valentine felt as if he had his heart in his mouth. It wasn't the same, he thought, when the money belonged to the group.

Crotchet won a little, lost a little — and then abruptly won a lot. The five hundred was all at once a thousand. A buzz of comment began to rustle all about the room, and men left other tables, coming to crane and watch. The thousand quadrupled; Crotchet could do nothing that was wrong. All the other tables were suddenly empty, and men were coming in from the street to watch. The only ones who seemed unmoved were Crotchet—and Abrigo, who was the croupier. The fat man made no comment, and no expression crossed his face.

His fingers moved like fat caterpillars, flipping cards, gathering them up, shuffling them so that they blurred. Then all at once Valentine heard Crotchet say softly, "Suh, I challenge for the tap."

Tap? For a wild moment Valentine could not even remember what the word meant. He heard Abrigo cough and clear his throat and then say, "Pardon?"

"Suh, I wish to tap for the bank."

Then Valentine remembered what the word *tap* meant, and he couldn't help it—he let out a grunt of pure horror. Crotchet was betting all that he had on the throw of one card, in the hope of taking the whole of that yellow shivering mountain of dust on the table. He looked about wildly, almost as if he were looking for escape, and became aware then of the perfect hush in the room. Men craned to see, from chairs, from the tops of other tables, and no one breathed a word.

Valentine returned his apprehensive stare to Abrigo's face. Abrigo looked unusually thoughtful. He had his head a little on one side, so that his neck on that side was fatly creased. He nodded. Then he shrugged and moved his hands a little. Four cards floated out from the pack by pure prestidigitation, one landing in each rectangle, tidily face up. They were the four of hearts, the two of clubs, the ace of diamonds, and the king of hearts.

Three red cards, one black.

Valentine held his breath, waiting for Crotchet's bet. His friend had his head on one side, too, and seemed as pensive as Abrigo. Then, with a casual motion, he put down their stake, the whole of their gold, the *Gosling* gold too, all in the square where the two of clubs lay.

Abrigo's face showed no reaction. He gave the stake an indifferent look, began to move—and Crotchet said, "Stop."

Abrigo stopped. "Señor?"

"I choose to deal the gate."

It was Crotchet's right to challenge if he wanted, but nevertheless it questioned Abrigo's honesty. Valentine heard a hiss of comment start up in the room, and then silence again as men strained to hear.

Still, the fat man showed no trace of expression. Without comment, he handed over the pack. The cards were greasy and well worn about their black edges, but Crotchet handled them with reverence, his flat gambler's palms smooth. He shuffled, while everyone strained not to blink, and then— flick! —- a card flew up, floated, arrived face up on the table. Everyone craned to see. The silence was taut.

The card was a court card, a woman on a horse. It was the queen of clubs.

The whole room erupted in a burst of incredulous laughter, while men shook their heads. Crotchet had won. Won! Valentine felt weak with relief.

Crotchet said in his diffident way, "And now, suh, I wish to tap again."

"But the bank, señor, is busted."

"I'll bet everything—everything on the table, against this fine establishment."

"What!"

The cry burst out, not from Abrigo, but from Valentine himself. In that shocked, horrified moment he was not aware that he had shouted. It went unheard, anyway, as other men were crying out their astonishment. For a moment there was bedlam, but then Abrigo opened his mouth. And it was abruptly quiet again.

Abrigo said, "You wish me to wager my café, señor?"

"I'm afraid I do, suh," said Crotchet. His smile was bashful.

Silence. Everyone waited. Abrigo was staring at the table. Perhaps, Valentine thought, the years of running this café-restaurant were parading through his mind. Then, with a shrug, he inclined his head. He nodded.

Taking the pack, he dealt three cards. They arrived face up on the table—the three of diamonds, the six of clubs, the knave of hearts. The fourth one seemed to stick. Abrigo's tongue-tip touched his lips as he freed it, and then it floated onto the table. It was that lady equestrienne again. She lay there and seemed to smile primly at them all, that queen of clubs, but most especially up at Crotchet.

Crotchet had his head on one side again. Valentine most desperately wanted him to bet on the lady of the clubs. Then, smiling faintly, Crotchet shifted all their winnings and put them by the jack of hearts. The knave, whose smile was insolent.

Abrigo murmured, "The heart, señor, you bet all on a heart?"

"Yes, suh—and I deal."

Abrigo again handed over the deck. Crotchet held it, looking not at the pack, but at the table. Then, with a swift decisive movement, he faced the top card without bothering to reshuffle.

It was the six of hearts.

"And now," said Valentine with great satisfaction to the shipkeepers on the *Gosling,* "we can drop this grubby boarding house business, and put all our efforts into running the café-restaurant." That, he mused, was bound to be much less tedious than looking after surly lodgers, and selling provisions.

And ah, he thought, that wonderful gamble—the gamble that Abrigo had fixed the pack, anticipating that Crotchet would go for his lucky queen of clubs again. The outcome had been marvelous, when it could have been so dreadful. For the first time, Valentine was looking forward to life in Pueblo San Marco—for the first time, he was grateful to the bear that had left them both stranded in the village.

165

SIXTEEN

"BEAR baiting," said Don Manuel Vidrie, in his excellent English. "You celebrate Christmas in London with such exciting sport, perhaps?"

"No, I don't believe so," said Harriet, and shook her head as she took his proffered arm.

For her, Christmas in London meant pantomimes, and certainly nothing that sounded as medieval as bear baiting. Pantomime was considered the lowest form of theater by the cultural elite, and was exhausting, too, as the performances often lasted five hours. Nevertheless, there had been a pantomime starring the Gray family every single December — for the simple reason that it brought in a lot of money.

As a toddler, Harriet had been carried about as a Babe in the Wood. Then, as she grew a little older, she had been a cherub in her queenly mother's retinue, trained not to laugh as her famous father, who normally played kings and tragic heroes, swept about in a vast and dowdy woman's gown, wearing a huge red wig and bawling satirical songs that made fun of political figures. At the age of thirteen she had been promoted to Principal Boy, and had donned tights to play Dick Whittington, which was when, because of the whistles and comments from the males in the audience, she had found out that she had beautiful legs.

167

At fourteen, she earned a different kind of applause as Columbine, endlessly fleeing with her star-crossed lover, Harlequin, while an enraptured crowd bawled encouragement. They had cried out warnings, too, she remembered, particularly the children. Each time the villain crept onto the stage, they had screamed with delicious fright, *He's behind you!*

The memories trailed on, because, oddly enough, life with the extensive Vidrie family reminded her often of playing in pantomime — because of the endless dressing up. There was a difference, however. Lavish costumes, whether comical or splendid, had been a large part of the attraction of pantomime, and costumes were changed so often that getting onstage at the right instant and in the right dress had often been a panic-stricken rush. But, though it had been nervewrackingly rushed, all that dressing up had had a purpose. Here, the Vidries kept on changing their costumes for no apparent reason at all.

Christmas, for the señoritas and señoras of the large family, involved a perfect frenzy of clothes-changing, or so Harriet was discovering. It had begun at dawn, with all the Vidrie women vying for places at the looking glasses, competing to see who could wind her raven hair the highest. Harriet had felt shabby as she joined the process to the church, and while that wasn't unusual, she had thought today that the women and their guests were adorned as if they were for sale.

Not only were their gowns lovely, though even less modest than the English styles that Harriet wore, but they were decorated to the hilt with flowers, feathers, combs, and silk ribbons. The women's bare arms were heavily adorned with bracelets, ungloved fingers equally weighted with rings. Parasols, mantillas, and lace handkerchiefs adorned their vivacious persons, and they had long trains to their skirts that were allowed to trail on the cobbles. And the men on whose arms they paraded were equally splendidly got up, looking as splendid as peacocks.

There had been another long-drawn-out change of dress for breakfast, which was served at noon. It was a vast meal of stews, soups, rice done many different ways, eggs fried in garlic, chocolate cups almost too sweet to drink. Ah Wong was one of the servants who waited at the table. He watched Harriet constantly, anxiously, but Harriet was so used to it that she paid little attention. She often felt, uncannily, as if she had disappointed him in some way, but did not have a notion how, and over the weeks it had come to have little significance.

What the women had to say had little significance, too. She listened absently to the Spanish clamor, understanding every word — though none of it was addressed to her — because she had become fluent in the language. The Vidrie women found her amusing, she thought. In the beginning they had paid her great attention, had vied for her company, had exclaimed about her golden hair, her slenderness, her manners, her clipped, clear diction, but now they were more apt to ignore her. Harriet knew that they gossiped about the fact that she was still here after all this time, while her husband was not. Did they ever wonder why Don Manuel hadn't politely sent her away — why he so gallantly tolerated her continued presence in their house? Harriet certainly did, but there was no sign that the puzzling question had ever crossed their butterfly minds.

Then, siesta, just as on any other day. The Vidrie women treated the rest as another social occasion, gathering in one of the bedrooms. Throughout the quiet hours the echoes of their laughter filled the stone walls of the great old hacienda. Harriet had sat alone in her bedroom, as usual, with Captain Schouten's journal on her knee.

Captain Schouten was the original owner of the brig *Gosling,* and not only had he been a pirate and a treasure-hunter, but he had also owned a wonderful journal filled with jottings and maps and stories of the conquistors. The

169

journal, inherited by Jake Dexter when he had acquired the brig, was a treasure in itself, and one of Captain Dexter's most cherished belongings. Yet she had found the scrapbook in the bottom of one of her baskets, when she unpacked them after arriving here.

Jake Dexter must have slipped it into the basket she had left behind when Bodfish took her to Sutter's Fort, she thought. She had no idea why, but it had been a great comfort to her. Now she knew the many tales of gold off by heart, and could have drawn the treasure maps from memory, but still she touched the book lovingly, while her thoughts revolved. She thought about many things, including Judas Island, which was one of the maps, and was the rumored repository of pirate booty — though there had been nothing to find but the evidence of old, cruel deaths when the *Gosling* crew had looked there for the fabled gold. The treasure hunt there was not a pleasant memory, but Harriet relived it often. She had too much time to think, she reflected.

Now, siesta was over. She had looked up from her seat in Don Manuel's garden, to see the Don walking over to her. It was her favorite place — she went to sit there every afternoon, as soon as it was decent to leave her bedroom. Because the garden was sheltered on three sides by tall stone walls, the flowers bloomed even at this time of the year, and from the bench where she sat the flower beds had been so designed that they drew the eye to the fourth side of the garden, which provided a fine view of the magnificent Vidrie mansion.

Built of quarried stone, slate-roofed, and with ornamental iron grilles over all the windows, the building was an image from ancient Spain, or so she often thought. It was huge, housing all the family, but she had explored just about all of it over the idle weekday afternoons, when she was not in her room or in the garden. She had even ventured into the cellars, where wine casks lay in fat rows, and the press house, with its cool stone walls and adzed timber ceiling, where the air stung with the smell of crushed grape-skins.

In the mornings, except for holidays and Sundays, she went out riding, escorted by Ah Wong. Her horse was the same horse she had ridden on the way to this place from Sefton's ranch, a magnificent gelding that would have been too spirited for her to manage if she had not been an expert horsewoman.

It was not one of Sefton's horses, she thought—though, she was not sure about that, as it did have a peculiarity, in that it would never gallop straight forward, but would prance in a sort of sidelong canter, its neck curved, and its beautiful head cocked wickedly. This meant that the gelding was spectacular to watch, but needed very skilful management from its rider, so she sometimes wondered if Sefton had deliberately chosen this steed for her, just in the chance that it would throw her off, and that she would break her neck in the fall.

The rest of the time she thought it was Don Manuel's own personal horse, not just because of the horse's bravura, or because it was caparisoned in the Californian style, but also because the saddle was not a side-saddle. Though it was decorated like a lady's saddle, with a seat that was upholstered in azure velvet, enriched with handsome embroidery, much of it silver, and with a head-stall that was ornamented with chased silver, too, it was definitely designed for someone who rode astride. She didn't mind, because riding astride for any length of time was easier than riding side-saddle, and this saddle was also so very comfortable, with a pummel that was as high as her waist, and stirrups that were cut out of solid wood, so were unusually wide and strong. But she did wonder what had inspired Don Manuel to be so remarkably generous, and whether the openhandedness might not have been entirely voluntary.

That the horse was strong and the trappings so sturdy

and comfortable meant that she and Ah Wong could gallop for hours at a time, exploring the vastnesses of the Vidrie lands. They always began by mounting the slopes where the lines of grapevines marched, brown at this time of the year, the vines twisting shapes on the wires, and then galloped beyond the vineyard toward the grassy hills that rolled into the distance. When Harriet paused, it was to gaze at the lofty fastnesses of California, the mountains that had mothered the golden lode.

Pine forests, gray granite cliffs, snow-topped peaks, birds rising, cawing, calling, rising in flocks from the distant silver thread that was the Feather River, where Don Roberto's fort crouched. On this side of the river, the Vidrie lands met the fringes of Sefton property, divided from them by a stony creek. Though Sefton's hacienda was another four hours' ride from there, the boundary was where Harriet always turned back, the nape of her neck stiff as she wheeled the horse around.

Thinking now about those lush, rolling hills and the multitudes of cattle that grazed under the great stands of red-leafed trees, she said to Don Manuel, "Do you never fear that the gold-seekers will invade your property?"

Though she could have phrased it in Spanish, out of politeness she deferred to his fluency in English, and spoke in that language. Understanding perfectly, he smiled with confidence, and said, "Don Roberto will make sure that they don't."

"He can do that? One alcalde, by himself?"

"The only access from Pueblo San Marco is past his fort, which guards the narrowest part of the river, and I hear he has some fierce deputies. If a man crosses the river at Pueblo San Marco," Don Manuel added, "he could ride here, as you did, but he would have to pass through the great property owned by your husband, Colonel Sefton."

"I see," she said, nodding, and wondered if that was the

reason that Sefton had such a hold over this Californian Don.

"It is good, no?" he said, and laughed. "It would be sad indeed if Cache Creek became another Eldorado. My poor cattle, they would be rustled, shot by the miners for food, and my country would become a tent city, like Captain Sutter's land. You know what happened to Captain Sutter's cattle?"

"No, I do not," she said.

"Not long after gold was first discovered, at his mill on the American River, a man rode in from Monterey, and staked a claim on the slope of a hill, just a few yards from the bottom — an excellent and most promising spot for prospecting. He erected a large tent there, and stocked it with provisions, which he sold at a very good rate to the miners as they came in. So reasonable were his prices, you have no idea, señora! Flour and biscuit he sold for just two dollars a pound, coffee and sugar, six dollars a pound, and beef at just one dollar and one half!"

"Goodness me," said Harriet. "It doesn't sound like the way to make a fortune."

"Yet, he was making a fortune indeed, Mrs. Sefton. He was rich with gold. It was a mystery."

"A mystery indeed," she said, but was back to thinking about another mystery — the ancient, chilling mystery of Judas Island. They were passing through the pueblo that belonged to the Vidrie property, a cluster of whitewashed cottages where the servants and vaqueros lived. As on Judas Island, the adobe houses were built around a little plaza with a turreted well in the middle — but on Judas Island the pueblo, like the island itself, was deserted.

On Judas Island, the church was broken, the flagstones cracked, and the cottages ruined, all wrecked when the people had been killed. They had been slaughtered when pirates had come hunting for the treasure of Panama — perhaps in a murderous rage, because no one had given up

173

the secret of the treasure, even when tortured.

Here, by contrast, the pueblo was alive with men, women, and many children, and the chapel was religiously maintained. There was no overriding sense of past terror. Only the architecture was the same.

Realizing that Don Manuel was waiting for her response, she said, "So how was that man reaping riches?"

"Captain Sutter found out when he came to the tent to buy coffee, having heard about the bargain price. As he stooped to get through the entrance of the tent, he blundered into an immense piece of raw beef, suspended from the ridge-pole. His own beef, from his own cattle! And at the rear of the tent were seven or eight Indians, hard at work digging gold, supervised by an American who was also a beef slaughter man. At night, Captain Sutter found, the American rode out in quest of cows and oxen, which he killed, cut up, and then carried back to the tent for sale."

"Merciful heavens," said Harriet, suitably horrified. "So what happened next?"

"He was run out of the territory," Don Manuel said severely.

"And I should think so, too," said Harriet. She wondered why the two entrepreneurs hadn't been slung by the neck from the nearest branch, but didn't like to ask.

The village was behind them, and they were nearing a sort of pit, which was surrounded by benches set out on slopes, so that it was like a little amphitheater. Harriet and Don Manuel were the last to arrive, she saw, because a chattering horde of Vidries and guests packed the benches, and stood at the stout, solid fence that surrounded the pit.

The Vidrie women had changed yet again, and were wearing shorter gowns, and shorter shawls, in the same rainbow colors, but more suitable for the dusty terrain. The men, by contrast, were dressed like bullfighters, in gold and braid and embroidered velveteen. The feeling of festival was palpable, the air full of excited talk.

174

Don Manuel urged Harriet right up to the fence, and she held onto the top of this, looking down into the pit. The posts on the inside of the fence were clawed and gnawed about, evidently by some large angry animal, some time in the past. Now, except for the body of a dead dog, the arena looked empty.

Then the bear moved, and she saw it. The great bear had dug itself a shallow hole in the sand, and had been lying inside it like a shaggy rug. Harriet saw the beast move, and her hands clenched on the top of the fence as she stared, horrified. The bear was huge. When it rose onto its hind legs it towered high. If it hadn't been for the depth of the pit, it would have topped the fence.

A rank smell rose with it, a charnel smell of rotting meat, and when its mouth gaped wide, she saw the yellow snaggled teeth and the bloody gums. Ropes of saliva dangled from its jaws. Then the bear lumbered over to the body of the dog.

To Harriet's horror, the dog came to life, and attempted to move its broken body away. The bear swiped, the dog flopped back, and screamed like a human. The bear swatted again, and the body flew over the fence into the crowd. Women scattered and screamed, and men jerked back and laughed.

Then, with a lurch in her chest, Harriet saw Sefton.

Like a warning from the past, here was an echo in her head — *He's behind you!* Frank Sefton was deep in the crowd, with men and women clustered about him laughing, as if he were the star of some drama.

Harriet sensed Don Manuel move, and when she looked he was leaving her, walking up the slope of the amphitheater to join Sefton. Had Don Manuel known he was coming—had he been unusually gallant, this day, because he had known that Sefton would be at the arena? It was impossible to tell, just as it was impossible to guess how long Sefton had been there.

Harriet turned her head away, but glimpsed him look in her direction at the same instant that Don Manuel arrived at his side. Every fiber of her body tensed, dreading the encounter. She thought he was moving through the crowd towards her, but then she saw him stop, distracted like them all as some large animal bellowed.

It was not the bear that had made the noise. The bear was back in its hollow. Men on the far side of the pit were harrying an animal through a gate in the fence, and it was this beast that bellowed. It was a bull, black, its powerful body shiny.

The vaqueros who harried it along were shouting and waving their hats, and cracking their whips. The bull charged, they eluded him, and then the bull charged again, at the gap in the fence. He charged right through, and down the ramp into the pit, and the gate was hastily shut.

At the sound of the gate being barred, he stopped short, and scraped the ground with his front hooves. His viciously horned head was low, swinging from side to side. His red eyes turned about in their sockets and women screamed in delicious fear. He was a bull in his prime, huge genitals dangling, horns lowered, perfectly wild. Then he caught sight of the bear.

The bull charged. There was no hesitation. The bear rose to meet him like doom, huge, upright, utterly fearsome—and the bull rammed his head right into the shaggy chest.

The sound was loud and sudden, like a butcher breaking into a carcass. One horn was buried deep. The bull's head twisted, but the horn was stuck.

The bear grunted, no more than that. It bent slowly over the bull's head and gripped the massive shoulders in two powerful forelegs, the long claws set deep in the thick black hide. Then slowly, inch by inch, the bear began to scrabble backwards, sinking slowly into the hollow, taking the bull with it. The bull's sharp hooves cut grooves in the sand as it resisted, but the bear's great weight prevailed.

176

Some of the men laughed with excitement, while others were shouting, and Harriet recognized Sefton's voice. Some were urging the bull to do its utmost, while others were shouting encouragement to the bear, and Harriet realized that bets had been placed on the outcome. She heard Frank Sefton cry, "Toss him, brave bull, lift high!"

The bull's neck muscles bulged and ran with sweat. Hooves scrabbled more and more frantically and clots of sand flew, but the bull was still held fast by its own horn, the horn that was buried deep in the bear's chest. Then, with a sick snap, the horn broke off at the root.

The bull lurched back, still on all four legs. The bear slumped, gouts of blood pumping out of the great hole in its chest where the impaled horn had torn, and Harriet heard the strange groan as it died. The bull was bleeding too, spraying blood from its nose every time it snorted furious triumph. One eye hung by a string. Harriet looked down, fighting faintness.

Frank Sefton cried, "The brave bull, he won! My brave bull, he prevailed!" The Vidries and their brilliantly clothed guests milled about happily, hailing each other, and shouting, "Merry Christmas!" Harriet seized her chance to get away, fleeing back through the village to the garden.

There she sank down on her favorite bench, the one facing the view of the mansion. It was shaded by a weeping elm, with a bed of rose bushes on either side. The roses were not in flower, but she sat there until it was too cold to sit there any longer.

Harriet had her head down as she went down the familiar corridor to her bedroom. She could hear the Vidrie women at their mirrors again, giggling as they prepared for the late evening dinner. Then, when she opened her door, her throat clenched. Frank Sefton was lounging on her bed.

He's behind you! When she turned to face him he looked at her with his cold eyes and his rosebud smile. He had been

177

there a while, she thought. She could smell the wine he had drunk, and the tobacco he had smoked while he lurked in wait.

He said, "Avoiding me, my dear?"

Harriet carefully closed the door, then stood with her back against it. She said, "My hostesses believe the reverse — that you are avoiding me."

"Nonsense! They know I adore you."

"And it's embarrassing," she said, as if he hadn't spoken.

"What? You missed me? What devotion, Harriet."

"As you know perfectly well, devotion has nothing to do with it. But the Vidrie women will be glad when I go."

"I trust you have done nothing to shame me?"

"I have done nothing at all, save play the grateful guest. I have played it for almost four months," she said. "Which is a season that is at least ten weeks too long, and is a role that I do not enjoy at all. I wonder if I am deserted again, and I know the Vidries wonder if I am an abandoned wife, too."

"Desert you?" he said, and she could see the secret laughter in his eyes. He sat up higher against her pillows, and said, "Tut, Harriet. I know the Vidries do not think that — how could they? I've told them often enough that you are my bright star, the adornment of my life. I only permitted them to keep you here because they pressed me so insistently. They are determined that you should stay here. Don Manuel declares that his wife, mother, sisters and nieces are fascinated — enthralled. How could they possibly believe that I have shifted my marital responsibilities onto their shoulders? For have I not come to wish my wife a merry Christmas, and have I not come bearing gifts?"

"I don't want them, whatever they are."

"But you must accept them — for they are beautiful gowns made of Chinese silk, gorgeous shawls created in the East. I insist that you wear them. As the devoted husband that I am, I must pay due homage to your beauty, and you, as a dutiful wife, must be an adornment to my wealth and reputation, too. The business acumen and commercial success of a man is best displayed in the person of his wife."

He swung his feet down as he spoke, so that he sat on the edge of the bed. His manner was expansive, and his smooth palms gestured in time to his words. Harriet looked with hatred at the round, unblinking blue eyes, and snapped, "I think the Vidries are already sufficiently impressed by your commercial success. Tell me, does Don Manuel owe you money?"

"You are insolent, my dear—for a wife should not ask about her husband's business affairs," he scolded—but he smiled at the same time, a little, secret, complacent smile.

Then he straightened and walked towards her, while Harriet stood frozen, her back against the cool wood of the door. His hand came out and touched her face, but not caressingly. Then he leaned forward so his breath engulfed her, and whispered, "Do I take it, my dear, that you are desperate to come back to my ranch?"

He paused, staring down at her taut expression, and then he nipped her cheek with his fingertips, and he hissed, "Or perhaps you plan to cross the river and get on board the brig? H'm? Perhaps you think to fly to Captain Dexter, and beg for his protection?"

She said, "How dare you suggest that!" But, to her fury, her voice trembled, because that was exactly what she had turned over in her mind during the long, solitary, lonely hours.

His expression became scornful. "You're trying to pretend it has never occurred to you? Are you really trying to pretend that you were nothing more than a passenger on the *Gosling* ... nothing more than that, when Captain Dexter's every manner speaks of jealous passion?"

She couldn't help it. The words spilled out before she could stop them. "Have you seen him?"

"Not since Sutter's, my dear—though I was told he was

179

in Pueblo San Marco for a few days. But it is useless to dream," he purred. "And I am sure you dream, for your brother revealed much more than he thought he did."

"What? You've seen Royal?"

"Not since early September — for in the second week of that month he and Captain Dexter headed into the hills. To the mines. To Bedstead Gully, or so Don Roberto told me," he said. And smiled.

So Jake was in the hills, and Royal with him. Harriet had never heard of Bedstead Gully. Then she saw Sefton's eyes become glassy with thought. "I remember … I remember that you had rather splendid limbs, and that you were unexpectedly agile, for a woman," he murmured absently, then smiled again as he saw her involuntary shudder. "Did you twine those long, slender legs about Captain Dexter's waist as you wriggled and thrust against him?"

"How dare you!"

"It's an enticing picture — so did you, did you?"

"You bastard!" Humiliated tears were leaking out from between her lashes. She said in a trembling voice, "I want a divorce."

He smiled. "But as you know — because I know you have asked — it's not possible for you to divorce me, my dear, because I have done nothing to bring a scandal on your name."

"You married an actress, didn't you?" she spat. "And that's a mystery, Frank — why you lowered yourself to do it. I'm sure you could have tricked any of the colonists as easily as you tricked me."

"Ah, but the colonists of New Zealand are a shrewd and suspicious bunch," he said with regret in his tone. "And, as you undoubtedly noticed, they gossip. But the Grays — the Grays were not just fresh from England, but also attractively naïve."

Harriet stood very still, concentrating on breathing slowly, imagining herself into one of the strong female roles she had played in the past. Then she said steadily, "I'm sure you have a great deal more to say about me and my family, Frank, and that none of it is pleasant. But it would be better discussed in your own house, not here."

"You insist on wanting to spurn Don Manuel's hospitality, when you are such a cosseted guest, where you have your own room, feminine company, your own servant—"

"Ah Wong is as unhappy here as I am. He is treated as a curiosity by the other servants, who have never seen a Chinese person before. I think they are cruel to him."

"Poor Ah Wong," he murmured. "And my poor, poor wife." There was mocking laughter in his voice. "Perhaps I will think about it—later. I have important business on my mind."

Harriet was silent. Then, to her surprise, Sefton stepped back, and said in a matter-of-fact, practical tone, "I've decided turn my bank into a public company."

"What?"

"I've decided to bring in other investors, by selling them shares."

Harriet frowned, trying to work out why he was bothering to tell her this. His eyes had gone glassy again, as if his mind was elsewhere, busy with faraway schemes.

She said, "But what has this got to do with me?"

Again, that secretive little smile. "Doesn't every wise woman want her husband to be rich?"

"This wise woman simply wants to leave this place," she snapped.

"I told you I'll think about it," he said. "I'll let you know my decision later."

And, with that, he left. Harriet watched him open the door and go out. After the door shut she listened to his footsteps retreat along the passage.

Later was a long time coming. It was March before she saw him again.

SEVENTEEN

IT was March in the lofty fastnesses of California. The trail out of Bedstead Gully was still blocked by the boulder and the shingle that had fallen with it, but, as winter turned to spring, it was also evident that the upper ravines were becoming accessible.

The *Gosling* miners thought deeply about it, pored over mildewed maps, and consulted at length. Jake was still very reluctant to split up the party, but the vote was against him. Finally he agreed that they should send out small groups of three men to prospect in the hills, three men being the minimum number needed to dig the fifty holes needed to prospect a site properly, and work a gold washing cradle.

However, he also made the proviso that they would never stray further than a two-day march from Bedstead Gully, and that the cabin should always be occupied by at least three men. The trails from Don Roberto's fort would be open again soon, and there would be men determined enough to find a way around or over the great boulder that blocked the defile. A deserted cabin would look attractive, and even with all their duds inside to mark the hut as the *Gosling* Company's property, cabins were as easily jumped as claims.

Each party took a tent, pans, shovels, provisions and a

cradle and tramped onward and upward until they found a likely spot—in a ravine, or a gully, or the bed of a stream, any little crannies where the gold could be expected to be hiding away like a rabbit in a burrow. Their instructions were that they should look for blue clay, which was reputed to be the richest, but to settle for red clay, if necessary. The idea was to camp there for a week, digging exploratory pockets, and then stake a claim once significant traces of gold were found.

The trouble was, as Royal complained, that all the places looked promising, and none lived up to their looks. It was like fishing, he reckoned. The backwater where you decided to cast your line might look ideal, the kind of spot where trout or salmon lined up to take your bait, but whether fish were caught depended entirely on the luck of the angler. And gold hunting was the same, in that one place looked as good as another. In these lofty fastnesses of Calafia's realm, all the gullys and valleys looked the same in their rough beauty, all equally disappointing, and the one where they were currently camped was a twin to all the rest.

Royal's party included Spanish Pablo, and the Portuguese seaman from the Azores, Joseph Fayal, and the three of them had chosen the site where they were working not because it looked promising or the clay was blue, but simply because they had stumbled on it at the time of day when men begin to think about pitching a tent and getting supper ready. This particular ravine was the usual long arroyo with a stream bubbling through rocks and sand at the bottom, and steep banks composed of red clay, though with blue streaks through it. There were the usual thick pines and gray rocks, and the usual sounds of bears and Californian dogs at night. It was rockier than most, and steeper than most, so it was a lot harder than usual to find a level place to rest easy for sleep, but they decided to stop on because this *arroyo* with no name was so close to the far-famed Dry Bones Gulch.

So much gold had been found at Dry Bones Gulch that a town had sprung up in that valley. It was a wild town, too, by all accounts, so Royal's party had avoided going through it. Though it was only a two-mile trek away it could have been a hundred, for all the noise they heard. Pines and oaks and thickets muffled any sounds on the wind blowing from that direction, and the ravine was noisy already, what with the cheerful babbling brook, the rustle of leaves and the growling of distant, prowling animals. And the sound of Royal's constant grumbling.

"Luck or no luck," he complained, "it's a rotten way to live. When we first heard those tales from Honest Mill Mason, back on the Tombez River, it sounded as if all we had to do was come to California, squat down anywhere, and pick away for a few days. Well, sirs, it isn't like that at all. I've played pantomime in London, and Hamlet in the provinces, and I've chased alpaca all over the bloody Andes, but I never knew what hard work was like until I came along on this golden gosling chase. For what does your typical miner do? He chooses his spot, and faithfully prospects, then abandons it for another and yet another, until he comes to the logical conclusion, that the whole damn business is a lottery. Come on, Joseph, this valley is as empty of gold as all the others. Why else would no other men be here? Come on, *vaya*, let's go back to Bedstead Gully, where we can get a decent night's sleep."

Pablo and Joseph didn't bother to answer, which was no more than Royal expected. He complained so much that the other *Gosling*s had given up listening to him long ago. Pablo was digging, while Joseph rocked the dirt-washing cradle, and both men were covered with a coat of dirt and dust, which stuck to their sweat, because though the air was cool even in the middle of the day, their jobs were the kind that brought out a heavy perspiration.

Joseph Fayal was at one end of the cradle, which he rocked with a handle, while Pablo dropped shovels full of dirt onto a perforated copper plate, which was hinged to the top, and had a four inch-high rim. Royal's job was to bring up water from the stream, and pour it on top of the dirt that Pablo had piled on the plate, so that the gold-bearing clay was washed through into the bottom of the cradle, and the stones stayed on the top of the sieve, which was hinged back after the stones had been inspected, to get rid of the useless layer. Then, as Joseph rocked, the muddy water sloshed back and forth, and any flakes and nuggets gold that floated in it were caught by wooden rods that were nailed across the bottom of the cradle. Well, that was the theory.

Royal straightened his stiff back after pouring the latest bucket of water into the cradle, and pleaded, "Come on, shipmates, let's pack up and go. Let's get back to Bedstead Gully, and see how things are a-doing."

This time, Joseph Fayal did hear him. But he merely said, "One more bucket."

"No," said Royal. "I mutiny."

His pants were wet to the middle of each thigh and his boots sloshed with icy water. His back and those thighs ached sorely, too, with the constant bending down, heaving up the icy weight of the filled bucket, trudging out of the stream and up the hill to the digging, pouring the bucket into the cradle, and then doing the whole damn thing all over again. He wanted the comfort of the cabin at Bedstead Gully; he wanted to warm his bones by a real fire. The sun was still high and the air had been growing warmer day by day, but there were dark gray clouds gathering, with a strong hint of spring showers. Bedstead Gully was twenty hours away, and Royal yearned to get there.

"One last pail," said Pablo, speaking at last. "For this pan."

The pan was where he put the dirt that had been rocked through the cradle, and he wanted to slosh it with water. Royal said with perfect confidence, with weary experience, "There isn't any gold in that there pan, my good señor."

185

"But why not try?" said Joseph, at the cradle. "Why not make sure?"

"No, no, no," said Royal, but despite his stubbornness he sighed and gave in, setting off with the bucket towards the stream.

And with a crack of thunder that set the ground to shaking under Royal's feet, the heavens opened in a deluge of rain that was no mere spring shower. All three men sprinted for the tent and vied to dive in first. It was a tight fit, but they were used to that. "When the rain is ended..." said Joseph Fayal.

"Yes," said Royal, and sighed again. They lay still and waited, stowed in the little tent as closely as three unfledged sparrows.

All three were heavily bearded. Pablo's long black hair reached to his shoulders, and Joseph's glossy black curls and Royal's straw-like locks were in no better shape. "And so we are reduced," said Royal, and paused in his theatrical speech. The rain had stopped with the abruptness of a tap turned off, a rainbow had spun into the sky, and his two comrades had left him.

Royal felt reluctant to quit the scanty shelter. "One more bucket," he muttered like a curse, and then he heard a wild shriek, a yell of EUREKA-A-A! that made the mountains ring.

The bucket of water was no longer necessary. The rain had done the washing for them. The pan of dirt lay where Pablo had dropped it, and the rain had exposed the scatter of pea-sized nuggets in the bottom.

EIGHTEEN

IT was March in Bedstead Gully.

Jake Dexter was boiling up medicine for his patients. Abner and Jonathan were stretched out on two of the wooden shelves built along the sides of the hut that served the men as berths, and while Jonathan was quiet, Abner muttered and tossed. And they were sick with not just one complaint, but two—both of which could be fatal.

When Abner and Jonathan had come in, with Davy supporting both of them, all three men had had bleeding gums, and when Jake had stripped the two Americans to get them into their bedrolls, he had found that their legs were swollen and discolored, with livid spots that were running together. The trio had lived entirely on ship's bread and salt provisions, reluctant to spare the time from prospecting in order to hunt for herbs or fresh fish or game. This was common enough, as Jake knew, because the dream that the next hole dug would be the golden one came to prey on a man's mind. It meant that not only did he skimp his meals, but he didn't get enough rest, as every hour asleep felt like a waste of time, though by logic it was too dark to dig. But the inevitable result was the disease that men in these parts called "mountain scurvy," and all three were suffering from this.

Even worse than the mountain scurvy, though, was the dreaded Californian ague, and Jonathan and Abner had got this badly, because the scurvy had weakened their systems. Some of the miners called the ague "mountain fever," while others reckoned it was an intermittent fever brought the California by the men from the Isthmus of Panama. Whatever it was called, over the last season it had laid hundreds of miners low, and Jake had heard that dozens had died.

The advice in his medical book was to take twenty-five grains of blue pill, twenty-five grains of quinine, and twelve grains of oil of black pepper, and make it up into twelve pills. One pill was to be taken every hour for six hours on the first day, every hour for four hours on the second day, and the remaining two an hour apart on the morning of the third day. And this was what he had to do for each patient.

The problem was that he had run out of quinine. All he'd had in his medical chest was what had been there when the brig arrived up the Sacramento, because when he had tried to top up his medical supplies in Pueblo San Marco, quinine had been an unaffordable one hundred dollars a twenty-five-grain dose.

For the scurvy, he was trying out an old folk remedy, which was spruce tips tea that he brewed from the tiniest sprouts of the many pines that grew along the sides of the gully. And to his great relief it worked. The men's gums had stopped bleeding, and their legs were returning to their normal state. The Californian ague was a different matter, however—and the fever had struck Abner and Jonathan very hard indeed.

Now, staring down at Abner's contorted face as he spooned the cooled tea between his cracked lips, Jake looked at the fine scar where he had sewn Abner's cheek back into place after he had ripped it almost entirely off during a fall from aloft, and wondered if Abner would survive to show it off to his grandchildren. At the moment, it looked a very dim prospect.

Then Jake heard his name being called. He put down the spoon and mug, and went to the open door. Royal Gray was coming down the narrow trail into Bedstead Gully, looking even worse than when he had left the cabin with Pablo and Joseph ten days before, being grimy, sweaty, and foully bearded. His clothes were torn, and he had evidently slept by the trail in the night. Worst of all, Pablo and Joseph Fayal were not with him. He was alone.

Oh God, Jake thought, something else had gone wrong. But when he shouted, "Where are Pablo and Joseph?" Royal didn't bother to answer.

Instead, to Jake's disbelief, he saw Royal's face crack into an enormous grin. "We've done it, Jake," he cried. "We've done it!"

"Done what?"

"We have made our find! And by God, Captain Dexter, you can spell that find with a capital F, the biggest capital F in the book. I've come to report a Find!"

"Find?"

"In a word," said Royal seraphically. "Eureka."

Eureka. The word proved to be better medicine than any dose of quinine or mug of spruce tips tea. Jonathan and Abner both sat up to take in the miraculous news, looking more alive they had ever looked since they had limped in from their doomed prospecting expedition. And Tib and Dan, who had been digging holes up the head of Bedstead Gully, proving beyond the last trace of doubt that the gully was all worked out, were delirious with delight.

"We dug all about the first find," Royal told them. "We dug east and west of it, and verily north and south, and running west we found the vein. It's four feet down, two feet wide, and a full fifty feet is accessible."

Tib demanded, "You're sure of that? You prospected all along that fifty foot vein?"

189

"We did indeed, we did, and the further we went toward the stream, the richer it became."

"And nobody else knows about it?"

"We were the only ones there. No one appears to have stumbled on that particular arroyo. Dry Bones Gulch is just two miles away, but it could be further than Peking, China."

"And you claimed it proper?"

"Of course," said Royal. "We've staked out a strip twelve feet wide, all the way down to the stream, so we've covered all those fifty feet of gold-bearing clay. And we've put a sign on it, just as the regulations say. And right now, as we talk, Pablo and Joseph are working it—so there are men on it, as well as tools. I tell you, Tib, we've covered every single eventuality, and every single little rule. The valley didn't even have a name, so we gave it one. We named it Gosling Gully."

Dan sighed and smiled at Tib, and Tib grinned and nodded at Dan. It was as if the name made the find more real. Jonathan and Abner sat straighter, grinning like fools, and though Davy was slower to understand, once he took in the great news he performed one of his rare clapping dances, to the words of *Gosling Gully*. An hour ago, Davy had looked as if he was going to succumb to the fever like Abner and Jonathan, but now he looked as well as he had ever been.

And though the men didn't get much rest that night, being too excited and talking too much, the patients looked even better in the morning. Jake studied them with a frown, however, because he wanted to take as big a party as possible to Gosling Gully.

Though he hadn't said so, the proximity of Dry Bones Gulch worried him, because two miles was less than an hour on a horse. That was on level ground, of course, and could be more, maybe a lot longer, if the terrain was difficult, but he knew how fast the gold yarns ran, and how often claims got jumped. So he wanted to take Tib and Dan—and had a good idea that they would mutiny if they were not in the party, anyway — but that meant leaving Davy to look after the two invalids.

Jonathan and Abner assured him they would be fine, as long as they had Davy to do the heavy work, such as gathering wood for the fire, and buckets of water from the stream. By the time Captain Dexter came back, they reckoned, they would be as hearty and hale as ever. And anyway, they said, they wouldn't be alone for long. Any day soon, the trail to Don Roberto's fort would be open again, and miners would come flooding back. Somehow, they would get around that great boulder in the defile, and the settlement in Bedstead Gully would spring up again.

That was a good point, Jake thought. He made sure that Davy had memorized the recipe for spruce tips tea, and knew when to administer the Peruvian bark, and how much was in a dose, and then made Jonathan and Abner promise to never leave the cabin empty, even after they recovered. After that, reassured by their bright, optimistic looks, he strode off with Dan, Tib, and Royal. They took the llamas with them, along with two more cradles, and plenty of empty parfleshes to hold all that gold.

However, the trek that began so sunnily turned out to not be easy. Before the day was six hours old, the clouds closed in and it began to rain, and then it became so dark that they were forced to camp by the wayside earlier than they had intended. They didn't catch much sleep, and were up before dawn next day, when the prospects seemed to improve. The sun came up, and the mists soon rose, and it became easier to see where they were going. The bells that the llamas wore rattled gently with their trotting.

The ground was becoming more and more broken, heavily timbered with oak and pine, while beyond the deep forests the snowladen caps of mountains rose against the sky. Near noon, they arrived at a small river, its water crystalline and icy cold with snow melt. Royal said that he and Joseph and Pablo had left the trail here, as the river led to Dry Bones Gulch and they had wanted to avoid company. Going through the settlement was quicker, however, so that was the way they went.

It was just past noon when they got there. It was a sizeable settlement, with ten or twelve clapboard buildings and wooden sidewalks, built less than a half mile from the river. At least six of the buildings were in the business of selling liquor.

Jake stared about, frowning, uneasiness shifting in his mind. The town was quiet … way too quiet.

He said sharply to Royal, "Gosling Gully is just two miles away?"

"That's what the map told us."

"And you didn't stop here on your way to Bedstead Gully — for a celebratory drink, perhaps?"

"I told you — I've never been here before."

"So where the hell is everyone?"

Royal shrugged, looking around. "Out prospecting?"

Jake said grimly, "At Gosling Gully?"

"Oh, God," said Royal. While Joseph Fayal was quiet and reliable, Pablo liked his liquor, and so it was very possible that Pablo had headed into town for a drink. And, when Pablo had been drinking, he was apt to become loud and boastful.

Trying to brace himself, as well as the others, he said, "It shouldn't make any difference, even if they have heard about our find at Gosling Gully. We did everything right. We named the claim, and we staked it, with a stake, a notice, two men and our tools. Even now, Pablo and Joseph are working it. What more could we do than that?"

Nothing, thought Jake, but the misgivings didn't fade. As he followed Royal out of town, he felt tensed, ready for something dreadful.

An hour later they were walking in single file along a ridge, and then Royal led a zigzag path down the other side of the hill. There were spruce trees growing in diagonal rows along the slope, and pines on the other side descended majestically to the stream … and the mining camp.

There were more than two dozen tents set up along the creek, and more than fifty miners were hacking at the clay. Every few yards men were washing out the dirt in pans, and picking out flakes of gold with muddy fingertips, while other men were passing spades full of dirt through sieves, some of them as simple as Indian baskets. Still more were rocking cradles, many of them made out of liquor boxes.

The fact that Jake had dreaded … expected … this, made it harder, not easier. A nudge of guilt made him feel even worse, because he realized now that he should have made a rule that if a rich claim was found it should be kept as secret as possible, by going away from it only under cover of darkness.

Hoping against hope that Royal had steered them wrong, he said, "You're certain this is the right gully?"

"Of course it damn well is!" Royal's voice was shaking, just as it had up the Tombez River when he had found that the Indians had stolen the herd of alpacas that were going to make a fortune for the Company.

Back then, his face had gone red with consternation and fury, and it was equally puce with anger and outrage, now. "I tell you," he shouted, "we had this whole goddamned valley to ourselves! We didn't see another soul the whole damn time we were prospecting!"

"Then where is our claim?"

"There's our tent—over there."

Royal's pointing finger shook when he thrust out his arm. Jake recognized the tent then, because it was gray, made of old sail canvas, rather than the usual blue calico. The tent looked mildewed and neglected. It sagged on its posts, and was pegged tightly, close to the ground.

"Then where is our *claim?*"

Royal said wildly, "That one!" He pointed surely, but the direction didn't make sense, because while there were men digging there, Pablo and Joseph Fayal were not with them. The men had long black Spanish hair, but they were not Jake's men.

Then Jake recognized them. He said, "Oh God, oh God," and began to run, slipping and sliding as he half-fell down the slope. He heard Tib and Dan shout out and then run after him, but didn't wait for them to catch up. Then he slid to a shuddering stop by the digging, and the three Murietas straightened and stared at him.

The Murietas. The filthy bastards who had created such trouble on the brig. The same men that the alcalde, Don Roberto, had insanely recruited as his deputies. The last Jake had seen of them was when the bear had struck, and the boulder had blocked the trail to Pueblo San Marcos.

One was Joaquín Murieta, and the others were two of his brothers. They smirked, and Joaquín said, "Capitán."

Jake shouted, "Where are Pablo and Joseph?" There was a sickness deep inside him. Pablo might be unreliable, but Joseph Fayal would guard this claim with his life. Jake could hear muttering and rattling behind him as miners set down tools and came over to watch the confrontation, and he slowly, warily, turned his head.

The miners stopped in a huddle, and stared back at him. They looked much the same as any other miners, attired alike in torn trousers and stained shirts, their feet in double-cleated boots. They were all heavily armed, but that was not unusual, either.

What was strange was the sense of bloodshed and crisis. The faces of the young ones were both excited and scared, and the eyes of the oldsters flickered warily around—at the trees and hills and creek, as well as the other men.

Something had happened. Then Jake heard Royal arrive.

He snapped at the Murietas, "You've jumped our claim, you goddamned thieves."

"We … have?" Joaquín queried. Jake had almost forgotten the South American's odd hesitant English, and how threatening it sounded. Joaquín's eyebrows were lifted derisively high, and his thick moustaches drooped on either side of his twisted mouth.

"There was no stake, no. No stake. No notice. No nothing," he smirked.

"By God, there was a stake, and there was a goddamned notice, too. I know it, by God, because I staked it myself — liar, *ahijuna!*"

All three Murietas stiffened. Jake's hackles rose, for every man had his hand on a gun. Then an oldster spat to one side, and said, "The Spanish scoundrel tells the truth, for all he is a scoundrel. There weren't no marked claim here, not when we arrived."

"Then where the hell are Pablo and Joseph?" Royal's voice was shaking, on the verge of running out of control. He shook his fist and shouted, "I left Pablo and Joseph here, right here, digging this very claim, and it was just three days ago!"

"Ah…" The old man meditated. "Would they be Spanish-lookin' fellows?"

Jake said tensely, "One is Portuguese, but the other is Chilean."

"Ah…" Then the crowd shifted as men shuffled out of the way and stared at Jake with open ghoulish expectation. The old man jerked his chin and said briefly, "This way."

Jake, sick foreboding inside him, followed the old man to the *Gosling* tent. The front was tightly tied shut. The oldster said nothing, but bent and gripped the ties, and jerked them apart.

Jake said, "Oh, dear Christ." The smell had hit him. It was too early for flies, surely, but flies buzzed heavily. The two pairs of feet stretched towards him were stiff, and in the shadows two pairs of glazed eyes stared, still open.

He staggered, kept himself upright with a grip on a tent pole, and said huskily, "Who murdered my men? Who killed them?"

195

"That be for the alcalde to decide — not that it'll be a hard matter." The old miner's tone was matter of fact. "If you take one good look, you'll see for yourself what happened to these poor fellows." And he bent and gripped one pair of feet and hauled with surprising strength. "Injuns," he said.

The body was Joseph Fayal's. Jake heard Dan Kemp swear and Tib go to a tree and vomit. The noise Royal made was like that of a stricken animal. Joseph's face was open-mouthed, frozen for ever in ghastly terror. His skull where his long glossy black hair had been was a clotted mass of blood and exposed bone.

Then the old miner bent again, and hauled Pablo's body out.

"Injuns," he repeated. Pablo had been scalped, too.

Jake swallowed on a clenched, tight throat, and the old man went on, "Them Injuns must have throwed away your stakes and tools, for there weren't nothing to show that claim were taken, not when I got here. There ain't nothing to show that claim were your'n. We found these poor boys, God rest their souls, off over there in the trees. They'd been struck down, no doubt, while trying to run away — and who can blame them for that, huh?"

Jake said nothing. He couldn't. Instead, in a kind of hopeless quest for mercy, he looked at the sky … and four men were watching them from the top of the slope.

One was the Cockney alcalde, Don Roberto. He was seated like a sack on his mule. The other three rode horses, and they were the other Murietas.

196

NINETEEN

IT was April in Bedstead Gully, and Davy Jones Locker was sick. Abner and Jonathan were worse, too, and kept on whining for water.

Davy did his very best to oblige them, but he was very thirsty, too. In the end he gave up the ship and rolled up in his blanket on the wooden shelf that served as his berth. When he woke up the fire had gone out and he was shuddering with cold.

He stumbled to his feet dazedly, not knowing where he was or what had happened. Abner was crying out ... Abner was fiery hot. Abner's blanket was soaking wet with sweat, and Davy didn't know what to do. He called out for Captain Dexter, but then remembered that Captain Dexter wasn't there. He didn't know what to do, so he built up the fire until the whole hut sweated. Jonathan was quiet, thank the holy. It wasn't until dawn that Davy found out that Jonathan was dead.

Davy went out into the early freezing cold and dug a grave. He talked to himself a lot, and crooned little songs. He hacked at the clay as he sang, and sweat ran down his naked torso. Jonathan's body seemed impossibly stiff and heavy, but somehow Davy wedged it into the hole. Then he covered it up with dirt the best that he could. He found a board to put at the head of the grave, but didn't know how to write, so called out for Captain Dexter.

Still Captain Dexter didn't come. Davy had forgotten that Captain Dexter had gone away, so he stumbled off down the trail in search of him.

There was an obstacle in the track, a great shifting pile of mud and gravel. It took Davy a long time to realize that it was the boulder that had fallen down and trapped them, so very long ago. It was raining—the cool rain fell down and soothed his hot dry skin. It ran over the mud and shingle, too, making it all slide and shift. More dirt and shingle came down from the cliff … the soaked cliff was collapsing over the rock, turning it into a hill.

It was a steep hill but, unlike the boulder, it could be climbed, so Davy climbed it. Twice he slipped, but it was easy to start again. Then he was at the top, and to his surprise he was sliding down the other side. The trail to Don Roberto's fort was open again. He, he, Davy, had opened it! Davy called out to Captain Dexter to come and see what he, Davy, had done, but still Captain Dexter did not answer.

But Davy did hear a voice. He blinked, astonished, when he heard it, because he had decided there were no people here. The voice was that of a girl, an Indian. Her small, rough hands were pulling at him. It was the woman whose husband had been burned on the pyre. Davy remembered her, and told her so, amazed.

She seemed pleased, though she also didn't seem to understand him. When she urged him along the track through the defile to the Indian camp, he obeyed.

TWENTY

IT was April at the Vidrie hacienda, and at dinner in the evening Don Manuel announced a fiesta to celebrate the improving weather.

The wild oats, grass and clover were growing with extraordinary luxuriance as the soil warmed, enriched with clover, and all his cattle and horses were in the finest possible condition. The whole extent of his holdings was a pleasure to the eye, the grasses waving high in the gentle winds, and the corrals were filling with an incredible number of calves and foals. The grapevines, too, were sprouting, and Don Manuel told Harriet that he knew in his bones, his very soul, that this would be a record vintage year.

Soon, he said, the river would drop sufficiently for the bridge by Don Roberto's fort to be crossed, traffic would move freely between the towns and the farms and the hills, and then ... then such a prosperous season would dawn, the memorable season of 1849, the year of the California gold rush.

While he did not wish to see prospecting on his fertile lands, he expected to make a fortune out of supplying the traders, the market for beef being inexhaustible. This coming year such wealth would be reaped in this land of Calafia—

and a bear baiting spectacle was a truly fitting celebration.

Harriet made no comment, though she was certain that she did not want to watch another bear-and-bull baiting. Instead, on the day, she had a sick headache — or so she said, and she even sacrificed her daily ride to support her story. She stayed in her room while the family went out to greet their guests and escort them to the arena, and instead of going out to the garden after they had left, she sat in her chair gazing out of the window.

That old pirate Schouten's book was on her knee, as usual, but — also as usual — she scarcely read it, knowing it by heart. Instead, she and tried not to listen to the distant shouts from the bear pit. Then at last, the far-off roaring of the crowd faded, and she heard steps and voices approaching through the gardens. The Vidries and their guests were coming to dress up for dinner. Harriet sighed, putting her mind to what she would wear.

And the door to her bedroom was jerked open, to reveal Frank Sefton.

He's behind you!

Harriet flinched, and the book fell from her lap to the floor. Sefton came into the room while she was reaching for it. He put a hand on her shoulder, and held her still while he reached down with the other hand for the journal.

Straightening with the book in his hand, he said blandly, "Did I frighten you, my dear?"

She was watching the journal, and not his face, and had to school herself not to grab when he handed it to her. She said shortly, still not looking at him, "I had no word that you were coming, Frank. I thought that perhaps I had seen the last of you."

"But I told you I would return, my dear — and I have brought guests, three guests. They are American speculators who have just arrived from the States. I hope to do business with them, so you must take great pains to enchant them. I have also brought gifts — more gifts, for you," he added, but then his voice became vague. With discomfort, Harriet saw that he was gazing pensively at the old journal in her hand.

He said, "What is that?"

"It's mine."

"A journal, kept by yourself, perhaps?"

She said again, "It is mine," and then, to distract him, said, "What do you bring this time? More gowns and shawls?"

"Gowns?" He still seemed preoccupied, but then as he gazed at her, his eyes cleared, and his expression became malicious.

He smiled, and said, "I'm sure you remember, my dear, that I had great ideas of turning my bank into a public company? Well, I have done it! I have taken the plunge! And it is so successful ... so successful that I want to celebrate by sharing my success with you. I have made you one of the principal shareholders!"

"Me?" She stared at him suspiciously, remembering the trick he had played in New Zealand — the trick that had left her penniless. "Why me?"

"But why should you ask such a question? Can't you guess? It's an affirmation of my affection, my undying love, and a celebration of a memorial year."

She paused, studying him warily. Then she said slowly, "I know you do nothing that is not to your own advantage."

"That can be said about any shrewd speculator, Harriet! Of course business is meant to profit the investor — it's not a humanitarian affair!"

He seemed angry, but then calmed down, and smiled, and sat on the edge of her bed, facing her, his expression indulgent.

"All I want is to share the profit with you, my dear. And so I have made you a gift of twenty thousand shares in my bank. It will make you wealthy. Even if I go bankrupt, you will be rich enough to rescue our fortunes. Even if I die a pauper, you will be my rich widow. With these shares, you will never have to exist on the charity of others."

"No?" she flashed. "I don't see your logic—not when I am living on the charity of others."

"Such melodrama!" He threw his head back and laughed. Then, sobering, he tut-tutted, saying, "Come, be tranquil, accept my gift in the spirit in which it is offered. Take the shares. See, they are in your name already."

He had the documents in a pocket of his tailored deerskin coat—four thick, folded leaves of parchment. They fitted tightly, and he had to heave himself around to pry them out. Harriet watched him suspiciously, while her bed bounced in time to his movements. Then, when he pushed the documents at her, she slipped Schouten's journal on the floor beneath the skirt of her chair.

She took them and looked at them. They were certainly impressive. As he had said, her name was inscribed in flowing copperplate at the top of each one.

There were four certificates, each one worth five thousand shares in Sefton's Bank for Miners. Twenty thousand dollars in total, a fortune. In the distance, she heard the bell that was the first summons for dinner. It chimed no more insistently than the alarm bells in her mind.

She said, "What am I supposed to do with these?"

"Why, keep them, just keep them. In a safe place, of course. Don Manuel will look after them, if you ask." He smiled. Even his cold blue eyes warmed. He was the picture of innocent benevolence.

Then he added, "To make it all lawful, you will have to sign for them, of course."

"I beg your pardon?" The alarm bells in her mind were ringing louder than ever.

"Scribble your name on this paper here—and this, and this, and this, and then you can sleep easy, knowing you are a rich woman, no matter what happens to me."

The dinner bell sounded again, but she scarcely heard it. She said, "Why my signature?"

202

"Only to make the gift lawful, my dear, so the charlatans can never rob you. It's just a precaution, and entirely in your own interests."

She said slowly, "But at Sutter's Fort, when you were taunting me about stupidly thinking I could sign the bill of sale for the piece of land for a theater, you made it plain, Frank, that my signature is worth nothing. That's what you said—emphatically. *Nothing.* You said that a married woman's signature has no standing in law. So explain to me why this is different."

"It's different because I will countersign the papers, in an affirmation of your signature. I will be your witness. If I had countersigned the bill of sale for the land, everything would have been fine. That's why you made such a blunder when you bought that lot at Sutter's, Harriet. You should have consulted me first."

But she hadn't even known he was in California, she thought—and would have fled, if she did. His tone was reasonable and even kind, but the hairs on the back of her neck were rising.

She said curtly, "I'm sorry, but if there is a difference, I don't understand it. My signature was witnessed in Auckland, the day before our marriage—by my father, by my brother, and a lawyer, but it made no difference to the outcome. And I still don't understand, Frank, how you found out not just the precise amount I paid for the theater lot, but that I borrowed the money from Captain Dexter's men … unless Don Roberto told you."

He paused, his eyes cold again. Then he said, "How did you guess?"

"So you do have the alcalde in your pocket," she said with disgust. "And yet you pretend to be a respectable businessman? So why should I believe you? I might be *just* an actress, but I can see that there is no logic in what you say. You're trying to tell me that though my signature was worth nothing at Sutter's, it is somehow valid here—but that

203

simply doesn't make sense. And the truth of the matter is that I don't trust you a single inch, Frank. I won't sign your papers, and you can keep your shares. I most emphatically do not want them."

The whites of his eyes flushed with rage, but to her surprise he made an obvious effort to control himself. With remarkable calmness, he said, "Think again, Harriet. You blundered at Sutter's, but you make no kind of blunder here, because you can rely on the shrewd advice of your husband."

Her eyes narrowed. He was very keen to get rid of those shares, she thought.

"No, Frank," she said steadily. "I remember the last time I signed your papers, and I remember how I regretted it."

Frank Sefton was silent. She was even more aware of his inner rage ... eerily so, because his smooth expression didn't betray it.

His voice, when he finally spoke, was equally mild. "Come, Harriet," he said. "It's no crime to avoid discriminatory legislation, if you can avoid it in a legal fashion. Your father approved, and your brother, too. They were realistic enough to know that the more wealth I managed to keep out of the British administrators' hands, the more prosperous you would be."

"*Prosperous?*" She laughed, rather wildly. "You left me penniless, Frank!"

Sefton stood up as if she hadn't spoken. The bland mask was firmly in place. "Think about it," he urged. "And keep those certificates in a safe place. Soon, I know, you will think better of your decision. But forget about it now, my dear, and set your mind to charming my guests—you must be your most beautiful self, for I insist!"

And he went. Harriet watched the door close. It was a long moment before she stood and put her mind to dressing for dinner. Sign his documents? Never, she thought, *never*.

TWENTY-ONE

BECAUSE she took a long time to get dressed, Harriet was the last to arrive at the dinner table.

The women usually gathered for a glass of sherry wine before parading into the huge dining room, but when she had looked into the salon, it was empty. Obviously, they had given her up, so she made a solitary entrance into the dining room. With a concerted grinding of chair legs on the floor, all the gentlemen stood. As she dipped a curtsey in response to their gallant bows, Harriet glimpsed Sefton's irritation. However, the three gentlemen he had brought with him didn't appear to notice her lapse of manners.

All three were true-blue Yankees, who had come by sea from around the Horn. One was a silent and dissipated-looking fellow by the name of Giles, who studied the assemblage with yellowed eyes while he ate everything that was put in front of him. The other two, by contrast, dominated the conversation, being anxious to tell Harriet all about their adventures. Their expressions were identically admiring as they vied to relate how they had hired horses in Sonoma, and then had ridden by stages to Sefton's ranch, and for quite some time Harriet found it difficult to tell them apart, even though they were not related.

One was Prenderwhite, and the other was Chaffey. "We

have not come to California to dig the shining gold, no indeed, Mrs. Sefton," said Chaffey, and lifted his wine glass in a salute to her eyes. "We have other schemes to improve our fortunes," he revealed, and then complacently sipped.

"And you will," said Sefton, smoothly seizing his chance to enter the conversation. "Some men—a few —will make vast fortunes at the diggings. But others, much shrewder, will make greater and surer fortunes out of trading and wise investment."

"And others by gambling," said Prenderwhite. His expression was rueful. "I brought two dozen roulette wheels with me and sold them within moments of landing — for one hundred dollars apiece! One hundred dollars, for wheels that cost me eight! Now I wish, by heaven, that I had brought two hundred!"

"Or waited to charge five hundred apiece—which you could have got at Sutter's Fort, or even Pueblo San Marco," said Sefton, and Harriet watched Prenderwhite's expression turn to one of chagrin.

"You're certain?" he said plaintively.

"I am indeed, sir. That was your first mistake—and it's a mistake men will make over and over again, if they don't have the wisdom to ask for the advice of the old settlers. If you'd asked Don Manuel here, or his brothers or his cousins, or even asked for my thoughts, you would have waited until the first lucky diggers came down from the hills, when your single roulette wheel could have been worth one thousand!"

He stopped to savor a mouthful of wine, his smug smile more superior than ever, and Don Manuel nodded, and said, "It's true, what my friend says is very true."

There was a babble in Spanish about the table, as the other Vidries repeated this in their own language. Mr. Prenderwhite's expression, Harriet thought, was quite a study. Then she wondered if he believed what Sefton and his Californian cronies claimed, or was as naïve as Sefton hoped, because he asked many penetrating questions, many of them echoed by his friend Chaffey. These two Americans were more wide-awake than Sefton assumed, she meditated, and thought that he might have more trouble persuading them to invest in whatever he had in mind than he had hoped.

Meantime, food arrived in the usual procession, soup first, then various fowls and meats cooked with beans and rice and highly flavored with garlic. Harriet ate in her usual silence, listening to the Americans, and casting a glance around the table every now and then. But then, quite abruptly, she noticed that Mr. Giles was watching Sefton with close but covert attention. There was something about her husband, she thought, that interested him extremely.

She looked at him with renewed curiosity. Mr. Giles had long and drooping moustaches, which made him look rather like a world-weary hound. They were stained with tobacco juice, and his eyes were jaundiced, too, their expression definitely jaded. He drank rather a lot, Harriet noticed, but what was most noticeable of all was that he watched Sefton all the time, even when Sefton wasn't speaking.

Then she leaned back, as the servants cleared the table, took away the tablecloth, and brought ashtrays, decanters of port, and bowls of nuts and raisins, which were all laid out on the highly polished wood. In England, the arrival of the port would have been the cue for the women to rise and retreat to the salon. But this was old California, where the women stayed to smoke tobacco with the men. There had even been occasions when the younger women had left—to return in beautiful embroidered jackets and splendid velvet calcineros, silk scarves tied about their waists with the ends artistically drooping down from one curvaceous hip, and their scarlet mouths newly painted. Then, returning to their seats, they had smoked cigars with the *sang froid* of a set of Dutchmen.

Frank's voice rang out above the commotion of decanters being passed around. "That is the best advice a

Californian settler can offer," he was saying. "To ask the advice of the old Californian hands. Only the men who live here and have observed the business that was done over the past year are fully aware of the potential of this gold rush. It is better to go into partnerships, or buy shares in businesses that are already established—for these established businesses are the substance in the rich brew that is California now, and not just the froth on top."

"You are a poetic persuader, Colonel Sefton," observed Prenderwhite, and laughed.

"Then allow me another flight of fancy, sir. You enjoyed the spectacle of bear-baiting today—and don't deny it, for I saw you. And I would like to think that the state of the California business market can be likened to that sport. Right now, like the bull that strives to toss the bear high, the California market is rising. Shooting up like a comet! Shall we call it a *bull market*? But next winter, or the winter after that, who knows? California may well be like the bear that endures to drag the bull down, and the market will plunge. It's hard to say how much gold is left in the mines—enough to fuel the gold rush for two years? Five? Ten? And the tales of the inexhaustible gold will certainly keep on attracting an almost inexhaustible number of migrants, but with every influx, the chances of picking up a fortune will diminish. And the failure must necessarily affect the traders and speculators, because the stores will be glutted with more goods than there are people who can afford to buy. So of course the market will fall. Perhaps we will call it a *bear market*, then."

"Bravo!" said Prenderwhite. Harriet couldn't work out if he was truly enchanted with Frank's little tricks of simile, or if he was being derisive, but Sefton's complacent expression didn't slip at all.

"Only those who have already made the largest fortunes will withstand the crash," he said. "The men who can afford to bide their time. You may depend on it, we will have enormous fluctuations, but there will be men who have speculated well, who will profit immensely in the end."

Don Manuel was lighting a cigar with tremendous care and smiling wisely at the same time, as if he understood Sefton's tortuous logic. The Vidrie women, sipping chocolate, smiled blankly, and lifted their white shoulders at each other in uncomprehending little shrugs. Mr. Giles, Harriet observed, merely buried his nose in his glass of port. His expression, as much as she could see of it, was more sardonic than ever.

Then he straightened, brushed limply at his damp moustaches, and spoke for the first time since Harriet had taken her seat at the table. "But how, Colonel Sefton sir," he asked, in a nasal accent, "do we brash newcomer Yankees persuade the settlers who are riding this here bull to shift over and make room? For, by your logic, sir, they would shove us off rather than share this bonanza."

"They will shift over willingly! And why? Because it is to our ultimate benefit to welcome new investment. The influx of new money is needed, sir. Only think, of paying a thousand dollars for a twenty-foot warehouse, or twelve hundred dollars for the use of a lot—to rent it, Giles, not to buy it. A mere shop assistant can now command between two and three thousand dollars a year. Few men can stand those kinds of risks and outgoings for long, sir, which is why new investment is welcomed—actively solicited! Why, I myself owned a fine flour mill in Pueblo San Marco until just six months ago. A Yankee miller worked the stones for me, on a percentage basis, and did so well that I gave him the chance of an eighty percent share, and even loaned him the money to buy it."

"Really?" said Mr. Giles. He didn't seem at all impressed, though an admiring murmur had set up round the table. "It amazes me that you should be so generous, Colonel Sefton sir, when you reckon there was so much potential profit there—and there are those costs you talk

209

about looming in the near future. Perhaps after you had a look at your account books, you revised your estimate of the figures?"

"You malign me!"

Sefton, Harriet realized, was more than merely insulted — he was furious, because she recognized the ominous flushing of the whites of his eyes. With what, she thought, was an obvious effort to calm his voice, he said, "That miller can't help but do well. Provisioning the miners is the most profitable business around."

"If you don't count gambling," Mr. Giles observed.

"That is true, yes — but the greatest profit of all is in neither gambling or trading. It is in buying up shares in the gold business itself, and by that I mean buying up shares in Californian banks."

"Banks?" Mr. Chaffey stared. "I didn't know there were any in California."

"I own one myself. Sefton's Bank for Miners, in Pueblo San Marco. As soon as the river can be crossed I shall be over there to check the accounts, and set the books to absolute rights, for I've turned that bank into a public company, sirs, and am prepared to sell shares to substantial and reliable men — and even lend them the wherewithal to buy those shares. It's a once in a lifetime chance. Those shares in my bank won't be on the market very long, I assure you!"

Mr. Giles's yellow eyes widened, so that he looked more like a bloodhound than ever. Then he said incredulously, "You have a bank, Colonel, that you can't even visit — because it's on the wrong side of the river?"

"That is immaterial!" Sefton's anger was becoming more apparent, Harriet thought. "The bank was established there because I saw the commercial potential of Pueblo San Marco! I saw the possibilities, sir, and I was right, because the town is at the gateway to the mines, sir! I live across the river, because my hacienda happens to be across the river, sir, but for most of the year that is no disadvantage at all."

"But for the rest of the year, when the river is too high to cross—as we found when we rode to your rancho, Colonel? What happens then, Colonel Sefton sir?"

"The river will be down in days, sir, and it may even be possible to cross the bridge at Don Roberto's fort now—and to answer your question, I feel no concern whatsoever that when I get to the bank I will find anything amiss, for it's supervised by Don Roberto Ross himself, the alcalde of this area!"

"Alcalde?"

"The administrator of law and order in this district."

"Something that is highly necessary in this here territory, I reckon," muttered Mr. Giles, and buried his nose in his glass again.

Sefton was openly irritated, now, so much so that he deliberately turned his shoulder to Giles, saying to Chaffey and Prenderwhite, "The bank, whatever its situation, is a prime investment—and for a very good reason. A bank is critical to this district, because within four months there will be an embarrassing over-abundance of gold."

The silence, Harriet mused, was everything Sefton could have wished for. Even the sardonic Giles looked surprised.

Chaffey said in a scandalized squeak, "But you can never have too much gold!"

"Indeed you can," said Frank Sefton, and smiled. He was back in his stride now, having successfully removed the general attention from the gadfly, Mr. Giles, and turned it back on himself.

Then Harriet saw that he was fiddling while he talked. He had spread a little piece of white paper on the table, and he had a jackknife in one hand, and was shaving flakes off the plug of tobacco that he held on the palm of the other hand. As she watched, the brown flakes fell neatly onto the paper.

She had seen this operation before, but never done by a

man. Don Manuel and the other Vidrie men were smoking cigars, and when the young and lively women were dressed as men, they smoked cigars, too. Otherwise, the Vidrie women smoked what they called "cigarettos," which they made by flaking tobacco from plugs, or even cigars, onto squares of thin paper, which they twisted at each end before lighting.

Now, just like the women, Sefton rolled the paper, trapping the tobacco flakes inside the little cylinder. Then he gave it a twist at each end, and set it between his lips. Flirtatiously, one of the women held a lighted taper to it, leaning across the table so that her generous breasts swelled in the low bodice of her gown.

Sefton thanked her with a charming smile, and relaxed back in his chair. "They tell me," he said in a conversational vein, "that the use of tobacco is popular with travelers — because cannibals dislike the taste of the meat of men who indulge in the habit."

Then he chuckled, while Mr. Chaffey and Mr. Prenderwhite grimaced.

Mr. Giles murmured, as if to himself, "Is that so, huh?" Then he said in a louder voice, "You were telling us, sir, about the terrible danger of digging too much gold."

"It is not that there is too much gold, sir, but that there is too little coin. Gold is all the currency here, as you have all observed, and because of that gold is becoming debased. Over the last eight weeks of the season, six hundred thousand dollars' worth of gold was collected up the American and Feather rivers, and commerce to the amount of two hundred and fifty thousand dollars was done in Sutter's and Pueblo San Marco — but all in gold dust. So can't you see why the precious metal has become devalued? Right now, gold of the finest quality fetches only nine or ten dollars per ounce in Pueblo San Marco, or even San Francisco, though it is well known that at the mint in Philadelphia an ounce of gold is worth at least eighteen.

Where a pinch would buy a drink, now a teaspoonful is demanded. The need for a mint is becoming critical, or else all the gold is lost from our national currency, going to Mazatlan, Chile or Peru, instead—for why not take it away, when it is worth so little here? Over the last season more than a million dollars' worth of gold, at the lowest computation, was taken from the mines every month, sirs, *every month*, and this quantity will be more than doubled when the emigrants from the States, from Oregon, the Sandwich Islands, and the Southern republics arrive for the season of 'forty-nine. *We need a mint!* The first bank to obtain permission from Congress to establish a mint and stabilize the currency will fill a great need and make a great fortune, and I intend that bank to be mine, sir. So now you see why I need investment from others."

Silence, as everyone stared at Sefton, mesmerized by his eloquence and his figures. Then Mr. Giles brushed his moustaches away from his mouth.

"But," he said, looking elaborately puzzled, "didn't I hear you say, Colonel Sefton sir, that you are willing to lend us the wherewithal to buy those shares?"

"That is so, indeed. You are not mistaken. I will lend the money—and take the shares that have been bought in the bank as collateral. That, sir, is a demonstration of how much faith I have in the scheme."

"A persuasive argument, Colonel Sefton."

"Then you will buy some shares?"

"No, sir, I will not. I have other plans, but I thank you."

"Plans?" Sefton echoed. He was staring unblinkingly at Mr. Giles, and Harriet saw that the whites of his protuberant eyes were flushing again as his temper rose. "But what plans could beat my offer, sir?"

"I plan to set up a weekly newspaper, sir, and I have all the doings organized. My little paper will be a page twelve by eighteen inches, and I reckon on a circulation of five hundred, at a subscription rate of twelve dollars a year. I

213

figure I should make two or three thousand each and every week out of advertising, and it will suit me fine if it is paid in gold instead of coin. It's going to be called *The Placer Times*, and I plan to set it up, sir, in the place they call Sutter's."

The women, having finished smoking and drinking chocolate, were rising from the table, but Harriet didn't move. Instead, she was watching her husband as he stared challengingly at Giles, fascinated by the interplay between him and the abrasive printer.

Sefton snapped, "Sutter's? Then you're mad, sir, because the town of Sutter's doesn't exist!"

"Really, Colonel Sefton sir?" Mr. Giles drawled, and didn't seem taken aback in the slightest. "I was under the strong impression that there was a fort with a story which I might even write and send back to the States, it being a fort with reason and substance."

"There is a fort there, certainly, but my wife can tell you that the land about Sutter's is worthless, being nothing better than swamp and overflowing river."

Was it? Belatedly realizing that in a minute or two she would be the only woman in the room, Harriet stood to follow the Vidrie women.

But her mind was busy. Worth nothing? That was not what Don Roberto had said when he had talked her into buying the plot of land, and not what he had said when he persuaded the *Gosling*s to lend her the money.

Then she froze in the doorway, as she heard Sefton say sharply, "Harriet, tell Giles that anyone who invests in Sutter's has lost their money. Tell him that Sutter's is doomed."

For a long moment Harriet was silent, her head bent as she looked at the polished parquet of the floor. Slowly, she turned, and looked at her husband. He met her eyes, staring compellingly.

In the voice that had been trained to carry very clearly,

she said, "All I can say is that I have heard arguments from both sides. I have heard what you say, and the Embarcadero, when I last saw it, was muddy, most certainly. But other men who know California equally well spoke to me in glowing terms about the future of Sutter's Fort. The day before I left I talked with army surveyors who were laying out streets and measuring off lots of land, and they assured me that the Embarcadero will soon be a city to rival New Orleans. And when I talked with the alcalde, Don Roberto Ross, he told me exactly the same."

Then she nodded regally, and left the room.

TWENTY-TWO

HARRIET woke with a lurch, her skin clammy with a presentiment of danger.

The house was as silent as the grave, but the light in her window told her that the sun was well up. She sat up in bed. She was alone — she had been alone all night. Or had she?

Her body was as untouched as ever, but she still felt violated, as if an intruder had been here. Or had she dreamed it? She had taken so long to fall asleep, listening apprehensively to every sound, knowing she had made her husband so viciously angry. Doors had slammed, and there had been sharp footsteps in the corridor outside — but the steps had passed on, and while she was listening to them fade into the distance she had suddenly dropped off, and then slept heavily.

And while she slept she dreamed that someone had been moving stealthily about her room. But she hadn't woken up, and now she didn't know if it was true.

It had just been a dream, she told herself, but she got up quickly, impelled by urgency. Things were not quite as she had left them, she was sure of it. Gowns had been shuffled on their hooks, and drawers were partly open. Her baskets had been moved.

Apprehension gripped her, and she looked through

them wildly, throwing out clothes, putting them back, and then turning them out again. Then she remembered that she had put Schouten's journal under her chair. She remembered Sefton watching her, and she remembered the expression on his face.

She fell to her knees, hunting on all fours, feeling about the underside of the chair, round the back, and then, in desperation, hauling out the heavy chair to look at the space where it had been. Nothing. She had not been dreaming, because Schouten's scrapbook of tales of gold was gone.

The book was gone. It belonged to Jake Dexter—what would she say to him, if she ever saw him again? She dressed quickly, and washed and brushed her hair with furious haste.

When she ran out of the room, she found the passage empty. There were still no sounds in the house, not even the movement and chatter of servants. The polished floor stretched ahead of her, as silent as a looking glass, patched with squares of sunlight from the windows. The quick rustle of her skirts seemed deafening.

Harriet stopped at the corner, where it led to the dining room, looking about, frowning as she tried to work out why the house was so quiet … so deserted, and a voice behind her drawled, "Good morning to you, Mrs. Sefton."

She whirled around. It was Mr. Giles. He looked even more played out than he had at the dinner table. The pouches beneath his yellowed eyeballs sagged, and his stained moustaches drooped to his chin, emphasizing his world-weary look. Then he lifted one hand, and nibbled thoughtfully, and she saw that he was holding a cold chop.

So he had been in the dining room. She said angrily, "You gave me a fright."

"So I observed, ma'am."

But neglected to apologize, she noticed. Then she put her mind to the immediate problem, and said swiftly, "Have you seen my husband?"

217

"That I have indeed, this very morning."

"Then where is he?"

"That's a little difficult to answer, ma'am, being as I don't know how far it is to Don Roberto's fort. The men could be there or not quite there, yet."

She gasped, furious that Sefton had left her with any explanation or excuse again, that he was still humiliating her by leaving her with these people. Worse still, he'd stolen Jake Dexter's book, and taken it with him.

Then she thought about what Mr. Giles had said, and demanded, "Men? What men?"

"Why, all of them, ma'am. Don Manuel and his showy male relatives, Chaffey and Prenderwhite, and all. Quite a little gathering for a solitary alcalde to entertain."

Mr. Giles paused, his attitude thoughtful as he studied her. Then, with decisive movements, he finished his chop, threw the bone out the nearest window, and headed back to the dining room. Evidently he hadn't finished breakfast. If she wanted further conversation, she was forced to follow him, and so she did.

There were bowls of fruit as well as platters of bread and congealed meat on the table. Harriet sat down in the chair she had occupied at dinner, and Mr. Giles sat opposite. She looked around and said, "Where are the women?"

"The women? I haven't seen them. Perhaps they are at church."

Or asleep, she thought. It was common for them to sleep until midday. As she watched, Mr. Giles reached out and plucked another chop from its quivering gravy. After gnawing at it a moment, he said, "Tell me more about this alcalde fellow, the one that everyone calls Don Roberto."

"He's a Londoner. His real name is Robert Ross. He has been in this country a long time, and is a Mexican citizen now."

"Mexican? Is that an advantage?"

"Maybe not now that the Mexicans have been defeated

by the Americans, but it has certainly allowed him to make a lot of money as an alcalde. He gives out advice, and makes judicial decisions," she said, "and charges fees for both."

"Advice? Ah," said Mr. Giles, nodding. "The fellow with such grand prognostications for Sutter's Fort. Did you say he's a Londoner, ma'am?"

"He's a Cockney, if that holds interest."

"Oh, it does indeed, ma'am. And you, by your accent, belong to that city too."

Harriet stared at him with dislike, and then took a plate and bread and preserve. She spread with emphasis and said, "I am not a Cockney, and there is no connection, I assure you of that. I met Don Roberto in California."

"But it's an odd kind of coincidence."

"Don Roberto is definitely odd, but there is no coincidence."

"Odd, is he? Ah," said Mr. Giles, and nodded wisely over his chop. "I reckon California will soon get acquainted with oddities. Don't you agree? Oddities will become the usual run of thing—if it ain't happened already. And you met your husband the Colonel in London?"

"I did not."

"Surely not in Canton?"

Harriet narrowed her eyes, thinking that Mr. Giles knew rather a lot about Sefton, or perhaps had been asking a lot of questions. She snapped, "I met him in New Zealand, if that holds interest."

"Everything you say is of interest, Mrs. Sefton," he said, but the way he said it sounded more inquisitive than gallant. Then he remarked, "I often wonder about your husband the Colonel."

So did Harriet. She said nothing.

"I wonder why he's so uncommon anxious to sell off shares in his bank, for a start."

"While he wouldn't say so in front of Don Manuel and the other Vidrie men, he probably wants to make California more American," she said, thinking of Captain Mervine of the frigate *Savannah*, who was so very outspoken on the topic. "It's a common sentiment among Americans here, that the wealth of California belongs rightfully to Americans, and not to those they call aliens, which include the Spanish who have been here for generations. You were not tempted to buy some of his shares?"

"Ma'am, those shares could well make some other man a fortune, but I am naught but a poor roving printer. Starting up a newspaper is the height of my ambition."

"Well, there is the coincidence you are looking for," she brooded. "For I am—was—naught but a poor roving player."

She saw his jaws stop short as his eyes opened wide. For the first time, she had startled him. He exclaimed, "You're an actress?"

"Well guessed, sir," she said tartly.

"Colonel Francis Sefton married an *actress?*"

"He stooped that far, Mr. Giles."

But he didn't seem to notice the irony. Instead, he was lost in meditation, chewing one end of a drooping moustache while the chop sat neglected in his fist. Then he roused himself and said, "I've met him before, your husband the Colonel, but he don't remember that."

"You did?"

"In New York, nigh on nine years ago, according to my recollection—which is usually impeccable, as I am always on the hunt for a story. There was a great deal of gossip going the rounds about Colonel Sefton. He was highly active in New York social circles, very wishful to better himself, for all that his family back in Philadelphia were so blue-nosed. Not rich—quite impoverished, in fact, but most definitely aristocratic. Old stock, if you know what I mean. He was chasing after a certain Miss Coffin, of the whaling and merchant lot. An heiress to a fortune."

Harriet paused, looking at him with her head on one

side. Then she said, "Mr. Giles, you might pretend to be just a poor roving printer, but I'm fast coming to the conclusion that you are much, much more than that."

He grinned. "Ah, a printer I am, and a printer's devil, too, and a compositor, sales clerk, and editor. I can write, and be critic at any acting affair, ma'am, and set up posters, too. If I had thought to print myself visiting cards, I would give you one."

"I think you write much, much more than critical reviews of plays, Mr. Giles."

"You are most perceptive, ma'am, because I confess that I do send stories back east. There's a large and lively interest in stories about this here golden territory. Publishers vie to buy the stories that come out of here, even those that take a year to arrive."

"I think you write more than stories, Mr. Giles. I think you deal in gossip. What about this Miss Coffin in New York, for instance?"

"You're jealous, perhaps?"

She laughed.

"So you're not," he said, and rose from his seat, brushing his hands to flick off the grease. "But even if you were, you have no need to lay awake at nights. Miss Coffin married a much more likely man. Your husband the colonel swore to make her regret it, though. He flew into a very public rage, but while people waited with riveted suspense for the explosion or the murder, nothing happened. He simply disappeared. He vanished. But," he added, "I do remember him."

Then he started on his way out of the dining room, but Harriet stopped him, saying quickly, "Whereabouts are you going?"

"Why, to pack, ma'am, having replenished my belly and soothed my spirits with conversation. Don Manuel," he told her, "has withdrawn his hospitality. His last words as he set off were a formal adieu—a courtly goodbye, but one that

221

made it perfectly plain that he did not expect to see me here on his return."

"But I thought you were Frank's guest here? That he vouched for you?"

"Not at all, Mrs. Sefton. Chaffey was the one with the letter of introduction. Prenderwhite and I were just bit players, so to speak. It was a most remarkable surprise … a coincidence, if you will … that my host was so unknowingly memorable." Then Mr. Giles looked around the empty room and lowered his voice. "Do you think Don Manuel withdrew his hospitality because I disappointed him in some way?"

"Because you questioned the wisdom of buying shares in Sefton's Bank for Miners?"

"Was I that blunt, Mrs. Sefton?" he said, and laughed. "I hesitate to think that I influenced Chaffey and Prenderwhite in any way."

"But I think you did, Mr. Giles. Did Mr. Chaffey and Mr. Prenderwhite also decline the offer of the shares?"

"Well, let's just say that by the evening's end they still hadn't made up their minds."

She paused, thinking, and then said slowly, "You seem to think that my husband's business dealings and Don Manuel Vidrie are connected in some way."

"Well, it do seem uncommon coincidental that my welcome should wear out so quickly after I declined to purchase those shares." Then he said slyly, "You've been here a long time, or so I hear, Mrs. Sefton."

"Since the start of September," she said moodily.

"Then Don Manuel is a very obliging neighbor, a good friend to your husband the Colonel."

She grimaced, thinking that the fact she had outworn her welcome must be very obvious, if this casual visitor had seen it, and said, "The Vidrie men are coming back soon?"

"This very night, or so Don Manuel revealed. That was the deadline, or so to speak, that he gave me."

Harriet's thoughts were flying. What did she want more,

to stay out of Frank Sefton's reach, or to escape this gilded cage? She needed to escape, she thought—for no matter how vile it might be at Sefton's hacienda, Pueblo San Marco would be within reach. When the Vidrie men came back, escape would be impossible, because Don Manuel would never allow her to travel without her husband's permission, or an escort. And Mr. Giles, while insinuating in speech and offensive in manner, was an escort, of a kind.

But was Frank Sefton coming back to this house, or was he riding on to his ranch? She said, "What about my husband? What is he doing?"

"Aha, that is the nub of the matter. My impression is that he intended to stick with Chaffey and Prenderwhite for as long as possible, maybe even all the way to Pueblo San Marco, in the hope of getting them to alter their minds about those shares. And then, that done—or not done, as the case may be—he will cross over the river to his rancho."

So the river was navigable once more, she thought. And that settled it. She said very firmly, "Mr. Giles, I would be obliged if you would wait little while."

"And why?"

"Because I am coming with you."

TWENTY-THREE

HARRIET didn't feel any misgivings until Don Roberto's fort came into view. Ah Wong had been openly unhappy about leaving the Vidries', but she had simply instructed him to load her baskets onto his horse and lead the way.

Mr. Giles, on the other hand, had been cynically amused. "I don't intend to go further than Don Roberto's fort," he warned her now.

Harriet was silent, studying the thick walls of the squat little fort and the bastions on the corners as they plodded down the slope towards it. Then she said, "And after that?"

"Down the muletrain road to Pueblo San Marco, and then by river to Sutter's."

"My husband didn't persuade you that Sutter's Fort is doomed?"

"Your husband the Colonel experienced little success in any of his persuasions last night."

"He was telling the truth, you know. The Embarcadero was under water and mud when I saw it last."

"Is that so?" Mr. Giles appeared to meditate. He rode a mule with his legs gangling down outside the stirrups, drawing a second mule along on a lead string. The mule he was riding was a most morose looking animal, and untidy and unkempt withal. To Harriet's secret amusement the animal and the man looked rather like each other.

Then Mr. Giles decided, "I'll see Sutter's for myself, I reckon."

"You've heard other reports, perhaps."

"All I know, ma'am, is that I believe what you said last night—that the future of Sutter's was highly recommended by folks who should know what they are saying. And I also know that a large crowd of men was waiting at Sonoma for passage up the river to Sutter's. And I also heard that there's a mighty crowd at San Francisco, waiting to get up the Sacramento, too. And I can look at a chart, ma'am, and half-way understand it, and the situation of Sutter's Fort seems sufficiently promising for men to want to settle it. So, until my mind alters, that is where I've concluded to set up my press."

Harriet looked at him thoughtfully. He and Don Roberto should have an agreeable conversation when they met, she thought, and she also thought that her purchase of the lot on the Embarcadero was looking less silly by the minute.

Then she looked back at the fort in its valley, and her mind stopped, while her body froze.

There was a cavalcade of men and mules and horses coming out of the gate of the fort. She could see the light spark off trappings, and see, too, the flag flying on one of the corner bastions that showed that Don Roberto was home. But the riders were not the Vidries. She knew that at once, because these men, while Spanish, were not at all showy … and the hairs were rising in warning on the back of her neck.

She reined in, scarcely aware of Mr. Giles's inquisitive look. The mule train looked tired, she thought. The animals' heads hung low, and their flanks were gray with the dust of heavy going … and yet it seemed that they were only just setting out on their journey. She wondered if the stop at the fort had been just a brief one, to allow the mules to drink and eat a little while the men drank, ate, and conferred with Don Roberto … about what?

225

Whatever it was, she was sure it wasn't good, that it could very well be evil—because the men were the Murietas.

To her great relief, they didn't come this way. Instead, they headed back over the bridge, and then along the broad muletrain trail towards Pueblo San Marco. Harriet heard distant shouts and whooping, and then they were round a bend and out of sight, taking the mules with them … mules that were carrying what?

She gathered her wits, clicked her tongue, and set her horse into a trot again. Ah Wong and Mr. Giles followed her down the track and through the gate of the fort. Echoes rattled off the walls as they clattered in over the cobbles.

Harriet slid down from the saddle, and looked about warily. The courtyard and stables were empty, but she could smell the manure and urine the mule train had left behind. The shadow cast by the block-shaped building in the middle was littered with straw and discarded papers and rags.

The place looked so neglected and deserted that she wondered if Don Roberto had gone with Frank Sefton, and forgotten to take down his flag before he left. But then, with a sudden clatter, the door of the house opened, revealing Don Roberto's comic figure.

He stared, rubbed his face, stared again, and exclaimed in consternated tones, "Mrs. Sefton! But your 'usband left a whole hour back, and he never said you was coming."

She said calmly, "There was a change of plan."

"What? What do you mean?"

"And I would like to speak with you about something that concerns me deeply."

He wavered. If she had come alone, or with just Ah Wong, he would have sent her away, she knew, but having Mr. Giles there as a witness made all the difference.

When Don Roberto very reluctantly led the way inside, Harriet followed. She missed a step in her surprise when she went into the first strangely empty room, and saw that Mr. Giles was staring about with some awe, too. Then they walked through an even vaster room that was furnished with just a billiard table and a dresser, and had a stairway at the far end.

"I ain't all primped up for callers," Don Roberto grumbled, and led the way up the stairs to a huge apartment that was as full of furniture as the downstairs rooms were empty.

Huge carved sideboards leaned against each other, their mirrors crooked, and there were carved wooden tables, too, one with a huge tarnished silver tray that held an assortment of pitchers and rows of dusty glasses. Harriet wondered where all this stuff had come from. Had it been looted from Spanish mansions during the past war? And how had Don Roberto got it all up here?

"One day," said Don Roberto, reading her mind, "I plan to turn this fort into a first-class 'otel."

Good lord, thought Harriet, and was reminded of Mrs. Marchant's swain, Mr. King, who had great prognostications for the hotel business. She saw that Mr. Giles was looking about with his brows high, too.

"And will do it," said Don Roberto, "when the alcalde business gives me time."

Harriet said nothing, being occupied with finding a place to sit. Dozens of large ornate chairs were stacked so tightly that she had to lift her skirts to clamber over one of them to find a seat on another.

Mr. Giles folded his frame onto a second carved chair, while Don Roberto bobbed about, muttering peevishly, as if to himself.

"Being alcalde ain't nobbut a theft of my time, I swear, and takes all my industry, too," he mumbled. "It ain't worth it, it ain't, not when other fortunes are a-beckoning. A doleful business, at the best. I'm all the time running about adjudicating crimes, hearing all the evidence, ensuring that the right reparation be made once I've made my decision, I am. Here, take this," he said in a louder voice, and handed a glass to Harriet and another to Mr. Giles.

Harriet took the tumbler absently, staring up at him as he continued his complaint. "You've not a notion how hard it is, and no mistake about it," he said. "Murder's bad, but claim jumpin' is the very devil, excuse me hard language Mrs. Sefton, but it makes me fair bad-tempered, that it does."

Harriet said nothing. She had just registered Mr. Giles's riveted attitude as he stared at his drink, and had had a look at the contents of her own tumbler. Like his, her glass was half full of murky water — *busy* water. Incredulously, she watched mosquito larvae tumble about in their dozens.

Then she heard Don Roberto say, "Just 'old it out a moment, excuse me."

Numbly, she held out her glass, and he produced a dark bottle and poured a liberal amount into the water, then did the same to Mr. Giles's portion. The contents of both tumblers immediately became frantic. The wrigglers all turned somersaults, and then, as one, they gave up the ship and sank to the bottom.

As Harriet watched, Mr. Giles lifted his glass, flicked an eyebrow, and took a swig. It did not seem to do him any harm, but nevertheless she put her tumbler on the nearest table, and returned her gaze to Don Roberto.

"Murder's bad, I admit it," he querulously repeated. He looked about and then planted his fat rump on a chair. "But when you got a corpse, at least you got a crime, motive, cause and effect, all lying there before your eyes. But claim jumpin'! I know you must feel bad about it, and want to 'ave your say, but what else can I do but take time to think over the evidence?"

Harriet frowned. "What does this have to do with me? Why would I have anything to say?"

"Well, I expect you feel bad on account of your brother, as I expect he rails enough about it, saying the claim were rightfully his, but how do I know that, when the tools and stakes was all throwed away?"

"Claim?" Her breath caught. "What claim?"

"Why, your brother's claim, of course. Ain't that why you say you want a word wiv me? The one at Gosling Gully, just two miles from Dry Bones Gulch, and the richest find so far this season. You saw the gold go out perhaps, on that mule train bound for the bank at Pueblo San Marco. A gratifyin' pile, wivout a doubt. My deputies dug out twenty thousand worth."

She blinked. "Did you say twenty thousand dollars?"

"All from just that one vein." The alcalde's tone was injured. He took a gulp of his own drink, and nodded at Mr. Giles, saying, "Perhaps you ain't heard of the system yet, sir, but when I get called in as alcalde to adjudicate on claim jumpin' offences, I get my deputies to dig out all the gold, and then stow it all safe in Colonel Sefton's bank, until the time I think I know the rightful answer to who owns that gold. It takes time, and we all get our percentages and fees, of course. Diggin' and panning's hard work, and so my deputies deserve to be well paid. But at least justice is done. and 'ow many east-side judges can boast of that, huh?"

Mr. Giles looked alert, as if he was on the verge of taking out a notebook, but Harriet scarcely noticed, because her mind was tugging at the coincidence. Twenty thousand. Sefton had offered her four five-thousand-dollar share bundles. Twenty thousand, the same amount that Don Roberto had been taken out of Royal's claim.

She said tensely, "You're telling me that the gold the Murietas are carrying into my husband's bank came from my brother's claim? That the Murietas dug it out after Royal's claim was jumped?"

"I don't say jumped, Mrs. Sefton, because that ain't proved," Don Roberto yelped. "There were no stakes or tools on that claim when the miners got there, and no notice neither, for they'd all been taken and throwed away."

"But surely the tools and stakes were there in the first

place?" she said acidly. "If men declare they were thrown away, then they also declare that those tools and stakes were there at one time."

He went red and shouted, "Oh, very clever, Mrs. Sefton, but dead bodies don't stake a claim, and in particular bodies what were not even lying on that place, and the Indians what stole the tools ain't even catched!"

Harriet's vision went dark. The room, most sickeningly, seemed to be swaying.

She whispered, "What bodies? What Indians?"

"Why, them Indians what invaded that ravine and massacred them two men! The folks at Dry Bones Gulch had only just learned that gold be struck there, and when they went to look they found them two corpses."

She cried out in agony, "What corpses? For God's sake, tell me."

"Two seamen what belonged to the brig *Gosling*. A Chilean and a Fayal man."

Pablo. Joseph Fayal. She said huskily, "Was anyone else hurt?"

"No, of course not. How could they be? The way your brother tells the story, the three of them was prospecting, 'im and the Spaniard and the Fayal man, and they turned up that rich find. So they staked and claimed it and he went back off to fetch the others from Bedstead Gully, leaving them two to work it while he was away. When he got back the murders 'ad been done and the ravine was all taken up, the Dry Bones Gulch people havin' moved in and taken their own claims."

She swallowed, calmed herself, and said, "So who was digging Royal's claim? Who are the men who jumped it?"

"I don't know if it had been jumped!" he shouted, puce in the face. "Don't you ever listen?"

She merely stared at him, and reluctantly, staring down into his glass, he said, "The men digging in the place that your brother reckoned was his was three of the Murietas, the same ones who be my deputies—but that ain't nobbut more than a coincidence. They 'ad it staked all legal, Mrs. Sefton, and they 'ad naught to do wiv the murders. Was definitely Indians what did that foul deed."

"Why Indians? What evidence do you have for that?"

"It had to be Indians, for the poor victims had been scalped."

"*Scalped?*" She shut her eyes as the room swung again. *The administrators of Sonora and Chihuahua pay a bounty for scalps…*

Pablo and Joseph had both had Indian-black hair. She opened her eyes, trembling, and cried, "How can you *bear* to hire bandits like the Murietas?"

"Because I 'ave to have deputies, Mrs. Sefton, and it ain't any use having men who ain't tough and not squeamish. The Murietas serve my purpose and it ain't no business of yours, ma'am."

Then he shouted, "What are you doing here?"

"What do you mean?"

"I thought you'd seen your brother, or someone had come out of Bedstead Gully now that it's open, but you knew naught of the gold, Mrs. Sefton, so why are you here with this newspaperman and your questions?"

She lifted her chin, and said sharply, "I've come to ask you about that land I bought at Sutter's, Don Roberto. I already know that you told my husband about it. Why did you do that?"

His eyes shifted, leaving hers. He shuffled on his seat and muttered, "If I'd known you was Mrs. Sefton I wouldn't have let you buy it, for all it was an excellent investment. It was your deception what done it, you can't say fair for one moment that you didn't deceive me about your married state. But Colonel Sefton would've found out anyway, even if I didn't tell him. And don't think for an instant that I didn't feel a proper fool for having sold a man's lands to his very own wife."

"What? The land was Frank's?" It was so unbelievable that she had to fight down hysterical laughter. Then she frowned, and said, "I don't believe you. You're telling lies."

"I am not!" he yelped. "It's the honest truth!"

"But it can't be. My husband would never own land at Sutter's. He tells everyone it's worthless. Ask Mr. Giles, if you don't believe me."

The little eyes were sliding around again, flitting over furniture and dust. Then he muttered, "Colonel Sefton did not get that land by purchase. It was collateral on a debt that Captain Sutter's son owed 'im, and the money never got paid back, so Colonel Sefton took the deed as was his legal due, and advised me at the same time to sell it, if I could."

Collateral. That word again. Harriet had the chance of twenty thousand shares in Sefton's bank, exactly the same amount as the confiscated gold—twenty thousand shares that Frank Sefton had taken away with him when he left her room. All she had to do was see Sefton again, and consent to sign his papers and take over those shares...

And then? She didn't know. Nevertheless, she stood up in a hurry, trying to hide her urgency.

Don Roberto saw her down to the courtyard. Mr. Giles didn't bother. He was down to the dregs of his glass and had declared he would try another before heading to Pueblo San Marco. The alcalde made no attempt at all to hide how pleased he was to be rid of her. He even helped Harriet mount her horse. Ah Wong, was waiting, already mounted.

It was all in such a rush that Harriet had led the way to the ranch-ward trail before she even noticed that the little Chinese man was sweating with what looked a lot more like abject fear than simple worry.

TWENTY-FOUR

HARRIET watched Ah Wong as they trotted along the hills and dales that led from Don Roberto's fort to her husband's ranch. At Don Manuel Vidrie's place he had usually followed her as she galloped ahead on her spirited horse, so she had never watched him as intently as this.

He rode far forward in his seat, crouched over the withers with his thin knees cocked sideways like a cricket, his pigtail pattering between his shoulder blades. Harriet had become fond of Ah Wong over the months, and not just because he, too, had been politely incarcerated in the Vidrie establishment. He was over-anxious and over-conscientious, and she still had a nagging feeling that she had disappointed him in some way, but she had found much pleasure in teaching him English, for he was such an apt and eager pupil. And, more than that, she had learned from him the strange enjoyments of Chinese poetry.

That poetry had taught her to look more closely at nature. Because of Ah Wong she had learned to look at California—pale spring sky, the misty horizons to late afternoon, the lines of dark purple pines on the gold-grassed slopes, the ethereal outlines of mountains. A skein of waterfowl flew high, flying north to the Siberian summer; perhaps they were the same birds she had watched last autumn in the Bay of San Francisco, flying in the other direction.

Six months, she thought, six months of loss and heartbreak and shame and waiting. She had changed, and so had California.

> *In ordered beauty, as the wild ducks fly*
> *Note follows note in melody*
> *The red-toothed plectrum plucks the strings*
> *Lily-like fingers hold the lute*
> *Delightfully, and in perfect accord, the new refrains*
> *Set to new melodies, echo among old pillars...*

Ah Wong's head did not turn, but she heard him whisper *Wan fu ... wan fu...* Happiness thousand fold. She often wondered about Ah Wong and his native land, for life, surely, must have been hard there. Otherwise a man would not have to search for *wan fu* in a string of ducks and a poem.

Ah Wong described his homeland's scenery as a never-ending tapestry of patches, centuries of landscape, made by generations of men and women who grubbed endlessly in the dirt of the Celestial Kingdom to keep that patchwork complete. Ah Wong had scrimped and saved and then sold something valuable to make up what seemed a pitiful sum of money to buy his way to San Francisco, the golden promise of a younger, less patch-worked land. She knew how harsh that scrimping had been simply by looking at Ah Wong's face. The shriveled little man she had thought was sixty had proved to be thirty-two.

He had paid that money to Sefton. It had been just a deposit. He had bonded himself as Sefton's servant for five long years, as the payment of the rest of the debt.

Harriet had often wondered if Ah Wong regretted that. Looking at him now, and his increased terror as they approached the ranch, she thought that he would have never made that bargain if he had known what lay ahead. Night was falling, the shadows swooping over the hills to touch them, evening mists rising from the river, and she heard Ah Wong hissing to himself as he jogged in his saddle, in a constant mutter of fear.

In the distance, over the other side of the river, she could see the town, the brig, the schooner moored at the embarcadero. Then night fell, and she could see the river no more. Ah Wong reined in under a tree. The gate to the ranch was a hundred feet ahead. Harriet reined in, too. When she looked at Ah Wong, she could see the drops of sweat gleam as they rolled down his cheek.

She said, "Ah Wong, what's the matter?" He did not answer. In the fields the goatsucker birds were calling. *Whip, poor Willy ... work, poor Willy, weep...* The house was dark and still. The air was scented with growing grass and early orange blossom.

Harriet tapped her heel on her horse's side, and the animal moved forward reluctantly. Then, from ahead, she heard whickering.

There were horses tethered there. She could smell their sweat, and hear the clump as one lifted a hoof, and the inquiring snort as one scented her steed. She slid down from the saddle and led her horse forward, round the corner of the garden to the path that led to the courtyard door. There, she found the other horses tied together under a tree.

There were four of them, with California trappings, high pommels on the saddles and broad stirrups made of wood. They were Vidrie horses; she recognized them instantly. And yet ... and yet the house was so quiet. Stealthy despite herself, she tethered her own horse, then opened the door in the side wall, the one that led directly into the courtyard.

The fountain rippled, and the leaves of the climbing plants whispered. Harriet stopped and listened — to male voices, soft and echoing from inside the house. They spoke in Spanish — the Vidries. She recognized the tones, but could not discern the words.

235

There was the same feverish excitement in their voices that she had heard around the arena where the bull and the bear battled for their entertainment. When she heard a step, her heart jerked, but it was only Ah Wong, come into the courtyard to join her. She began to speak—and heard his whine of utter fear.

She thought he was going to scream. His eyes bulged and his mouth opened wide, but only that whine of abject terror came out. His face in the faint light had gone as pasty as cheese and his mouth was still open, but all she heard was that sound of superstitious fear. She stared at him in bewilderment and pity—and Sefton's hand shot out of the shadows and gripped her arm.

He's behind you! She almost screamed herself. She had heard not a sound to warn her.

Frank's fingers bit into her arm. "What the hell are you doing here?"

Horrifyingly, Harriet's mouth was too dry for her to speak. She stared up at him. Sefton shook her hard, with fury, and he said, "Who brought you here? Surely not Ah Wong? He wouldn't dare!"

Ah Wong had gone, disappeared as completely as if he had never been in the courtyard. Belatedly, she heard the sound of his running feet. He had gone into the depths of the house. Then Harriet heard a giggle—Mei-Mei's teasing laughter. She had forgotten the pert depravity of the girl's laughter, and the sound gave her the strength of fury.

Harriet snapped, "It was not Ah Wong's idea for us to come here. He did not want to come at all, so please do not blame him. He merely obeyed my orders."

"Your orders—when he happens to be *my* servant?"

"And," she flashed, "I had an escort."

"An escort?" She saw his head turn towards the sounds of the Vidrie men and Mei-Mei, and she could feel his consternation, along with his anger. The fingers bit cruelly, and he hissed, "Who was your escort?"

236

"The journalist. Mr. Giles." Her voice came out more unsteadily than she would have liked. She was afraid, she thought, which made her more angry than ever. "I've come to sign your papers," she spat. "I've come to take your shares. What more do you want? I've come to sign your goddamned documents!"

She shouted the last sentence, unaware that her voice had risen. Then she heard the horrified hush in the room where the Vidrie men had been … flirting? … with Mei-Mei. She saw Sefton turn his head, too, and heard him mutter, "Giles. The reporter. Giles."

Then, silence, broken by Sefton's sharp intake of breath. Had he remembered where he had seen Giles before, perhaps? She didn't ask. Instead, she was forced to go with him as he moved in a rush, hauling her out of the courtyard and into the kitchen, along a back corridor to the room that had been her bedroom for that one night. He didn't want her to see the Vidries, she thought, and he didn't want the Vidries to see her. Then they were in her room, and Sefton let her go so abruptly that she stumbled.

Everything looked just the same as the dreadful night when she had first arrived. The fireplace was as cold. The furniture was just as black and huge. The same quilts were on the same canvas-bottomed bed. Steadying herself with a hand on one of the posts, she looked warily at her husband.

Forebodingly, he was smiling. She said very quickly, "Please do not punish Ah Wong. It was not his fault." But the cruel smile merely widened.

"I'm pleased you obeyed me, my dear, and have given more thought to my gift of the shares. Sleep well," he invited, his hand on the latch. "And we'll discuss the matter in the morning." Then, before she could move or say a word, he was gone. The door shut firmly behind him.

The room was dark, but she found a lamp, and managed to light it with trembling fingers. Then she slumped on the side of the bed, thinking that now, at this distance, the Vidrie mansion looked like a most comfortable prison.

The Vidries. Outside, she heard subdued voices, and then the sounds of horses being hastily galloped away. She didn't want to wonder what kind of entertainment she had interrupted. Every time the question entered her mind she pushed it away.

When at last she lay down, she fell asleep at once, more exhausted than she had realized. She dreamed uneasily of Pablo and Joseph Fayal and woke up with a start when she heard herself crying out Jake Dexter's name.

In the blackness, she thought she heard Ah Wong sobbing. She got out of bed and rushed to the door, but the door was locked.

Ah Wong brought her breakfast. He looked the same as always. Colonel Sefton was not in the house, he said. He had gone over the river to Pueblo San Marco, on bank business. Harriet thought grimly that she knew what the business was — the stowing of twenty thousand dollars' worth of gold.

After she had finished eating, she washed and dressed and went into the house, listening to the waiting silence. The rooms were all empty, and there was no sign of Mei-Mei. There was nothing to stop her ordering Ah Wong to have her horse saddled, and then riding with him back to the Vidrie place — nothing but the memory of the Vidrie men's excited voices. She couldn't ask Ah Wong to take her over to Pueblo San Marco, either, for Sefton was there.

She tried the door to Sefton's study, but it was locked. She went for a long walk, and then came back and ate another meal, and then, after sitting for an hour in the courtyard, she decided to try the door of Sefton's study again. She pressed stealthily on the latch — and it opened. It opened so suddenly that she gasped. Swinging wide, it revealed Sefton sitting at his desk.

To veil the gasp of fright, she said, "I didn't hear you

come back." Then, seeing what he was reading, she cried, "That book is mine!"

"Your book?" His voice was unstartled. "When I first saw you with it, I thought that perhaps it was a diary you had kept yourself, perhaps from the moment we met in New Zealand…"

"Did you indeed?" she said more calmly. She wished now that she had kept a diary in New Zealand, as she could have used it as a weapon, but didn't say it.

"But I see that it belongs to the brig *Gosling*. Perhaps you stole it, because it certainly isn't yours."

"I did not steal it!" Then, more quietly, she said, "It was loaned to me."

"By Captain Dexter, no doubt. But he wasn't the man who kept this journal."

Harriet pressed her lips together.

"So who, pray, was the man who wrote all this … and drew these maps?"

Still she did not reply, but it didn't seem to worry him.

Calmly, Sefton looked down at the book, his smooth hands turning one page after another. "I have read it with great interest," he said. "Such scribbles, so tantalizing, such a preoccupation with gold. Your brother told me that when you joined the *Gosling* the brig was at Judas Island, and the men were digging for treasure there. Pirate treasure."

She snapped, "That is nothing but rumor and gossip, and Royal had no right to tell you. He wasn't even there."

The blue eyes sharpened. "But you were, my dear," he murmured. "And tell me—was that treasure found?"

She shrugged. "There is no gold on Judas Island."

"So Judas Island does exist? It's not a figment of your brother's overheated imagination? Ah yes," he said, and his smile was sly as he watched her face. "I believe so indeed, even if the map is so ornately concealed. For I believe, dear wife, having read this journal with immense attention and interest, that this chart … this one, here … is of Judas Island.

239

Am I not right?"

Her skin crept. How did he know that? Sefton was clever, as she remembered uneasily. Had he heard of the treasure Captain Morgan had hunted, the gold from Panama that was rumored to have been carried away by the nuns? The memory of the skeletons in the pit the *Goslings* had uncovered was vivid in her mind. There had been wooden crosses among the tangled bones, and scraps of ancient black cloth.

She hid her feelings, shrugging again, saying nothing.

"And you were with Captain Dexter and his crew while they were searching for gold on this island?"

She snapped, "Many people have searched for treasure there, from the pirate Henry Morgan onward. For all I know, there may have been treasure, but if so, it was found and taken away a long time ago. There is certainly no gold there now. Why are you asking me these pointless questions?"

"Because this book intrigues me, my dear," he said, as smoothly as ever. "Perhaps the gold was so well hidden that no one has found it … that it truly is buried treasure. Do you think this book just might hold the answer to the puzzle of the whereabouts of that gold?"

The hairs on her forearms were rising again. She said sharply, "No, I do not. And if I did, it wouldn't signify. A man who wrote down the secret of the treasure would be the same man who dug it up. Why would he leave it there, if he knew where it was?"

"Why indeed," he agreed affably.

Then Sefton silenced. She watched him set the journal to one side, and lay out a little square of white paper. His expression was abstracted as he scraped tobacco and twirled the paper into a tiny cigaretto, and for some moments she wondered if he had forgotten she was in the room. Then he looked up, his eyes as sharp as ever.

Lighting the cigaretto, he leaned back in his chair, studying her through the acrid puffs of smoke. "So you have reconsidered and come to sign the papers and accept the shares," he mused. "Can it be that you see the economic sense of my gift at last? I don't believe it's because you can't bear to live away from me any longer."

His tone was taunting. She snapped, "I wouldn't give a damn if I never saw you again, Frank. Marrying you was the most lame-headed thing I have ever done. You fooled my father, somehow, and you certainly fooled me, and I may be a fool even now, to sign your papers. But I will sign them— on two conditions."

"What?" He looked thunderstruck, genuinely shocked. "You—you, my lawfully wedded wife, you, a woman—you dare to make conditions?"

She shrugged. "You seem very anxious to get rid of those shares, Frank. I'm completely at a loss to guess the devious workings of your mind, and I swore never to sign another paper of yours, because I suffered so much from signing those papers in New Zealand. But, I will sign for these shares, Frank—if you give me back the journal, and if you give me back the deed for that land at Sutter's."

He stared at her, his eyes veiled with thought again. There was definite menace in his expression, and for a moment she was aghast at her foolhardy courage. She kept her own stare level, however, and finally he said slowly, "I understand what you're saying, Harriet ... but I still wonder what made you change your mind about the shares."

She lifted her brows and spread her hands.

"And why the deed for that land?"

"After talking with Mr. Giles, I decided I hadn't made such a very terrible mistake when I bought that land on the Embarcadero at Sutter's."

"Giles!" The word was like a curse. He had definitely remembered meeting Mr. Giles before, she thought.

Then he snapped, "You're a fool."

"Am I? I don't believe so—and neither does Don Roberto. I know now that the deed was collateral on a bad debt, that it wasn't one of your own investments. You've told me repeatedly that the land is worthless — so giving me the deed is hardly a condition at all."

"No?" He stared at her as the silence dragged on. Then, so suddenly that she recoiled, he laughed. "And what are you going to do with the deed to this worthless patch of dirt?"

"I'll give it to Captain Dexter."

"And I'm not supposed to mind when you publicly shame me?" He laughed again, even more cruelly. "Do you really believe the good captain is going to build you a theater? What have you got left to sweeten the deal?"

"I don't know what you mean."

"Do you not? But I think I read your mind very accurately, my treacherous little bitch of a wife. I think you plan to escape me, now that the trail to Bedstead Gully is open, and the good captain can return to his brig. I think you want to make your adultery public."

"That's an evil, baseless slander!"

And he laughed. "You mean to tell me you haven't fallen into Captain Dexter's bed? You, an actress? Do it, my dear, seduce the poor fellow," he urged. "It's not before time. You should have found yourself a protector after you found yourself alone in New Zealand — I had every expectation that you would!"

She exclaimed, "*What?*"

"Ah, don't try to tell me that you, the sweet little ingénue actress that you were, didn't have plenty of offers. Well, you have left it very late, but it's not *too* late, so do it. Go across the river and take up your residence on the *Gosling*, seduce your captain, and flaunt your adultery. And … I may decide to be kind, and generous … and fulfil your heart's desire. I might … if I feel like it … sue you for divorce."

She shouted, "If there was justice for women in the world, I would be suing *you* for divorce!"

And the door opened, and Mei-Mei glided into the room.

Sefton's smile became warm, almost human. "Mei-Mei, my little Mei-Mei," he said lovingly, and beckoned, and she went over to him, and leaned on his shoulder, her tiny mouth pursed triumphantly at Harriet.

"My beautiful little ward," he said, caressing Mei-Mei's hip, her waist, her breast, and Harriet glimpsed adoration in his eyes. It was the same adoration that he had pretended to feel for her, back in New Zealand, but this worship looked real, as if her sadistic husband was genuinely besotted.

When he stopped stroking the girl to take the documents out of one of the drawers in his desk, the gesture looked reluctant. "Down to business?" he inquired.

Harriet took a deep breath to steady her voice, and said, "Of course."

She signed the papers, and took the shares. Then she looked at him again, and said, "And now the journal."

"Of course," he said, mocking her.

"And the deed."

"That, too." There was pitying derision in his expression as he handed them both over. Then he leaned back in his chair, his arm around Mei-Mei, his hand lovingly straying over her body.

He said, "And now, dear Harriet?"

For a moment she said nothing, because there was a horrible blank in her mind. One step at a time, she thought then, and said calmly, "In the morning I will go into Pueblo San Marco and deposit all these in a very safe place—your own bank."

"So wise, my dear," he said, and was still laughing as she turned and left the room.

TWENTY-FIVE

HARRIET was dreaming. She dreamed she heard horses and men moving about in the darkness outside her window. She dreamed she heard a distant scream, and woke with a jolt, sweating with fear, and realized that someone was in her room.

She leapt up in bed, her throat too dry to cry out. It was Ah Wong. He touched her shoulder with a shaking hand and said in a low voice, "Please come, please, please, come very quickly."

"Wh-what?"

"Quick. I beg you, do not talk. Please dress and come quickly, quietly."

The hushed plea seemed jerked out of him. She realized that his teeth were chattering with panic. Her own voice shaking, she whispered, "Wh-where?"

"Away, far away. Quick. Quiet. No time to pack."

She scrambled out of bed and pulled on a shift over the one she was wearing, grabbed two petticoats, put them on, hauled a gown over her head, and then put another on top of that. Then she added two shawls, and tied a third about her waist, before she hauled on her cloak.

It was like the times the family had fled from boarding houses in a hurry, wearing as many of their clothes as they could, to avoid a bill her father did not want to pay. Then she stuffed the shares, the book, and the deed into a cloth bag, added the wallet of lotions, salves, rouges, powders and creams that she, an actress, always carried, and slung the bag over her shoulder.

It had taken just five minutes. She whispered, "Where are we going?"

Ah Wong didn't answer. Instead he opened the door and peered out into the passage.

The corridor was dark. He seemed to stand there for ever, rigidly still, listening. When he moved, she tiptoed after him. She carried her riding boots, and with her other hand she held her skirts to stop them rustling.

They were halfway along the passage when voices echoed outside. She heard Ah Wong suck in a terrified breath. They both stood frozen, waiting, while Harriet listened to the thunder of her heart in her ears. Then the voices moved on into the garden. Ah Wong crept forward again, and Harriet followed him through the bare kitchen and into the courtyard.

There were horses under the same tree where the Vidrie men had tied their steeds, but these were not Don Manuel's. One snorted on an inquiring note, and Harriet heard Ah Wong's faint whine of fear. A fraught pause, and then he kept on moving, sidling through the dark, past the tree, along a hedge into the pool of shadow under an oak.

Again they froze. A loud voice had sounded from inside the house. Not Sefton—for Sefton was in Pueblo San Marco, but another man, one who spoke in Spanish. He came out of the house by the same door from the courtyard that they had used, and went over to the horses. He took down a saddle bag. It looked small in bulk, but seemed heavy. He was smoking a cigar. The end glowed redly when he puffed. Harriet saw his face. It was Joaquín Murieta.

He looked around, apparently straight at her. Her breath stopped in her throat, while she waited … waited. He didn't move ... didn't move—and then he turned and went back into the house.

With an almost unheard sigh, Ah Wong moved. Taking a steadying breath of her own, Harriet followed his shadow along another hedge to a barn, and then into the barn's interior. Two horses were there, already saddled. Ah Wong led them both out.

Ah Wong helped Harriet mount to the saddle, because she was hampered by her layers of clothing. It was not a side-saddle — she had to haul up her skirts so she could ride astride. Then Ah Wong vaulted up onto the other horse.

The sounds they made seemed deafening, but there were no shouts from inside the house. They walked the horses along the grass until the trail crested the first rise, and then they started to gallop. It was like the mornings on the Vidrie estate, except that Ah Wong was in the lead.

Ah Wong led the way upriver towards Don Manuel's holdings. Was he taking her to their old prison? Surely not— but Harriet had no chance to ask. Then he took a side trail, and the going became rugged. On into an unknown night they galloped.

After some hours Harriet's horse began to labor, but Ah Wong kept up the smart pace. He looked back every now and then, and Harriet could see his lips drawn back over his big teeth. She kept on looking over her shoulder herself, afraid she would glimpse men in pursuit, but the miles went by and the night was silent except for her panting and the snorting of the two horses as they pounded on.

Then the edge of the night was paling to gray. Dawn would soon be upon them. Ah Wong galloped faster, faster, as if he were in a race with the sun, and Harriet had to work hard to keep up. Then all at once they were zigzagging down a steep hill, and she could see the river and Don Roberto's fort.

When they reached a level place, about a hundred yards above the river, Ah Wong reined in his horse.

Harriet stopped, too, and looked at him inquiringly.

He looked back at her with beseeching eyes, and said, "Mrs. Sefton, please, I must ask of you to dismount."

"Here?" she said blankly.

"I must return with both horses, before ... before it is seen that you are gone."

"But you can't go back there!"

"I must."

"But surely ..." But he met her protests with a stubborn silence, just waiting, so in the end she gave in and slid down from her mount, landing hard because of her stiffness and her layers of clothing.

Leaning down, Ah Wong took the bridle from her. Then he galloped off without a word.

Harriet stood and watched until Ah Wong and the two horses were out of sight over the top of the hill. Then she turned, and walked down the slope to Don Roberto's fort. One step at a time, she thought. The muscles of her stiff legs loosened as she walked, but her thoughts remained uncomfortable, for she was so very worried about Ah Wong. Would she ever see him again? Tragically, she doubted it.

No one called out as she passed the big studded door in the wall of the fort, or hailed her as she walked across the bridge to the other side of the river. When she looked back she could see the first dawn breeze shake the flag on the corner bastion. She supposed that meant Don Roberto was home, but the fort was so silent it was easier to believe it was empty.

When she reached the other end of the bridge she turned left, instead of right. Without a glance at the well-worn muletrain road to Pueblo San Marco, she turned onto the trail that led to the mines. It was much narrower than the muletrain road had looked, and much more winding, but was easy to follow. The eager feet of men had marked it plain already, even though the season was only weeks old.

As it wound up into the mountains, and the sun rose in the sky, the going became more difficult. Harriet persevered doggedly … one step at a time. She was sweating and shivering by turns. It was icy cold in the shadowed clefts where she had to step carefully through rushing streams, holding up her layered skirts, and suffocatingly hot in the exposed ravines. Her cloak and her shawls were alternately a curse and a blessing, and her petticoats a constant cursed encumbrance.

Time passed … passed, and then she found herself creeping along first one cliff face, then another. She looked down, and gasped. Turning so her face was against the rock wall, she edged along sideways, hanging onto cracks with hooked, desperate fingers. If the wind gusted…

She swallowed and shuffled along faster, increasingly terrified, moving more and more quickly.

But instead of a gust, it was a blast of swallows that flew at her, flapping their little wings as they swept out of their burrows in the cliff and attacked her hands and face. Harriet shrieked. The tiny birds were like moths with claws.

She scrabbled for finger holds and screamed again as her nails tore loose. Little talons caught in her hair, and wings beat madly. Pins dislodged, and her hair pulled loose and stuck to the sweat on her cheeks and the tears of pain that were running out of her eyes. She sidled faster and faster, put one foot on a ledge that gave way—and fell, rolling, tumbling, shrieking with terror as she fell through empty air.

A sickening moment passed, and then—crash! She was caught by rough clutchings, which turned out to be the twigs and branches of a tall tree. She bounced, crashed down further, was caught and bounced again. Then her momentum stopped. The air was full of a resinous smell. She was suspended in a giant pine, partly in the hammock of her snared cloak.

The tree rustled—the world was full of the rustling of

the rough, tangy, springy pine branches, and her own loud sobbing. Her cheeks were sticky with her tears and her blood, and there was dust and pollen in her mouth. Her hair hung snaggled, and one of her shawls dangled like an exotic bird from a branch four feet above her. It was a long time before she could stand, let alone climb, but eventually her trembling eased just enough for her to move. She heaved herself up, grasped the lowest corner, tugged at the shawl and heard it rip. Then it came free. She fell another few feet when it came away, but when she was caught by another branch, she still had the shawl in her hand.

After another long while she managed to climb down the rest of the tree, and stagger away from her savior pine. It wasn't until she looked up ... up ... up, that she realized how miraculous her survival had been.

She couldn't bear to look at the high cliff. Instead, she turned and trudged on down the valley, though she did not have a notion where she might be, or if Bedstead Gully was anywhere within reach.

The ground under the trees was slippery with needles, and so the going was still not easy, even though the valley floor was level. At the next stream, she knelt down and drank thirstily, first to clean her mouth, and then because it tasted so good, like the best champagne. Then she stood up and marched on, one step at a time.

A long time later, at a widening in the trail, she stopped, amazed at the sight of people. There was a flat space at the side of the valley, about an acre in extent, and people were living there. Indians. They looked like the Indians who had lived further down the river, the ones she had seen from the deck of the schooner. Like those other Indians, these were just women and children. There were no men, she thought— but then she saw a few oldsters. And Davy. *Davy.* Davy Jones Locker. She stared a long disbelieving moment, and then rushed towards him.

He was sitting on the ground, watching some women

who were grinding a kind of flour and making flat cakes, which they baked on flat stones. The women were grinding acorns, Harriet saw with wondering pity. The acorns were blackened, having been roasted in a fire, and the women ground them up with rocks and sand. Other women took the dust they made, and put it into bowls of water, so that the sand fell to the bottom and the flour floated to the top. Then the flour was skimmed off, slapped into shape and baked. Harriet was hungry, but the smell as she approached was not good.

She stopped and said, "Davy?"

He took a long, long time to look up. When he did, the nape of her neck crawled, for his eyes were so blank. One of the women left her work and came and stood close to him, her manner protective. She had a board on her back, and a baby that looked about eight months old was strapped into it. The little bright eyes looked at Harriet inquisitively, but the baby made no sound.

Harriet said, "Davy, what are you doing here?"

He frowned. "I live here, mistress."

Mistress? That shiver touched the back of her neck again.

Harriet looked about the encampment. Like the river Indians, this tribe lived in huts that had been built over pits in the ground. The walls were built up with dried mud, and topped with a kind of thatch. That was all they seemed to have—the huts, the earthenware bowls, the baskets, and the acorns.

She looked back at Davy and said, "Where is Captain Dexter? And why are you here?"

Two questions, she saw, were one too many. Davy frowned painfully, and didn't answer.

Then someone touched her arm. Harriet jumped with surprise, and then saw that the woman with the baby was offering her a cake of the baked acorn flour. The other women had drawn away, and were gathered in a tight group, eyeing her. Was she the first European woman they had seen? Perhaps, she thought.

When she looked back at the girl with the baby the cake was being offered again, even more insistently. Harriet didn't want to take it, because these people looked so very poor, but she pulled off a small corner, to be polite. When she put it in her mouth it was gritty with sand, and almost impossible to swallow.

Then Davy said, "Bedstead Gully. That way."

He pointed up the trail. She said, "Captain Dexter is there?"

"Yes, mistress," he said. "You go."

He was smiling politely. Harriet stood for an uncertain moment, watching him, but then gave up and walked back to the trail.

Within ten minutes Davy and the camp were out of sight. At each stream she stopped and drank, but still there was sand in her mouth. She wondered what it must be like to live so poorly in this land with its promise of gold, and wondered if it was so very different from the life Davy had led on the slave plantation in Guyana.

The Indians, Davy even, became distant and meaningless, as her thoughts drifted in circles. She still had the bag hanging over her shoulder, and the book, the deed, and the share certificates, with her wallet of cosmetics, knocked every now and then on her back. She would give the book, the deed, and the documents to Jake when she found him … if she found him … and then … and then…

He would know what to do, she decided. The sun was at its zenith, but she was walking in the cold shadow of a long, narrow defile. Then all at once she found she was climbing a steep hill. It seemed to go up for ever, but she managed to claw her way to the top, and then she slid down the other side on her seat, cushioned by her petticoats and cloak. It was a long slide, but it was restful to sit down.

At the bottom, she stood up stiffly, and trudged on. The trail left the ravine, and wound about the trunks of trees and

251

outcrops of rocks. Then all at once she emerged from the shadows of a copse, and Bedstead Gully lay before her.

It was green, and very pleasant, overlooked by slopes of pines and oaks. There was a neat little log cabin in a clearing on a terrace on the side of a slope, and beside the hut there was a square corral, with four llamas grazing inside it, and there was a stream running through the bottom of the valley.

And Jake Dexter was standing knee-deep in the middle of the brook, pouring pails of water over his head. He was fully dressed and his clothes and hair and beard were streaming. Harriet stopped short in utter astonishment, and said, "Jahaziel, what the devil are you doing?"

Lowering the bucket, he turned and looked at her. "My God," he said. "It's Harriet. Now I know for sure that I'm feverish."

Then he looked down at the water he stood in, and clambered unsteadily out. He stalked over to her, and stood looking at her, and she stared back at him, and they said not a word. Then Abner came out of the cabin and came running down the slope to the stream, crying out. Jake Dexter turned his head at the noise, and that unbalanced him entirely. He sat down on the grass with a sudden bump, and his head slumped on his chest.

When Harriet felt his forehead it was burning with fever. He was very ill, she thought with horror. The realization that she had come so far just to watch him him die was terrifying.

She cried to Abner, "What's wrong with him?"

"Californian ague, miss, what they call mountain fever."

Abner was staring at her, his expression horrified at her appearance. But that meant nothing, because she was trying so hard to remember what she had heard about the Californian fever.

Abner then said, "I had it, too."

So he had survived. Thank God, she thought, for it

252

offered hope. Apart from the heavy beard that hid most of his herringbone scar, Abner looked much the same as she remembered.

But then he said, "And Jonathan had it too, before he died."

Oh God. "He died of the fever?"

"Yes. I woke up, and found his grave. Davy had buried him, before he went away, but he hadn't done a good job, and I could still see Jonathan's face, what the animals hadn't eaten. I covered him all up," Abner added.

Oh dear God. Harriet looked at Jake with dread. He was still sitting slumped. Despite exhaustion, she was abruptly filled with nervous energy.

With Abner's help, she got Jake up on his feet, and then they guided him up the slope to the log house. Inside, it was clean and cozy—just as expected, she thought wryly. Jake Dexter could be relied upon to build a shipshape house. There were shelves along the walls that served as bunks, and with Abner's assistance she managed to get Jake undressed and inside the bed roll that Abner said was the captain's.

Jake said nothing. Instead he watched her feverishly, every second of the time. Abner made up for his silence, for suddenly he found words, and oh, how he talked. "Davy was sick, too, but he got better enough to look after Jonathan and me when the others went away," he said. "Cap'n Dexter and Tib and Dan and Royal went off to the hills to the claim that Pablo and Joseph were digging, and left us with Davy to look after us, but then Davy got sick again, and Jonathan died, and when I woke up Davy was gone and Jonathan was half-buried."

He was babbling, Harriet thought, and sounded so young, so pathetically relieved to have someone to listen to his confidences, and take over his worries and fears. And Abner, Harriet thought wearily, was three or more years older than she was, the second mate of the brig.

"So why are you alone with Captain Dexter?" she asked.

253

"When he came back with the llamas, he found Jonathan dead and only me alive, because Davy was with the Indians. And he was all by himself because he said that Pablo and Joseph were dead, and the others had followed the alcalde to Pueblo San Marco, and that they would tell Mr. Martin what had happened, how we had lost our claim, and lost all our gold. He said the Company would give up on the hunting for gold, and so we was to pack everything up on the llamas and head back to the *Gosling*, so that we can get out of this godawful country and try our fortunes somewhere else, but he only found me, and Jonathan's grave, and then in the morning he was sick himself. And I didn't know what to do, Miss Gray!"

She said slowly, "I saw Davy at the Indian encampment. He wasn't in his right mind."

"Brain fever," said Abner, nodding wisely. "The fever burned his brain all up, and now he thinks he's an Indian."

Poor Davy. Harriet looked at Jake with more foreboding than ever.

His eyes were bright as he watched them talk. Now that they were silent, he said, "How did you get here?"

"Walked."

"But why?"

She tried to smile. Her mouth was still gritty with sand and her smile was stiff. Her whole body was stiff, for that matter, she thought.

However, she said lightly, "Perhaps I thought you might be sick and trying to medicate yourself out of your dreadful book. I've watched you medicate the men, you know." And sew them up, too, as he had sewn up Abner's cheek, so long ago.

She watched him smile and shut his eyes. He looked like a desperate stranger with his beard. She heard him say, "The same young Harriet. I think you came to argue."

Then his face smoothed out. She thought for a horrible moment that he had died, but when she touched him, he

254

was merely asleep. Then she envied him. She would have given her soul to sleep, but felt too tired to even sit down.

She looked around the hut. The floor was beaten earth, but it was swept clean, with old flour bags for mats. There was a hearth made of stones, with a fire burning and a wire spit over it, and pots and pans hung from wire hooks on the wall to the side. The cabin looked very well used, with the smoke-smudged roof of a long, cold winter, but well tended, too.

Then she heard Abner worrying on again. "The captain said that Pablo and Joseph were murdered, Miss Gray. They were working the mine of gold they had found, and the captain and the others went to help them, but when they got there they found them dead. Murdered. He said it is time to give up, that the gold is not for us. That we should get out of this godawful country. Is that right, Miss Gray?"

His face mutely begged her to tell him it was wrong. She sighed, and said, "I didn't know about the decision to give up the hunt for gold and leave California, but the rest is right, I'm afraid."

"Jonathan's dead," he said for the dozenth time, after sadly shaking his head, and then he took her outside to show her the grave.

Jonathan's name was written in charcoal on a board at the head, and Abner told her he had done it. Harriet stared at it with sore, dry eyes, remembering the lanky, true-blue Yankee, and how he had told her he was making a fortune so he could marry his Mary-Jane. She wondered if Mary-Jane still waited back in New England, unaware that her swain was dead.

When she went back inside the cabin, Jake was still asleep. To escape Abner's revolving conversation she went upstream, stripped, and bathed, and washed the gown she had worn on the outside, along with her outside petticoat and the inner one of her shifts.

She felt a little better with the dust gone, but even more

255

troubled in her mind about Jake, because the water was so very cold. Shivering, she put on the shift that had been on the outside, and the petticoat that had been on the inside, and the gown she had worn on the inside over that.

Then she hung her laundry over bushes, and went back to the cabin. Sun set behind the long purple mountains, and Abner lit a lantern and cooked bacon and flapjacks while Harriet read Jake's sea captain's medical guide.

The book held many suggestions for the treatment of agues and fevers, but she did not have gelsemium or aconite root, or even know what they looked like. There was no quinine in the chest. The little bottle was empty. When she looked up helplessly, Abner told her that Captain Dexter had boiled spruce tips and added molasses to make a medicinal tea, so she made some.

When Jake woke they gave him some tea and coaxed him into eating a little, and then, to Harriet's relief, both Abner and Jake went to sleep. Gratefully, she lay down on a bunk on top of her spread cloak, with one shawl as a blanket and another folded to make a pillow. She meant to think, but fell instantly asleep instead.

She was wakened by a voice. For a confused moment she thought it was Ah Wong and she would have to start escaping again. Then she remembered where she was, and realized that the voice was Jake's. She fell off her shelf and stumbled over to him.

He said, "Harriet?"

"Yes." She groped about in the light of the embers, built up the fire, and found the tea. Jake drank it thirstily, but when she took the cup away he held her other hand. His fingers were hot and dry and he would not let go. Finally she set down the cup and sat on the floor by his berth, and reached out for the shawl she had used as a blanket and dragged it about her shoulders, holding onto his hand all the time.

He mumbled, "I thought you were a dream."

"No, 'tis I, Harriet, myself, me, complete with bumps and bruises."

She heard the ghost of a chuckle. Then Jake was quiet. She thought he slept, but he would not let go of her hand, so she leaned her tired head against his side, and drifted off herself.

In the night he whispered, "Why didn't you tell me you belonged to another man, Harriet?"

She thought about it. She could hear the slow bump of his heart, and feel his warmth against her cheek. Her eyes were too heavy to open. It took a long time to wake up enough to answer. Then she said, "Because I didn't feel as if I did, Jahaziel."

He said nothing. Perhaps, she thought, she had dreamed it. She went to sleep again, and slept all the way through to a stiff and cramped morning.

TWENTY-SIX

Jake woke when she tried to tug her numb hand away. His green-brown eyes were bright, but not with fever. The improvement was astounding. As she thought ironically when she checked him over, he seemed to be in a great deal less pain than she was.

He ate a small breakfast, and then he ate a much larger midday dinner after sleeping the morning through. Then, instead of going back to sleep, he asked that the cabin be made a little more tidy, please. That offended Abner, because he had taken such pains with the hut while Captain Dexter was sick, and he muttered and grumbled endlessly while he swept and scrubbed.

To escape him Harriet went out and checked her washing again. At last it was dry, so she stripped off the dirty clothes she still wore, bathed again, and washed the dirty gown, petticoat and shift. Then she washed her hair, and sat in the doorway of the cabin in the hot, late sunlight until it was dry, aware of Jake Dexter watching her. Then, at supper, Jake ate ravenously, and complained about the food with each and every mouthful. Obviously, the man was getting better at a tremendous rate, Harriet thought rather tartly, and was glad when he went to sleep after drinking yet another mug of spruce tips tea.

Jake was just the same at breakfast, just as hungry and just as tetchy. "Do you think he'll be well soon?" said Abner.

He and Harriet were cutting grass for the llamas. "Not quite well enough to walk out yet," she said. "But well enough for me to nurse on my own."

She looked at Abner thoughtfully, and then she said, "Do you think you could find your way back to Pueblo San Marco? And tell Mr. Martin what has happened? He will need to send a party here, to pack the llamas and close down the cabin. Do you think you can do that?'"

"Of course, Miss Gray," he said, and looked insulted. Then he thought again about what she had said. "But would you be able to manage, with just you and the captain?"

"I think so."

"What about the Indians?"

"I'm not afraid of the Indians," she said, and pushed the thought of the Murietas out of her mind.

"What about other miners?"

"You told me Bedstead Gully is all worked out."

"Yes, but…"

She knew what was in his mind. There were new gold seekers coming in all the time, and a girl and a log cabin could look enticing, particularly when their only protection was a convalescent man.

However, she said, "I'll be fine."

Abner didn't look convinced, but finally he said, "Shall I head off in the morning, then?"

She nodded, and said, "When you get back to the brig, would you do me a favor?"

"Of course, Miss Gray."

"Across the river from the pueblo, there is a ranch, owned by Colonel Sefton. It's easy to get there—there's a ferryboat, and then a track over the hill. It's not far—and there is a man who works at the ranch … my Chinese servant, Ah Wong. It would be a good idea to take some friends with you for protection … to check on him … and if he seems to be in danger, bring him back to the brig."

"In danger?" Abner looked a lot more interested.

"Yes," she said, and nodded emphatically, but without explaining.

Then she wondered if she should give him the deed and share certificates, to hand on to Charlie Martin or Bodfish for safe-keeping, but thought of the incoming miners again. They could include bandits, she thought, which scotched that idea.

Abner collected together what he could carry back to the brig, and was ready at dawn. Jake was asleep still, so she went with him as far as the place where the boulder had fallen, and then stopped and watched him climb.

It was a long way, and he was far above her by the time he reached the top. Then he turned and waved. Abner, despite his doubts, was glad to leave, she thought. She wondered nervously if she should have kept her silence about Ah Wong, because of the risk that Frank Sefton would find out that she had taken his cynical advice and gone to Bedstead Gully. But her worry about Ah Wong wouldn't have allowed her to keep silent, not when she was so certain he was in danger.

Then Abner disappeared down the other side of the hill. Her head down, Harriet trudged slowly back to the cabin, to find Jake Dexter waiting impatiently.

He had been awake for hours, he said. He wanted to know where Harriet had been. But then he didn't seem interested in the news that she had sent Abner back to the brig, frowning at her instead. She gave him more tea, and fed him more food, but he didn't go back to sleep. Instead, when she sat on a bench out in the sun, he came and sat beside her.

The beauty of California surrounded them, roofed by a warm spring sky. Pines wafted pollen and tangy scent, and birds caroled in the oaks. The brook babbled as it ran through the holes that had been mined last season, and Jake grizzled and grumbled about the food he had eaten, the tea she forced him to drink, and the aches in his rapidly mending body.

Then, mercifully, he went back to his bed roll and back to sleep, and smiled as he slept. Harriet surveyed him with weary fists propped on her hips. She'd forgotten how much she loved him, she thought wryly, and went to the stream to fetch water for the llamas. They were very tame, nibbling grass from her hand, and clicking and humming when she talked to them, waving their long lashes attentively as if they were trying to understand. They were much nicer company than Jake, she decided, and hoped that when he woke he would be in a better mood.

But when she got back he was awake and as tetchy as ever, demanding that she shave him. His beard itched, he complained, and made him feel dirty.

Harriet, feeling martyred, fetched more water and set it on the fire to boil. When she mixed the lather her fingers hurt where the nails had torn and rocks had scraped off skin. She concentrated on the pain and her irritation, to avoid the weight of Jake's attention as he sat on the bench and watched and waited. She wondered if he had any idea how tired she felt.

The shadows were growing long, the late afternoon cooler. Birds gave long crying calls, unlike the bird chatter of full daylight, and their solitude weighed on her mind. The long rows of blue mountains seemed to watch as she sharpened scissors on the neck of a bottle, and then inspected the bushy brown beard, kneeling upright in front of Jake.

He frowned at her. Only the crooked brows and the bright brown-green eyes were familiar. Otherwise, he looked like a bear, she thought. To match his mood.

Leaning forward, she clipped carefully. She could feel his breath on the back of her hand. The scissor handles bit into the sore cuts on her fingers, and she was glad when she'd removed enough to start shaving. She brushed on the lather, twirling the soap into fluffy peaks and valleys, and then she stood and went behind him.

His head leaned back, pressing into her waist. It was years since she had shaved a man, and that man had been her father. And shaving her father, she mused wryly, had not been like this.

She scraped slowly and very carefully, afraid of cutting him. It felt strange to see the familiar creases reappear as she stroked hair and soap away. She stretched the skin with the tips of her fingers to get at the creases, gently smoothing his cheeks straight, and wondered if he was enjoying this. Other men, she thought tartly, paid to be shaved, and seldom had the privilege of being shaved by a woman.

To her ironic amusement, when she had finished, and went around the front to inspect her work, he complained. Instead of bothering to thank her, he grumbled. She had taken too long, she had made his face stiff. Good lord, she thought, and leaned forward and shut him up with a kiss.

She felt the lurch inside him. Then he jerked back as if he'd been struck. It was an instinctive rejection—a rejection that hit hard, far more cruelly than the impulsive kiss warranted.

Harriet looked around quickly, grabbed the shaving bowl, and fled to the stream. She heard him calling, but ignored it, and it was a long time before she returned to the cabin.

TWENTY-SEVEN

THE atmosphere was just as strained next morning. Jake was much better, but quieter, too, and neither of them made any comment. He dressed and washed and shaved himself without a word, while Harriet made breakfast. When she fetched more wood for the fire, he silently helped her, and when she poured coffee he took the mug with only a nod of thanks. Then she went upstream to bathe, and wash more clothes.

Jake stood in the doorway, watching her go, watching the slim figure hungrily. He had forgotten the way her hair tangled and caught the sunlight, the twinkle in her dark eyes, and the sparkle in her smile. She had changed, become older and more wary, he thought.

Then he thought, no, because this was the same Harriet who had boarded his brig at Judas Island, tricked off the *Humpback* and onto his ship by the dishonest Captain Smith, who had taken her money, and then decided to get rid of her. She had the same hungry, careful look, like a waif who dreaded what life would throw at her next. All these months he had remembered the carefree Harriet, the Harriet who had loved life on the brig, and had teased him to distraction all the way from Valparaiso to Tombez, but this Harriet belonged to an earlier time.

Reunion with her husband had not been good for her. Jake wondered where Sefton was, and whether he knew that Harriet had come to Bedstead Gully. He thought of the scratches on Harriet's arms and face, and the way her nails were torn and her fingers scraped. Her appearance was a testament to the ordeal of her journey to join him, but he'd welcomed her like a grudging miser, parsimonious with his welcome and his questions because he remembered her husband the whole time. Jealousy had torn inside him, and that kiss had been like mockery.

He stood looking around, at a loss to know what to do. The cabin was tidy, the way he liked things, the way he liked his brig. Something tiny gleamed on the floor. He bent and picked it up, and it was one of Harriet's hairpins. Even here, he thought miserably, he was collecting her pins. He turned it over in his fingers, looking at it, such a simple thing to mean so much, a mere scrap of wire that would stop in her hair so much longer if someone put a crimp in it. Then he put it in his pocket with all the other pins he had collected.

Her shawl was crumpled in the corner by the head of the shelf where she slept. Harriet, he mused, was not tidy. He picked it up to shake it and fold it, and found a cotton bag underneath. The bag had a strap, designed to go over her shoulder, and as well as her wallet of cosmetics it held objects that were hard and rectangular. He hesitated no more than a moment before tipping the bag over her berth.

First came the wallet, a pretty embroidered wallet that held her potions and creams, and he smiled involuntarily to think how feminine that made her seem. Then that old pirate Schouten's logbook fell out. Jake had almost forgotten poking it into the basket she had left behind when he had sent her off to Sutter's Fort. Why had he done it? To remind her of the good times they had shared, he thought. Now he opened it greedily, because it was so long since he'd turned the pages of this book.

It fell open naturally at the map of Judas Island. The light from the door fell across it, lighting up faint grooves. Jake cursed softly, anger rising. Someone had made a tracing of that map, he was sure of it, and instinctively he knew, beyond doubt, that it had been Sefton. Her husband. Harriet had betrayed the secret of the Panamanian gold … the treasure on Judas Island.

Then he looked at the documents that had been in the bag with the book, and the fury overwhelmed him.

Sefton had sent these, he knew it. The deed to the land at Sutter's was another taunt—undoubtedly because Jake had never cashed in that note for one thousand dollars. And the share certificates—in Sefton's bank!—added up to exactly the value of the gold that had been dug out of Royal's lost claim, according to Don Roberto's estimate. Jake dropped the papers as if they stung, and ran off after Harriet, stumbling in his rush, furiously determined to have it out with her—to make her listen to his accusations.

Harriet was out of sight, but he knew which way she had gone. He stumbled again, but didn't pause to think that it was because he was still feverish. The ground was pocked with holes, ferns and grasses springing up to hide them now the miners were long gone, and that was reason enough for stumbling. Then Jake was in the trees; he was shoving his way through undergrowth.

He swore as he shoved through, only vaguely aware that he had strayed off the path. It was like his delirium. A briar swiped across his eyes. He shouted Harriet's name, "Harriet, damn you!" —and heard her answering cry of fear.

Then the roar, the hungry roar. A bear. A grizzly, just out of hibernation. Oh God, that terrible snorting roar. Jake's gun was back at the hut. He ran faster, not back, but forward, crashing through the thicket. Branches sprang at his face, snarled his clothes, and then he burst into a clearing and saw the bear.

It was huge. It filled his vision. It reared on its hind legs, high above him, standing on top of a great boulder, just like the nightmare bear that had trapped him in Bedstead Gully. Its shaggy hide hung in rank folds, and the light struck on the great claws and jagged teeth. When it bellowed, the roar was deafening.

Harriet was below the beast, facing it, frozen with terror. Jake shouted, "Run!"

His cry was hoarse, feeble in his ears, and his legs felt heavy. He seemed unnaturally weak, held down by nightmare, his feet mired as he tried to run.

Harriet didn't move—she seemed deaf, or paralyzed. Then at last Jake managed to hurl himself forward, and his fingers reached Harriet. He bore her with him in a crushing fall, over and over and into the edge of the undergrowth.

The bear plunged off the boulder, and roared in pursuit, swiping at branches as it came. Jake scrambled to his feet, hauled Harriet up with him, shoved her into a stumbling run. She ran zigzag, her hair flying out, seeming as dazed as he felt. The bear snorted at Jake's heels. Harriet turned her head and screamed. Jake saw the panic in her eyes. Then she stumbled and fell headlong—and disappeared into a hole in the ground. Ferns parted and she was gone, with scarcely a sound.

Jake roared, "Oh God, no, oh God!" and fell after her. His boots shot out from under him. He fell in a series of crashes. His legs and shoulders hit stones, ferns, bracken, dirt, while ferns sprang back over his head, hiding the top of this seemingly endless tunnel in the growth.

The bear bellowed from above. Jake frantically turned over onto his back as his fall crashed on, and he saw the bear's shadow overhead. He smelled the beast's rank smell, and heard the thunder of its inexorable pursuit.

Then, all it once, it was gone. It had blindly vaulted the top of the hole and kept on going.

And then, while Jake was still trying to comprehend that the pursuit had stopped, he landed on top of Harriet, and came to a stop.

He shook his head dazedly, and rolled over and looked down at her. The light filtered green and pale gold into this cleft in the scenery, and illuminated her furious expression. There were tears running down her cheeks.

He said huskily, "Oh Hat, are you hurt?"

"Of course I'm not hurt! And don't call me Hat, I hate it."

"Then what's wrong?" he said.

"Nothing. Everything." She began to sob loudly, and then she wailed, "Jake, everything has gone wrong, and I don't know what to do!" So he kissed her.

Her mouth was open, moist. She was still panting from the chase, and he could feel her heat. She wanted him, he was abruptly sure of it. Harriet was shaking violently, so he held her tight, hugging her close while his hands moved of their own accord, pulling away fabric, searching, cupping. He thought he heard a cry of protest, so he kissed her again, a kiss of mindless hunger, thrusting his tongue into her mouth.

His hands moved faster, faster, greedily. Her petticoat and skirt rustled like desperate leaves. Then her skirt and petticoat were all up in a heap, and he was on top of her, squirming between long, endlessly beautiful legs. Another cry, another mouth-stopping kiss, and then the blood was pounding in his chest, hammering in his ears, so all he could hear was his own pounding need. He thrust, missing, and then with a jolt of sensation so brilliant with delight that it hurt like a pain he found his mark and entered the tight, hot flesh, thrusting, thrusting for ever.

Then he stopped, buried to the hilt, tight against her. Oh God, such exquisite vanquishment, such piercing delight. Jake stilled, shivering, lost in pleasure, his entire being concentrated in the damp heat where their bodies merged, where he possessed Harriet. He kissed her and her cheeks were wet, so he kissed and licked her tears, nibbling at the

267

salty tracks as she squirmed frantically against him and he held her tight. Then mounting pleasure necessitated another thrust, the slow suspense of drawing out and then the triumphant lunge. If she had cried out, he would not have heard it, if she had been dying he would not have been able to stop. The delight was unendurable. He yelled out wildly, and then one last thrust, too soon, too soon … and he foundered in unstoppable crisis, spending for ever and ever.

Then, slowly, he came to his senses. Harriet lay still and rigid beneath him, as still as death, her eyes shut. Her face was so white and shocked that he could see the pink of the scar on her cheek where Joaquín Murieta had once cut her, along with the more recent, redder, scratches.

Jake moved back, and said numbly, "Oh God."

"Please…"

"That was…" He stopped, unable to find a word to match the terrible, despicable thing he had done to her.

Then, when he thought of the word, he couldn't bear to say it. He rolled away, sat up, and and stared bleakly up the green cleft in the ground, thinking that one awful word over and over, knowing that he had committed it. He had committed the same crime that the foul bandit, Joaquín Murieta, had had in mind when he had attacked her with a knife. An eagle floated in the mile-high blue, and at that terrible moment Jake envied the bird.

He said numbly, "I have no excuse."

Her voice was toneless. "You don't need an excuse. You're a man."

Oh God. "But I knew you were married."

"Please don't blame yourself," she said bitterly. "My marriage died the night of our wedding."

He watched her as she arranged her crumpled clothing, making herself decent. She moved stiffly, as if her body hurt, but even when wounded he thought she was beautiful—so beautiful that he couldn't believe her.

He said jealously, "Your husband would say different."

For the first time she looked at his face. She frowned and said, "What do you mean?"

"I imagine Sefton will be furious, when he finds out you came to Bedstead Gully. Naturally, he will believe you have betrayed him — humiliated him. He is your *husband*, for God's sake! He's the man who had every right to reclaim you, when he found you had come to California!"

He could hear the blackness in his voice, the rage and longing he had lived with for so many months. Then he saw Harriet's eyes widen incredulously.

"I'll tell you how much he wants me," she spat. "Oh, he put on a good show, but underneath he was furious that I came to California — I was an embarrassment! He has a mistress who can do everything I can, and entertain his friends as well. He sent me off to live with those friends — for months I lived with them, and was an embarrassment there, as well. Then, when I came back to his hacienda, he told me to get out and live in sin — with you. If my adultery was blatant enough, he said he might do me a favor and sue me for divorce."

"*What?*" Anger rose again, and he exclaimed, "Is that why you came to Bedstead Gully? He sent you here to *seduce* me?"

With a sick lurch, he realized what he had said, and wished he had cut out his tongue. He hoped, with fierce grief, that she would refuse to answer, or lie, or shout at him. He stared at her white face in silent entreaty, and saw her eyes shine with bleak pain.

She said very calmly and clearly, "Yes, that is exactly what he advised, and I, like the fool that I am, thought that you might want to go along with the idea."

Jake flinched. He said bitterly, "And is that why he sent those shares along with you — and the deed to that land?"

Harriet stared. She said, her tone bewildered, "But he didn't send them along, I brought them of my own accord. How did you find them, Jake? Were you looking through my things?"

He didn't reply—he couldn't. He numbly watched as Harriet brushed herself down with sharp, angry movements.

"If you found them, Jake, why didn't you look at the documents properly while you were at it, and see that my name is on each and every one? Those shares are mine, Jake, they were gifts to me from Frank, and I signed for them. I had sworn never to sign anything of his ever again, but when I heard that you had lost that gold ... oh, damn it," she said. Her voice was weary. "And no doubt you didn't want the deed to the land, either, and Schouten's journal was yours to start with."

She turned her back. She was crying, he thought, but she had turned her back before he was sure he had seen the tears. "He hates me!" she cried, without turning. "The first night of our wedding was a nightmare, but the second night was even worse—because that was the night he told me in detail how much he loathed me. And then, though I tried to stop him, he ... he took me, he possessed me. By force. Without love, without tenderness, without asking. So now you have the whole story, Jake, and I hope you're happy!"

His mind staggered with the shock of what she was saying, trying to comprehend it, so he didn't move as she scrambled up the tunnel to the light, but watched her numbly instead. Her husband had *raped* her? And he... *oh God, what have I done?* When he tried to call her back, it was too late. Harriet was gone. He knew when she reached level ground, because he heard her begin to run.

He followed her slowly, marshalling his thoughts into arguments so he would know what to say when he arrived at the cabin. The trees rustled about him but he gave no thought to the bear. He wondered what Harriet would be doing when he arrived. If she was grimly setting about domestic tasks, they could go back to the awkward silence, until he found the courage to say ... to say... But it would be so much better if she were weeping, because then he could, with all honesty, take her into his arms, and comfort her, and say *Oh God, Harriet, I love you so much, I have been so goddamned jealous, I think at times I am out of my mind...*

He was prepared to find her angrily silent, and he was prepared to find her in tears. What he was not prepared for was to find she wasn't there. He looked about incredulously, and everything she had brought with her was gone. The cabin was as clean and vacant and tidy as if she had never come. He swore in a mutter, and then desperately launched himself into a run.

He caught up with her on the path to where the boulder had fallen. She had got *so far*, in such a short time. She was wearing all the clothes she had brought with her, and her oddly bulky figure was walking determinedly up the trail.

He stopped beside her. She turned her face away and kept on walking so he ran around her and stopped in her path. She halted. He said grimly, "Where are you going?"

"To Don Roberto's fort, for a start."

"Why Don Roberto?"

She sighed. "It's only a start."

"But the trail—"

"I've walked that trail before, Jake, and survived it."

So she had. He thought about her torn nails and the scratches on her arms and loathed himself.

He shouted, "You're not bloody well leaving me, Harriet—"

And saw the men come into sight. Abner was at the front. Behind him were Tib and Dan and Royal. Abner must have met the others on the way to Pueblo San Marco, he thought. Then Jake felt Harriet push past him. She ran to her brother and took his arm.

The jealousy took hold again. It took him a moment to calm himself and move, and by the time he was up to them Royal had his arm about Harriet's shoulders.

Royal was saying to his sister, "Hat, what the devil are you doing here? Sefton told me that you were staying with

271

the Vidries."

She said without expression, "Oh, I left them."

"And came here?"

"In a manner of speaking."

Puzzled, Royal stared at her, and then turned to Jake. He said, "What the hell is going on here?"

Jake made no movement, and kept silent. He was standing with his legs and shoulders braced.

Royal looked back at Harriet. He said, "But what about your husband? Surely you ain't left him?"

Harriet paused. After a moment of deep thought she said, "I think the right word would be *escaped.*"

Jake's belly cramped. Royal said, "For God's sake, Hat! What do you mean?"

Harriet said nothing, simply shrugging.

A long moment, and then Royal sighed. "Jake Dexter and I, we were worried," he admitted. "We discussed you much. We wondered about that business in New Zealand, how you've been alone since Father was killed." He waited, and when she did not respond, he said with concern, "You're shivering, Hat. Are you well?"

Still, she did not answer. Jake watched her turn her head and meet his eyes, her expression remote.

Finally she said, "It was a bear, that's all. A bear chased me."

"A bear? My God! Hat, no wonder you're shaken. Are you all right?"

"I'm fine," she said.

Tib, Dan and Abner had their hands on their guns as they stared at the hill-tops and the trees. Tib said, "Was it after the llamas?"

"No. The llamas are fine."

Royal looked at his sister, and frowned and said, "Hat, you seem so strange. Were you hurt?"

"I'm fine," she woodenly repeated. "Jake chased the bear away."

Jake shifted, uncomfortably aware that Tib, Dan, and Abner were regarding him with expressions of deep respect. Royal, by contrast, was frowning. He opened his mouth, but Harriet forestalled him, her voice holding intonation at last.

"Royal," she said with obvious urgency, "when did you last see Frank?"

"Three days ago, in Pueblo San Marco."

"Three days! And he didn't tell you—"

"I didn't have much chance to talk. He was preoccupied enough with bank business, in and out of his vaults with his ledgers in his hand. My God, though," Royal went on, suddenly looking animated, "the whole town is so busy and alive-oh! God's thunder, Jake, just wait until you see it!"

He was as lively as if he'd never lost the richest claim this season, as if he had not found his sister in this very strange situation, as if she had not been chased by a bear. And Tib and Dan were grinning, too.

Puzzled by the abrupt change of mood, Jake demanded, "What are you talking about?"

"The town is full as a boot with adventurers, Jake! Men are paying small fortunes to come upriver from 'Frisco, and right now the Pueblo is bulging with men with nothing better to do but drink and fight and gamble, while they get set to trek into the hills. They're all on the hunt for fun and entertainment. It is a nipping and an eager air, by God! I tell you, Jake, this Californian gold rush is fated to be the greatest adventure yet! It's the Crusades all over again, but without the restrictions of piousness and religious pretence."

And without the restrictions of law, Jake meditated, Don Roberto being nothing than a legal bandit. With a growing sense of dread, he said, "And how do they fare on the brig?"

"Oh, good lord, Cap'n" said Tib. "You won't believe it." He winked at his captain, and poked a gleeful finger at the sky. "We may have lost our good vein of gold, wasted a winter and lost good men, too—but good lord, sir, how they make up for that on the *Gosling*."

"What are you saying?" said Jake. Every suspicion was alive.

"Why, they are making a fortune, sir," said Dan. He shook his head, grinning. "They're reaping a fortune, sir, and in the merriest way possible, too."

Dire forebodings were growing with every ebullient word. He should never have left the *Gosling*, Jake realized. Charlie Martin was a fine seaman, but … And Valentine and Crotchet … whom he would never have left in town by choice … were flighty-headed and silver-tongued.

He said sharply, "I hope the boarding business is going well."

"It's not going at all, sir, and that's the wonder of it!" Tib exclaimed. "They don't need no boarders, sir, and better still we've made up for all our lost gold! All that and more! And all on account of the café-restaurant."

"The *what*?"

"Abrigo's, sir. Crotchet won the place in a monte game, after the Company staked him for the gamble, and he and Valentine have been running it ever since — with Bodfish's help, of course. And that little gambling house has proved to be a goldmine, sir, business being so booming."

"Oh God," said Jake.

TWENTY-EIGHT

THE whole of Pueblo San Marco was, it seemed, crowded into Abrigo's gambling house, now owned by the *Goslings*. Though the evening was unseasonably chilly, the café-restaurant was remarkably hot, packed by more than a hundred men. Some played, but many more watched.

The atmosphere of anticipation was palpable. Valentine kept on glancing questioningly at Crotchet, but Crotchet was as quietly suave as ever. Then Abrigo came in.

The fat Californian looked just the same as he had the night Crotchet had won this place. He even seemed to be wearing the same grimy damp shirt. His fat face was as expressionless as a pudding. He nodded to those who spoke to him, but never smiled, never frowned, and he said very little. He looked around and breathed heavily as he watched the play but did not join the game for quite an hour.

Then he played at Valentine's table, where his luck was indifferent. He bet on black all the time and then just on clubs. It was the quick way, Valentine thought, to lose his money. But slowly, slowly, slowly, Abrigo's luck turned. Clubs, clubs—the gate turned up clubs three times in a row. Abrigo's mountain of winnings rivaled the mountain in the middle of the table.

Valentine surveyed the two heaps of gold thoughtfully,

then roused himself and sent for grog.

"Pisco!" he cried. He snapped his fingers, and Bill, the cabin boy, who served the fine meals created by Cookie in the kitchen, came over with the jug, and poured.

Abrigo merely nodded, and drained the glass. Then he bet the lot on spades — and won.

His pile of dust and nuggets glittered. There were little coin landslides on the slopes. The crowd pressed close, craning to see. Men were whispering in other men's ears. Giles, the reporter, was there, a notebook propped in the crook of his left arm while his right hand wielded a pencil.

Abrigo did not bother to look around. Instead, he took off his left boot and shoveled in the golden hill. Then he limped over to Crotchet's table, and plonked the boot down.

Crotchet was waiting, his hands in his pockets, standing easy, whistling under his breath. The whole crowd moved round to watch Abrigo, and Crotchet smiled at them all.

"*Buenas tardes!*" he said to Abrigo. "I thank you for the unusual pleasure of your custom, señor!"

Abrigo included his head. Then, breathing heavily, he set his paunch against the edge of the table. His little moist eyes watched the forty-card pack and Crotchet's deft fingers as Crotchet shuffled.

Despite the boot, Abrigo played as cautiously as if he were down to his last ounce. Crotchet smiled each time the coins were squeezed reluctantly onto the chosen places, and he dealt the cards with equal care. Then Abrigo began to win again, slowly, betting all the time on black.

Crotchet could not recollect any time in his gambling experience when the gate had turned up spades or clubs so often. Soon, he gambled, the deal would turn up red, and Abrigo's luck would turn bad too, but as relentlessly as time the gold and the coins and the nuggets shifted, the profits of weeks of gambling and restauranting moving as if by magic toward Abrigo's boot.

The pile rose high and equaled the bank. Abrigo's only

reaction was to take off his other boot, shovel his pile into it, and set both boots beside each other.

"I challenge," he said, "for the tap."

"Aha," said Crotchet. He listened to the babble that ran around the room, and felt the excitement. All of Pueblo San Marco, he meditated, had waited for this moment. The men in the hills who had passed through here would say to others as they arrived, how goes it between Crotchet and Abrigo? And even those who were digging a fortune would regret that they were not here tonight.

"The bank," he said regretfully, "is bust, suh."

"Then I challenge for this fine café-restaurant, señor."

"So I expected," sighed Crotchet. "So I thought."

"You refuse?"

"Of course not."

Then Crotchet whistled a line from *Yankee Doodle*. He surveyed the table with his head a little tilted as he whistled, flashed a glance at Abrigo—and dealt four cards, two from the bottom of the pack, two from the top. They floated with style, each to its proper place.

Every man in the room craned to see what cards they were. The two of hearts, the seven of clubs, the three of hearts, and the seven of diamonds. "No tiny faces smiling," hummed Crotchet. And only one black, he thought.

Abrigo wheezed and grasped his boots. Everyone fell silent.

The fat man deliberated … deliberated for ever, while all the time Crotchet waited, holding the pack, waiting for Abrigo to place his bet on that one black card.

Then, grunting, Abrigo placed one boot by the two of hearts, and the other on her sister three.

Everything bet on just one suit. The air was hushed and steamy. Crotchet was poised, ready to deal the gate—and Abrigo coughed, and said, "I deal the card, señor."

Crotchet didn't hesitate, not for a second. "Certainly, suh."

Some of the crowd had climbed on stools to see better. Abrigo received the pack with apparent indifference. Once in his hands, though, he handled the cards as a lover fondles his mistress. Everyone knew Abrigo's magic with a deck. He could pick and deal at will, it was whispered, and those plump awkward fingers could move invisibly, like fluttering wings in the night.

Crotchet's eyes, however, were very sharp, his concentration merciless. He whistled insouciantly but that meant nothing. Abrigo's hand moved slowly As Crotchet watched, a droplet of sweat began to run down the fat man's nose.

It glistened. The fingers paused, bent like caterpillars.

The door crashed wide. A man shouted, "Fire, fire, Colonel Sefton's house burned all down, nothin' but ashes left! The Colonel's dead and gone, a burned-up corpse, with the corpse of his wife beside him!"

And Abrigo had dealt the gate. Crotchet's eyes had shifted for the tiniest instant, and in that infinitesimal pause Abrigo had tossed down the card.

It was the knave of hearts. The saucy fellow was riding a roan and white horse, and his grin was evil.

Abrigo said, "*Lindo el overo rosao, sí?*"

Crotchet began to laugh. He couldn't help it. The steed the Jack of hearts was riding was definitely a pretty mare in her roan and white. The only pity was that the crowd, too, had been too distracted to see that melodramatic drop.

"Thank you, señor," he said. "A brave gamble indeed. And I wish you good fortune with this fine establishment. May you keep it longer than we did."

"I will," said Abrigo, and for the first time in history, Californians heard Abrigo laugh.

End of book two

LOOK OUT FOR THE NEXT BOOK IN THE SERIES

A Promise of Gold

BOOK THREE

DEAREST ENEMY

Chapter One Follows ....

ONE

FRANK Sefton's ancient hacienda had burned down more thoroughly than Harriet would have believed possible.

Even the most massive adobe walls had collapsed with the heat, and now they looked like blackened sand dunes. Huge oak rafters had fallen higgledy-piggledy, and were piled on top of one another, crusted with shining charcoal.

The rest was rubble and ashes, well raked over. Harriet could see tracks in the black crumbling dust where men had fossicked for anything worth looting. If any of her clothes had survived the fire, she thought wryly, they were certainly gone. Which meant that her wardrobe was severely depleted—she was down to two sets of undergarments, three shawls, two gowns, and a cloak, all of which she had piled onto her body when she had fled from her husband. Rather inconvenient, she decided, but not particularly significant. Otherwise, there was nothing for her here at all.

Everything that had happened to her in this house had been a nightmare, yet it had been possible to admire the old mansion. She turned to the newspaperman, feeling angry.

"Why did you want me to see this?" she demanded. "It used to be a fine house, you know. A hacienda in the traditional style, with a rather nice courtyard in the middle.

It had a fountain, and mosaic tiles, and hanging plants."

Mr. Giles was standing in his customary slouch, studying the ruins with a straw in his mouth. He was nibbling at that straw like a rodent, so that his moustaches revolved, and now his eyebrows lifted.

"Why," he said, "perhaps I wanted your thoughts on the subject. After all," he pointed out, "it was your husband the Colonel who lost his life in this fire. How do you feel about being a widow?"

How did she feel? Harriet turned away from the ruins and looked at the meadows and corrals, now empty of cattle and horses. She wondered where all the livestock had been taken, and then thought about how she felt. She was sad about the devastation, she supposed, and certainly angered by the way Mr. Giles had phrased the question. She didn't feel like a widow, but she had never felt like a married woman, either.

Glancing back at Mr. Giles with dislike, she snapped, "You want to record my feelings for a story?"

"Story, Mrs. Sefton?"

"The story you are sending back east—and don't pretend there isn't one."

"Wa-al, of course there's a story in it, Mrs. Sefton, for wasn't your husband the Colonel a prominent figure—in New York society, as well as in the blue-nosed ranks of Philadelphia? He came from an uppercrust family, as you know very well, and was respected in much higher circles than folks like you and me will ever aspire to. And after all, for quite a while people thought you had expired in this fire as well—that is, until you mysteriously materialized out of the hills, in the company of the *Gosling* gold prospecting party. What do you think about your miraculous survival?"

Harriet said, "As you've just pointed out, I was nowhere near here when it happened."

"And neither were you supposed to be, Mrs. Sefton—for didn't your husband the Colonel send you off to his good

2

friend Don Manuel Vidrie and his charming family, right after you arrived here in California? Even though you had been just reunited after more than a year apart?"

Harriet's eyes stung, forcing her to look away. Frank Sefton had humiliated her by sending her away the morning after she had arrived at the hacienda, and now the whole world was about to know that she had been dumped on his Californian friends just one night after getting to his property in the Sacramento Valley.

"You seem to have been asking questions, Mr. Giles," she finally said. "And getting some interesting answers."

"And I have eyes in my head, Mrs. Sefton, and I have ears to listen, too. I might not say much while I am eating, but I watch and I listen, and it didn't take more than one or two courses of that great feast at Don Manuel's dining table before I'd worked out that you had been a guest in his house for a mighty long time, and that you resented it, too. And why else would you have seized your chance to escape while Don Manuel and his showy male relatives were off out riding with your husband the Colonel? You reckon I've forgotten how you badgered me into escorting you out of the Vidries' territory?"

"I don't think you ever forget anything, Mr. Giles."

"You're right again," he said, with one of his sardonic sniggers. "But think, Mrs. Sefton, think!" he went on. "By insisting on coming back to this here house, you could have sealed your doom. According to my deductions, the fire happened only the second night after you galloped here. So how do you feel about your narrow escape from being burned to death, huh? How do you feel?"

"I feel astonished, if that holds interest," she retorted, having no intention of telling him that she had escaped the fire by pure good luck, as she had run away from Sefton earlier that same night. "I'm astonished that it took so long for the fire to be noticed. Why did no one see the hacienda burning? I know it's out of sight of Pueblo San Marco, being over the hill and across the river, but it must have gone up like a torch."

"That's true," he conceded, mumbling at his straw. "Mind you, ma'am, and I apologize that I beg to differ, but those adobe walls were mighty thick. The fire could have smoldered for hours without anyone noticing. It burned like a baker's oven, if you see what I mean. Roasting inside, you understand, but without apparent light and heat."

That could well be so, Harriet thought with a grimace. The chief clerk at Frank Sefton's bank had had just one thing for her—the ring that Frank had always worn. It was a half-melted lump, silent testimony to the heat of the blaze. It had been taken off the corpse, the clerk had said; that was how they had identified her husband's body. She winced even now, thinking that the ring must have been chipped off the finger bone.

Mr. Giles was watching her closely, she saw. "You were meant to be the other victim of the drama," he pointed out.

Harriet shifted uneasily, and said, "Perhaps."

It had been Ah Wong, her Chinese servant, who had made her run away, that night. He had been in a state of utter terror when he had woken her up and told her to her flee—and yet the fire had certainly not started then. Had Ah Wong known that something dreadful was going to happen? She had assumed that he had seized the chance to get her away while Frank was across the river, in Pueblo San Marco. Obviously, Sefton had returned just in time to be killed in the fire. It was unlike Frank to have such foul luck, but it had happened. And, if Ah Wong had not helped her run away, she would have been unlucky, too.

Mr. Giles was saying, "And I do wonder about the identity."

Harriet blinked, dragged out of her preoccupation. "Of what?"

"The identity of the woman who was burned to death in your place."

4

She flinched with shock. "There was another body?"

"Indeed, Mrs. Sefton. The second body was beside the body of your husband—in your bed. That's why everyone thought you were dead."

"What?" She stared incredulously. "That can't be true! How do you know it was my bed?"

The writer's grin was sly. "Ah, Mrs. Sefton, as you observed earlier, I know where to ask questions, and how to find answers. It was your bed and your bedroom, and the woman's corpse lay blackened beside the equally blackened corpse of your husband, so of course folks assumed the second body was yours."

Harriet stared at him, unable to take it in that Frank should have been found in *her bed*. It was utterly impossible.

Mr. Giles took her elbow, and led her to the oak tree where the bandit Murietas had tethered their horses the night that she had escaped. It was not far away, close to the ruins, and the ends of the branches were scorched, their leaves withered with the heat of the fire. As they walked there, she remembered how she and Ah Wong had hidden in the shadows, holding their breaths for fear that Joaquín Murieta would see them, and drag them inside—that her escape from Sefton's hacienda would be foiled.

There was a broad raked mound under the tree now, with two boards at its head. One board informed her that here lay the remains of Colonel Francis Sefton. He had belonged to Philadelphia and he had been forty-two years old at the time of his death.

So this was the end of Frank, she thought, the miserable end of his devious dealings. All he had wanted was to get back to New York with immense riches, to make a certain Miss Coffin regret her decision to turn down his gallant proposal of marriage. And what had he got? This humble grave.

The other board was blank. "Folks do whisper," said Mr. Giles musingly, "that your husband the Colonel kept a

Chinese mistress."

Beautiful little Mei-Mei, Harriet thought, Mei-Mei of the camellia-like complexion and the rosebud mouth. Frank had likened her gold-colored, pouting breasts to pigeons, and had shared her with his friends.

She snapped, "Mei-mei was his ward."

"But the feet of the second skeleton were all twisted up, like bird claws. I hear that's what they do to Chinese girls, to make them attractive to men."

Mei-Mei? *In her bed?* It was the ultimate humiliation, Frank taunting her from beyond the tomb. Harriet stared at the reporter, feeling sick.

Mr. Giles's head was tilted as he watched her, so that he looked somewhat like a bird himself. So the whole of the Feather River district knew that Frank Sefton had kept a beautiful, exotic mistress, she thought with shame, and now the whole eastern seaboard of America was due to learn that, too.

She said sharply, "Who told you that Frank had a Chinese mistress? Was it Don Manuel Vidrie? Or Don Roberto?"

"I don't divulge my sources, ma'am."

"Do you not? Then where is Don Roberto now?"

"Who knows, Mrs. Sefton, who knows?" The reporter let out one of his characteristic grunts of sardonic amusement. "No sooner had the alcalde signed the death certificate and looked for his fee than he skipped the territory, ma'am, and who can blame him? He scarpered off for the hills, and no doubt over the border to Mexico, on account of a posse of disappointed gold miners was all baying at his heels, crying out for their gold."

The gold, the vanished gold. No one wanted to find that gold more desperately than Harriet herself. The bank had been the first place she had stopped after arriving in Pueblo San Marco that late morning, for Sefton's bank was where the *Gosling* Company's gold had been stowed after Royal's claim was jumped — by the Murietas.

Instead of gold, though, she and her brother had found a shouting mob outside the door. It had been impossible to tell what all the men were baying about, but after Harriet and Royal had managed to shove through the crowd and get inside, the agitated bank clerk had told them what had happened. All the gold that had been deposited there by Don Roberto — the gold that he had confiscated from God alone knew how many disputed claims — had vanished. When the clerk had come in, the morning after the fire had been discovered, he had found the vaults empty of all the bulging parfleche bags. Thousands and thousands of dollars' worth of gold dust, gold flakes, and nuggets were gone.

Royal had stormed into the vaults, and found them swept clean. Then Captain Jake Dexter had arrived, carrying the documents for twenty thousand dollars' worth of *Gosling* disputed gold, plus Sefton's signed draft for one thousand dollars, repayment of the money Harriet had borrowed for the plot of land she had bought at Sutter's Fort. Jake had listened grimly to what Royal had to say, and then had demanded to see the ledgers. Harriet remembered how nervous the clerk had looked as he had handed them over, and how he had stammered as he said that the last man to write in the ledgers was Colonel Sefton … who had made a lot of alterations in the lists.

While Jake Dexter was going through the accounts, Harriet had found Mr. Giles at her elbow. Despite her chilly demeanor, the printer had persuaded her to come with him to her dead husband's hacienda … and here she was, avoiding his insinuating questions while mayhem and panic were still holding sway at Sefton's Bank for Miners. What a waste of time, she thought.

Harriet turned on her heel and set off decisively for the path to the ferryboat. She didn't care if the reporter came or not, but heard his hurried steps as he joined her. Then Mr. Giles was slouching along at her side.

She looked at him briefly, and said, "My brother told me he saw Sefton in Pueblo San Marco, the day after you and I left the Vidrie place. As you know, I arrived here that same night, and was still here that next day—but Frank didn't tell Royal that. Instead, he led Royal to believe that I was still staying with Don Manuel Vidrie. Can you think of any reason he would have lied?"

Mr. Giles was silent a long moment, lost in contemplation. Then he brushed his damp moustaches and said, "No, ma'am, that I cannot guess, other than he wished to keep you and your brother apart."

"Perhaps Royal was mistaken. He said that Frank was very busy in his bank, working away with his ledgers."

"Yep," said Mr. Giles, and nodded emphatically. "That is exactly how your husband the Colonel was spending his last day on earth."

"What? You saw him, too?"

"That I did. Right preoccupied, was he." Then the journalist let out another sardonic grunt, and said, "If he'd known he had only hours to live, he might have been doing something a mite more entertaining."

Harriet ignored this, saying, "What about Ah Wong? You remember Ah Wong, my Chinese servant? Have you seen him at all?"

"No, ma'am. That I have not. I remember him well, but have not seen him since you and he left me at Don Roberto's fort, after galloping away from Don Manuel Vidrie's estate."

"Poor Ah Wong," Harriet said.

She shivered, remembering how frightened poor Ah Wong had been when she insisted on leaving the Vidrie estate, and coming back to the hacienda. She remembered how she had dreamed that she heard Ah Wong crying and sobbing in the night, and now she wondered if it had truly been a dream, or whether Sefton had been punishing Ah Wong for bringing her back to the ranch.

She had begged her husband not to blame him, saying

that it was all her own fault … that coming back to the hacienda had been her own decision. That Ah Wong had just been following orders. But Frank Sefton's rages had been terrifying.

Forcing her mind away, she said, "What do you think Frank was doing in the bank?"

"But you should know that already, ma'am, because you can work it out for yourself. I recollect quite plainly how we both did wonder about those shares in his bank that your husband was so anxious to sell—and we wondered, too, why he was so strangely willing to lend men the monies for the purchase … with the shares in the bank as collateral."

Collateral. The last word held more meaning than all the other words put together.

Harriet said, "Go on."

"When he was busily at work with his ledgers, he was converting all those loans he'd made, declaring the debts all bad. With one stroke of the pen he was taking back those loans, and claiming the gold as the security for those loans. It rightfully belonged to others, but there it was in his vaults, and somehow with his legal chicanery he made it legally his. In a word, ma'am, your husband was collecting on bad debts."

The reporter nodded to himself, but apparently not because he was so pleased with his detective work. Instead, he looked world-weary, as if this kind of confidence trick happened every day.

Harriet said bitterly, "I had twenty thousand dollars' worth, you know. I was a major shareholder."

Mr. Giles, for once, looked astounded. "You bought them?"

"No, of course not. That wasn't possible—I had no money of my own, and even if I did, it would belong by law to my husband. No, he presented them to me as a gift. I had to do was sign for them."

"Sign for them?" echoed the reporter. "But that doesn't

9

make sense. Because you were his wife, the shares were still legally his."

"I know," said Harriet wearily.

There couldn't be many women in the world who had fallen for the same trick twice, she brooded, but kept silent. She had no intention of revealing to this inquisitive fellow that Frank Sefton had swindled her once already, in New Zealand, when she had tamely signed the deeds to all his properties, the day before they were married. Just as in California later, he had pretended that he was giving the deeds to her as a present. And then, the morning after their wedding night, he had gone off into town to sell all the properties those deeds represented—at an enormous profit, because they were now in her English name. Because of a loophole in the law, he had made a huge fortune. She had been a fool, a double fool, she bitterly thought, and the prospect that the whole world might get to know about it was mortifying in the extreme.

Like the men who had bought shares in Sefton's bank, she should have taken legal advice, she thought—and at that her thoughts stopped short. The only legal advisor in the district had been the alcalde, Don Roberto.

She said to Mr. Giles, "Don Roberto must have been party to the swindle. He was the one who deposited all that disputed gold in Sefton's bank."

"The way you put it, that makes sense, but who knows, Mrs. Sefton, who knows?"

"He might even have been the man who stole it, after Frank was dead."

"Wa-al, you could be right on both counts, Mrs. Sefton. A lot of the men who claim to own that gold certainly reckon that Don Roberto and your husband the Colonel were working in cahoots, and that's why they are hot on Don Roberto's trail. But it stands to reason, don't it, that he couldn't have carried all that gold away without help. While I've never had much gold myself, I have it on good authority

10

that the stuff is very heavy."

But Don Roberto had six deputies — the bandit Murietas. Harriet stared speculatively at the reporter, and he nodded wisely, and said, "Do you want to know what I think, ma'am?"

"Knowing you as I do, Mr. Giles," she said tartly, "I'm certain you have a theory."

"Ah, Mrs. Sefton," he said, "you know me well," and grunted with cynical laughter. Then he said in a matter of fact voice, "I think Colonel Sefton was the one who carried the gold out of the vaults. I think he got the gold across the river to this ranch here, and then the men who stole that gold from him murdered him and his mistress, either on purpose or accidentally, depending on whether they were dead or not when the house was set on fire."

"*Murdered?*" Harriet could think of many people who would be glad to kill Sefton, but none who would have had the courage to actually do it.

"Murdered," Mr. Giles repeated with satisfaction. "And what could be a better motive for murder than all that confiscated gold?"

"But no one has suggested that the house was deliberately fired."

"No? Wa-al, ma'am, I suggest it now, because it would give us another reason for the long delay in reporting the blaze. After all, if folks who saw it also knew that it had been deliberately torched, their own good sense would advise them to keep shut about it."

Such as Frank's vaqueros, she thought — who had fled, taking Sefton's cattle and horses with them. It was something they certainly wouldn't have done if they hadn't known he was dead. Sefton's iron will and his vicious outbursts of temper had kept them well under control. And naturally they wouldn't have reported either his death or the fire, as the delay gave them time to get away.

So who was the murderer? And who had helped Sefton

11

carry the gold out of the bank and across the river?

Suddenly, the night she had escaped was vivid in Harriet's mind. Again, she heard Ah Wong's terrified gasp as Joaquín Murieta had come out of the courtyard of the hacienda. She remembered how they had cowered in the shadows of a hedge as Joaquín walked to the same tree where Sefton now lay buried, and the red glow as he had drawn on his cigar. She remembered how he had seemed to stare right at her, as she cowered with Ah Wong in the darkness. And Joaquín Murieta had five brothers, all evil, all bandits...

She was suddenly, tragically, certain that poor little Ah Wong was dead. The Murietas would have caught him when he returned with the horses, after taking her to the safety of the hill that overlooked Don Roberto's fort—were probably waiting in ambush as he arrived. She had pleaded with Ah Wong not to go back to the hacienda, but he had been obdurate—because he had to return the horses, he'd said. So it would look as if she had never left the house.

Tears stung her eyes. To hide them, Harriet turned and set off to the ferry landing again.

At the riverbank, to her surprise, she found that the ferryboat was in requisition. It was worked by hauling on ropes and pulleys that were attached to a double line that stretched from the riverbank of the ranch to the embarcadero of Pueblo San Marco, and it had been strictly for Sefton's private use. While it was easy enough to draw it back from the other side of the river by hauling in the line, the villagers had never dared use it. But, while Harriet had been talking with Mr. Giles, some opportunist had evidently realized that Sefton's dominance over the river crossing had ended with his death. So instead of lying on the bank where they had left it, the boat was mid-river and coming toward them.

It was moving very slowly, because it was packed to the gunwales with miners. As Harriet incredulously watched, bearded, weatherworn men in flat, wide-brimmed hats and checkered shirts and buckskin trousers disembarked. After the briefest look around their surroundings, they passed her as they headed off up the slope, with every obvious intention of digging gold-prospecting holes in the land that had once belonged to her husband. Bedrolls and folded tents were packed on their backs, and mining tools rattled around them, and they strode with confidence, because there was absolutely no one to stop them from invading the territory and hunting for the yellow stuff. Some even tipped their hats to her as they passed.

Mr. Giles was watching, too, she saw. He touched his hat to one in return, and then said to Harriet, "Ain't you the rightful owner of all this now?"

"I strongly doubt it," said Harriet, knowing how convoluted Sefton's dealings had been, and how much he had hated her. "But even if I do own it, what can I do to stop them?"

"Nothing," said the reporter, and bent to pluck another straw, which he nibbled. After another meditative moment, he said, "What do you reckon about Don Manuel's fine and fertile property?"

"I beg your pardon?"

"Those miles of Vidrie hills and dales could be invaded by prospectors, too."

"But Don Roberto's fort guards the bridge to the Vidrie lands," Harriet protested—but then she remembered that the alcalde was a long way away from his fort, maybe as far as Mexico. Which meant that the bridge was open to all, and that Don Manuel Vidrie's lush pasture lands and vineyard slopes were now fair game for men who were crazed for gold.

"All it takes is one report of a big find up Cache Creek, and every soul in Pueblo San Marco and further downriver will be fighting to get into these parts," Mr. Giles prophesied. "And it will take more than those showy Vidrie caballeros to stop them."

"You're right," she said, and grimaced.

"How refreshing that you should agree with me," he smirked. Then he took Harriet's arm, and urged her down to the water. The ferryboat, now emptied except for the man who had appropriated the ferrying business, was about to cross the river again.

To her disgust, the new ferryman demanded a fee of two dollars a head, boasting at the same time that he expected to make two thousand this season out of this here venture. However, Mr. Giles paid it with only a token complaint, and the waterman had good reason to be so optimistic, Harriet saw. When they arrived on the other side, there was a packed line of men waiting to board for the next crossing, while many others were settling in for the night, resting up before heading over in the morning. The broad riverbank had sprouted thickets of tents, all the way from the landing place to the junction of the river and the stream that rushed down from the watermill high on the slope above the village.

Mr. Giles was standing beside her as men pushed past them to get to the ferryboat. When he saw her look at him, he smirked again, and said, "What now, Mrs. Sefton?"

She pointed to where the *Gosling* was moored up tight against the embarcadero. Close up, the brig was a sad sight, Harriet thought. With her topmasts struck and her running rigging down, the *Gosling* did not look at all like the dashingly piratical vessel she remembered.

"You're going to live on board?"

The reporter's tone held salacious curiosity. Which meant that insinuations about her adulterous relationship with Captain Jake Dexter were likely to be printed, too.

Harriet gave him one inimical glance. "I'm going to a meeting," she snapped. "And it is just a business meeting, I assure you." And with that, she turned on her heel.

End of chapter one…

AUTHOR'S NOTE

Many books, newspapers, and journals were read in the quest for background for the *Promise of Gold* trilogy. The following were found to be particularly useful.

Kelly, William, J.P. *An Excursion to California over the Prairie, Rocky Mountains, and Great Sierra Nevada, with a stroll through the Diggings and Ranches of that Country.* London: Chapman & Hall, 1851.

Robinson, Fayette, *California and its Gold Regions,* in, *The Gold Mines of California.* New York: Promontory Press, 1974.

Ryan, William Redmond. *Personal Adventures in Upper and Lower California in 1848-9.* New York: Arno Press, 1973 (first published 1850-1851).

Shaw, William. *Golden Dreams and Waking Realities.* London: Smith, Elder, 1851.

Street, Franklin. *California in 1850,* in, *The Gold Mines of California.* New York: Promontory Press, 1974.

Taylor, Bayard. *Eldorado, or, Adventures in the Path of Empire.* New York: Putnam, 1850.

The Friend, Honolulu, December 1, 1849, pp. 81-83. Account by a Hawaiian missionary (probably Rev. Damon) of a tour in Alta California.

Tyrwhitt-Brooks, J., M.D. (Pseudonym of J. Vizetelly, printer.) *Four Months among the Gold-finders in Alta California.* London: David Bogue, 1849.

Woods, Daniel B. *Sixteen Months at the Gold Diggings.* London: Sampson Low, 1857.

JOAN DRUETT is an independent maritime historian and writer who has published many award-winning maritime studies, including *In the Wake of Madness*, *Island of the Lost*, and a biography of the extraordinary Tahitian high priest and navigator, Tupaia, who sailed with Captain James Cook on the *Endeavour*. Her novels include *A Love of Adventure* and the Wiki Coffin mystery series, as well as the three books of the "*A Promise of Gold*" trilogy.

A proud author-member of Old Salt Press, she lives in New Zealand with her husband, Ron, a well-regarded maritime artist, whose works are exhibited internationally.

www.oldsaltpress.com

Old Salt Press is an independent press catering to those who love books about ships and the sea. We are an association of writers working together with the aim of producing the very best of nautical and maritime fiction and non-fiction. We invite you to join us as we go down to the sea in books.